Things are sweeter when they're lost.
F. Scott Fitzgerald
The Beautiful and the Damned

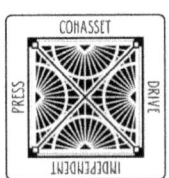

Copyright © 2020 by Arly Carmack

All rights reserved.

No part of this book may be reproduced in any form or by any electronic or mechanical means, including information storage and retrieval systems, without written permission from the author, except for the use of brief quotations in a book review.

This is a work of fiction. Names, characters, businesses, places, events, locales, and incidents are either the products of the author's imagination or used in a fictitious manner. Any resemblance to actual persons, living or dead, or actual events is purely coincidental.

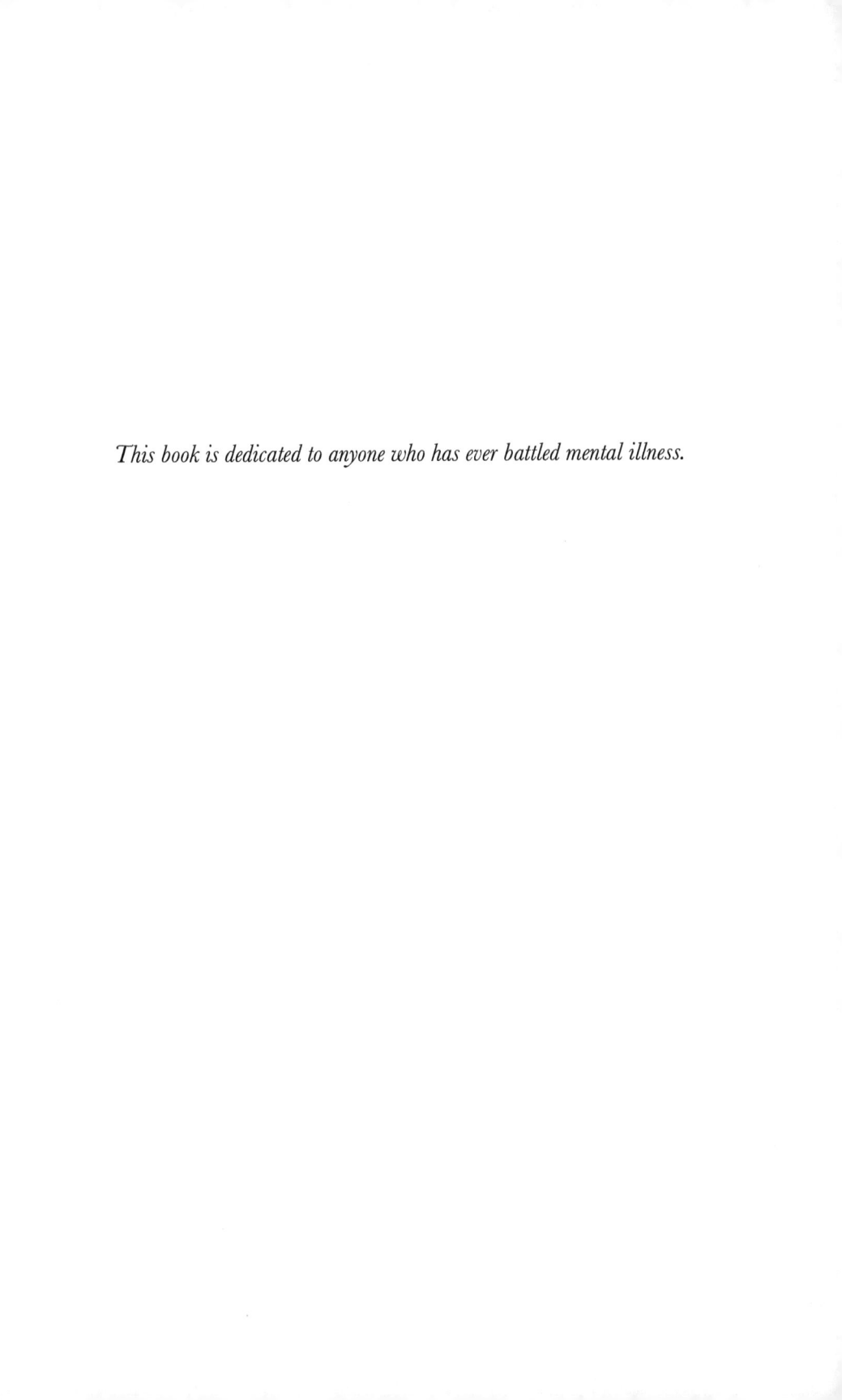

This book is dedicated to anyone who has ever battled mental illness.

THE PASTEL EFFECT

ARLY CARMACK

PART I

Caroline
FALL 2009

1

A Routine

WHEN I SET foot into a building, I always wondered about all the people who walked the halls before me. I especially thought about it at school. I imagined all of the things that really mattered in high school: winning the big game, getting the grade, going with the cute boy, and having your heart broken. I wondered about the years and years that the old plaster walls had seen. Then, in the grand scheme of it all, it didn't seem that important that I was there, doing the same thing. I closed my locker and walked to class, feeling the only thing that any normal high school sophomore could ever feel: utter boredom.

My life consisted of getting up in the morning, walking to school, shuffling through classes, and coming home. Then I ate dinner, watched TV, did homework, and went to bed. Every day was exactly the same and part of me liked it that way. I liked my routine of curling up on the couch during increasingly darker fall days, and knowing the day of the week by the television program I was watching. I'm sure my dad loved it, too. I was boring and predictable, and he didn't have to worry about me. Although, at the same time, something else was happening to me. I wasn't sure what it was, but it was something inside that just wasn't completely right. I had an idea of what it was, but I didn't want to give it a name.

During my sophomore year, I was lucky enough to gain two of

the most fundamental experiences of being a teenage girl: my first best friend and my first proper crush. Lilly Waters was my best friend, and her twin brother, Skip, was my crush. Lilly was gorgeous. Her blonde hair framed her heart-shaped face, and blue eyes peered out from behind long bangs. She had a small button nose and a radiant smile. She looked like a *Seventeen* magazine model, but in conservative clothing. The guys loved her, but none of them stood a chance because her father was a pastor, a strict one, and she was exceedingly obedient to him. Additionally, Skip was always there to reinforce her moral standards if she even thought about straying from them. Skip was an all-muscle, good-natured boy with the same shade of blonde hair and blue eyes as Lilly, and dimples that melted my heart.

Every other Friday I broke my usual routine and spent the night at Lilly's house. We talked about clothes and school and boys. We were both boy-crazy in our own way; she had celebrity crushes and I had Skip. Lilly knew about my crush on her brother, but it didn't bother her because neither of them were allowed to date, and she knew that Skip took Pastor Waters' rules seriously. He would never cross his father. Never. Even if it meant breaking my poor little adolescent heart.

On that same every-other-Friday, my dad had a standing rendezvous with a waitress named Kristi from Alice's Pizza. During my formative years, my dad tried to hide things like that from me. I never thought about him dating anyone because I knew that he was still in love with my mother. It never occurred to me that he might have other needs to fill. When he did finally tell me he was seeing someone, it took me a while to figure out it was her, but I put it together after I noticed the way my dad liked to go out for pizza every-other-Thursday night, and the way she touched his shoulder when she took our order, and the fact that not only had I found a pair of pink panties in the laundry, but also an Alice's Pizza t-shirt.

I didn't hold it against him. After all, my dad became a father when he was nineteen and had given up all the better years of his life taking care of me. I decided that he should have his fun now at age thirty-four. I never brought up the Kristi thing and neither did he. It was known, but unspoken, when I neatly folded the forgotten articles of clothing and left them on his bed. At least she was a nice girl.

It had just been the two of us since I was four years old. My parents met when my dad was in college and my mom worked at National Record Mart. She was way out of his league, but he built the courage to ask her out, and they fell in love. It was no secret that he fell a lot harder. My mom was a manic depressive, but by the time he found out, he was invested. When she got pregnant with me, he tried to marry her. She never accepted his proposal, and five years later she died of a drug overdose. We didn't talk about Tressa very much. I learned about her by chance, like when one of her favorite songs would come on the radio and he'd be reminded of her and say, in a barely audible voice, "She loved this song." The truth was that he was still in love with her, and still heartbroken that she was gone. He couldn't bear to think about her too often. He still cried when he did.

I didn't look like my mother. She had brownish-blond hair that fell down to her waist, and pale blue eyes. She was tall, slim, and beautiful. In pictures, she never smiled. She never really looked happy, just lost. I had inky dark hair that always looked jagged around my face, no matter how I tried to soften it. I wasn't as tall as her, but the same height as my dad, and I had his brown eyes too. My dad smiled even when he was breaking on the inside; I had a harder time concealing my feelings, more like my mother. I tried, even when I knew I was showing all the signs of depression, to hide it from my dad so he wouldn't have to go through it again. I dragged myself out of bed for him, I pretended to be interested in things for him, and I laughed for him even when I didn't feel like it. I saw my dad as fragile, and I didn't want to break him. And I saw my mother as heartless for doing so.

2

Getting Cody

"YOU'RE SO lucky that you got Cody Kirby as your Geometry partner. I was jealous, I have to admit."

"Jealous?" I asked. "Over Cody?"

"Yes. He's cute. Don't you think so?"

Lilly flipped through the *Cosmopolitan* magazine that I had smuggled in, one of many forbidden items in the Waters' household. Amongst the others were tampons, televisions, and mainstream music.

"I don't know. He doesn't seem very interested in being my partner. He looks disgusted, actually."

"I don't think so."

"He is totally incapable of smiling."

"It's that jock thing."

"He's a jock?"

"He's on the wrestling team with Skip. You never noticed? You've been to the matches."

"I guess not." It was hard to notice anything else when Skip was around because everything paled in comparison to him. Cody was just under six feet tall, muscular and slim, with a baby face that hadn't totally changed with his body yet. His cheeks were still chubby and he wore braces. He had short, dirty-blonde hair and blue-green eyes. He always looked mad, or unhappy, or both. He was a trendy dresser, but always wore things a bit too tight. He usually looked good from the neck down, and I gave him credit for having his own style. "You think he's cute?"

"Yes. I think he likes you. He's always looking at you."

"No he's not."

"Yes, he is. I've seen him staring."

Lilly always tried to say encouraging things to lift my self-esteem, like telling me that I had shiny hair and a well-proportioned nose. Trying to convince me that a boy liked me was a thoughtful next step.

"Cody and Caroline. It sounds good together. And if you get married your name would be Caroline Kirby, and that doesn't sound too bad."

"We've skipped to marriage now?"

She smiled. "We always have to skip to marriage around here," she said, alluding to the fact that sex before marriage wasn't an option for her. So, if we wanted to think about boys in that way, we had to think up a wedding first. "He has some fashion sense. I would say he'd opt for a non-traditional tux. Maybe a nice baby blue or something."

"OK. Sure. And what song are we dancing to at our wedding?" I asked sarcastically.

"I would say he's traditional in that matter. Let's go with something tried and true. Like Whitney."

I flopped down onto her bed. "I'll ask him on Monday."

"Ask him what?"

"What song we'll be dancing to at our wedding." I had never before thought about Cody Kirby as a boy I would ever like and oddly enough, it felt possible.

The Waters' allowed us to have ice cream on Friday nights, and I volunteered to get it out of the deep-freeze knowing that Skip practiced worship music on his acoustic guitar in the basement where the freezer also happened to be located. I got about halfway down the steps when I saw him: Skip Waters. He was leaning against the washing machine in the dull light, his pants pulled down to his knees. I couldn't believe that the holy Skip Waters thought about sex, let alone allowed himself to feel anything. I watched quietly until he finished. His cheeks were pink and it was a good shade for him. He used a sock to wipe down his abdomen, then threw it in the washing machine and pressed the start button. He pulled up his pants and put a shirt on, and as he began to pray (probably for forgiveness), I finished my descent and excused myself for interrupting his evening prayers.

"Do you want to pray with me for a second?" he asked.

"OK," I said eagerly.

He took my hands and I had to wonder if there was any residue left on his hands that was now transferring to mine. Instead of praying, I played back what I'd just witnessed in my head. I always knew there had to be some kind of a real boy under his wholesome, perfect persona. After that night, I always wondered who he thought about while he masturbated.

That moment led me into a string of thoughts: for the entire weekend I imagined every boy I liked doing that and wondered who they thought about, and then I imagined Cody doing that and wondered who he thought about.

On Monday at school, I paid attention to Cody. He had a tight-knit group of friends that had been inseparable since kindergarten. Everyone at school referred to them as the Golden Circle. Some girls, some boys, all loyal to each other. I had heard that his group was impenetrable. I wondered if it was true.

Geometry class was seventh period, the last class of the day. Cody always smelled good, and after spending the weekend thinking about him, I looked forward to his scent. I looked at him for a long time and decided he looked different. Maybe it was because I had been thinking about him differently.

As partners, we didn't talk much. I wanted to break the ice. "What's different about you?" I asked.

He looked up from the graphing paper. "I lost a contact lens."

"Oh, you're wearing glasses."

He nodded, unsmiling.

"I like you better in glasses," I said, realizing it was a bold statement.

He looked back down.

"Can I ask you a question?"

He looked up again, probably annoyed.

"Do you ever think about what song you'll dance to when you get married?" I felt spontaneous, and Lilly would get a kick out of it if I came back to her with the answer. Of course, there was always the chance he'd roll his eyes and go back to graphing.

He barely had to think about it. "Bryan Adams. *Heaven.*"

"Right. You've thought about it?"

"Who hasn't?" he asked.

"Me, I guess."

"Well, clearly you thought about it. You asked the question." He put his pencil down, giving me his full attention. "So, what is it?"

"Can I get back to you? That's hard to compete with."

"I guess," he said. He picked up his pencil again. "Look, when are we going to get this big project done? I know everyone else is doing it over Thanksgiving, but I have a wrestling invitational and I can't do it then."

"Any time is good for me, really."

"I'd rather not do it at my house. My parents are annoying."

"My house is fine. You can come over tonight if you want to."

"I have wrestling until seven."

"After seven is fine. My dad won't care." I scribbled down my address on a piece of paper and he shoved it in his pocket without looking at it right as the bell rang. "See you then," I said, a little too enthusiastically. He just looked at me and walked away.

I walked home, beating myself up over the fact that I was looking forward to seeing him again. All of a sudden, something about Cody was attractive and I hated what I was feeling for him. Feelings were a downfall. I had to be careful with them. Having feelings for someone meant that they had the power to hurt me. Losing someone could cause grief. The only person I had ever really loved was my dad because I knew that he would never go away. I really didn't even think God would take him away from me. I knew that he would always be there for me and it was safe. Trusting someone like Cody was risky. I was suddenly crushing hard on a boy who had never even looked at me, and I couldn't figure out why.

"Pheromones," Lilly said. "Those are the things that people give off that make them attracted to each other. It's science."

"I know what pheromones are," I said. "But they don't work both ways, I'm assuming."

"I don't know," she said. "I can look it up, though."

"Why, why, why?" I asked. "Why do I have to like him? Why?"

"I think it's natural to like someone so opposite from you. And let's face it, he's accessible right now. Maybe it's our natural instinct to take what's available."

"The problem is, I doubt he's available. He's in the Golden Circle, remember? The Circle dates within the Circle."

"Cody doesn't seem to fit in the circle. Not completely."

"I don't know, Lil. There are rules, you know?"

"You've never broken rules?"

"Rarely. Have you?"

She laughed. "Please. Between my dad and my brother, how could I? I just don't think Cody's part of that flock, though. He's different. He answered the question, didn't he?"

"I didn't think boys thought about things like that."

"I think boys are needy and afraid to be alone and attached to their mommies and they can't admit that they want to get married as soon as possible so they have someone to cook and clean and take care of them and give them unlimited sex without having to try too hard to get it."

I thought about it, and it sounded plausible. "Did you read that in *Cosmo*?"

"No. I gathered that through observation."

"Bear!" my dad called. That was his nickname for me — my mom used to call us Teddy Bear because we were inseparable. He still called me Bear. "Your study date is here."

"Gotta go," I said, hanging up on Lilly. I instantly blushed and ran out to the living room.

Cody was wearing shorts even though it was cold out, and a too-tight sweatshirt with our school logo on it. He stared at the wall where my dad had his outdated-but-loved stereo equipment, and his hundreds of vinyl records, cassettes, and CDs. My dad loved music.

My palms began to sweat when he looked at me. "Want to go in the kitchen?" I asked, trying not to let my nerves get the best of me.

"Aren't you going to introduce us?" my dad asked, smiling.

"Cody, this is my dad. Dad, this is Cody."

"Are these all your records, Mr. Bryant?"

"Yeah, they are. I've been collecting for years."

"What was the hardest one to get?"

"Well, I have an autographed Zeppelin album — Plant *and* Page. And I have some early blues recordings that were fairly hard to get."

"Zeppelin?"

"Led Zeppelin. You've never heard them?"

He nodded that he had not. Once my dad got on the topic of music, it was hard to get him to stop, so I gave him a look and he retreated. "Well, I have some papers to grade. Listen to whatever you want, Cody. Really. Anytime."

"OK," he said.

My dad went up the steps to his home office-bedroom, and I looked at Cody, hoping he would say something first. He didn't.

"Sorry about my dad. We don't get a lot of visitors."

"He's cool."

"Yeah, I guess."

"You're lucky."

"Having a cool dad isn't as easy as it seems."

"Why not?"

Cody followed me into the kitchen. "Slutty college girls are always hitting on him. It's weird. I guess because he's young."

"My dad is fifty-nine."

"Mine is thirty-four."

"Why college girls?"

"He's their teacher."

"Your dad is a teacher?"

"An English professor at the college."

"At Hayes?"

"Yes."

"Is that why you moved here?"

"Yes."

"Oh. That's cool."

I shrugged. "I guess so. What does your dad do?"

"He inspects construction sites for safety and stuff."

"And your mom?"

"A nurse." He unzipped his book bag. "Your mom?"

"Dead," I said. I never liked to go into detail about it because dead mothers were instant conversation stoppers.

"Sorry."

"It's OK."

"What was her name?"

I don't think anyone had ever asked me that before. "Tressa," I said, and it felt weird coming out of my mouth.

I started to watch the Golden Circle at school. It seemed like a ring of vicious flirtation that led nowhere. The girls would always find a way to touch the boys: hugging them, playing with their hair, sticking a tag back into their shirts. I usually wasn't comfortable touching people, and it always amazed me how some people did it with such ease.

I questioned Skip about Cody vaguely, acting like I didn't actually care about the answers he gave. Cody was Skip's grappling partner and he said that Cody was a serious and dedicated wrestler, but not much of a talker. He also mentioned the Golden Circle, and the more anyone mentioned it, the more it irritated me.

The next time Cody came over, he drew the graphs while I did the math, and that combination seemed to work for us. I liked math, and he was more meticulous about drawing. We barely spoke, but the Golden Circle predicament continued to bother me. Eventually, I had to say something. I could tell myself a hundred times that there would be no benefit to saying things, but I usually said them anyway.

"You have a lot of friends," I said.

"I guess so," he agreed, not looking up.

"I know I only came to Newbury a year ago, but everyone says you've all been friends since kindergarten."

"Something like that."

"Everyone says you all only hang out together and only date each other and stuff like that."

"Yeah?"

"Is that true?"

"Generally, people hang out with their friends, yes."

"True, I suppose." I hesitated but couldn't help myself. "I think it's a little weird that you only date each other. I'm sorry. I just…"

"We don't date each other," he said matter-of-factly.

"Oh. OK."

"I mean, I suppose we could if we wanted to, but it doesn't go there."

"It just doesn't seem like you guys talk to anyone other than each other."

"I don't date anyone," he said. "I'm not dating. Is that even a thing anymore? Dating?"

"Well then, what is it called when people go out with romantic intentions?"

"Hooking up. That's all people do anymore is hook up. There's nothing romantic about it." He said it as if he knew it for a fact.

"So, I guess you don't hook up with each other, then?"

He laughed. "No. *God*, no." He finally looked at me. "Why do you care?"

"I just have a hard time understanding these high school demographics. It's hard — I haven't been here forever like you have. I don't get it sometimes. Who's dating, who's friends, who's hooking up. It's hard to tell."

"Is that how you like things? To be exactly what they seem?"

"Clear cut? Yes. I don't like to be guessing all the time."

"No guessing with me. I'm not hooking up with anyone and nobody is hooking up with me."

"Well, thanks. Now I sound like a creep for asking."

"No, you don't. Girls are very…"

I waited patiently for him to finish the sentence. We had forgotten about our assignment.

"Confusing. They act like they like you when they don't. They act like they don't when they do. They can be all over you and only want to be your friend. They text you for seven days straight and never text you again."

I smiled at his frustration.

"Sorry."

"Don't apologize to me. I'm not one of them."

"Right."

"I'm serious."

"Why do you think you're different?"

"Well, for one thing, I don't throw myself at anyone. If you think I like you, it's because I genuinely like you. And if you want to text, I'll text you back. I'm a very easy person to get along with."

"Well, that's not how most people are. You usually have to guess."

"Then maybe you need to go out on a limb and say it first."

"No way."

"How do people get to the point of hooking up if they can't even say they like each other?"

"Ask someone who does that."

He went back to his graph. I tried to keep my mouth shut for a few minutes, but I couldn't leave it alone.

"You've never had a girlfriend?"

"No."

"Why not?"

"It just seems like a super-complicated thing to navigate right now. Why do you seem surprised?"

"I guess because you're popular."

"See, we have warped perceptions of each other. Isn't that sad? Everybody is so fake that when one person gets real, we're skeptical. We can't believe it."

"I'm starting to realize how messed up things are and we're only in tenth grade."

"This girl I know, she posted on Twitter the other day...*I want to hook up with one of my friends*. She had seven hundred friends on there. There was a one in seven hundred chance she was talking about me, right? Am I going to take that chance and ask her out? Doubt it. The odds aren't in my favor."

"The chance it was you was like a tenth of a percent."

"Right. You see? Why would a girl say that? Why not just say — and not online, but in person or on the phone — 'Hey, you, I want to hook up with you.'"

"The same reason you don't assume it's you."

"How can you ever find the right person? There are seven billion people on earth."

"The chances that you'll meet your soul mate are one in seven billion. That's depressing."

"I guess it's depressing if you want that sort of thing."

"Says the person who has chosen their wedding song."

He smiled, finally. "I'm not cut off from the possibility of it happening."

I felt reflective and oddly close to him. "What do you want out of life, Cody?"

He contemplated it for a while, went back to his graphing, then finally answered, "I just want something real."

God, that was a good answer.

After the project was done, I scrambled for ideas on how to keep the flame alive with Cody. In my brain, it was a flame. In his brain, he probably hadn't even manufactured the match that started the fire yet. Skip seemed less attractive to me. Skip was just Skip. I thought about Cody non-stop. I knew it was like an obsession, borderline unhealthy, and unrealistic. I wondered if my obsession was yet another sign of my impending mental illness, and I beat myself up over it. I couldn't imagine that any normal person felt that way. Obsession was for psychopaths. It was what they made those murder shows about. It was for stalkers. It wasn't for me. I shouldn't think about Cody every waking hour of every day, looking forward to school and Geometry and everything else I shouldn't look forward to.

And then, one day it happened. Sort of.

I purposely sat with my back to the Golden Circle at lunch, partly because they annoyed me, but mostly because I would be compelled to stare at Cody the entire time. Instead, I made Lilly face them and tell me every move he made.

"Weird," she said. "He looks like he's coming this way."

"Really?"

"Yeah." She looked down. "He is, for sure."

I got nervous and looked at my apple sitting alone on the table. I thought that perhaps I should seem occupied, so I took a bite of it, which made my mouth full when he approached me.

He sat beside me. "Hi."

"Hi," I answered, trying not to spit apple on him.

He looked at Lilly. "Hi."

"Hi," she said.

"So. There's a party tonight. Zack Fortner's parents are out of town, like on a cruise or something."

I gazed at him with a blank stare.

"I'm telling you about this because I want you to come." He looked at Lilly. "And you."

She smiled. Of course, she couldn't and wouldn't go.

"So, nine. I'll see you there."

"Uh…"

He was already walking away.

In geometry class, he texted me the address.

3272 Forrest Green Avenue

Just replying because I'm not one of those girls.

I know you're not.

"You could have just told me that," I whispered.

He smiled. "I could have."

"You have to go," Lil said.

It was the Wednesday before Thanksgiving, and traditionally a big party day, according to the kids at school. Someone always had an epic party the Wednesday before Thanksgiving.

"What if they're drinking?" I asked, trying to chicken out.

"Don't drink," she said.

"What if it's drugs? What if everyone is making out on every piece of furniture, like in the movies?" I tore through my closet like a maniac, trying to find something to wear.

"That's the movies. It's fake." She held a necklace up to a dress that I had tossed on the bed. "What are you going to tell your dad?"

"I'll tell him the truth."

"I think this means Cody likes you," she said.

I had already spent an hour staring at the text and wondering what it meant. Now she was fueling the non-existent fire. "You think?" I asked, wanting to revel in it for a moment.

"Yeah, I do," she said thoughtfully. She held up one of my dresses against herself and looked in the mirror. "I can't pull off dark colors like you do."

"I can't pull off light colors like you do," I reciprocated. "You know, maybe he likes *you*. Maybe he wanted you to come to the party and invited you through me."

"He doesn't like me. Come on, now."

I was nervous, and when I got nervous, I could feel my armpits sweating no matter how much deodorant I caked on, then my hands got clammy. My dad seemed happy that I was being a normal teenager and going to a party; he even dropped me off there. I had a feeling he'd be seeing Kristi since I wouldn't be home, and that was another reason he was glad to get me out of the house. There were people standing in the yard with red cups, cars everywhere, and loud music. All he could say was, "Have fun, Bear."

I looked at him in one last attempt to let him change his mind. "Have fun, Teddy," I said.

He just laughed, then drove away.

I hesitated before I went in, straightened my necklace, patted down my hair, and pulled down on my dress, which I felt was a little too short. As I approached the door, somebody swung it open, ran outside, and puked. I went in and walked around for a little while. Someone handed me a cup. I put it down as soon as I got the chance. People were yelling. I heard a commotion coming from the basement, and that's where I finally found Cody. He was wrestling with another guy on a mattress that was on the floor and he was only wearing a pair of short, pink, terry cloth shorts. The other guy was Zack Fortner, the wrestling captain. Zack had a large tattoo on his back. Everyone was screaming and Cody had him pinned for a while. Finally, a short, stocky kid acting as referee called it.

"Best two out of three," Zack said, and everyone cheered.

"You owe me ten bucks," Cody said.

"How about this? You win, I'll give you twenty. I win, you wear my sister's shorts all night."

"Let's go," Cody said.

The cheers erupted again. They began another fight, and I watched Maia DeFelice edge her way to the front. I wasn't sure if she was angling towards Zack or Cody. At one point Cody looked up at me and I thought we made eye contact. Zack took him down hard, but he got out of it and pinned Zack once again.

The referee called it.

Cody helped Zack up and held out his hand. "Twenty bucks, dude."

Zack reached for his wallet on the end table, and a creepy smile spread over his face. "I'll give you fifty to keep the shorts on."

Cody stuck his thumb in the waistband, allowing room for the money. "Do it," he said. Zack stuck a bunch of bills in the waistband of the pink shorts then smacked his butt.

Everyone laughed and cheered and Maia put her hand on Cody's back. He pulled away awkwardly. Once the commotion died down, he walked towards me, acting like he had just noticed me.

"You came," he said. "Where's Lilly?"

"Her dad is strict."

"Yeah. I guess I knew that."

He still smelled good, even after the wrestling bout. I was falling in love with his smell. "Nice shorts," I said, noticing what the skimpy shorts revealed.

"Do they make my ass look good?"

"They make your ass look great," I said, then immediately wished I could take it back.

He smiled and walked away.

I was not great at socializing in situations like parties. I couldn't find a really sober person to talk to, and Cody was completely preoccupied. I didn't want to seem like I was stalking him, so I tried to be in another room most of the time.

After an hour and a half of Cody and I ignoring each other, I found him sitting on the couch with Maia. I texted my dad and asked him to pick me up. He didn't respond, so I walked home.

It wasn't the coldest night, but I could see my breath and pulled my jacket tight. I liked the feeling of the cool air on my flushed cheeks. I wasn't sure if it was just hot inside, if I was nervous, or if my crush on Cody was exploding inside of me. I watched my breath in the air and I pictured the night turning out differently, with Cody being happy to see me and taking me under his wing and teaching me the ways of high school parties. I pictured him in that flannel shirt that I liked to see him in, wearing his glasses, walking me home. I pictured him liking me.

It always hits me all at once, that feeling of worthlessness. The world comes crashing down because I got one bad grade, or one person made fun of me in the hall, or one stupid boy didn't like me. It's always something small that brings on the darkness. I think I let myself melt in it because it's the only way I can be close to my mother. Her life was full of despair and paranoia and sadness and when I get a taste of it, I drink the whole glass because I know I feel how she felt.

My dad's car wasn't in the driveway; he must have decided to go to Kristi's. I went straight to my room and climbed into my bed, sweaty pits, makeup, and all. I thought, *who cares if I stink and get zits? Cody Kirby doesn't love me. So who really cares?*

When I got into those moods I stayed up, mind racing, then shut it down and went to sleep for a long time. Once sleep came, it was a nice escape from the misery. I beat myself up for feeling upset over petty things like boys and tests, and then my shallowness depressed me further. I knew I would have to tell Lilly every detail, but I didn't want to recall the pain of not being wanted.

I heard my dad come in, then a woman laughing.

"Come on, Teddy. We never do it in the kitchen."

"What if Caroline comes home?"

"Who comes home from a party this early?"

Even my dad's waitress-fuck-buddy thought I was a loser.

"It's weird, Kristi. It's like…we eat here."

"You're so vanilla, Teddy. So vanilla. Take a risk. My gosh."

I could hear them kissing. *"I'm not vanilla. Not at all."*

"Right here, then. Come on."

"OK. OK."

Zippers. She laughed. *"I can't believe you got me so drunk."*

"It was your idea to go for drinks."

More kissing. I was intrigued and grossed out at the same time. She barked out orders and my dad said nothing. She moaned and he still said nothing. I'm pretty sure she faked it, because according to *Cosmopolitan*, we usually fake it, and then it seemed to be over.

"Another drink?" he asked.

"Oh, what the hell. Who cares?"

I imagined my dad reaching for the bottle of Johnny Walker he kept in the cupboard above the refrigerator, barely able to reach it. I heard the glasses clanging and she laughed again.

"Have a drink with me."

"I have to drive you home."

"You're getting so rigid and professor-y."
"I am not."
"Why aren't you into it today, babe?"
"I don't know."
"You're thinking about her?"
"Huh?"
"I think that's why you're always so far away. You're thinking about your wife instead of me."
"We were never married." He said it thoughtfully and I wondered why he had to point that out.
"You still love her and you always will. No one will ever compare. That's why I don't even try." She said it in a drunk, slurring fashion.
"We shouldn't talk about her."
"You are physically incapable of saying her name."
My dad didn't respond. Probably because she was right.
"I thought you weren't drinking."
I heard the glasses moving around again.
"Let's go to bed."
"You're letting me spend the night?"
"Sure."

That was the first time it occurred to me that on that level, you didn't have to be alone even if you loved somebody else. Maybe that was the definition of hooking up.

3

Messing Up

NOTHING IS MORE awkward than the first time your dad makes breakfast for you and his lady friend. Especially when she's wearing nothing but his Gorillaz t-shirt and purple panties.

"Let's see. Oh, look. Bacon!" he said with genuine excitement as he foraged through the freezer for food.

My dad and I were both hopeless at things like grocery shopping and meal planning. To find enough food to make a meal really was a miracle.

I started the coffee, and he put everything on the stove in various frying pans while Kristi looked at the newspaper. My dad and I usually did the crossword together while we ate breakfast. Now what were we going to do?

We sat down together at the high-top kitchen table and began to eat. I couldn't look either of them in the eye.

"What time did you get home, Bear? I fell asleep and didn't hear you come in."

"Ten-thirty," I said.

They looked at each other, guilty, knowing I had busted them officially.

"That's early," he finally said, choking down some food. "Must have been some party."

"I guess parties aren't for me."

I kept quiet about all the things I wanted to say, like how disappointed I was in Cody and how much it hurt not to fit in.

"Do you have somewhere to go for Thanksgiving?" Kristi asked, changing the awkward subject.

"We're staying in. I'll make turkey sandwiches," my dad said, looking at his watch. "Oh. Let's put the parade on."

He went into the living room to turn on the TV and Kristi and I finally exchanged a glance. I tried not to have an expression on my face. I wanted to be cool about it, but I wished my dad would have talked to me about her first. He could have told me Kristi was going to start spending the night and that maybe they were a thing now. Instead he just got tired and lonely and didn't drive her home.

"You're always welcomed at my folks' house." She raised her eyebrows and lifted her coffee cup to her lips.

"Yes. And then what would we tell them?"

"About what?" she asked.

"About us. You know, the questions that don't really have answers. Where did you meet? How long have you been seeing each other? What are your intentions with my daughter?"

"All questions that are going through my mind right now," I said, unable to hold it back any longer.

They both looked at me, my dad maybe a little hurt.

"What questions do you have, Bear?"

"Spending the night? I mean, come on, I know what you do every other Friday. But we skipped right to eating breakfast together." I put my fork down and waited for an answer.

"It's different," my dad said, faltering.

"What's different?"

"Relationships are different when you're older. You don't have to follow all these...rules."

"People my age don't have relationships either. Maybe there is no such thing as love anymore. Or maybe everyone is afraid to say it."

My dad just stared at me, puzzled.

A knowing smile spread across Kristi's lips and she reached across the table and put her hand on top of my hand. "Honey..." she started. I hated when people called me that. "We're certainly not in love with each other. If you're worried that I'm going to take your dad away from you, I'm not. We never wanted you to feel that way."

I pulled my hand away. *We.* As if they had discussed it. That seemed so pretentious. And rehearsed. And so very wrong. "That's not what I was talking about," I said quietly, and stuffed another forkful of food down.

My dad looked at me throughout the rest of breakfast like an alien had taken over his child. I never talked to him about my innermost feelings — the ones I really kept hidden. I had a fear that I could never learn to love because I had never seen it first hand. I doubted that I could ever trust anyone enough to share anything about my mother. And then there was the real fear — the fear that I would turn into her.

I announced that I was taking a walk, bundled up in a big black sweater, and went out into the crisp November air. There I was, alone on the street while everyone else was inside watching the parade and preparing for a feast and complaining that it was too early for the Christmas commercials on television. My mother was in a box in the ground too far away to even visit. I wondered if my grandmother put flowers on it like she promised she would.

Walking around Newbury became boring quickly; I felt a fleeting rebellion and considered taking up smoking so I would have something to do while I walked. I let go of it quickly at the prospect of death. I got ignored by the boy I liked at a party and my dad had just made a severely lame attempt at explaining to me why he was having casual sex with a pizza waitress. My phone vibrated in my sweater pocket and I had to partially unwrap myself to retrieve it.

Did you have fun last night?

I started typing:

By inviting me to a party, I assumed you liked me. You barely looked at me, spoke to me even less, and completely ignored me. I thought you weren't like that. I thought you were different. I thought there was a spark. You're a liar. All guys are liars. What is the definition of a relationship? Do you think it's OK to invite a girl to a party and just ignore her? Did you momentarily forget I existed? Were you that drunk? No, really. WHAT. THE. F—

I decided that a knee jerk rant-response wouldn't be the best idea. I deleted the message and went with:

It was OK.

You never see that side of me. I wasn't sure if you hated me now.

Don't you have some wrestling thing?

Saturday.

I don't hate you. Why would I hate you?

I act like a complete dick when someone eggs me on enough.

I like that you have a personality.

What's that supposed to mean?

You're always kind of dry.

Moist.

What?

I'm not exactly dry. Maybe moist is the right word.

Look. I'm sorry.

Damp. Moist sounds like something bad. Damp is better.

I've apologized. Forgive me.

I have a damp personality. Shit. That sounds worse than dry.

SORRY.

Are you smiling? Are you laughing? I'm trying to make you laugh.

No. I thought you were mad at me.

You wouldn't exactly be the first person to say that. I'm used to it.

So you overcompensate for your dryness at parties then?

There is just so much shit to deal with. Sometimes I just want to be stupid and have fun.

Shit?

Wrestling. Grades. Parents. Teachers. Unclear relationship boundaries. You name it.

I know. I have some shit, too.

Then why not loosen up sometimes? Take off your clothes and wrestle someone.

I'm as stiff as you are dry. Also, I'm not athletic enough for wrestling and not confident enough for taking my clothes off.

That's too bad. It's pretty fucking awesome.

I'm laughing now. You win.

What's your wedding song? Figure it out yet?

Jesus. No. Don't pressure me.

Fine. I guess you have some time to think about it. I wasn't going to propose until Christmas anyway.

That only gives me a month.

We have two more years of high school and four years of college to plan the wedding.

Guess we'll just have to use your song.

Maybe by the time you're on your second husband you'll figure it out.

What's with Maia?

What do you mean?

I saw you sitting with her at the party.

With drinking comes courage and poor judgement.

Maybe she likes you.

Maybe I tried to kiss her after homecoming, she turned her head and I kissed her hair which got tangled up in my glasses. Maybe she told me she doesn't like me like that. And maybe I only kissed her because that's what they do in the movies.

Maybe. Or maybe she likes you now.

Do I detect a hint of jealousy or something?

I had a rough morning. I'm just man-hating and you don't deserve this.

What happened?

My dad didn't know I came home early and brought home his fuck-buddy. We all just ate breakfast together while he tried to justify casual sex to me.

Whoa. I just thought of something gross.

What?

I wonder if my parents still do it.

Do you kind of hope not?

Yes and no. I mean it is gross. Yes. But I would probably still want to do it when I'm that old. Especially since I probably won't get laid until I'm thirty with my shit personality and all so I'll need to make up for lost time.

You're popular. You'll get some.

I can't imagine doing that with just anyone. I can't see people as just bodies. And then there's fear. I don't want to be a dad for a long time. And I don't want to get fucking herpes or something.

You ever heard of condoms?

I don't carry around Trojans with the expectation that it will happen.

Maybe you should, because maybe there is.

Your dad is wrong. Don't compromise.

I'm glad that you're different.

My mother is calling for me. I think she wants me to stick my hand up the turkey's ass or something.

Happy Thanksgiving. Good luck at the wrestling thing.

I'll wear the pink shorts for the win.

You do that.

When I got back, Kristi and Teddy weren't there. I sat on the couch re-reading the texts from Cody. I heard my dad's keys hit the table and didn't look up. I was becoming the master of sneaking in when people weren't home.

I heard him go up the steps, come down, and shuffle around. Finally, he was at the edge of the couch with a copy-paper box. "We need to talk."

"Why?" I asked defiantly. I knew I sounded bratty. I didn't want him to talk any more.

He sat the box on the coffee table and pushed my feet aside so he could sit down.

"Holidays are hard for you. Especially this one."

I guess I had pushed it back into the recesses of my mind.

"It's hard for me, too. I guess that's why I messed up with Kristi."

"You didn't mess up. You thought I wasn't home. I mean, it's your house, right? You pay the bills."

"That was the worst Thanksgiving of my life. I swear, I still wait for her to come home every Thanksgiving. It's like I wait, and I wait, and I wait. Like she's going to walk in and time will warp back to that day and this was all a bad dream. And I've never been quite honest with you about your mother."

"I think you have."

"You don't know her and that's not fair."

"She took that from me. Not you."

"If you blame her…if you have any anger towards her…you should try to let it go. Maybe she deserves it, but it's a hell of a lot easier to miss her than to blame her. I made the choice the first day that I would never blame her. It was a disease and there is no cure for it. So I miss her. And I wait for her. Because my heart tricks my brain into thinking she's still out there." He leaned forward and looked down. "She left in the middle of the night. I woke up because you woke up and that's when I realized she was gone. For years I was mad at myself because I didn't hear her get up, and maybe I could have stopped her from leaving. We went over to Gram's without her. Gram never made me lie to her about Tressa. She knew enough about it not to ask. You and Gramp fell asleep in the evening and I confessed everything to Gram and Jen, and Gram thought Jen and I should go out to look for her. Gram said she would help me find a good hospital for her and we would get her better. So we went and we looked. I had some ideas of where she could be. All day Friday we never stopped looking. I showed her picture to anyone who would look at it. I begged every crackhead, every homeless person, every convenience store owner to tell me if they saw her. I begged them and told them that she had a little girl. And finally someone recognized her. It took twenty-two hours to find her, she had been gone for more than thirty-six hours, and I was too late."

I had never known that he went out and found her.

"You know, it was weird. She wasn't any less beautiful. Even the drugs couldn't take that from her." He wiped his right eye. "Jen and Gram went out and bought her a nice dress that would hide the needle marks. Something she would have liked. Gramp had gone to school with the mortician and when he came over to see us, I gave him a picture so he could make her look right and it was fucking amazing. She looked like she was sleeping. I almost wished she would've looked worse because it would have been easier to accept the fact that she was dead. I remember how her hair was lying over her shoulders... how perfect it was. She would have liked it that way. She was just so pretty, you could forgive her for everything else."

He broke down crying and I felt a responsibility to comfort him.

"We stayed with Gram for a week or so," he said tearfully, "But I knew I had to learn to do it on my own. I had to go back to work. And I had already been doing it on my own for a while, really. So we went back to Cleveland. It was easier than I thought it would be. Working and taking care of you distracted me from the pain of it. Every day got better, and I got to the point where I only thought about it in bed at night. I kept busy. That was my fix for it all. Staying busy. Over a year went by and Christmas came around again and it got so lonely sometimes. We went home to see Gram for Christmas and I don't know what happened, but I hooked up with my high school girlfriend. We ran into each other at the grocery store and she asked me if I wanted to get drinks and I said yes because I wanted to see if I could still function like a normal human being — if I could have friends and go places and not just spend my time trying to forget her. I had lost your mom and Becca had just gone through a painful breakup with her fiancé and it just happened. It just filled something. I don't know, a dark spot. It was a little less time I had to think about Tressa. I just wanted to fill up all my space so there was no room to mourn. That's how it started, Bear."

"How many of these people were there?'

"Enough," he said.

"Did I know any of them?"

"Miss Baker."

"My third grade teacher?" I felt betrayed.

"Yes. I'm just going to be totally honest with you."

"Did you love her? Did you love anyone?"

"Well, I guess I loved them all a little. I just still loved your mother more. I never wanted a relationship and neither did they. I just wanted to put my arms around someone who was nothing like her. I wanted a woman that would not remind me of her in any way."

"Did it work? Did it fill the space?"

"Sure, for as long as it lasts until they get sick of sneaking out at four in the morning."

"Why didn't you just have a girlfriend?"

"I couldn't risk putting you through losing somebody else. Relationships are temporary. You needed something permanent. You were always so sensitive about losing things. You didn't cope with change well after she died. I realized it one day when we were watching a commercial — it was like a car insurance commercial and this girl was going off to college and her parents were left in the driveway waving. The girl had blonde hair, and maybe she looked a little like Tressa. And you were crying, crying hard. I asked you what was wrong and you said they would never see each other again and I couldn't figure out how to explain to you that some people don't stay in your life forever and that's when I realized I couldn't bring anyone else into our lives who was capable of breaking us. I liked them all, maybe I loved them a little, but I couldn't invest in any of them and I was so dedicated to you that none of them wanted to invest in me. But that's all OK. I wouldn't change any of it. You needed me more than any of them did, and I needed you more than I needed any of them."

He put his arm around me. "I always promised her that I would take care of you and everything else. I made her that promise... and I will always keep it. I knew that she couldn't do it. It wasn't that she didn't want you. She was sick and she knew it and she knew she couldn't do it. I promised her that I would be responsible for you, because once we found out about you, we wanted you. She was scared. She was so scared and I just promised her that it would be fine. And I had to make it fine. I always knew that you were my job."

"I never really thought she wanted me."

"She wanted you. Before you, she would live in a moment. She would get caught up in one good thing and everything else was shit and she would get sad. And after you, she had this vision that someday we'd have the picket fence and the dog and the kids and the swing set and she'd cook dinner and I'd come home and we'd be a big, happy family. She wanted it to be the way I grew up. She was in love with the idea."

"Then why didn't she do it?"

"She was too sick. Depression is like a brick wall, I think, and it separates you from everything." He looked at me. "But I think you know that, don't you?"

"I don't have a wall."

"I apologize for Kristi. It's not a good example for you and it's not something I condone doing. I don't want you to think that's what I was doing. God, no. I don't ever want you to be that to a guy. Kristi and I are good friends. Neither of us wants a relationship. It's a mutual feeling. Sex — I never wanted to be the one to talk to you about it. It makes me totally uncomfortable. I don't know what to say about it. Respect yourself and be with someone who respects you. And ultimately, you should be in love. And don't do it when you're young. Don't — it doesn't matter as much as people say it does. And me, I do it for all the wrong reasons. I thought I was doing an OK job of hiding it from you. Last night, it was just the night, you know? Like, eleven years. I just kept thinking, eleven years. Twelve Thanksgiving mornings I've woken up alone, if you count the first one. Eleven entire years. I just wanted to wake up with someone and that was horrible and I'm sorry. We definitely should have talked about it first."

"I want you to have a girlfriend, Dad. I want you to be happy. I'm not jealous. I want you to wake up with someone every morning. I want you to be in love again."

"Eleven years, but I'm not ready for all of that. So, I'll just promise that there will be no more surprises. I'll keep those types of relationships under wraps and we'll go back to normal."

"I don't mind it. I don't mind her being here if it's what you want." I handed him a tissue, because he was crying again. "Like, maybe you could consider getting her some pajamas, though."

He put his face in his hands and laughed. "Oh, Bear. Where did you come from? Huh?"

I smiled. "I came from you."

"I guess you did."

He put his hand on the box. "When we came back to the apartment after she died, I decided I'd put a couple of things away every day. I couldn't do it all at once and I didn't want to do it at all, really, but they were constant reminders. She wasn't a person who had a lot of stuff. Here it is, though. I don't remember what's in here, but it was hers and you should have a piece of her."

I found it hard to accept that an entire lifetime could be stuffed into a copy-paper box. She lived for twenty-four years and that's what she had to show for it.

4

How Not To Kiss

I took fifth because they wouldn't let me wear the pink shorts.

They need to relax their dress code.

That's not why we need to talk. I've been thinking about this thing with girls.

Which girls?

The girls who don't text back.

What about it?

I'm also irritated by girls who never text me first.

I promised I would always text back, not always text first.

Right. Why don't you though?

What if you're busy or sleeping? What if you're the boy who doesn't text back?

I'll eventually text back.

I don't want to set myself up for the fall.

I'm not going to NOT text you back.

You've probably got the phone numbers of a hundred girls. None of them text you?

Nope. Just you. Unless they want something.

What do they want from you?

Usually homework answers. Or another guy's phone number. Or to ask me if I think another guy likes them. Occasionally a slutty selfie, for tease only.

That's a lot more than guys text me. Zero. Plus one. So one. You.

Skip Waters doesn't text you?

Skip doesn't have a phone. And he wouldn't text me if he did.

He's a weird dude.

He's a nice person.

Do you like him?

Not like that. He wouldn't be into it. He doesn't date. Or hook up. Or whatever they're calling it these days.

Unclear boundaries. You know. Can we kiss or will I get a mouthful or hair? I don't know. Have you ever kissed anyone?

That's a personal question.

So? Have you?

Have you?

Yeah. A couple.

How was it?

Hard to navigate through teeth and tongues. Never sure how much pressure to apply. Never sure when to end it. Also, depth is an issue and also breathing.

Breathing?

It's weird to breath onto somebody's face.

That's a lot of issues. Must have taken a lot of kissing to get there.

Not really. You could easily screw up one kiss with all of that.

How?

OK. So I went in for the kill, we bumped teeth, I went waaaaaaay too deep and she told me it was gross.

Was it a blast to your ego?

No. I learn from my mistakes. I did the next one a little better. I decided to not go past the two front teeth and I held my breath. But I ran out of breath and that looked stupid.

Isn't it supposed to be natural? Not a thinking thing?

Oh. You answered my question then.

What question?

Did you ever kiss anyone? You would know how unnatural and technical it is if you had kissed someone before.

Kissing is so unnatural. Invading someone's mouth is so unnatural. I'd rather hold hands or something.

Maybe I had a kiss and it was natural.

Lie.

OK. You're right. I've not been sucking face. Secret is out. Are you surprised?

Yes and no.

Why?

No because I never see you talking to guys. Yes because you're nice.

Is it normal to kiss people just because they're nice?

When it gets there, yeah.

Is that how you got there?

No. It was an eighth grade game of spin the bottle. The second one was my cousin's neighbor and I think she just wanted to get some strange.

What is strange?

It's just doing stuff with someone you don't know and probably will never see again. The first one though, I had to take it in front of everyone. She literally said it was gross. In front of like twenty people.

Have you had a good kiss?

One. Remember the freshman trip to Cedar Point at the end of the school year?

Yeah, but I didn't go.

The Pastel Effect

I stood in line with this girl for like four hours and we started talking. We hung out the rest of the day. I decided to kiss her goodbye. The trick is to dominate the kiss, but be gentle at the same time. I felt like a genius when I figured it out. Breathing on someone's face is still weird, though.

What happened to her?

She lives in Michigan. She went into the 'doesn't text me back' box.

So kissing is like wrestling.

How?

To dominate, but with finesse.

Maybe you're right. I'm not always so smooth with wrestling either. The coach says I'd make a better boxer. I kind of tend to want to hit people.

Wow. I can see that.

You think I could come over and listen to those records someday?

Of course. My dad would love it.

I thought we were mad at him.

We talked. It was a hard day for him. My mom died on Thanksgiving.

Last year?

It's been eleven years.

I'm sorry. That sucks. Are you OK?

Yes. It was a long time ago and I don't even really remember her.

My mother is calling me.

Your mother is always calling you.

I know. She's always bossing me around like she's my birth giver or something.

Jesus. You're not right.

I know.

One more thing.

What is it?

Maybe when you run out of breath, or when you want to breathe, you could go for the neck. Then come back to the face again. It makes it seem more passionate and I think that's why they used to call it necking.

You're a fucking genius.

I DECIDED NOT to open the box until my mother's birthday. I wanted to wonder about it and build up to it and then make it a ceremony of sorts, or a remembrance. I thought it would be more meaningful. My dad gave me the box on her death date and I would open it on her birth date. Her birthday was February twenty-fifth. I had almost three months to go.

Cody still spent his time at school with the Golden Circle. Seventh period was ours, though. Sometimes when we sat at the table together, his knee touched mine and I wondered if he was conscious of it. Every day he smelled good. Every day I liked him more. I wondered if the Circle knew about us, and if they did, were they going to accept that he had an outsider friend? I spent way too much time and energy analyzing the dynamics of the inner and outer

Circle relationship. They intimidated me, though. A lot of them were snobbish about it, had no other friends, and wanted to protect it. Cody seemed more willing to stray than the others. He seemed interested in finding an identity beyond his high school clique.

Maybe, in an act of rebellion against Maia DeFelice, or maybe to prove to me that he didn't like her, Cody invited me to her sixteenth birthday party. It was a Golden Circle event, but he wanted me to come. For three weeks running we had spent Wednesday nights watching *Broken Blue* together. We found out it was practically the one and only thing we had in common, a favorite TV show about cops who were always on the cusp of being bad, but for good reasons. It was my favorite show because the lead cop was hot. It was Cody's favorite show because he was going to go into law enforcement.

He picked up the remote and paused the show at a pivotal moment.

"Did you pause for commentary? Lopez is about to shoot that drug dealer in the face."

"He won't do it," Cody said, disappointedly. "He'll pistol whip him and kick the shit out of him and arrest him."

"OK. So you paused it to do a spoiler."

"A prediction. But that's not why I paused it."

"Why, then?"

"You want to go to Maia's birthday party?"

I raised my eyebrows. "Do you want to throw me to the wolves? I'm not part of the gang."

He was still trying to deny the Circle. "She texted out the invite and it clearly states to bring a friend."

"She only said that because everyone who got that invite would only bring someone else who got that invite."

"Not me. I'd bring you."

"Why?"

"Because I thought you liked my party-boy side. You said you did."

"I think you're funny."

"I promise to be funny. I swear."

"Some of that group is pretty exclusive."

"You're going with me."

"So, by that you mean, we're walking in together, you'll not completely ignore me, and we're leaving together?"

"Coming and leaving together, yes. If I ignore you just come find me. I'm a dick. I can't help it."

"And those girls — what if their claws come out?"

"I'll handle it."

"You're putting me in a vulnerable place if I go."

"I will protect you. I will protect you like Lopez protected Shields when he almost got caught stealing cocaine from the evidence locker before he went to rehab. The world's shortest rehab because he was back on the job the next Wednesday. Cocaine must be an easy habit to kick."

"That makes it sound like I'm going to steal her mother's diamond earrings or something."

"No. What I'm saying is I'll protect you like a bro would protect a bro."

"We're bros?"

"Kind of. It's a little different. It's kind of like that, though."

"So, am I in the category of girls who text you back or bros?"

"You are…a bro-friend."

"What is a bro-friend?"

"The stuff we talk about is a little deeper than bro conversation. And you were the only one in the 'girls who text me back' category anyway. You're a girl. You're a friend. We're not dating, but we hang out because we like the same shows and the same music. You're really good at math and you tend to be a problem solver, and I like it when you figure shit out for me. And I like it when you laugh."

"That does not explain bro-friends."

"I trust you like a bro and you're the first real person I've met in a long time. It's our own thing. It's a C thing," he said, putting his arm around my shoulders.

It felt good, but I didn't want to let it feel too comfortable. I looked at the TV. "I will bet you a dollar Lopez shoots him."

"Two dollars says he pistol whips the dude."

"Fine. Two says he shoots him."

He was truly competitive. "It's on."

On the Thursday before the party, Cody approached me at lunch — the social mecca of high school. I figured he was trying to ease the Golden Circle into the idea of an outsider crashing their party. He sat beside me and took a bite out of my granny smith apple. "Sorry. Did I ruin that for you?"

I took a bite out of it, maybe to prove that I wouldn't mind swapping spit with him.

"Can I come over again tonight?"

"It's Thursday," I said, matter-of-factly.

"And your point is?"

"It's not Wednesday."

"We have all that math homework. We could get it done twice as fast if we split it."

"Of course you can come over."

"What are you wearing Friday?"

"Don't know yet."

"If you want to fit in with the other girls, you'll probably want to showcase your boobs. Something to think about."

"Thanks for the advice."

He picked up my apple again, bit a chunk off of it, handed it back and walked away.

"He likes you *so* much," Lilly said.

"No he doesn't. We're just friends."

"Uh-huh," she said, as if I were trying to hide something.

"Good friends, but not romantic."

"Uh-huh. What do you call that?"

"As of yesterday, he calls it the C-thing."

"He has a name for your relationship? Like Brangelina? Like Bennifer?"

"No. That's for couples."

"You are well on your way to Codaline."

"That sounds like a medicine you take when you have diarrhea."

"It sounds like love to me."

"He does NOT love me," I said, my frustration peeking through.

"He's coming to your house two days in a row, taking you to a party on day three. Do you know how lucky you are?"

"I'm just going to picture your brother shirtless right now. OK?"

"You're going to waste your time in some fantasy where Skip

forgets that he loves Jesus more than he loves you? Do you want to know what the aftermath of that hook-up would be? He would probably hang himself on the cross for three days because he wouldn't want Jesus to have to die for that sin. He would take it upon himself."

"He is literally the absolute hottest guy in school. A sophomore guy, hotter than any junior or senior guy, turning down offers from every girl ever. I think Jesus would expect him to cave. Imagine the nudes he'd get if he had a phone. My goodness."

"You are a horrible person," she said.

"Sorry," I said. "I'm just saying, Cody is about as likely to love me as Skip is to go on a date. With anyone."

"I don't even think my brother has a penis," she said, looking away.

I could have commented on that one, but I didn't.

Thursday nights weren't as exciting for television as Wednesdays were, so after we did our homework, we muted the teen drama that was on and listened to music. Cody seemed introspective and discontented, and I was afraid he was getting bored with me.

"Is something wrong?"

"This shit on TV is so unrealistic."

"Why?"

"These actors make it all seem so normal and easy."

I glanced at the television where two of the teen characters were engaged in a steamy sex scene. "It's not normal and easy?" I asked.

"No. It's all really complicated. Do kids our age really act like this?"

"I don't know. Do they?"

He gave me a look.

"You're asking someone who hasn't even kissed anyone. You're the one with experience."

"I've never even been to second base."

"Really?"

"No. Why would I? I can hardly even get through a kiss."

"You don't want to progress to second base?"

"Of course I *want* to, but I've never kissed someone and had it feel right to go there."

"We're only fifteen," I said. "Those actors are like thirty."

He looked at the screen and laughed, and finally he seemed like himself again.

Maia DeFelice lived in Cody's neighborhood, so my dad dropped me off in front of his house. I knocked on the door and he opened it. "Come in. The parents aren't home."

"If they were home, you wouldn't invite me in?"

"Do you seriously want to be the first girl I bring over? I mean, the first girl I bring over that I haven't known for a million years that doesn't come with seventeen other people?"

"Why would that be bad?"

"My mom would be all like, 'Do you have a girlfriend? Is that your girlfriend? You don't even tell your own mother that you have a girlfriend? How dare you not share with me every last detail of your miserable life?' And then I would spend six weeks explaining the C-thing to her and in the end, I'm still her baby and she doesn't want me to grow up, which means, she doesn't want me to be interested in girls and it would be a big shitty mess."

"And what about your dad?"

"He'd just be like, 'Use a rubber, son.'"

I laughed, and he appeared to get some pleasure out of amusing me.

"Sit down for a second. I have to brush my teeth."

The Kirbys' house was modest, but nice on the inside and well-landscaped on the outside. More than I could say for my yard and house. I sat at the kitchen table, wondering why he had to brush his teeth, analyzing the possibility of a kiss.

After a few minutes, he emerged from the bathroom wearing my favorite of his flannel shirts and glasses. He *still* smelled good. He must have a naturally good smell to him. Pheromones, like Lilly said.

"Let's hang out a minute. I want to be a few minutes late. I hate being there at the beginning, when everyone is still square."

"How do your friends get away with these drinking parties?"

"Maia's parents will keep an eye on things." He pulled a flask from his back pocket. "But we have our ways."

"Are you going to get trashed?"

"No. I probably won't even drink. It's for looks. The point is to make everyone *think* you're drinking and being cool and stuff."

"So you never drink? You just pretend?"

"I've been wasted before. It's weird."

"Why?"

"You know the conversations you and I have?"

"Yes."

"Well, I try to have those with other people when I'm wasted and they're just not that into it. When everyone else is wasted they are wrestling in girl shorts, but I do that shit when I'm sober and get all serious when I'm wasted."

"So when you're with me, you feel like you're wasted?"

He smiled. "Yeah. Sort of."

I thought about it. "You look nice," I finally said.

"Yeah. You, too. Good choice with covering the boobs. You'll stand out from the crowd. And you still look hot."

"Look, I know we're going to this party together, but don't let me stop you from second base. Don't feel like if you get an opportunity that I would…I want you to have what you want. I don't want to bring you down. I just don't want to feel like an outsider at the party."

"I know exactly what I'm going to do to break the ice. I know the right person for you to talk to."

"Uh-oh."

"And I'm not smooching with anyone tonight, so there will be no second base."

"How do you know you won't get the opportunity to smooch?"

"I have standards, and one of those is to not kiss drunk girls."

"Even Maia?"

"You have beef with Maia, don't you?"

"No. Not at all. I just don't like her with you is all."

"Who would you like with me, then?" He asked it as a challenge.

"I don't know yet. I have to think about it."

"I want you to be single," he said.

"Why?"

"I don't think there's anyone good enough for you. You're

special and that would be wasted on anybody that I know. Anybody that goes to our school, at least."

I wanted to tell him that I wanted him to be single, too.

We walked slowly down the street, probably because we were both dreading it a little.

"You pick our wedding song yet?"

"No. I've been busy naming our kids."

"Enlighten me."

"Shawn and Emily."

"What?"

"What?" I asked back.

"Shawn and Emily Kirby? Whoa. That's harsh. But at least you've been planning for our future."

More than you know, I thought.

"Wait a minute. You've not put any thought into that. Shields' first name is Shawn and Lopez's girlfriend is Emily. You're playing with my emotions, here. I thought you went to bed dreaming about our kids."

"No wonder you're going to be a detective someday."

"CIA," he said.

"Right."

"Well, if this outfit is your idea of sexy, I can't wait to see your wedding dress."

"It's going to be reminiscent of a hospital gown. Because I don't mind showing off my back."

He laughed. "That's OK. It's what's underneath that counts."

"You're sick," I said.

"I know."

Cody introduced me to Gus Garrett, the one kid in the Golden Circle who would even talk to me. Gus was a bit weird, really obsessed with anime, and had a knack for drawing surprisingly accurate sex cartoons. He was only in the Golden Circle because he was somebody's cousin, and that somebody was Cody Kirby. Cody and Gus were in the crib together, and it was only natural for them to be in the Circle together. Gus wore square plastic Ray-Ban glasses and sometimes a Karate-Kid-style bandana around his forehead.

He showed me his YouTube channel while we sat on the couch, and went into descriptive detail of the Ghostbusters parody he was filming with Cody and some other kids.

"How do you parody a comedy?" I asked.

"What?"

"How do you parody a comedy? Like, *Spaceballs* is a parody of *Star Wars*. And *Scary Movie* is a parody of *Scream*. How do you make fun of something that's already a comedy?"

"I'm not making fun of it."

"Are you just doing a reenactment then?"

"Well, there are going to be more jokes."

I quit trying to figure it out.

"Do you want to see the time I dared Cody to put a toad in his mouth?"

"OK."

He queued up the YouTube video on his phone. "The toad pissed in his mouth and he barfed all over himself."

"You just gave me the spoiler."

"Yeah, but it's still funny."

I took the phone and watched a younger Cody almost chicken out of it, gag, then finally do it, legs first and head sticking out. Then the camera movement went shaky as the barfing and laughter erupted. It became steady again while another guy from the Circle washed out Cody's mouth with the hose on full blast. There was blood, more vomit, and then Cody looked up and said, "That was for you, Mom." Then it was over.

"Funny stuff," Gus said. "A lot of people don't know that he's a super-funny guy. And he's nice, too. He's always making girls talk to me. Like now."

"Me? I thought he was making *you* talk to *me*."

"He told me to, yeah, but I thought it was because he had already told you to listen."

"Wait. What is this?"

"I mean, he did tell me you were awkward about the party because of the Circle and stuff." Gus looked down. "Don't worry. I don't fit into it either sometimes. I annoy them, but they put up with me."

"Why do you come to this stuff then?"

"What else is there to do? Sit at home? Alone? I'm the dweeb and the girls know I'm safe so they tell me all their shit and I get to be the friend-zone guy and I get to cop a feel every once in a while when someone is vulnerable. 'Oh, I would never do that like your boyfriend did that. He was so wrong and you are so right. Now let me touch your boob.' Yeah, that's me."

I laughed at his honesty.

"Why does Cody like you enough to bring you here?" he asked.

"You're the friend-zone *guy*? I think I might be the friend-zone *girl*."

He nodded as if he agreed with me. "You wanna make out?"

"Um. No."

"Whatever," he said, shrugging it off.

After talking to Gus for an excruciating length of time, I found Cody on the sun porch, just finishing a swig from the flask. He motioned for me to sit beside him. "Hi," he said and started laughing.

"What?" I asked. The paranoia was setting in. The feeling that I wasn't wanted there, not even by him. He slid over on the couch, though, into the girl beside him, and made room for me on the edge. I could smell her perfume over his good smell and it bothered me.

"What's up?"

"Nothing." I was going to tell him about the make out offer from Gus, but the room was too quiet.

"Now I'm going to ask her. I'm going to ask her because…"

Everybody groaned.

"Shut up," he said. "Shut up. I'm going to ask her because she's smarter than any of you."

They chuckled a little. I hated being in the spotlight, and on top of that, put up on a pedestal.

"Do you believe in reincarnation?" he asked.

"I guess," I said.

"You never commit to an answer," he said.

"I do when there is a right answer. I don't know on this one. I want to believe."

"Oh my God. You want to believe. I love that answer."

"You're an idiot," one of the girls said. "There is one life and it's now."

"No, no." His blue-green eyes got wider and greener when he

was in a serious mood. "There is a parallel universe. There has to be. How else do you explain deja vu?"

"But then in the parallel universe you would have to be you," I said.

"Maybe not. Maybe I could be you and you could be me. If it was a moment of deja vu between the two of us, we could have switched bodies or something."

"Then how do you explain deja vu with other people?" the girl asked.

"Maybe we're constantly switching, jumping back and forth between space and time."

"That's not reincarnation, though," I said. "And you wouldn't have memories. Reincarnation is more plausible."

The girl beside him and the one across from him got up. "Come on, Jules. Let's let the nerds hash this one out."

"Fuck you, Libby," he said, reaching for the flask again. I stopped him because I saw Maia's mother pass by. The other two guys got up and left, too. He took another swig and stretched out on the couch. "Who needs them?" he asked.

"What happened to party-boy? Am I meeting drunk-boy for the first time?"

"You certainly are," he said, smiling.

"What happened to no drinking?"

"Sometimes being fun gets too heavy for me. It's like a burden sometimes, to entertain people. They don't like the real me. See? Everybody leaves."

"This isn't the real you. This is the drunk you."

"Where is the real me?"

I thought about it as he put his feet in my lap and got even more comfortable. "I think the real you is sitting on my couch watching *Broken Blue*. Being jealous of me for being able to eat popcorn because you have braces. Worrying about Lopez's never-ending cycle of poor life decisions. And wondering when I'm going to wear a shirt you can look down."

He laughed. "You are probably right, C-dog. You are probably right. Except I like booty."

"I know you do."

He looked at his watch. Another thing I found odd and endearing about Cody was his eighties-style calculator watch that was big and bulky and dorky, and I loved that he just wore it anyway.

"So, I had no intentions of getting drunk tonight and here I am and my mom is *not* cool with this. You think you could get me home before eleven?"

"It's ten thirty and they haven't even had the cake yet."

"You need to have my back right now," he said.

"You were supposed to have *my* back," I countered.

"Be my bro-friend, C."

"OK." I squirmed out from under his feet and pulled him up, then I happily headed for the door.

He wrapped his coat around me as the chill of fall enveloped us. "Are you warm enough?" he asked.

"Yes. Thanks."

"I'm sorry I got drunk. I'm a little shit of a drunk. I can't even drink the bitchiest amount of alcohol and I'm shit-faced. I'm not a good drinker."

"It's fine."

"Looks like I sat the bench in this game."

"What do you mean?"

"Second base."

"I got asked to go up to bat."

"No way. Who?"

"Gus. I didn't kiss him."

"Good. He's kind of a douche."

"I gathered that. Why did you put me with him?"

"I wanted to show you that the Circle is not as tight as people think it is. It's more like a…" He made a spiraling motion with his finger. "Like one of those." He laughed. "You call it a circle, but you thought it was like a twenty point star and we were all porking each other. You see now what it really is? One of these." He did the spiral again.

He couldn't manage to put his house key into the keyhole, so I did it for him, and when we got inside he announced that he was going to puke. He made it to the kitchen garbage can, then crawled to the bathroom to finish it off. I hesitantly followed him. He vomited into the toilet for a couple of minutes, then flushed it.

"You OK?" I asked.

He groaned. "No. Maybe."

"We need to wash your face and hands."

"I can't stand up."

"OK. Let's do this."

I turned the cold water on in the bathtub and he stuck his head under it. I found a towel.

He crawled to his room and spread out on the floor.

"Come on, we have to take this off," I said, pulling his arms out of his wet and vomited-on shirt. Then I carefully pulled his t-shirt over his head. The flask was still in the pocket. I pulled his shoes off and tried my best to lift him onto his bed. He groaned through most of it. I tried to towel-dry his hair and he finally opened his eyes.

"Thanks," he said as I covered him up.

His whole room smelled like him, and I realized he was my favorite scent. I was so in love with him at that moment.

"You were the best thing at that stupid party," he said.

"OK. That's the alcohol talking."

"No, that's me."

"You won't remember this in the morning."

He sat up beside me, wrapped his arms around me, and hugged me. It was a tight hug and he was stronger than he looked. "You're the best."

"Thanks," I said.

He continued to hold onto me. "And…"

"And what?"

"I can totally feel your boobs right now."

I let go of him and he flopped back down laughing, sighed loudly, and immediately passed out. I gathered up the clothes and the flask and decided to walk home. I thought about the hug, and the way his arms felt around me, and the way his hair tickled my cheek. He was drunk, but I felt high.

My dad and Kristi were cozy on the couch watching a Christmas movie, and it was a little less weird when they seemed like they were just hanging out. Our tiny tree decorated with my childhood ornaments that were made in Sunday School twinkled in the window, and he looked back at me, really smiling for once. "Hey Bear. Home early from a party *again*?"

"Cody got drunk and puked all over himself. I'm going to go wash his clothes now so his mother doesn't find out."

"Sounds fun," my dad said.

Sometimes having a cool dad was OK because I could tell him things like that.

I sat on my bed in a face-off with the flask. It was old and tiny and silver and monogrammed with the letters AGB. I wondered who it belonged to. I was crazy like that, thinking that I could somehow get closer to him by holding something that belonged to him. I tried to remember everything about his room, even though my senses were overwhelmed with his smell. I took out my journal and wrote down everything he had said, then I fell asleep thinking about his embrace.

In the morning, I took his shirts out of the dryer hoping they would still smell like him and they almost did. I contemplated life while holding them against my face, imagined putting my head on his shoulder, and thought about kissing him. I wanted that kiss. I wanted it more than ever.

That morning at the breakfast table, my dad and Kristi were fully dressed and it was a relief.

"We're going Christmas shopping. You want to come?" He scooped some scrambled eggs onto my plate. Kristi sipped on her coffee and hogged the paper again.

"I don't know," I said, falling back into my deep thoughts of Cody. "I might hang out with Lilly."

"Right. Your party life is messing up your sleepovers with Lilly."

"That thing I have, I'd hardly call it a life. It's an existence. An uneventful one."

Kristi looked up at me. She didn't understand my humor.

"I'm kidding," I said. "I need to talk to Lilly, though."

"Fine. But if I mess up on Gram's present, I'm totally blaming you."

"What is there to mess up? Buy her a knick knack or a sweatshirt with a cat on it."

He glared at me.

"The Beautiful perfume from Estée Lauder. OK? That's what she wears. That's what she could always use because she won't buy it for herself. It costs too much."

"Thank you, Bear."

"And a cat sweatshirt."

"Keep pushing it and I won't allow you to go to teenage drinking parties any more."

"That wasn't even supposed to be a drinking party. It was legit."

He finally sat down beside Kristi. She wasn't paying any attention to him.

"Cody was drinking. I don't know why. He said it was heavy. He's super complicated, I think."

"Boys aren't complicated," Kristi said. "They only think about like two or three things. Ever."

"Cody isn't like that, though. I mean, he sort of pretends to be like that, but he's not actually like that."

"He's a teenaged boy. Give it some time. You'll see his true colors."

A light went off in my brain, like a revelation. That would be my wedding song. I had to tell Cody. I scarfed down my food, rinsed my plate, and excused myself. I retreated into the bathroom so it wouldn't just seem like I was trying to avoid Kristi, even though I was.

I am texting you first. Good morning.

It took him about five minutes to respond.

I feel like shit. And I'm starving. But I'm shitty.

I have some awesome news.

What's that?

I have chosen the song.

Did our Lord and Savior come to you in a dream last night and tell you?

No. It just came to me.

Give it to me.

The Pastel Effect

Cyndi Lauper. True Colors. You know it?

I am dragging my ass out of bed to Google it as we speak.

So, what do you remember?

You watched me puke, didn't you?

Well, once on video, via Gus, and twice at your house.

Sorry.

It's OK. I did a Lopez for you and disposed of the evidence.

Sweet. How?

I washed the puke clothes and I have the liquor.

I'll come over tomorrow and get my stuff if that's OK.

Sure. Whenever.

Thanks for covering for me.

I'm thinking that's what bro-friends are for.

You can always count on me to drag your drunk ass home and wash your clothes.

I know that.

Holy fuck. I think you nailed it with this song.

I know. Right?

This is so you. You are Cyndi Lauper reincarnated.

She's totally not dead.

Parallel universe. Trading bodies. Shit happens.

You remember that much?

You see, the problem with the "circle" is that they don't really like to think outside the box.

So, popularity problem number one. Your friends don't have ideas.

Sure, they have ideas. Should we go to Orange Julius in the mall or in the plaza? Big questions. So big. So important.

What is the answer?

Wherever the hell your mom drops you off. So it's not even really a question.

Let me say it differently. Circle rule number one. Don't think outside the Circle.

It's not a circle. It's something else.

I know. It's more like a spiral.

How'd you know?

We've already been over this.

Maybe there is no parallel universe and deja vu is just remembering the things you did when you were drunk.

Great theory. Do you remember anything else?

Did you take advantage of me in my drunkenness? It seems like you want to tell me something.

No. That's all. You crawled around your house puking, then I tucked you in.

God, I didn't try to kiss you or anything, did I?

No. Nothing happened. Geez.

I can be a real idiot sometimes.

When things get heavy, you know we can talk, right?

I know. But I'm not the one who holds it all in, you are.

What?

You always look like you want to say more than you do.

I don't have much to say.

I'm going to listen to this song again.

OK. You do that. My dad is calling me.

Really?

No. But if I'm the first to text I gotta be the first to go. See how it works?

I will see you tomorrow.

See ya

5

A Time To Wait

LILLY SAT in front of the mirror while I tried to braid her hair. I was never good at doing hair or makeup or any of the other things girls did when they spent time together.

"I feel like I'm missing out on so much, Caroline. I wish my dad would just let me do things. I wish I would have the guts to sneak out. I wish I could be a good liar so I *could* sneak out and get away with it."

"The party sucked."

"Really?"

"Yeah. I mean, the only reason I went was Cody. And he was the only good thing about it."

"When do you think he'll just break down and ask you?"

"Ask me what?"

"To be his girlfriend."

"I don't think he will. I think he just wants to be friends. It's weird, though. He's not like you would expect him to be. He has standards. And he's really a lot more open than most people."

"How?"

"He told me every detail about every kiss he's ever had."

"Wow."

"Even when it wasn't flattering."

"Has he done a lot of kissing?"

"Surprisingly, no."

"More than us, obviously. No one will ever kiss me."

"You're the prettiest girl at school."

"No, I'm not."

"You are, totally. I think the boys just know about your dad."

"It's Skip's fault. I don't wear my religion on my sleeve like he does. I'm not such a goody-two-shoes like he is. But nobody knows it because they associate him with me."

"You *are* a goody-two-shoes."

"I would take opportunities. I would *jump* at opportunities. He's perfectly fine where he is."

"What opportunities?"

"A chance with someone like Cody. A chance with anybody."

"Do you think he's cute?" I asked, seeking approval.

"He's not the worst, that's for sure. I mean, he's cute in his own kind of way."

Skip knocked on the open door before coming in. I always got a little flustered when Skip came into a room. "Lilly, I left my calculator in my locker. Do you have yours?"

"In my desk drawer."

"Thank you," he said, smiling. "You're doing a good job with the braid."

"No, I'm not. But thanks."

"I can show you how to do it," he said.

"What?"

"French braid. I've been doing her hair since we were kids."

"OK." I moved over on the bed, making room for him.

He undid my attempt at a braid and skillfully divided her hair into exactly the right pieces. He didn't even have to think about it. He was good. I watched as he put the hair together, precisely, and perfectly, like someone who had had a bit of practice. It must have been a twin thing, the way their eyes locked in the mirror. The way they didn't even have to speak. I had to wonder how different my life would have been had I had a brother or sister to share everything with, to read my mind, to braid my hair.

"Aren't you good at math?" Skip asked, breaking up the twin-braiding silence.

"I'm OK at math."

"Don't you take the honors courses?"

"Yes," I said.

"Do you think you could help me with Algebra?"

"Sure." I had taken Algebra two years ago, when we still lived in the city.

He tied off the hairdo and went back to his room to get his book.

"Does Skip still seem attractive now that you got Cody?" she asked, laughing.

I shushed her as Skip came back again.

"What about Cody now?" he asked, then a knowing smile came to him. "Does one of you like Cody?"

"Caroline does," Lilly said, quickly, and with a giggle.

"I don't like Cody. We're friends. That's all."

"Cody is a nice guy," Skip said. "He's a good grappling partner and he's a serious wrestler."

"Caroline will find out how good he is at grappling," Lilly said.

Skip blushed. "You guys."

"It's not like that at all. We just watch TV together sometimes."

"And share every detail of his—"

"Nothing like that," I interrupted. "It's simply very friendly. Totally platonic."

"You don't have to justify it to me," Skip said.

"You have to justify it to Jesus, though," Lil chimed in. She liked to poke fun at her brother's conviction. "You have to apologize for those impure thoughts and seek repentance. Right Skip?"

He looked at his math book, thoughtfully. "It's natural at our age to be curious about that stuff. I don't necessarily believe thinking about it is a sin. Acting on it is."

I took his math paper and began to correct his work. "Isn't it hard for you, though?" I asked.

"Hard for me how?"

"Every girl in school likes you. Isn't it hard to keep saying no?"

"It's not hard at all. I don't have to say no. They want me to do the asking and I just don't."

"Why don't you find out if Cody likes her?" Lilly said, leaning against him. "Why don't you ask?"

"No. Don't do that. He'll think I put you up to it." I panicked, simultaneously hoping that he would and wouldn't do it.

"Listen. If he says anything, I'll let you know. OK? Now help me with my homework, please. And I'll owe you one."

Sometimes I went to church with Lilly, mostly to see Skip dressed in his nicer clothes with a clean, close shave, and that certain glow he had when he felt closest to God. It was almost as good as his orgasm glow. Almost. Sometimes he would play the guitar and sing and I almost never missed those services. I wasn't crazy about Pastor Waters' sermons. They were always full of fire and brimstone. I was a Presbyterian and we were pretty open-minded about most things. I didn't believe the devil was everywhere waiting to pounce on me. I didn't believe the Holy Spirit would slam into me one morning in church and make me pass out. They weren't quite that spiritual, but they were close. In fact, one thing Skip had always struggled with was why that sort of thing had never happened to him. He opened his heart and his mind to Jesus, and he couldn't figure out why Jesus didn't want to enter into him. I always believed that Jesus was simply in my heart, and the best way for anyone to know that was through how I treated other people. Skip believed it would be a spectacle, and a testimony, and a miracle when he felt Jesus in him. He believed his mission was to tell people about it. I believed my mission was to be a decent human being.

I sat through it, though, for Lilly's sake. And for the loveliness of Skip. And for the music because sometimes the music was good.

My dad wouldn't go to the Waters' church because he did not want to fear the Lord quite that much. When he attended, he went to the chapel at the college. When we went to Gram's house we went to Pleasant Corner Presbyterian, where Gram and Gramp got married and where my dad had gone all his life and where my mother's funeral had been. In the narthex, there was a huge book with a page for every funeral and every wedding and every big celebration they had, and when I was eight years old, I snuck away from a Bible school class to turn the page back to 1999 and see my mother's name in the old handwritten script.

Tressa Kovalchek

The Pastel Effect

*Born 1974, Died 1999.
I know that everything God does will endure forever; nothing can be added to it and nothing taken from it. Ecclesiastes 3:14*

I closed my eyes and memorized it and closed the book again. I always remembered that verse and wondered what it meant. I tried to tell myself that it explained why I was born. It was so their love would endure, so there would be proof she existed, and so my dad wouldn't be alone. When I made my confirmation two years ago, I chose to memorize Ecclesiastes 3, the entire chapter, and when I had to recite it in front of everyone, my dad cried and I immediately felt bad for choosing such a meaningful verse. He didn't want me to feel bad, though. I think he just cried because for some reason, when he sat there in the church, he felt closer to Tressa.

I walked home after church in the familiar chill of fall, leaves crunching underfoot. As I approached my house, I heard my dad's music and I wondered what kind of mood he would be in. Sometimes it was a good sign, and other times not so much. I opened the back door, which led into our kitchen, our drab gray kitchen with its cold stainless steel appliances and blue dish towels. Our whole house was drab and gray and when Gram came to visit she complained that it looked like a bachelor pad. My dad would laugh and explain to her that he actually *is* a bachelor, and she would tell him that was no excuse.

It was during the drum break of "Whole Lotta Love" when I looked up and saw my dad and Cody air drumming together. It was a long drum break and I watched them go at it, as my dad switched to air guitar, and eventually to lip-syncing. Cody continued drumming. I just watched, wondering who Cody really liked: me or my dad.

When the song ended, my dad said hello to me and Cody jumped up, probably not expecting to find that I had just witnessed the majority of their air-jamming session.

"Wow," Cody said. "That song."

"You liked it?" my dad asked, carefully putting the record back into it's well-preserved sleeve.

"*Woman!*" he said, trying to imitate Robert Plant, but failing. "I loved that part."

"I know. John Bonham's drumming is just amazing. *Amazing.*"

Cody nodded and looked at me. "You look nice," he said, awkwardly and only half-meaning it.

"Thanks," I said. "I'll get your stuff."

He shoved his hands into his pockets and waited for me. I put the items into a bag and gave them to him.

"You're a life saver, C-dog."

I shrugged. I heard my dad creaking up the steps. I think leaving me alone with Cody was his way of giving me his approval. He obviously liked Cody a lot.

"What are you doing right now?" he finally asked.

"Probably nothing."

"You want to, like, go somewhere?"

"Like where?" I asked.

He seemed to be faltering. Where could or would the two of us go together? There was nothing to do in Newbury on a Sunday afternoon. We would have to get a ride to someplace else. That would mean involving parents and that got awkward.

"Do you want to just watch a movie?" I finally asked.

"Yeah, OK."

"You eat lunch?"

"No. I've not been quite up to eating right, yet."

"How about some soup?"

"Alright."

He sat at the black high top table, which didn't help our drab kitchen cause, and watched me take the solid block of icy soup out of the freezer, put it in a pot, and pour broth over it. "My Gram sends this home with us because she thinks my dad doesn't feed me. Or that I don't feed him. I'm not sure which way it goes."

"That's nice of her."

"Are you close to your grandparents?"

"They're mostly dead. And not really."

"Since my dad was a teacher, we could pretty much spend the summer at Gram's house every year. She still has my dad's old bedroom and everything. It's pretty fun. We ride bikes and go for ice cream and it's like a super-long vacation. And it's almost like having a brother sometimes."

Our eyes met and he smiled.

"I'm sorry. I'm talking your ear off."

"No. It's cool. I wish I was closer with my dad."

"You're not?"

"I don't know. I love him and I respect him, but we just don't have a lot in common."

"What do you do together?"

"I mean, I kind of like to follow sports, but he's into it more so I pretend to be into it more."

"Like wrestling?"

"No. Like football and stuff. I like wrestling, I love it. But it's not the sport that I love. It's the discipline and the achievement and the goals. And it's my ticket to college, probably."

"You get good grades."

"Yeah. I guess."

"Where do you want to go?"

"Baylor looks nice."

"I saw the poster in your room. That's in Texas?"

"Yeah. My dad's not cool with it. He says if I want to go to a Christian school I should stay in Newbury and go to Hayes. He wants me to get a good state university education because it's cheaper and he says I'll get more networking and contacts and all of that. He wants me to go to Ohio State. He says college isn't just about education; it's about the experience. He thinks it'll be like *Animal House* or something."

"I'll probably go to Hayes. My dad's discount, you know."

"Yeah. It's not bad, I guess."

"Neither is Baylor," I said. "If you want it, you should try for it."

"We've got time to figure all of that out. Don't we? A couple of years at least? Maybe I'll change my mind."

"What made you choose Baylor?"

"I saw it on TV a couple of years ago when my dad was watching football and they did a sky view and the campus looked nice and so I went online and looked it up and it just fit me. That's all."

"I've never even thought about going anywhere but Hayes."

"Where would you go, though, if you could go anywhere."

"Maybe UCLA. Maybe because it's warm and sunny."

"I never took you as a warm and sunny liker."

"No?"

"No. I take you as a sweater weather girl."

"I like a little bit of everything. I like fall because it's pretty, but it's kind of suffocating, too. You know? Everything is dying and falling down. And winter is the same way, but everything is already dead. Spring is just an extension of winter. In summer, everything is alive and that's what I like about it. Everything is warm and living." I dished his soup out to him. "What season do you like?"

"Summer. Less clothes I have to wear. Somebody pointed out the other day that in every picture I post I'm never wearing a shirt."

"Oh. I don't go online much."

"How the hell do you stalk people, then?"

"Lilly does."

"I'm surprised she's allowed."

"As long as she only posts Jesus-y stuff."

"Your grandma makes good soup."

There was a *Die Hard* marathon on cable and we decided to watch it because Cody liked cop stuff. He didn't want to be a cop, but FBI or CIA or a detective instead. He wanted to outsmart people, not write them tickets. He *said* he wanted to outsmart people, but I felt like injustice bothered him, too. He got excited during the movie when there were close calls, and he laughed really hard when there were funny lines. My dad came down to check on us every once in a while, and it was always about that time when Cody would look at his phone and ignore all of his messages. I had no messages, and when he shoved his phone back into his pocket, he would smile at me apologetically for being so popular.

When it was dark, and the first three *Die Hard* movies were over, he decided to go home, making me promise to watch the next ones with him sometime soon. I went into my room and took out my journal and started to gush about Cody as if he were the only boy on earth. It would be harder and harder to hide my crush on him from everyone else. It would be hard to hide it from him, too.

On Christmas Eve, I lay in my Aunt Jen's bed staring at the ceiling. I was using her room since she wasn't coming to Rocky Ridge for Christmas. She was part of some big, selfless organization that was helping a third world country get clean water and baby vaccinations. Aunt Jen was a hippie through and through and she didn't care about things like having money or a car or a place to live, and I think that's why Gram kept her room up. She kept up my dad's room because he was always coming back to it.

I don't remember the first Christmas after my mom died. I imagine it was solemn and unhappy. The twinkling lights were just a reminder of how her light had gone out. Gram had an ornament for my mother on her Christmas tree — it was silver with Tressa's name spelled out in glitter. Gram had bought it the first year my parents were dating to go with the other four on the tree. Edie, Carl, Jen, and Teddy each had a bulb specially decorated in some way or another. I always stared at the sparkling bulb, liking the way it twinkled.

Gram loved my mother a ton, and desperately wanted her to marry Teddy. She even gave Dad the ring that belonged to her mother for proposing, but Tressa just didn't want to marry him. Gram thought if she could get on my dad's good schoolteacher insurance, she would get a good doctor and real help, but Tressa said no, and Gram told me that Dad came to her tearfully one day, gave back the ring and said, "She told me to stop asking." And Gram had to accept that.

When Jen would go out to do something dangerous or crazy or ridiculous, Gram would always say, "I can't stand to lose another daughter." I guess the ring didn't need to prove it. If the Bryant family wanted you, you just had to be a part of them. There was no choice.

Where are you right now?

I'm at my Gram's. Where are you?

Oh shit. I'm home.

It's two o'clock in the morning.

I know. You up?

I was up, yes.

Why?

Thinking.

Bout what?

My family and how good they are.

Oh, that's so nice and Christmasy.

I know. So, what's up?

I just was thinking about how I was going to propose to you tomorrow. But you're out of town.

Oh, yes. I forgot about that when I left to come here yesterday.

I guess I'll be putting it off until Valentine's Day now. That's OK.

It's fine. You know, maybe we shouldn't be engaged while you're at Baylor anyway. I've always heard a lot of nice things about Texas cheerleaders.

OK. I guess I can give that a try. Maybe Texas girls are a little more straightforward, the way I like them.

I think they are known more for their boobs than their butts though.

You're probably right. And UCLA guys are all stoners, if you want to go with stereotypes.

Where did you hear that?

The movies. TV. They're just hanging out on the beach smoking pot all day.

I actually think it's LSD.

Do people still do that?

Probably.

I don't want you to go out with the UCLA guys.

That's fine because I'm going to Hayes.

With Skip Waters.

Yes, he'll probably go there because he won't leave his church or his dad.

I don't want you to go out with Skip Waters either.

That's fine because he doesn't date.

He likes you.

I think I would know that.

He talked about you a lot at practice the other day.

I don't know why.

He said a lot of nice things about you.

He's a weird dude. You said it yourself.

Is there something going on with you two?

No, of course not. I was at Lilly's house and he heard us talking about you. Lilly desperately wants us — you and me — to be together. She can't grasp the bro-friends thing. She asked Skip to try to find out if you liked me. I told him it's not like that, but Lilly probably couldn't help herself and told Skip to interrogate you anyway. Now I'm humiliated and embarrassed. Are you happy?

Yes. I'm much happier now knowing that you're still hopelessly single.

Why does it matter to you?

If you had a boyfriend, we couldn't hang out anymore. It would be weird. I can't really be friends with a girl who has a boyfriend. It feels weird.

There is no way Skip is ever going to be my boyfriend. He's married to Jesus at the moment.

You've thought about it.

Skip is attractive. Lots of people are. You know this.

Those aren't real people. Not for me, at least.

How long have you been thinking about this?

A couple of days.

Don't hold back from me. God, I hate that. When people don't just say what they feel.

I had to figure out what I wanted to say. And if I even had a right to say it.

I'm not out looking for boyfriends if that's what you think.

I want you to be single.

You've said that before. I know.

Do you want me to be single?

If you found someone, I would understand. And I would want you to be happy.

I am happy and I don't need a girlfriend to be happy.

I don't need a boyfriend either.

OK. Merry Christmas C-dog.

Merry Christmas to you.

I couldn't sleep so I went to the kitchen to get a glass of water. The logs were still crackling in the fireplace and the tree was twinkling and I felt lucky enough to be in a place that resembled a perfect Hallmark television home. Maybe I had lost a lot, but it didn't change the fact that I was pretty damn lucky for what I still had.

I looked out the kitchen window and saw an unfamiliar car in the driveway. Snow was falling gently, and I noticed that the windows were fogged up. I heard someone talking. Or maybe laughing. I opened the basement door and heard the soft lullaby of Christmas music. When I reached the bottom, I knew the laughing was coming from the couch in the makeshift game room.

"Hello?" I said.

My dad's head instinctively popped up over the back of the couch.

"Bear. What are you doing up?"

"Waiting for Santa," I said sarcastically. "I was going to bust him for breaking and entering."

"You're watching too many cop shows." He awkwardly rearranged himself so he was sitting on the couch.

"What are *you* doing?" I asked.

He looked down, and his old high school girlfriend, Becca, sheepishly sat up. They had clearly hit the eggnog a little too hard. "You remember Becca. You've met each other before."

I had met Becca before and I knew that she was my dad's "senior year" girlfriend, as he called her. The girlfriend you know you are going to break up with at the end of senior year because you're going to different colleges. My dad had had two "real" girlfriends before my mom. Veronica was a short-lived three-months-while-we-were-camp-counselors relationship. They didn't live near each other, or it might have worked out. He had alluded to the fact that she was his first time. Then there was Becca. She was always a little too good for him, he thought, and he wondered why she ever even liked him in the first place. He ran over her cat in his Chevette, and that's how they met. They formed a relationship over a dead cat. We would see her in the summer sometimes, and they tried to hide their seasonal romance of convenience. We were always bumping in to her. It was almost a little uncanny.

Becca was OK. Gramp had liked her, but Gram always thought she was a bit snobby. When I had run into her with Gram, there was usually some tension. When we would come across my dad with Becca in the photo albums, Gram barely gave them a second glance. She always lingered on pictures of Tressa, though. Probably because Tressa could steal the picture from everyone else in it. You couldn't help but look at her. Gram keeps a gorgeous picture of her wearing a white sweater on the mantle. Gram says she looks like an angel in that picture, and that maybe God needed her.

Gram could forgive Tressa for killing herself with the poison she shot into her veins, but she would never forgive Becca for being a snob. Gram didn't apologize for that, either.

I stared at her awkwardly until my dad cleared his throat, breaking the silence.

"Well, I should get going," Becca said, standing up and straightening her skirt. It was good to see you again."

She went around me and quietly made her way up the stairs.

Teddy stood up, picking up some beer bottles on his way past the coffee table.

"Did I mess that up for you?" I asked, sorry but not sorry.

"She'll be here next time."

"What about Kristi?"

"We're not a couple," he said. "Bear, you know all of this. I thought we were OK now."

"I'm fine with it. Why does everyone think I'm not fine with it? Kristi thinks I'm jealous of her. I'm not. Now you think I have a problem with Becca and I don't."

I followed him up the stairs.

"OK. I believe you."

"You should," I said.

He threw away the beer bottles and washed his hands in the kitchen sink. I wondered where they had been that they needed washing. Finally, he turned around, leaned against the kitchen counter, and crossed his arms. I could smell the faint odor of sugar cookies in the air from earlier in the day. "What are we doing now?"

"Nothing," I said.

"I know this is hard on you. Coming here, you're thinking about your mom, it's Christmas. Gram talks about her like she was a saint. I loved her. I *love* her. I love her with every fiber of my being. But she is not here. She isn't here and a part of her chose not to be here and I am *lonely* sometimes. Sometimes, to bring back memories, even if they aren't great memories with Becca, it makes me feel better. God, Bear. I hope you never have to be in love with a dead person. I hope you never do."

"I'm sorry, Dad," I said. I felt bad that he felt bad. "It's not that I don't want you to have a life. Just, why do they all have to act so awkward around me? Why do they all have to be so weird around me?"

"Maybe it's because I love you more and I'll always love you more."

"I thought you said there was no love."

"Maybe there's got to be a little bit, you know? Maybe."

"I don't know, dad. I don't know anything about relationships. You keep treating me like I'm judging you. I'm not. I just really don't understand." My lip trembled and I tried not to cry, but we had the same tells and he knew it was coming, so he hugged me. I could smell Becca's perfume on him.

"It isn't your fault. You never got an example. I'm always teaching, teaching, and I never taught you anything that you needed to know."

"Yes, yes, you did." I looked up at him. "Let's blame it on Tressa. It's easier."

His face formed a weird smile and he started to laugh. "Are you serious?"

"Yes, I'm serious."

He laughed harder and I didn't know why.

"What?" I asked.

"When you said that," he said, trying to stop. "When you said that, you sounded just like her. I mean, that was just something she would say and this is the first time you ever reminded me of your mother." He laughed some more. "And it was just delightful. I've been waiting for this moment for years. I knew you had to have something of her in you. And, my God, there it was. She was always just jumping to some rash conclusion so she didn't have to deal with the hard stuff. I mean, here we are, me trying to figure out how to explain love to you, something I'm clearly not equipped to do, and you just say that. It's classic Tressa. She never wanted to work on the hard stuff. Never. With her it was either a very genuine all or nothing. I think the only thing she ever truly thought about was whether she really ever loved me or not. I think she stayed up at night wondering if she loved me. But everything else was all or nothing. And the only reason she thought about me was because she certainly couldn't give me her all, but she couldn't give me nothing either. Here, I thought you were me, but you *are* her. And there it is."

He hugged me again, and I was limp because I had finally been compared to my mother and it sounded like I reminded him of the worst part of her.

"But, didn't that drive you crazy?" I finally asked.

"Actually, I always found it quite amusing that she could write things off so easily. It was her way of not being able to deal with the injustice of things."

"You just said that she didn't even know if she loved you. That didn't hurt?"

"I loved her. And she cared enough to consider it. Does it even matter now? What happened, happened." He sat at the kitchen table. "God, we've talked about her more in the last month than we have in the last eleven years. I'm turning a corner on this, Bear. I can feel it."

I sat across from him.

He seemed to snap back to himself again. "Can I ask you something?"

"Yes."

"Is all of this about Cody? Is this why you're so perceptive to it all now?"

"No." I had to deny it. "Cody and I are friends. Just, kind of, oddly enough, friends."

"Well, it was when Cody started coming around that you started getting annoyed with my sex life."

"Dad, please don't use that term to describe…that. Just, say anything but that."

"OK. My love life. You've been annoyed with my love life."

"I'm not annoyed. I guess I just never realized it was really a thing in your life. And now it's obvious and I have to realize that you're my dad, but you're also a guy, a guy who is just like almost every other guy. And it's normal and it's fine."

"I still think you like Cody. Or he likes you. Or something is going on."

"Maybe he's more than just a friend. He's the one person that gets me and he wants me to laugh and he wants to protect me and he tells me things that he doesn't tell anyone else and I tell him things I don't tell anyone else. Maybe we're best friends. I don't know. He has best friends. This thing is different, but it's not that."

"Well, I like him. He's a good kid."

"I think you should get a girlfriend."

He smiled. "Please. There are no single ladies in Newbury that are even close to my age. And all the ones that are too young for me, well…been there, done that."

"Please. Stop."

"So, who do you have in mind?"

"A nice Christian girl."

"No way."

"Yes way."

"You want me to go from slut to saint just like that?"

"I want you to find someone who deserves a guy like you. Because you are a really good guy."

He took my hand. "Can we get you through high school first?"

"Look. I'll make you a deal. I'll tolerate Kristi. I'll even try to get along with her. When she hogs the paper, when she gives me that look like I'm pathetic, and even when she insists on touching you throughout breakfast. But try to keep your other escapades under wraps. I can only deal with one at a time. I mean, do what you want, but can you not do it around me? I'm a big girl. You can spend the night with people at their house. You can go to a hotel. You can do it in the car if you want to, just don't park it where I'm going to find you."

"OK. This just makes me feel like a shit parent."

"You're not a shit parent. You're just a man and we all know that men are weak. But you're my dad, and I can't know that about you. OK? You have to make me think that men are awesome or I won't want to marry one. That's kind of your job."

"So, you know I suck, but you're OK with it as long as I pretend I don't suck?"

"Precisely."

"When this is all said and done, I think I'll write a book for single dads."

"I wouldn't go that far," I said, and finally I went back to bed.

6

The Dawn of a New Year

WE WERE WATCHING *Donnie Brasco* with that terrible feeling that you get when you know you have to go back to school after Christmas vacation. When you go back after summer break, you have Christmas to look forward to, but when you're in tenth grade, Christmas to summer seems like an eternity. For Christmas I had bought Cody a Baylor t-shirt, but I didn't want it to seem like I had bought him a Christmas gift, so I decided to give it to him like it was an afterthought, although I had put tons of thought into it.

"Hey, I got you something," I said, casually.

"What do you mean?"

"I bought something for you."

"What? Like a present?"

"No. Like, I was thinking of you."

He smiled and sat up. I didn't even wrap it so it would seem less like a gift.

I went to my room and got the t-shirt, which I hadn't even folded properly to seem like I had put even less thought into it. He looked surprised and happy about it.

"You went to a lot of trouble to get this."

"No, I didn't. Not really."

"I like it. It's awesome."

I had found something out when I bought the t-shirt and it was something that I had wondered about for a while. "You didn't tell me that Baylor doesn't have a wrestling team."

"Yeah. They don't."

"I thought you loved wrestling."

"It's not my life. I'd rather use my brain than beat up my body, to be honest."

I was still waiting for something to go further with him. He was painfully slow if he liked me. I just stared at him, smiling, though. I couldn't stop smiling at him since I had unwillingly fallen in love with him.

He looked at the shirt. He looked at me. He looked at the shirt again. "Fuck," he said, finally.

"What?"

"I fucked up," he said.

"How?" I was still stupidly smiling.

"Why do you have to be so goddamned nice?"

"I don't know." I felt the conversation turning in a different direction.

"Fuck."

"*What?*" I asked again, impatiently.

"I wanted you to be home so I could take you to Caden's New Year's Party."

"Why? Because me and parties make a great team?"

"No. Because I wanted to take you."

"Why?"

"Because I thought it would be fun and special because…" He trailed off into his thought.

"Why?"

"Because aren't you supposed to kiss someone at midnight? I mean, that's the thing; that's what you wait for."

"Who? You and me?" I asked, surprised he was bringing it up.

"You never kissed anyone and I thought it could be really memorable."

"So? I wasn't home. Don't beat yourself up. It's not your fault."

"We're just friends, but I thought it might be cool."

"I know. I mean, it's cool that you even thought about it."

"I'm not beating myself up over that."

"What then?"

He looked away, more worried than I had ever seen him. "I fucked up and I kissed someone else."

I knew what my dad meant when he said that I knew something about putting up a wall. I did it at that moment to protect myself. Suddenly, it became the most important thing in the world to not let Cody know how I felt about him. "Everyone kisses at midnight. No big deal."

"Yeah, well, it's a big deal to me. It doesn't feel right to be kissing other people when I was supposed to be kissing you. It doesn't feel good and it's been eating away at me and, God, it gives me a stomach ache."

"You're single, Cody. It's fine. Do you apologize to your other friends when you kiss someone?" I said that, but I desperately wanted to know who it was.

"You're not mad?"

"I can't really be mad. Do I own you? It's not like we were in some kind of kissing relationship and you've cheated on me."

"I would be mad, I think, if I found out that you kissed someone."

"Why?"

He stood up and shoved his hands in his pockets. "I don't know. I don't know how to explain it. I just would."

"Was it good?"

"What?"

"The kiss. Was it a good one or a bad one? Did you breathe on her face?"

He looked at me, a little surprised, and sat down again a little closer. "No. It didn't last that long."

"So it was just a quick thing. Like…like you'd kiss your mom or something?"

"No. I tongued her."

"Oh." I deflated a little bit more. "Were you drinking?"

"No."

"Oh." I was nearly flat. "So, it was good then?"

"No. She clenched her teeth and my tongue just hit them and I guess I was thinking of one type of kiss and she was thinking of another."

"Why'd you do it? She was pretty?"

"I don't like her," he said.

"Then why?"

"Because she was standing beside me and she turned towards me when the music started playing and I thought…I guess I thought it was the thing I should do. Or I thought that she wanted me to. I don't know. I was missing you, though. You know, when you build something up to be something…something it's not, or it can't be for whatever reason, and you take the next best thing, but you realize you'd rather have nothing at all than the next best thing."

"Yeah. I know what you're talking about."

I stared at the television for a minute, wishing I could switch to the parallel universe and go to that party. I willed my eyes to stay dry long enough to finish our conversation.

"I changed my mind."

"About what?" he asked.

"About the face-breathing. I think you should just do it, just go for it and breath on her face. I mean, it's part of kissing. It's messy and it's sloppy and you get breathed on. I mean, if you can't take the heat, get out of the fire. If you like the person, you're going to want all of that anyway."

"The first kiss should be good, though," he said. "You can't take back a bad first impression. I think someone important said that once."

"Who cares about first impressions? I mean, isn't life just about second chances?"

He ran his finger around the corner of the couch pillow. "You're probably right."

I hated him at that moment. But he put his head on my shoulder and we watched *Donnie Brasco* even though he broke my stupid heart.

I tried to tell myself to get over it. My dad told me it's easier to forgive than to blame, and I knew he was right. And by the next Wednesday, when Lopez and Shields were roughing up an inmate to find a missing baby, I had almost come full circle to liking Cody again. But I wondered who he had kissed.

I thought about Cody and the girls in the Circle. My rumination turned into a fact in my own mind. I thought it had to be Libby and I grew jealous and bitter. I never wanted to feel that way towards another girl. I never wanted to be possessive, especially over something that wasn't mine. I hated myself for my thoughts and they spiraled down into my life like a funnel cloud.

I couldn't hide all of those feelings, though, and by four in the afternoon, I was exhausted, in bed, and sleeping away the sadness and the rejection and the loss.

After about a week of that, my dad approached me and told me that he wanted me to see a doctor. I wanted to try to fix myself, and for a little while, I could fool my dad into thinking that I was OK. I could do that because it came naturally — something I got from my mother. Even when things seemed to be going well, when my grades were up, when I spent time with Lil, and as things evolved between me and Cody, I still couldn't shake the feeling of doom. It got harder to hide what was happening to me.

Did you notice?

Notice what?

The shirt. I was wearing it. I waited all day for you to say something. You're about to go into the girls who never text first box. What is wrong with you?

I haven't been feeling good. I'm tired.

Maybe you have mono.

Ha. Ha.

What?

Was that a joke?

No, why?

They call mono the kissing disease.

I seriously was not trying to be an asshole there. For real. I'm sorry. I was just worried about you.

Why?

Ever since Christmas you've seemed off. Did I piss you off or something?

(I couldn't tell him the truth because I had lied about *not* being pissed off to cover up my secret infatuation with him. What could I say?)

I told you I don't feel good.

As long as it's not me. If it's me, be straight about it.

I would and it's not.

Are you on your period?

You should really never ask that question. Just some advice.

No, I want to be in sync with my woman's cycle.

Fine. When you get a woman you can keep track of that.

They have apps for that.

I know.

I am failing miserably at cheering you up.

I'm just really worried that Lopez is not going to find the missing super-diabetic baby that needs his insulin.

I was a little more worried that Emily thinks she might be pregnant.

See how they did that? Lopez is tapping into his nurturing side just in time to get the positive test so he can act like he wanted to be a dad all along.

He does want to be a dad because his dad wasn't there for him growing up.

His dad was a serial rapist.

Still a deadbeat dad.

I bet when Emily finds out the secret about his dad being the Candlelight Rapist, she'll abort the baby on account that it could turn out to have that rapist gene.

You're fucking good. Why is it when I want to make you laugh, you always make me laugh?

If serial rapists and abortions make you laugh, you've got problems.

You're still at it, girl. Go, go.

I'm out of jokes. Even those shitty ones.

Cheer up, OK? Get out of this funk.

I will. It takes time.

I get it. I want your smiling face back.

My smiling face?

You have a cute face.

I will take it as a compliment. I think I hear your mom calling you.

So funny. Good night.

Good Night.

I felt good enough to get up in the morning, put on a little makeup and curl my hair some. I put on jewelry and a cute dress, too. He looked at me like I was a super model and I had to admit, it felt good. We mutually ignored each other at lunch, but in Geometry, he kept his shoulder against mine. "What happened?" he asked.

"I woke up feeling better."

"It was my jokes."

"It was my brain," I whispered.

"I'm so ready for tonight," he said.

I just looked at him.

"*Broken Blue*," he reminded me.

The teacher began talking, but I was drunk on his smell and couldn't hear a word.

I attempted to wear my cutest lounging clothes, if there could be a such thing, and hoped that things would get back to normal between us, but every night I prayed for the crush to go away. It was coming back in full force, little by little. *Broken Blue* always brought it out tenfold.

He was hiding something behind his back when he knocked on the door, and he always had a certain twinkle in his eyes when he was up to something. He came in, put a brown paper bag on the table and threw his coat over the chair.

"What's that? Chinese food?" I asked hopefully.

"No," he said, excitedly. "It's so much better than that."

"Italian food?"

"No, open the bag."

"OK."

I opened the bag, peeked inside, and looked back at him. "What is this, exactly?"

"So I Googled *What to do when your girl is on her period*."

"There are so many things wrong with that sentence."

"So, let's see, because I didn't know what your favorite snack really was, I kind of thought, since we're so alike, you might like my favorite snack. Which is —" he pulled it out of the bag. "Macaroni and cheese." He looked deeper in to the bag. "And, of course, strawberry milk."

The Pastel Effect

"Together?"

"Why not?" He finished unpacking it. "How did I do?"

"This is the weirdest thing anyone has ever given to me."

"And?"

"I'm sorry to disappoint you, but I'm *really* not on my period."

He took out his phone. "I'm begging you. Please tell me so I can put it in this app."

"Geez, I'll let you know, OK?"

"How will you let me know? Will you wave a red flag, or like, draw a red X on my locker?"

"I will somehow let you know if it's that important to you."

"Can't you at least tell me it's the thought that counts?"

"It's the thought that counts."

Our school hosted an invitational wrestling match every year in January, and Cody got super busy practicing for it, so our relationship dwindled down to nothing but texting. When he had a chance to think about what he was going to say, it brought out the best in him. He was funny, thoughtful, and open. He was all the things he couldn't be in the Circle. I went to his match and watched much more eagerly than I ever had before, trying to understand it, trying to pay attention. Cody and Skip each won two, then lost one.

Cody's mom, dad, and brother were there and it was the first time I had ever seen them all together. He looked a little bit like his brother, but like neither of his parents. His brother, Ricky, seemed like the kind of guy who thought he was really cool and suave and in fashion; he was the complete opposite of Cody. He was put together and matching and seemed like he spent a long time on his hair. His mom and dad were typical, but older like he said they were. After they got their medals, the school newspaper took a picture of Cody and Skip together and at that point, I decided to go home.

My dad was at the kitchen table when I came home, books and notebooks and highlighters spread out around him. He was a good teacher and he always put a lot into teaching.

"How was it?" he asked, looking tired. He had spent the night before at Kristi's, and he came home in the morning looking like shit. I didn't ask why.

"It was OK. A little boring, I guess, when you're not that into it." I sat across from him and picked up the newspaper that he had left for me. He closed his books and pushed them aside.

"Crossword?" he asked.

"Of course."

I loved doing the crossword with my dad. It always amazed me how many words he knew. If I knew that many words, I would use them to impress people in my everyday language, but he kept his vocabulary a secret weapon only to use when needed. My dad's intelligence was vast, but never on display. He saved it for the genius little things he did, and every once in a while he let himself be noticed, like when he won the Tally-Webber teaching award, an award given to one teacher who was recognized as an outstanding arts mentor to teens. Only one person won per year, and my dad was the first person *ever* to receive the award for teaching Language Arts. He was recognized by the organization when his students' standardized test scores went up an average of two hundred points in reading comprehension. He was asked to write an essay about how he did it, and he instead wrote an essay on how to make literature relevant again by finding a parallel that kids could connect with, or even better, to let them find one themselves.

My dad started his teaching career taking the first job that was offered to him since he had a kid and a girlfriend to support. That was the job in the juvenile detention center. Gram thought somebody would kill him, but she tried to keep from getting too upset. He liked his job there because the classes were small and he could really *teach* (he always said it with a lot of emphasis) because nobody cared enough to stop him from teaching. When my mother died, he went to a regular high school because we needed more money and some stability and even though he loved his job, there were fights and stabbings and he had to keep himself safe for me. He had to follow more rules and guidelines, but he found ways to bend them and that's how he became so good at what he did.

When I was in eighth grade, he got a teaching job at a Presbyterian college and we moved to Newbury, away from the city, where he said he finally felt totally safe, just like he did in Rocky Ridge when he was growing up. He was given several classes to teach, and he liked to give them nicknames. "Influential Authors of the Twentieth Century" became "Books You Should Have Read in High School." "Literature of World War II" became "You Would Have Heard This From Your Grandpa If You Were Listening." "Female Authors During the Sexual Revolution" became "Pay Attention Boys, And Maybe You'll Learn Something About Women." Everyone liked the nicknames. Not the faculty, but everyone else.

I had to sit there sometimes and just look at him and silently thank him for being who he was and equally thank God for making him my dad. He was just a good person. He had a huge heart, and I couldn't have ever hoped for anyone better. I wondered sometimes how he lived that heartbreak day after day, missing her, and thinking maybe he could have done more. I once heard Gram telling him, "You are only one man, Teddy Bryant, and I've never met one man who was capable of saving two women. One of them didn't want to live, and the other one still has a chance. You made a choice and it was the right one." I always thought about that when I thought about my dad. I always knew he would do anything for me, and I guess I would always want that from every man.

We both decided to go to bed early and it jolted me awake when my phone buzzed in my ear.

Where did you go? I looked for you.

I went home when it was over.

I really wanted to talk to you.

You looked busy with the pictures and your family and I know you're weird about me meeting your family.

I hate losing.

You won more than you lost.

I lost because I was stupid and distracted.

How were you distracted?

Doesn't matter. I just was.

Who is AGB?

What are you talking about?

On the flask. Who is AGB?

My great-grandpa. He was a cop. I used to be obsessed with him when I was a kid.

Why?

He was killed on duty in 1929. I found this box once with all the clippings and then I got the flask when my Grandma died a couple of years ago and it's always like, he's the one person in my family I think I would have connected with. I don't know why. I never knew anything about him.

You don't connect with your family?

I'm a little different is all.

Why?

I like to think. Hey, can you make me laugh?

You put me on the spot. I can't.

 He stopped texting me and then I couldn't sleep. I wondered what was bothering him. I always put a lot of thought into what was bothering people and felt like it was my personal mission to make people feel better when they were down. I used to desperately try to cheer up my dad on particularly bad days, and it was always a little ironic how down I allowed myself to get when I wouldn't allow anyone else to get down. I just hated seeing other people unhappy; I didn't care how unhappy I was myself.

 I held my phone waiting for him to respond. I was too stubborn to text twice in a row. I sat up in bed, went to the bathroom, got a drink, and went back to bed. What on earth could be bothering him? What could it possibly be? I spun my wheels trying to think of something funny to say, a way to cheer him up and I just couldn't. I felt like a failure. I stared at the blank phone in the dark, willing it to vibrate, needing to hear him say good night.

I almost screamed when I heard the tap on my window. I was so lost in my thoughts that I wasn't conscious that things were going on outside of my brain. I jumped out of bed, the prospect of a burglar never entering my mind until that very moment. I always felt safe, even with all the cop shows I watched. I heard the tap again and decided to confront it. I pulled open my sheer curtain and backed up quickly. And then I saw that it was Cody. I pushed the window open, trying not to make too much noise.

"You scared me!" I loud-whispered.

"I'm sorry," he said, coming through the window. He must have gained that expertise from all of the predator shows we watched. Or maybe he had practice. I hoped it wasn't the latter because something made me want to be the only girl who's window he crawled through.

I sat on the bed and turned on the dim bedside lamp. His face was beat up, not really bruised, just red with pressure points from wrestling. He looked sad. "I've not thought of any jokes since we texted," I admitted.

"It's OK. You can't always be on your A-game."

"What is it?"

"Huh?" he asked, looking around my room.

"What is bothering you?"

"I thought your room would be darker than this."

"You've thought about my room?"

"Yes. I've thought about it a lot, actually."

"What did you think? It would look like a dungeon?"

"I thought you'd like gray and dark things. Like the rest of your house."

"That's my dad. We'd live in an easter egg colored world if it were up to me."

"You come off as gray."

"But I like pastels."

"This is a surprise."

"You aren't making sense."

He touched my jewelry box, and the sweater hanging on my desk chair. "You are dark inside so you try to fill your life with light, don't you?"

I looked down and he sat beside me. He brushed my hair away from my face. "I don't know what you mean."

"Do you try to hide it?"

"Hide what?"

"Everything you feel because it feels crazy to feel the things you feel? The dark. Everything you think about."

"I don't know what you mean, Cody. These are walls. This is paint. It hardly speaks for who I am." He was starting to scare me. He looked a hundred times more serious in the dark and he never talked like that.

"It makes sense for you to be pastel. You're trying to cover up your hurt with something bright, but the color doesn't shine through. It only makes it to pastel. I understand."

In a way, what he said made perfect sense and I thought for a second that he might be the one person who totally understood me.

He ran his thumb around my face, around my chin, and I thought maybe he would finally kiss me. "You are a pastel girl," he said quietly. "I get it."

"Do you?" I asked.

"I don't want to be alone right now."

"Then stay," I said.

He took off his shoes and pulled his hoodie over his head, exposing an old, worn wrestling shirt, like it was the most natural thing in the world. Then he got under the covers and wrapped his arms around me. I wondered if he knew that my heart was beating out of my chest. I think it was the first time in my life I ever felt like I could surrender to someone else, to actually trust someone. His smell was like a drug though, and I fell asleep happy.

7

Monday Always Comes

HE WAS GONE in the morning. I was usually a light sleeper and I wondered how he left without waking me up. I wondered if he used the window or the door. And I still wondered what was wrong with him.

It's funny how Mondays always come and somehow the weekend was like a different life. It's like you leave behind a piece of yourself in certain places and times, pieces you can never get back. And then there's the parallel universe where you scatter things about, too. And after you lose all of that, what is left? What is even left of us? I wonder how adults get to adulthood without completely running out of whatever it is that's inside of us. I guess things happen to fill us back up and we have no choice but to pour it all out again. And when we're happy, we're just bursting to let that out, and when we're sad we're just trying to keep it all in.

When Monday came, he could barely look at me. I didn't know if he was embarrassed that he showed me a side that he usually kept to himself. Cody had a hundred friends, but he came to me saying he didn't want to be alone. I knew as well as anyone that there was nothing better to remind you that you're alone than being with a bunch of people. He had spent the day in the spotlight, mostly winning, surrounded by family, friends, coaches, teammates, and at the end of the day he had nothing left to say but, "I don't want to be alone."

I began to feel like he saved me for the weekends, then on Monday morning he watched Libby sashay down the hall, and he talked to Gus and Maia in the hallway, and we sat back to back at lunch. I wondered if he might skip Geometry just to get away from me. He was too serious of a student to do that, though.

He gave me an awkward smile and I decided it would be best to say nothing. The teacher droned on and on and I welcomed it since words couldn't seem to form.. I leaned towards him to smell him and something about it made me want to close my eyes, and I'm sure I looked stupid, eyes half-closed, inhaling like I was taking my last breath, but I didn't care. I needed it.

That night he didn't text me. It hurt, but I was used to that feeling.

When I couldn't fix a person, I always somehow blamed their original pain on myself.

I always found an odd satisfaction in getting my period. I treated it like a cleansing and felt like I could ditch a lot of things with the rest of it. On my period, my skin got clearer and brighter and I always felt prettier. The cramps didn't bother me, rather reminded me that I was alive and my body was working. It always felt like a fresh start to me. I guess that's why I was amused with the idea of Cody thinking it was my problem. Of course, most girls hated it and I'm sure that's where he was coming from, but I actually kind of liked the whole ritual.

He wanted to know, though. He said he wanted to know. And I was going to let him know.

Dear Cody,

Perhaps I should write you a letter, I thought.
Everything is fine, just wanted to try something new.
Regarding Wednesday, are you coming over?
I can make mac and cheese.
Or we can get Chinese food.
Decision is yours.

Your Friend,

C

I even wrote it in red. He would appreciate the irony. I had my dad take me to school early that day so I could slide it through the vents in his locker without any of the Circlers seeing me do it. At that point, I wasn't even sure who was trying to hide it from them more — me or him. I didn't give the details to Lilly. I told her some things about our recurring Wednesday night routine and his little pet names for me. I didn't tell her about Saturday night or the way he touched my face or the way he understood certain things without me having to tell him.

I waited in the hallway, reading *The Catcher in the Rye*, our English assignment. I'd already read it several times, as it was one of my dad's favorite books. I knew more about Holden Caulfield than he knew about himself. I knew more about going mad than a lot of tenth-graders did.

Cody Kirby finally came down the hall and I watched him from behind my book (suddenly wishing we'd been assigned a bigger book for hiding behind.) He always took a load of books with him and sometimes I wondered how he had time to study when he was always wrestling, or being in the Spirit Club, or hanging out with me. He was carefully stacking them in his locker when he found my letter. My heart skipped a beat as he unfolded it.

Libby Harman said hello to him and he never even looked up. I had his undivided attention and it felt great. For the amount of time he looked at it he could have read it three times. He turned around and looked at me across the corridor. (My locker was at the end of A-Hall and his at the end of C-hall and the crossroads of the two halls divided us.) He folded the note in half, put it in his pocket, and retrieved his phone. He truly was going to use that app. I felt that if I was important enough to track in an app, I must have been pretty damned important.

I decided to walk away while he was preoccupied with it. I had his attention and that was all I really wanted.

I miss you, pastel girl.

You don't act like you miss me.

I do, though. Do I always have to wear my heart on my sleeve?

No. Saying hello is nice, though.

I'm sorry. It got weird.

It wasn't that weird for me.

Sometimes I feel like I'm fucked. Like right is wrong and wrong is wrong and I can't do anything right or keep anyone happy and it just wears me out.

Maybe you put too much pressure on yourself.

I just want to be good at something. Anything, just one thing.

You're good at everything you do. Wrestling, school, everything.

I'm never the best, though.

Do you have to be?

Maybe once in my life.

You are one of the best people in my life.

You are my best friend.

You're mine.

How's the period going?

It's going fine.

Tell me. Do you have cramps?

Not really.

Bloating?

Not really. What is your fascination with this?

I'm just entering this into my app.

Can I tell you something?

Yeah.

Wednesday is my favorite day of the week.

Mine too.

Good night.

Good night.

That was as close as I could get to telling him that I liked him.

8

What to Expect When You're Not Dating

I WOKE up one morning in February and realized I was coming upon a new crisis in my life: Valentine's Day. What do you do for a person when your relationship has unclear boundaries? I thought we were too close to skip it altogether, but not close enough to make a big deal of it. Things were starting to change between us, and our friendship finally went public. It came about easily and without too much of a fuss from the Circlers, maybe because Cody eased into it. It started with him coming to my locker every day before Geometry class so we could go in together. After about a week of that, he started sitting with me and Lilly at lunch on Thursdays so we could discuss *Broken Blue*.

To me, Valentine's Day was never a big deal. Gram would send me a card with twenty dollars in it and my dad, being the romantic he was, would buy us some chocolate and we would watch *Casablanca*. That was our tradition, year after year, and sometimes we would talk right along with the movie in the good parts because we knew it so well. I never knew why we did it, we just did it.

With Cody, I knew I was playing in a different ball game. After contemplating it far more than any person ever should, I decided to go with a cheap and generic gift and make a card. The card would say, "I thought about you…" and the gift would say, "…but not too much." And I could always back off and chicken out if nothing about it felt right. Sometimes I was one of those people who did things even when they didn't feel right, though. I was a poor judge of what felt right and what felt wrong, because everything felt a little wrong most of the time and I feared regret as much as I feared rejection. That led to irrational decision making sometimes.

At least Valentine's Day was on Sunday, so at school it would be celebrated on Friday, typically a day when Cody and I had little contact and if I humiliated myself I would have the weekend to recuperate and maybe by Monday, the slate would be wiped clean. Taking this into consideration, I decided to make the card and buy the gift, but only give it if he did something first. Not being sure of where I stood with him, I didn't want to come on too strong.

After the night in my bedroom, he hadn't done anything like that again. He hadn't touched my face or my hand or any other part of me. He hadn't looked at me like I was the only girl in the hallway. He hadn't said anything about any of it. His lonely and worthless streak must have been over. Sometimes I wished mine would end.

At our high school, there was this horrible tradition of a thing called Candy-grams. They were used as fundraisers by the Cheerleaders who sold them for a dollar so you could send an anonymous (or not-anonymous) note to your crush. There was a box you could drop your note into with your one dollar bill so it truly would be anonymous, or you could order one in person. And the name Candy-gram was a misnomer, because years ago when it became unprofitable to attach the candy to the note, it turned into just a paper heart that was taped to the recipient's locker.

It was no surprise at all last year when I arrived at school and found zero paper hearts attached to my locker. Even Lilly had received two anonymous hearts. I received nothing, zip. I suffered through the humiliating holiday knowing that I was going home to the best dad in the world, and he knew the meaning of romance, and I would never sell myself short on a guy who didn't.

Even though I sometimes hated school, I liked being there early when the halls were nearly empty and I could hear the fluorescent lights buzzing. I quickly wondered how many Candy-grams had passed through the halls in the last forty years or so. I didn't linger in front of Cody's locker, but I certainly had to look at it, jealousy settling in when I saw his hearts. I took in as much as I could without gawking and noticed that most of his were signed. Maia.

The Pastel Effect

Libby. Tabitha. They were mostly from Circlers, and a couple of anonymous givers. From that angle, I didn't even want to look at my locker because I knew there would be nothing there. Year after year, there would be nothing there. I was willing to bet that if Holden Caulfield had attended Newbury High, he would have had a nice blank locker, too.

I didn't want to be like everyone else, but there was no denying that when eleven hundred people went to your school, approximately half of them boys, and not one of them cared to send you a Candy-gram, it stung a little. Especially when one of them claimed to be your best friend. And especially when, a month and a half ago, he claimed to want to kiss you and never had. All of it piled on like a swarm of bees and the sting got harsher.

I didn't wait in the hallway to watch Cody receive his Candy-grams. I went straight to home room and tried to pretend I wasn't miserable. Then I beat myself up for letting something so petty make me miserable. After all, I couldn't expect anything from Cody, and I didn't deserve anything from Cody. He wasn't my boyfriend and he never claimed to want to be and I never told him how I truly felt, either. I guess what I wanted from Cody was some grand gesture where he proclaimed his love for me. I wanted something big and heartfelt and that just wasn't Cody. That just wasn't Cody at all. Cody was in the little details, not the grand gestures.

The more bitter I got throughout the day, the less I wanted to give him the card, so at the end of the day, I didn't. I knew it. I was the angry teenager who was shunned on Valentine's Day, the most idiotic day of the year. I was a man-hater, a love-hater. God, how so much changed in the course of eight hours. I put on my best happy face in Geometry class, and he was his usual self, listening diligently, taking notes, double checking the teacher's work on his calculator. At the end of class we said good-bye and I walked home on the slushy sidewalk, thinking this muck must be the stuff that was sloshing around in my cold, cold heart.

Did my father seriously think it would make me feel good to tell me he turned down a date with Kristi to keep up our tradition? It made me want to punch him. I imagined myself eating chocolate and watching *Casablanca* alone while my dad wined and dined with Kristi and while Cody sat at home organizing his millions of Candygrams. People made me angry sometimes. Why was I the girl that never got looked at? I felt ugly. God, I hated Valentine's Day.

Half-way through the movie, I was seething with rage, albeit unjustifiable rage, and I decided to take it out on my dad since he was the most convenient male to direct it towards. I paused the movie.

"What's wrong, Bear?"

"Why do we watch this? Every year. Year after year. You should have gone out with Kristi."

"That wouldn't feel right. This is our special day."

"It's a horrid day. It's a day of humiliation and rejection for any girl that hasn't got the attention of a boy and that in itself is stupid and crazy. Who invented this day? And why do you think it should be special to us?"

He sat up, trying to chew his chocolate turtle, which he had driven thirty minutes out of his way to get at my favorite candy store. He certainly didn't deserve my bad attitude. "It's special, I guess, because it was the day…" He looked down, then around, then down again. "It was the day your mom got pregnant with you. I always remember that day. We were watching this movie. I had bought her some chocolates. She didn't want to go out — she didn't like going out too much. I don't know. It just happened like that and then every year after, we watched the movie, like a tradition, a little moment we shared. We didn't have an anniversary because she wouldn't marry me, so it was like an anniversary of sorts. We didn't even call it Valentine's Day. We used to joke around and call it Conception Day." He shrugged. "I never wanted to let go of that, I guess."

I felt like an asshole.

"It's just an excuse to celebrate her. A good memory of her. Maybe it's time to let go."

I burst into tears and wrapped my arms around him. I never meant to hurt such a precious person. "I love you, dad. I'm sorry and I love you and I'd never want to stop doing this."

He held me for as long as it took to stop crying, then he looked at me, seriously, and gave me probably the best advice of my life. "You don't need a boy to validate you. Don't base your self-worth on that. I can tell you from personal experience: boys, especially at that age, are self-centered and weak and scared. How can you base who you think you are on the opinion of someone who doesn't know who they are?"

"How do you get over it when you like someone who doesn't like you back?"

"Oh, I think he likes you. He just can't quite figure out what to do with it. So in the meantime, he watches television with you and he does homework with you and he ignores you when it gets too real. He's your friend and I think that's all you need right now. Relationships are complicated. You're young. He's immature. You two have something nice and I think you should enjoy it for what it is. You probably have feelings for him — he's the first boy you've ever been friends with. He probably has feelings for you because you're awesome. But I don't think he's stupid, Bear. If he thinks he can't handle it, he's probably right. And I think you shouldn't see it as a rejection, but a compliment that he respects you enough not to put you through that."

It made sense, and all of a sudden, my feelings for Cody found a place inside of me. I couldn't liken it to anything but somebody who thought they missed their boat, then realized that they would have been on the Titanic. I had the ticket. That was all that mattered.

That night when I got in bed, I noticed my phone on the nightstand. I always checked it just in case Cody texted me. That night, I let it be.

I guess the tapping didn't startle me the second time because I knew it would be him. Why did he have to be so weird? Why, in the middle of the night, and not during one of the hundred opportunities he had to talk to me during the day? What was it about the dark that made him miss me?

I opened the window again, not quite as amused as I was the first time. He climbed in, quietly, as if he had thought it through. I flipped the little light on again. Here was deja vu.

"What's the matter?" I asked.

"You didn't text back. I wanted to talk to you."

"I was hanging out with my dad. I never looked at my phone."

"I thought you were mad at me," he said.

"For what?"

"I don't know."

I glanced towards my desk and realized the forgotten Valentine was sitting in plain sight. It hurt a little to see it there, wasted. It hurt a little to know that I cared more than he did. I think, in general, I always cared more than most people did, and I always got high on the feeling of pleasing somebody. I imagined people thinking about me throughout the day, about the nice thing I did for them, and letting all their bad feelings melt away over the one nice thing that I had done to save the day. It probably never happened like that, though. Maybe I have a savior complex.

"Why did you think I was mad?"

"You *always* text back."

I looked away from him. "I said I didn't look at my phone."

"OK."

"You know, you don't even talk to me some days at school. At all. But then you have something to say later? I don't get you, Cody."

"I don't want to talk about things in school. I don't want anyone to know the things I tell you."

"You can't even say hello sometimes."

"You're more than hello."

I shook my head, wondering if he'd rehearsed that line. "Please."

"You are, C. All day I have to talk to these fakes, these *friends* of mine and I don't just want to treat you like one of those drones. Our time means something to me." He began walking around my room, like he did the last time. It was like he was looking for clues as to who I was and what he should say to get things right again. It was only a matter of seconds before he saw the stupid Valentine that I had spent hours making. It seemed like nothing big, but it was big for me. I rarely opened up to people that I couldn't completely trust.

As he made his way towards it, I decided to confess. I waited until his eyes fell upon it. "Is this for me?"

"It *was* for you," I said.

He picked it up, looked at it for a while, and smiled.

"I was embarrassed to give it to you. I'm always going a little further than what's normal. I'm always wanting to take twenty extra steps. I'm always making up for the other things I lack by taking one thing too far."

"Too far? Why is this too far?"

"Sometimes I just wonder where my mind goes compared to other peoples' minds."

"This. These are the kind of things…this is why I like you. Nobody ever made me feel special before you came along."

I knew that I should've given the Valentine to him without expecting anything in return, but how many times could I try to tell him that I loved him without any reciprocation? That was it. I was going to control myself going forward. I was going to quit going over the top for him. He got the card. It was his move.

"What is it that you feel inside?" he finally asked. "I always want to know what you feel."

"Why?"

"Because you're the most interesting person I know. It's like, did you ever read a book, start reading a book, and you want to know how it ends? Or you want to live in it? Just holding it in your hands and putting it down again isn't enough?"

"I suppose."

"What do you call that?"

I didn't know what that was called because I liked to jump to conclusions. I liked to make inferences. When I went into his room that night, I didn't wonder about him. I came home, wrote everything down, and guessed what it all meant. He gathered evidence, enjoyed the mystery, like reading a book. I wanted a poem, I wanted it all in a couple of words, tidy and contained to one page.

He sat beside me and reached for my hand. I watched his hand consume mine, and that's how I wanted it to be. I felt fragile and I wanted that protection. Maybe it wasn't love I was looking for, but to know that someone could stop me from breaking. That was a huge responsibility, though, and nobody should have to be burdened with that. Especially not somebody who was trying to hide their own cracks. We would only be friends, that much I knew. But it was time for us to be equals. It was time for me to quit having expectations and it was time for him to quit expecting me to sit around like a book until he wanted to open it again.

"I don't even know what I feel anymore," he said. "It's all so messed up, so confusing. I never used to be complicated like this. I never used to have a hundred thousand feelings and thoughts going through my head. What happened to me?"

"I don't think we really change all that much, Cody. I just think at some point we stop denying what was already there."

It was weird, then, what he did. He got on his knees in front of me and put his head down in my lap. I pushed his hair out of his face and he wrapped his arms around my waist and he stayed like that for a long time. I never knew what Cody wanted from me, only that he somehow needed me and maybe being needed was as close to being loved as a person could get.

9

How to Meet Your Mother

I GOT UP EARLY, five o'clock to be exact, to take the lid off the box. I expected to open the lid and know my entire life story, because I always wanted everything all at once. A little part of me wanted to take it slow, though. I took a mental inventory of the contents, like I always did of new and strange things.

- 1 Aerosmith T-shirt
- 3 Journals
- Jewelry, mostly necklaces
- 4 Cassette tapes
- 5 Polaroid pictures
- Small box containing ticket stubs from movies and concerts
- Perfume
- Several cards from Teddy
- 1 framed picture of Teddy and Tressa when they both looked unbelievably happy

I almost hated to open the journal; it felt like an invasion of privacy, but maybe I needed to see it. Maybe I could learn something about the woman who had eluded me for most of my life. Maybe I could figure out something about myself. I opened the leather-bound book and a dried daisy was in between the cover and the first page.

June 3, 1993
 I'm starting a new book because I feel like I'm starting a new chapter today. New medicine. New life, I hope. Doctor says this is going to work. It's new and it's working on others. I met a guy today. He's been watching me for a while. He wants to go out. I see the way he looks at me, like most men look at me. When they get to know me, they can't handle it. I said yes out of boredom. We will see.

June 5, 1993
 Teddy took me to the movies. He's polite and kind. He doesn't know me yet, though. We walked around the park and he spent the whole time trying to get the courage to hold my hand. I could make it easier on him, but it's so cute. The medicine is working and I haven't had bad thoughts yet. It's not a good time to be in a relationship. He doesn't know any of this and if I turn for the worse, he will be disappointed.

June 10, 1993
 He doesn't even know that he's a light in the darkness. He's so scared and I don't what of. I've been scared of so much — the fear of waking up or the fear of never waking up. Either way, it's all so scary to me. To get up and get dressed and walk out the door, all tasks robed in fear. At least I know what I'm scared of. Living. Is he scared that a woman like me will hurt him? I've never hurt a guy. Nobody has ever wanted me bad enough that it would hurt to be rejected. So I've decided to stop giving him a hard time and tell him how I feel.

June 13, 1993
 Admitting it felt so good. I told him that I liked him. His smile was priceless and he breathed a sigh of relief. He didn't kiss me right away, but at least he finally kissed me. I asked him if he always moved that slowly with girls and he said that he did. I asked him why and he said we had all the time in the world. You can't quantify time like that. Even all the time in the world could be one second or forever. How will we ever know?

. . .

June 15, 1993

Teddy bought me tickets to see Aerosmith in July! Nobody has ever been so good to me. I feel like I owe him something. I guess I've always had to pay my way with the guys I've dated, but he's different. He's actually a good man. He took me to his crummy one-room apartment and I thought he was going to make a move, but he didn't. We listened to records all night and I woke up in his bed under an afghan and he was sleeping on the floor. We drove out to Carbon Lake and sat on a rock and when he finally took me home, I was so happy that I cried.

June 18, 1993

The problem I'm having with the medicine is that I seem to be numb to everything. I can't feel it when he touches me. I can't laugh as hard as I want to, but I'm not crying anymore. Is this what I have to sacrifice to have a normal life? Is it true joy that I have to give up to avoid true pain? I don't want to hurt like I did, but I don't want to miss what it feels like to really fall in love. Is it fair to him that he doesn't even know who I really am without this medicine? He doesn't know the rage and sadness. Surely, there must be a way to feel everything, and control emotions that you don't want. Surely, it can be learned and not just chemically suppressed. There has to be a way to live and feel the good parts.

I closed the book, unable to go any further. Her life was a struggle. Her own mind was destroying her. I wondered what it felt like to know that the disease you had couldn't be cut out of you or cured, only slowed down and covered up. And then I realized that I knew a little bit about it. I knew what it meant to barely persuade myself to get out of bed. I knew what it meant to hurt like that, just never to that degree. And for the first time ever, I wished I was nothing like her.

Oddly, he was standing in front of my locker when I got to school. Stranger yet, he was alone. He didn't have the Circlers following him. Maybe because he was on the wrong side of the tracks in my hallway.

"Hey," he said, looking happier than usual.

"Hey," I said feigning interest. Normally, it would have excited me, but I was still thinking about the journal.

"What are you doing tonight?"

Really? Was he finally going to ask me on a date on the night I had planned to discover my mother? "I don't know yet, really. I mean, I had this project I was working on…"

"Anything I can help with?"

"No, I don't think so."

"Because you could skip the project and do it tomorrow and go to a party with me."

"Who is having the party?"

"Gus. His parents are out. He says it's just going to be a small group, but I know what he's up to and I wanted you to be there."

"What is he up to?" I asked as I turned to put away my things in my locker. I didn't want my eyes to give away the fact that I didn't really want to go.

"I'm sure it's my birthday party. I threw one for him and he drops enough hints that I know what's up."

"Wait. When is your birthday?"

"Today is my birthday."

"Today?"

He looked confused. "Yeah. Why?"

"It's my mother's birthday," I said. I knew he couldn't have a response for that, so I just went on as if I hadn't said it. "Happy Birthday. I had no idea."

"Thank you." He leaned against the locker beside mine and faced me. "So?"

"So?"

"Party? Yes or no?"

I felt like I owed it to him. "What time?"

"Eight-ish." He looked at his silly calculator watch.

"Whatever you want, Cody. It's your birthday."

All day, he kept looking at me, smiling at me, and normally I would eat up the attention, but of course he had to do it on a day when I was so preoccupied with my mother that I couldn't even enjoy it. That morning I had slid the framed picture into my dresser drawer.

I wanted it to be out of the box, but I didn't want it out where Teddy would see it and a flood gate of memories would wash over him. Teddy had a hard time looking at her, unless we were at Gram's. At Gram's he was OK with it. I guess because he felt safe with Gram.

When I went home, I sat on the couch looking at the Polaroid pictures of them. Clearly, Tressa knew her best angles, something I had never been able to figure out. I bore no resemblance to her. She looked good in whatever she wore, had perfect hair, and won over the camera without ever trying.

At five o'clock, Teddy came downstairs looking rather dashing and informed me that he was going to a faculty dinner at The Tavern, the nicer restaurant in town. My dad always looked nice in his tweed blazer. Gram had bought it for him years ago on Christmas, and that was always his dressy/casual go-to piece. "I'm staying with Kristi tonight," he said cautiously. "Are you going to be OK?"

"Yes, dad. Of course. I'm going to a birthday party, but I'll text you when I get home."

"OK." He opened his wallet and put two twenties down. "Enough?"

"Yes, plenty."

When he walked out the door, I went back to the box and took out a cassette tape. It was Soul Asylum and I remembered my dad telling me that one of her favorite songs was "Runaway Train." I fell asleep waiting for it to come on.

I woke up to my phone buzzing on my chest.

Let me in, please.

I jumped up, mad at myself for not getting ready. I opened the door and Cody came inside. I attempted to fix my makeup and hair in the bathroom while he waited. I ran from the bathroom to my bedroom to change my clothes and then I told him I was ready.

"Can we hang out a minute?"

"Sure," I said.

He sat down. "What are you listening to?"

"Soul Asylum. I found this tape…well, it was in my mom's stuff."

"You're distracted today. Is that why?"

I couldn't answer right away.

"I'm sorry," he said, attempting to save the moment. "I just never knew anyone who had a parent die. I mean, when they were so young. I don't want to bring it up, I just hope you know it's something we can talk about."

"I didn't know her. I can hardly remember. There's not much to talk about."

"I'm sorry," he said again.

I looked down at the polaroids, now sitting on the coffee table. "Do you want to see a picture of her?"

"Yes."

I didn't show him those ones. I guess I wanted him to see her for the first time at her happiest, as if they were actually meeting. "Come with me," I said, leading him to my bedroom.

I opened the drawer and moved my socks around until I found the picture again. I showed it to him. "Wow," he said.

"Do you think I look like her?"

"No."

I put the picture down. Her favorite song finally started to play. I tried not to get emotional.

He touched my necklace, a long one with a moon and star charm hanging from the chain. "This is the necklace she's wearing in the picture."

"Yes. It is."

He held it in his hand, inspecting it, and finally, our eyes met. He was wearing his glasses, his right eye bloodshot from a faulty contact lens. His hair had grown a little. He was always getting better looking and I was staying the same. He finally dropped the necklace and put his hand on my waist. It had taken longer than usual, but I let his smell intoxicate me. Oh, God, how I wanted all of him.

He stared at me and I stared back at him for an awkward moment and finally, he slowly leaned towards me and pressed his lips against mine. That was all. Just a kiss. It must have startled him, or he felt something, or he didn't feel anything at all, because he looked at me, scared. I just smiled. We headed towards the door, then I remembered that I had left the money on my dresser. I went back to get it, and when I returned to the kitchen, Cody was gone.

I was starting to notice a pattern with Cody. As soon as we

shared a sentimental moment, he would run away. I hated it. It was the one thing I hated about Cody. I always ended up alone. Why did everyone always have to leave so quickly?

I spent the weekend trying not to be upset over the kiss by being more upset over my mother. I was afraid to know her because I was afraid to notice the same traits in myself. Maybe it would have been better not to know her at all. I wanted to, though. I wanted something from it. Maybe I thought I could find the fire in her, the strength, and figure out where to get mine. This was the person my dad talked about, the outgoing one, the crazy one, the magnificent one. The one who wanted to live and know and be. The person in these books was scared and tired and introverted. How could I draw anything from that?

June 23, 1993

I stay on the medicine for fear he'll figure me out. I can fake a lot of things. I can't fake not feeling the misery I feel most of the time. He bought me a present last week, a Soul Asylum tape to listen to in the car. Sometimes when I can't sleep I put on my headphones and listen to "Runaway Train" over and over again. It's my favorite song. It feels like my life, like they're singing my heart. I'm afraid this will all end. This is too perfect to be true. Teddy is too perfect to be real. He's short and nerdy and quotes things constantly, but he loves me somehow. He's too good. He wants me to meet his mom. Mothers have a way of seeing through things. Will she see through me?

June 27, 1993

Teddy grew up in this big old house in a place called Rocky Ridge and it's by these train tracks where you can always hear the trains going by and he said he used to lie in bed at night wondering where they were going and if he would ever go anywhere. Teddy has dreams. He's going to write for Rolling Stone *someday. He's going to do interviews and then maybe he'll even write somebody's memoir. It made me realize that I never think about the future. I have no idea what I'm going to do tomorrow, if I'm even getting out of bed. I want Teddy to know me. I almost felt like telling him all of it. I stared at the ceiling in his* sister's room waiting for a train but I didn't hear one. Alone with my thoughts, I couldn't fall asleep, so I tiptoed back to Teddy's bedroom, which was full of interesting stuff and he was lying in bed awake, too.

I think he was surprised and a little nervous that it unfolded like that. I mean, all the opportunities we had. And I knew he thought it was too soon, but I needed him.

June 28, 1993

Teddy looks different today. I think I know what it is. I think this is it for him. He knows that he loves me and that he hasn't loved anyone else like this before and he won't love anyone else like this again. He keeps staring at me like I'm a stranger. Well, that's because I am one. I've stolen his heart and he doesn't even know me. It's not really fair to Teddy. I'm going to find an identity and stick with it. I'm going to make one up for myself and not tell him about the lost girl that I am. As far as he knows, I'm whole.

July 3, 1993

We never went to sleep after the concert. We drove back to Teddy's apartment and talked all night and ate breakfast in the morning. I dodge personal questions by asking him the same question he asked me, but with a different inflection. I can't tell him that my parents kept sending me away, that I was promiscuous on manic highs, and that I take medicine just so I don't feel like I want to hurt people. The sad thing is, Teddy would love me if I were crazy. He would love me no matter what. I just don't want him to have to.

July 7, 1993

We both had a long weekend. We spent it lying around. Lying around the park, the apartment, wherever. Teddy's favorite book is The Bell Jar and we took turns reading it out loud to each other and I never felt something so real in words. I know what it's like to fall so far you feel comfort. The difference for me is, I know what it's like to fly so high I feel like I'll never come down. I didn't go home for days, which meant I didn't take the medicine for days, and I think he saw it in me. When we went for breakfast, I kept feeling like someone's eyes were on me. I kept insisting a man was watching me, staring at me. I knew it was crazy, but I couldn't help it. I have to tell him sometime, some way. I have to tell him before he can't make the decision to leave. Teddy is a lover. He already talks about someday. Someday is too far away for me.

July 12, 1993

    I just had a horrible fight with Teddy. I know now that I was wrong. He wrote me a poem about how beautiful I am and it just felt like he was patronizing me. I told him that I knew what he wanted from me, the same thing everyone else did. I told him to get out and he wouldn't leave. He begged me to tell him what he had done wrong. He said he didn't want anything from me but to be in his life. If it couldn't be love, then he still wanted to know me. He said he would wait. He said he didn't care. I continued to accuse him of anything I could think up. I hit him. I told him to leave or I would call the police. And in tears, he finally left. I hurt everyone I love. I hurt everyone who tries to help me. I can't sleep and can't eat and the medicine is making me sick. I've lost weight. I don't even recognize myself in the mirror.

August 30, 1993

    Every visiting day he comes here. On Sundays, Edie comes, too. I never knew what it meant to have a mother. Mine was too busy for me. I was always alone, or left with him. There is some safety, some security there, just knowing that a person is out there for you. Edie brings soup and makes me eat it. She watches me eat it. I guess you'll have that when you've forgotten to eat for ten days and you end up in a mental hospital. I'm not sure if she knows or not. She brings me other things, too. Slippers. A night gown. Something pretty for my hair. Nail polish. She is truly kind and I know where her son gets it from.

    Teddy brings long letters and leaves them with me, one for each day he's not here. I have a confession: I read them all as soon as he leaves so I can get a feeling like I'm drunk on him. Then I read them over and over again because I just can't seem to believe he loves me unless I keep hearing it. I'm addicted to it.

September 15, 1993

    I've moved in with Teddy. He thinks it's better that way because he can take care of me, and since I've lost my job, my roommates needed somebody who would pay rent. I think they didn't want me around any more because I was crazy. I can't even deny that. The new medicine makes me feel like I'm on a constant high. I feel everything a hundred times to the extreme. I don't want to sleep. I try not to keep Teddy up all night. I wait for him to come home — it feels like decades — I just want to feel him. I always had a side effect to the high side of it, being insatiable. That's why I could never have a relationship. I had to find somebody, somewhere, to fill that desire, and if one person wasn't available, I would move on to the next. I can't do that to him, though. So I wait for him. I clean and cook and draw and read. He doesn't ask for any of it. I just can't sit still. I am electrified. I am always up. It is hard to control how high up I go, but it is better than nothing, and it's better than the alternative.

September 19, 1993

Today we were in Cleveland for my appointment and I saw something I wasn't too familiar with — a prostitute. I asked Teddy to stop the car. He didn't want to, but I opened the door and he had to. I started to ask her questions, but she didn't want to talk to me. Teddy gave her some money. I asked her how she does it and what she thinks about and how many men did she think she had been with. I asked her a hundred questions and she answered them, only because Teddy gave her twenty dollars. I asked her why she does it, and she told me she does it not to starve. She told me that once she did that, she forgot everything else and it was the only way to live. She was only twenty. I am curious to know what makes people tick because I don't know what makes me the way I am. If I can get out from under this, I'd like to be a person who can help someone. Then I started thinking about the fact that we live in a world that allows people to starve and that was painfully real.

September 24, 1993

We went home for Teddy's birthday. What a life that is there in Rocky Ridge! We canned some of the last vegetables from the garden and had the biggest meal I'd ever seen prepared before. I made mashed potatoes, enough for an army, and Edie showed me all the secret tricks to cooking that all of the real tried-and-true housewives must know. I feel normal there. I feel like there is so much to do that it satisfies me. Of course, the other craving never stops, and Teddy and I have to sneak off every so often and that's OK. He's more relaxed in his own environment and he seems to enjoy it a lot more. Also, I found my favorite place in the world! There is a hammock in the back yard and it is amazing just to sit in there and swing and relax. I can actually relax! All the sounds, trees in the wind, kids laughing, lawnmowers, cars on the street. Oh, it's amazing to know that all this life is out there. I can really open up and absorb it all and nothing scares me, nothing at all. And when we're there, I really know we're in love. I think when somebody shares their safe space with you, they must love you.

October 1, 1993

I got a job at Wasp today. I guess because their clothes are OK and I get a discount, it will be decent. They made me try on some of their stuff, because I guess it's important to make sure the salespeople can look good in the clothes. The district manager gives me the creeps. I felt like he was watching me change, but I told myself it was just my brain and I was able to get through the interview. We'll see.

October 12, 1993

Gary's advances are getting old. He comes around more often than any D.M. I've ever had. I tell him I have a boyfriend. He offered me money. Now I know how that prostitute felt. I haven't told Teddy, nor do I plan on it. He would probably kill the guy. He gives me all the slutty clothes for free and tells me he has to see me in them. I thought women have come a long way, but they really haven't. We are still just objects to most men. The only way to get even is to objectify them back, but the weaker ones who will take your shit don't deserve it, so it is never fair. Bullies know who they can pick on and just how far they can push it. He doesn't know me and he doesn't know what happens when someone pushes me too far.

October 15, 1993

How do you ever know how another person truly feels? God, do I love him, but I just can't trust love, never could. It's a tricky thing, always loving someone who can't or doesn't love you. Always thinking love is something it is not. Always hiding behind a mask because you're afraid to tell people how you really feel. Do your feelings match theirs? It's like taking a huge risk every time. Why is Teddy so confident to tell me everything? Why am I so scared to tell Teddy? I've heard "I Love You" a lot before and it's never what I think it is. Why can't I totally trust him? He probably thinks I don't appreciate him, and I can never quite reciprocate what he puts out there. Maybe some hearts are incapable of going into something one hundred percent. Then there's also this: Nothing good ever lasts.

. . .

I sat there, just staring at her stuff. I washed the couple of pieces of clothing that were in the box and I hung up all the necklaces and I put away all the other jewelry. I arranged the pictures in a small album that I had. I wanted it all to have a place, to feel natural and organized. For some reason, the rumble and hum of the washer and dryer was soothing and it was the chore I loved to do. I did all my dad's laundry, carefully hanging and folding it. He always thanked me for it, too. There was something about it that made me feel useful. It was the one domestic task that I thought I could probably please a husband with someday — clean clothes.

When everything was tidy and had a home and the box was empty, I finally had time to lie down and think about Cody. Why did he leave? Was it a terrible kiss? Was it a sudden realization that we were in two different worlds that would only collide? How would the Circlers understand? How could he break the Circle?

I didn't get too sad when he didn't text or call or come tapping on my window. Thinking about Tressa filled up that space. My dad came home early Saturday morning and we did our crossword. I couldn't help but wonder if he missed my mother every time he looked at someone else. On Sunday, I spent most of the day lying around developing the story of my parents in my head as if she had never died. I thought of her recovering, them having a wedding, and maybe having more kids. I thought about us all living in a house in Rocky Ridge and my dad being a high school teacher and my mom staying home and being a novice fashion designer who sold clothes on Etsy. I imagined us jumping in the family SUV on a Saturday afternoon and going for ice cream. I imagined vacations to the ocean and a monumental trip to Disney World. I imagined her being at all of my school functions and parent-teacher conferences and church programs. I imagined her and Gram baking cookies for Christmas and canning tomatoes at the end of summer. I imagined that she never aged one bit and neither did Teddy. They looked like nineteen year olds and everybody envied that.

On Sunday night, my dad suggested we go out for dinner. We chose a diner that was a couple towns away and it was one that had a jukebox on each table. We played songs and laughed and even ate dessert. I imagined it all over again when we got home, but instead it was a birthday celebration for Tressa and she was there with us. I wondered if my dad had done that for the last eleven years — imagined everything over again as if she were there. It was almost comforting and a bit satisfying to reinvent all your memories and insert the missing person into them.

It was working so well for me that I decided to try it with Cody. I knew it was dangerous, but I wanted to see what it would feel like. I closed my eyes. He was taking me to the Homecoming dance instead of Maia DeFelice. We went to the movies and held hands. When we watched *Broken Blue*, we were cuddling on the couch. I went to his parents' house and his mom liked me. We held hands at school and he really didn't care what the Golden Circle thought. They just had to live with it.

All of that didn't stop me from knowing that Monday was coming and I would have to face him again. Then it would be the reality that he kissed me and ran. And who knows what he did at that party? He probably kissed someone else to get me off of his lips. He probably got drunk and another girl had to take him home, clean up his vomit, and hide the evidence. He probably does that with all the girls he likes.

10

Too Much or Not Enough

HOW DO YOU FIGHT AWKWARDNESS? With normality. Let's act like nothing ever happened. Let's act like you did not ask me to a party, you did not kiss me, and you did not ditch me for the party after the kiss. Let's just walk up to him and say, "Cody, how was your weekend?"

That wasn't normal, though. I never approached him, and if I were going to approach him, it certainly wouldn't be in the company of the Circle. Perhaps I was going to have to text first. Maybe a simple, *we need to talk*. But that sounded so ominous. Question about math homework? He knows me better than that. Maybe the text could be the *how was your weekend?* Why would I even text him that when we were standing twenty feet away from each other? Avoidance would be the best bet, but that would just make seventh period hell. None of that was my style, and why should I change?

I went to homeroom and took out my notebook and pen.

Dear Cody,
    You can just talk to me, you know? I'll never be a person you have to run away from or hide from. You can say anything to me. We are friends. Maybe I like you a little too much, but we are still friends.
    Caroline

. . .

I slid it towards him in seventh period. He looked at it, then at me, then folded it up and put it in his pocket. He didn't say anything, and looked straight ahead at the teacher for the rest of the period. When the bell rang, he looked at me as if he wanted to say something, but he didn't. I went home and went to bed. It was the best thing to do when I couldn't stand to figure out the motives of the world any longer. My head hurt. My palms were sweating. I couldn't cope with it. I tried to sleep. Every time I closed my eyes, I listened for a tap on the window. Every time I opened my eyes, I could feel his lips. Feeling like that was hell.

I, no longer sane, picked up my phone to text him.

P.S. I liked it.

I waited for a response. I hated waiting for a response. I stuck my head under the pillow, regretting it, and hoping it was lost in space somewhere.

I never got out of bed. My dad brought me a sandwich. He asked me what was wrong. I told him I was catching a cold. Maybe he believed me. It didn't matter. At ten thirty I decided to force myself to sleep.

Why?

I picked up my phone and saw it. Should I make him wait, too? I couldn't be that kind of girl.

Why what?

Why did you like it?

Your lips are soft. You always smell good.

I don't know what to do sometimes.

About what?

I'm mixed up. It's our age, I guess.

I guess. I wanted you to do it, though. I have wanted you to do it.

Do you think it's the best thing right now?

I don't know what's best. If you don't feel like it, then we shouldn't.

Shouldn't do what?

Shouldn't do anything that makes you uncomfortable.

I wasn't uncomfortable. I don't know what it was. I was just not ready for that.

For what?

Nothing.

How was the party? Did you wrestle anyone? Wear women's clothes? Tell me about it!

I stayed for an hour, went home, and held my phone for two days waiting for you to text me.

I'm sorry. I shouldn't have been stubborn.

Me neither.

Should we talk about it?

Nah. Let's just let it keep festering. I'm not up for getting real. Let's talk about something else.

Like what?

It's weird how much I miss you when we don't talk for a day or so.

Yes. Same here.

Good night.

Good night.

It's funny how wounds will heal if you let them. I never mentioned the kiss to Cody again, and he never brought it up either. We immediately went back to normal. He still ignored me in the halls for the most part, we still had our Wednesday nights and Thursday lunches, and we still touched knees or shoulders or hands in Geometry class. Sometimes he would just show up on a random day and jam with my dad or watch a movie with me. He went to parties with the Circlers and didn't invite me along. My dad went to Kristi's. I was alone and I used those nights to read about my mother.

November 15, 1993
  Gary cornered me today and he put his dirty body against me. He doesn't know what kind of person he's dealing with. He doesn't know that I will snap. I've given Teddy clues about it but he's so damned diplomatic. I'm not the only one, either. He does it to everyone, but he does it to me more. I want to catch him, to bust him. I want to make him pay for what he's doing to me. I shouldn't have to be scared or ashamed to show my body. It makes me feel like crawling out of my skin when he looks at me that way. On Monday, I'm going to call his boss. She's a female and I'm sure she'll be appalled at his behavior and take care of it as soon as possible. Soon, it'll be safe for all of us to go to work without fear that we'll be man-handled by him.

November 24, 1993
  Thanksgiving at Teddy's! I love his mother. I ate so much. Jennifer is such

an intelligent and educated woman. Teddy pokes fun at her about her "Liberal Arts Education" and insists that it turns people into hippies. He picks on her all in fun because he's her brother and he's supposed to. It's like a sleepover when I go to her room. I painted her nails and she braided my hair and she told me that she can't wait until we're sisters. I wonder why she said that. I don't think Teddy is that serious about me. Why would he be? We've only known each other for a few months. She's probably just saying that.

Teddy watched the football game with his dad…he was actually reading a book the entire time. He knows what to say and when to say it, though. His dad seems to be more of a typical dad-type. Nothing like Teddy, but a very nice man. He was a marine. He went to Vietnam. He showed me his photo albums and he was a pretty dashing guy in his day. I don't know who Teddy looks like. He's not exactly dashing, but more exactly what his name sounds like. He's like a cuddly little Teddy Bear. He couldn't hurt a fly, I swear. He'll never hurt me, either. Tomorrow we are going to meet up with some of his high school friends. He's like a little boy sometimes. He told me that they are all going to wonder how he snagged a girl like me. They don't know me on the inside. Neither does he.

November 30, 1993

It all miserably back-fired on me. A woman in power in a man's world might as well just be a man. They have to be rude and heartless and cruel. Climbing a ladder in the name of feminism only means that you have to become a misogynist yourself. Leave me on the bottom of the heap, then, and give me my dignity. I filed a complaint with the corporation and Cora came to investigate the claim. Supposedly, she was going to investigate the claim. She came to tell me to keep my mouth shut because we were in a busy season, trying to get into the black, and she couldn't lose her highest performing DM. She said I'm the only one with a complaint and that I'm so full of myself that I think every man who lays eyes on me wants me. Gary found out, and he cut my hours to nothing; the other girls are pissed at me. I confronted him and I just went into a rage, like before the medicine. The next time he put his hands on me, I screamed at him and I smacked him in the face. He called security to escort me out, but he didn't press assault charges. Funny how he could have pressed assault charges against me for defending myself against his advances. I can't press any type of charges against him. The security guard told me that I had to expect that when I dressed that way and I told him that Gary made me wear the clothes. He smugly told me that nobody can make me do anything, so I slapped him, too. He didn't care too much for it and Teddy ended up having to get me at the police station. I was lucky that the police officer was a woman, and she understood. She told me that the only way to be a strong woman in a man's world is to remember that you're a woman. Don't act like a man. She convinced the security guard to also not press charges.

Teddy wasn't mad at me. He told me that I'd never have to work a job like that again and show my body when I didn't want to and take advances that I didn't want. He told me that he'd work two or three jobs before he would let me go back to that. He's what a man should be.

I got my old job back at NRM and I'm sure I'm going to be pretty happy there, although the memories from before might mess with me. We will see what happens, I guess.

By the end of March, spring was trying to break through and my spirits were a little higher since we were out of the dead of winter. Maybe it was the turn of the season, or maybe it was just poor judgement, but Cody, once again, decided to drag me along to a Circler event. I insisted on not going, until his heartfelt confession of why he really needed a date: Sylvia Blickman. I didn't know her. She was somebody who moved away in eighth grade and had just recently come back. She was busty, dressed cute, and her tight jeans showed off her round butt. It turned heads, and I'm sure Cody was looking, too. He finally confessed to me that Sylvia Blickman was the kisser from the game of spin the bottle.

I, soft and understanding, decided that I could be his hero and accompany him to the party.

Right from the beginning, it was weird. I dressed a little sexier than usual because I knew I had competition. She was pretty and they had a history. I tried to keep my raging crush on Cody under wraps, but when he was always texting me pictures of my "wedding dress" and asking me if he could start calling Teddy "Dad" it was hard to control the burning inside of me. It was all in fun, I knew that, but part of me wondered if something about it all wasn't real. Sometimes we'd look at each other a little too long. Sometimes he would start to tell me something really deep. Sometimes he was so honest that it hurt a little to hear what was really on his mind. He wasn't a stranger to anger.

It didn't make it easier to stop liking Cody when he suddenly quit looking like a child. His face thinned out and his hair got longer and he ditched his contacts for glasses full time. He got his braces off, too. He was turning into a man and I was watching the transformation. It only made him seem more of an unlikely boyfriend for me. I wondered if, at some point, we would no longer be friends. Once he got a girlfriend he would talk to her about all the things we talked about and we would have to end it. It wouldn't be right to have that kind of relationship with somebody's boyfriend.

When he came to the door, he was wearing my favorite shirt, a t-shirt underneath, and ripped jeans. It was the "I'm not even trying" look, but I knew he was trying. I got close enough to him to know that he still smelled good. We walked to the party quietly.

"Next time, I'll drive," he finally said.

"What?"

"I'm getting my license tomorrow."

"Oh. Wow." Suddenly, he seemed even more mature. I was still only fifteen because of my October birthday. The age gap seemed wide.

"*If* I pass, which I will."

He was confident most of the time, and I liked that.

"Are you nervous?"

"No. I'm sure I'll pass."

"No, I mean about tonight. About Sylvia and stuff."

"Nah." He sighed. "I just harbor resentment towards her because of the kiss-shaming."

I laughed. "Oh, boy. Do I know how you feel."

He smiled. "Shut up."

"Nope."

"We must never speak of that."

"You left that one wide open, Cody."

He shrugged. "Maybe I did."

"So, what is the end game here? Make her fall madly in love? Make her jealous? What is my role in it?"

"I just didn't want to go alone."

I tried to understand where he was coming from, but I was a creature of avoidance and didn't understand his need to face the kiss-shamer.

The only thing I liked about going to parties was watching. I wanted to solve the mystery of people, and he gave me access to that. I was a watcher, not a participator, and I would go home that night and recount all of the best parts in my head looking for significant meaning to life in trivial moments from a tenth grade party.

If any part of Cody shined through when we were listening to records or watching *Broken Blue*, it quickly scurried away into the recesses of him when he was at a party. He was interested in fitting in, and that made it even harder to understand why he took me to parties. I felt like he wanted to stay in the Circle, but he wanted to have some kind of identity outside of it, too. I was his connection to the outside world and he was my connection to the inside world.

It was a smaller party than what I was used to and not just a Circler party. Gus, Libby, and Maia were there, but the rest of them, including Sylvia, were outsiders, like me. It made me feel a little less special to be in the majority for once. It was a quiet gathering in the basement of Libby's house. Everyone had their secret booze stash. Cody had the flask, as usual, but I only saw him take one sip.

Libby made an announcement that we had to sit in a circle. We were going to play a game.

Cody grabbed my hand and sat beside me nervously. His palm was sweating. What would it be? Spin the bottle again? I hoped not because I really would have to think of a quick way to get out of it if I was chosen. I would say I have a cold. That sounded plausible. Sylvia sat beside him to his right and I was on his left. She nudged him and nodded towards his pocket and he handed her the flask. It made me horribly jealous for her lips to touch the thing his lips had been on. She was so pretty that it made me sick inside.

Libby put a beer bottle in the center of the circle and smiled. "Just like old times, right Cody?"

He didn't respond.

"Since it *is* the game you're infamous for, why don't you spin first?"

All of the color drained from his face, but he had to play along. He *had* to or he would surely be ridiculed.

"OK," he said, trying to sound confident. I knew he was nervous. He reached for the bottle. His eyes dropped, then looked to me. "I don't want to spin," he said quietly.

"What's that?" Libby asked, surprised that he'd defy her.

"I don't need to spin. There's only one girl I'd go in there with anyway."

"Who?"

"Caroline," he said, quietly.

Everyone paused in anticipation of what Libby would do to a rebellious Circler. She bit her lip, probably trying to think of a way to punish him.

It was Gus who finally saved him. He began chanting, "Co-dy! Co-dy!" until everyone joined in the quiet and persuasive chant. Cody, fueled by the cheering, stood up and held his hand out to me.

"You know the drill," Libby said with disinterest. "Seven minutes."

The closet was small and smelled of long-stored winter parkas from years gone by, but his black and white nearly threadbare flannel shirt smelled good. He fumbled around until he found a string to turn on the light.

"So," I said, not knowing what else to do, "What was that all about?"

He raised an eyebrow.

"Sorry," I said.

"I don't really think stuff like this is a game."

"Yeah. Neither do I."

"You don't have to kiss me."

"OK," I said, even though the idea of kissing him was exciting me. We were quiet for a minute. "Did our kiss even count?" I shouldn't have said it, but I thought it out loud.

He shifted around uncomfortably. "I don't know. Did you have to bring that up again?"

His hesitation to talk about it made me realize it must have been something he truly regretted and suddenly I felt like the ugliest girl in the world. "I'm going..." I reached for the door knob.

"No, don't." He grabbed my arm.

"Why not? You don't want to kiss me."

"Don't you know how shit like this works? If we don't stay, we'll never live it down."

"They are *your* friends, not mine. I don't have to come to another party like this. You do. I don't have to be fake and phony and pretend I was kissing you for seven minutes."

"I don't have to either."

"Prove it, then," I said, again reaching for the door.

"OK," he said, and in one quick motion he stopped me from

opening the door and locked his lips to mine. He opened his mouth and I felt his tongue find its way past my teeth. His lips were soft and he was good at kissing. He pulled me tight against him and his hips moved with the rhythm of the kiss and it wasn't too wet or too sloppy like I'd imagined it might be when I imagined kissing. I didn't mind him breathing on my face, either. It tickled, actually. It was a new feeling, to be weak over somebody, to want somebody. My mind raced, thinking of what all we could do with each other and he became the most attractive guy in the world to me. I couldn't believe I was allowing myself to feel so much.

Eventually, we were on our knees, and then, somehow, he was on top of me. The kissing part became less important and I concentrated more on his lower parts. I wondered how far it would go. My judgement was highly impaired by my intoxication from his smell. I didn't know much about boys, but I wondered if he was aroused.

I lost track of time, and finally someone knocked. Cody didn't stop. They knocked again. "Come on guys. Ten minutes? No, eleven."

He pulled his face away from mine, leaving me breathless, and he smiled. "Is that enough proof?"

"Of what?"

"That I wasn't trying to fake anything."

His usual pout curled into a coy half-smile and I didn't know what to say. He took my hand and opened the door and his friends erupted into a mocking cheer. He laughed and let go of my hand. I wasn't sure if I should be humiliated or proud, so I chose to be angry and I left.

Leaving was probably not the best idea. It started to rain and I ducked into Alice's on the way home. The brilliant white walls and checked floor hurt my eyes after coming in from the dark. All I could think about was what he might be doing with Sylvia after I left. His kissing had improved, and she might have wanted to give him a second chance. Or maybe we were just so compatible that I enjoyed his kissing, no matter how bad it was.

I sat down at the counter, an old-fashioned lunch counter, and Kristi came around the corner. "Hey, you," she said. I had never encountered Kristi without my dad. It felt odd.

"Hi," I said.

"Where's Teddy?" she asked.

"Home, I think. I don't know. I was at a party."

She smiled. "Do you ever stay very long at a party?"

"No. I guess I never have much reason to."

She poured a Sprite out of the fountain and leaned against the counter, sliding the drink my way. "Boy trouble?"

I had to make a decision whether or not to tell her. I hadn't been telling Lilly about my relationship with Cody because I didn't think it was fair to talk about it when she couldn't date. Plus, she was always encouraging me to be with him and I didn't need the false hope that we could become something. I didn't want to talk to my dad about it for the obvious reasons. I didn't want to talk to Gram about boys, because she still saw me as a little kid. I guess my pickings were slim.

"Yes," I admitted.

"You want to dish? Or no?"

"It's kind of weird. You're sleeping with my dad."

"Why is it weird?"

I shrugged. "I don't know." I quickly flashed back to him and Becca on the basement couch and I wondered if that's what was making it even weirder. "Do you have a boyfriend besides my dad?"

"Your dad is not my boyfriend, and we have an open relationship. He can do as he pleases and so can I, but we're available if we get lonely."

"And what if you want to stop having that type of relationship?"

She shrugged. "Then I tell him. And he either does something about it, or it's over."

"But you're OK with it?"

"Yes, I am."

"Why?"

"Because I'm not in love with him. I don't feel jealous over him. It's a different thing than love."

"I'm tired of being an if-girl. *If* I don't have anything to do or anyone to hang out with or anyone to text. *If* I don't have wrestling, or *if* I don't have homework. If there is nothing else on this earth to do, then you're my girl. Sort of. Not even."

"Why not call it quits?"

"He wouldn't understand because he doesn't know how I feel about him."

"Why not tell him?"

"He's the king of mixed signals. I don't know what he wants. And he knows that I like him."

"All guys are the kings of mixed signals. They don't know what they want either."

"Do you feel that way about Teddy?"

She smiled. "No. Teddy isn't like that. He's pretty easy to understand. He doesn't really hide anything."

"Why can't you just be his girlfriend?"

She came around the counter and sat on the stool beside me. "Woman to woman?" she asked.

I swiveled towards her on my stool. "OK."

"He is madly in love with your mother. I'll always feel like the other woman, Caroline. I don't want to be that forever. Every week, every other week, sometimes a couple times a week, I can put it out of my mind. He used to come in here without you at first. He'd bring a book, always. Eat by himself. One day I just sat down across from him and I said, 'Who *are* you?' And he got the biggest smile on his face and we started talking. He talked about you and I asked him where his wife was and he told me that he had never been married, that he had wanted to but she passed away. That's all he had to say, because in the way he said it, I knew she was the one. I would never be the one. I can be second. But not if he's going to try to put me first. I'll never catch up. So I take my spot and it's OK like that. You see?"

"Maybe I'm at the point where I want to be first to him."

"Then you should probably just ask him if he feels the same way.

"You see, the difference between you and me is that I don't think I can take the rejection. I don't want to hear it."

"You'll find strength in your first heartbreak. Trust me. You will. But then again, maybe he is wild about you, too. You don't know how pretty you are. When you figure it out, you'll learn how to use it."

I stewed over it, staying up all night, upset that I had let myself like him as much as I had. He had acted like he hadn't kissed me for so long because it was supposed to be special. Seeing him made me fall for him, so I didn't want to see him any more, study with him any more, or hang out with him any more. I was angry that my first real kiss, my first real make-out session, was only a joke to him. I was hurt and angry and I wanted to put up a new wall so I wouldn't have to see that mistake any more. It was hard, but I tried to train myself to loathe him. He wasn't boyfriend material, I couldn't hold a candle to the other girls he had liked, and it was over between us. Not even friends, and certainly, not more.

It was a long weekend off school, and I didn't speak to him for three days. At the end of the third day he showed up at my house in the new-to-him Jeep Wrangler that he had been saving up for. He was wearing new glasses that suited him well, and I could feel my heart in the pit of my stomach as my crush on him resurrected at full strength. I looked over his shoulder at the car and pretended not to be interested.

"You want to go for a ride?"

"I'm busy."

"Fifteen minutes."

"Fifteen? Not seven or ten or eleven?"

"You're mad."

"Yeah. A little."

"I thought you wanted to kiss. It's not like I do that all the time."

"Why don't you go pick up some of your real friends?"

"I came to see you because I wanted to see you. If I wanted to see them, I would have gone to see them."

He looked ridiculous in his too-tight Spirit Club sweatshirt, and something about his juvenile sense of style made me feel sorry for him. I only wanted to hate him, though.

"I could promise to never kiss you again, but I don't really want to say that. I like being with you. I thought about it a lot. We could be a little more than friends, the two of us."

"What does that mean?"

"I'm not pinning you down," he said quickly. "But we could be each other's go-to. It wouldn't be the worst thing ever. I'd be here if you were ever lonely and for school dances and boredom and dating and stuff."

"And when a game of spin the bottle comes around?"

"Count me out," he said.

"Aren't relationships all or nothing?"

"It's not the fifties."

"Oh. I can't wear your letterman sweater, then? Come on, Cody. I need a little more than, 'I'll call you when I'm bored.' I think I'm worth a little more than that."

"We could be a couple with the option of telling each other when we're ready to be over it. How about that?"

"Over it?"

"Let's face it. We're not madly in love. We're not even *in* love. So, if you believe in love at first sight and that person happens to come along, I wouldn't hold it against you and you could tell me you found someone more suitable. And the same goes for me."

"So, in other words, the first time you get offered sex somewhere, it's over."

He was amused with me. That was always the look he had on his face when we disagreed — like I was the only person who ever fancied arguing with him. "No. I'm not into body count."

"What?"

"Body count matters. I don't think people should do it just to do it. I'm not like that. Not all guys are the same and you seem to think they are, which is weird for a girl who was raised by a single dad."

"You're accusing me of making generalizations by making a generalization. What if my dad is a man-whore?"

"Your dad is not a man-whore. Neither am I. Now, let's go for a ride."

He had a no-nonsense way about smoothing things over, and I appreciated that, so I got in the car. As he drove, I contemplated having a relationship with him. He was polite. He was good-looking enough. He was an athlete. He was smart and hard-working. Being Cody's semi-girlfriend wasn't the worst thing in the world. I just knew I couldn't like him more than he liked me. I always got the feeling my dad loved my mom more than she loved him and I didn't want to be on the receiving end of that disappointment. I vowed I wouldn't fall any harder for him.

"If I agree to this, are you going to stop looking at Sylvia Blickman's ass every time she passes you in the hall?"

"Are you going to stop looking at Skip Waters?"

I crossed my arms. He drove a tough bargain.

11

Will the Circle Be Unbroken

AT SCHOOL, we didn't hold hands. We didn't kiss. We didn't act like a couple. He would pick me up in the morning, carry my book bag to the Jeep, open the door for me, and shut it behind me. Then he would get in on his side, lean over the center console and kiss me. He always had freshly brushed teeth, but the faint taste of strawberry milk always remained on his lips. Once we got to school, he opened the door for me again, got my book bag out of the back seat and put it on my back. He held the door open for me when we went into the school, he walked me to my locker, then he went to his locker and the Circle. They looked at us with sideways glances. They didn't say anything to me, and if they said anything to him, he didn't tell me. I didn't push the issue. I didn't care if they knew about us or not. I was happy enough with what we had outside of school.

    At my house, we had heated games of Scrabble. We listened to Motown records and Cody sang along. We took long walks together, usually around the lake at the college. We sat in the amphitheater and talked about silly things, like how we were going to get married and be normal and be parents and how our kids would hate us because we were uncool. Shawn and Emily, our children, almost seemed real. He talked about how he would always wear his gun when guys came around for Emily. He told me that I would seriously need to learn how to cook. We laughed about it because it was all fun and games, but something about it seemed plausible. I tried not to fall in love with him, but when we were together something felt so good and so natural that it was almost impossible not to feel a lot for him.

I still had my sleepovers with Lilly, and she quizzed me about him and about everything we did together.

"We don't kiss much," I confessed.

"Why not?"

"I don't know. My dad is around a lot. Or we're out in public. Or we're at school."

"If I were you, I'd want to kiss him all the time."

"I don't know who likes him more, you or me." I laughed.

"I don't like *him*, per se. I just wish I had someone to care about *me* like that." She sat cross-legged in front of me on the floor beside her bed while we drank Diet Pepsi and read *Cosmo*.

"What's the best thing about Cody?"

"The best thing is that I know a side of him that the Circlers don't know."

She smiled. "You're always so you-versus-them. You should try to get along with them."

"I don't need to get along with them."

"They are his friends, though, Caroline. Eventually it's going to cause friction."

"I don't make him hang out with my friends."

"Me. That's me. You only have one friend. It's different."

I contemplated that for a moment. "What kind of friction?"

"I don't know. I mean, I know you, but what if he thinks you're being snobby because you never want to be around them. The truth is you're an introvert, but maybe he'll think you're being stuck up."

It was a possibility. It was definitely a possibility, but I tried not to think about it.

It was the middle of May, and after the season finale of *Broken Blue* we had a pretty intense make out session since my dad wasn't home. We scarcely did anything but light kissing, but I saw the way he watched the sex scene between Emily and Lopez after she found out that his father was, in fact, a serial rapist. He watched it with intensity, on the edge of his seat, as if his life depended on not blinking until it was over. They stumbled around his apartment, kissing sloppily and aggressively until she stopped and stared at him, maybe in fear or maybe in lust. He ripped off her clothes and bent her over the arm of the couch and manhandled her. When it was over, he lit a cigarette and stood in front of the window. She came out of the shower, wet and flushed and told him that he was going to be a father.

Cody breathed a huge sigh of relief and flopped back onto the couch. "Holy shit! I thought we'd never find out the truth. Every episode was like, is she or isn't she?"

"I was kind of hoping she wasn't," I admitted.

"Why?"

"Because everything is going to change now. He'll have to think about the baby every time he's about to do something stupid or dangerous or wrong. He's going to grow a conscience."

"I guess you're right. Well, anything could happen before they write the fall premier, right?"

"I guess so."

He looked over his shoulder. "What time is your dad coming home?"

"Late. It's some big meeting they have before commencement. He told me he'd be home at eleven or later."

"That's an hour."

"Yeah."

He smiled and shut off the television.

"What's that for?"

"Let's listen to some music."

"OK," I said.

"You pick."

"What are you in the mood for?" I asked, looking at my dad's collection.

"Let's do nineties since we both like it."

"OK," I said, and immediately chose a CD.

He eventually started to kiss me and as the songs went on, he kissed me passionately. Harder. Then on the neck. His hand crept up under my shirt, but he asked first, and I allowed it. Another song went by before he unhooked my bra. I'm not sure where he thought that would go, since I still had my shirt on. Once he realized it, he laughed. "I'm sorry."

"It's OK," I said.

"It's just, that's what they do in the movies, you know?"

"I know."

"Can I take off your shirt?"

A wave of panic came over me. I was self-conscious. I never knew if what I had compared to what anyone else had. My body was nothing special and the only person I had ever really compared myself to was Lilly and she was perfect.

"Oh, God. I'm sorry. I shouldn't have said that."

He pulled away from me, but I didn't want that. I wanted to be close to him. I had never known what it was to be wanted before and I liked the way it felt. So I did what most girls my age do when they are feeling desperate to keep a boy close. "Yes."

"Huh?"

"Yes. You can take it off. Just turn off the lamp first."

He looked at me cautiously before he slowly reached for the lamp. I lifted my arms and he pulled the shirt over my head. I let the bra fall down in front of me. He kissed me again before he touched me, and soon he was on top of me, his hand between us, squeezing, his lips mashed into mine, his tongue in my mouth. He was breathing on my face and I doubted he even realized it.

"Is this OK?" he breathed into my ear.

"Yes." I wrapped my legs around him.

"Do you like this?"

"Yes," I said, now trying to kiss his neck, too. "I really like it. Do you?"

"Yeah."

I held him tighter. I kissed him harder. I put my hands under his shirt and I felt the muscles in his back. He was perfect. I ran my hands through his hair. He took his glasses off and put them on the coffee table, then his hand found its way back to my chest. An hour had gone by. I heard Cody's watch beep. It was eleven. "Hey. My dad might come home soon."

He sat up and flicked the light on.

I covered myself with my hands.

"Sorry," he said, handing me my bra and turning away. I was glad that he knew I didn't want him to look. Cody was intuitive like that. I dressed myself and he turned back to me. "I guess I should go. Huh?"

"I guess so," I said.

He suddenly turned shy and was unsure what to do next.

"I'll see you tomorrow," I said.

"I'll pick you up."

He left awkwardly, not even kissing me good-night.

I turned off the CD player and went to my room. I began gushing it out in my journal, every last detail of it. From the shape of his tongue, to the fact that he squeezed a little too hard, to the way I could feel him getting hard against my leg. A couple of minutes into it, my phone rang and it startled me to the point that I dropped my pen.

"Hello?"

"Hey. It's me," he said, softly.

"Hey. Is something wrong?"

"No. I just wanted to talk to you some more."

"About what?"

"That was intense," he said. "It felt awesome."

I was relieved that he felt the same thing I did. "Yeah, it did."

"It wasn't too much, was it?"

"It's not like we do that all the time."

"No, I mean, the boob thing? Was it OK? Did I hurt you? When I thought back on it, I thought maybe I was a little too rough."

"Well, you might have squeezed a bit much. But I wasn't complaining, was I?"

"Look, I was really into it. I have never seriously thought about it before."

"About what?"

"About sex."

"Sex?" I asked, surprised.

"Yeah. I was, like, thinking we would end up doing it."

"Really?"

"I mean, we're too young. We can't do it, you know?"

"Yeah, I know."

"You don't want to do it, do you?"

"No. I mean, yeah, but no."

"Yeah?"

"I mean, yeah. Like, when it feels good like it did tonight, yeah. But realistically, no. I know we shouldn't because, you know, we're too young."

"Right. I mean, there's so much stuff that could happen."

"I'm only fifteen."

"Right. And, I mean, I think you should be in love. You know?"

"Oh," I said, feeling deflated because, at that moment, I *was* in love with him. "No, you're right."

"Kids our age, they don't take it seriously. You take it seriously, don't you?"

"Of course I do."

"I mean, I think we should. Someday. Maybe after high school. You think we should do it after high school?"

"Yeah. I think so."

"We should be cliche. We could do it after the senior prom or something."

I laughed. "OK. That sounds good."

"So, now, we don't even have to talk about it. We can just have this mutual understanding that we'll do it on prom night."

"Sure. That gives us two years to figure out what we're going to tell our parents about not coming home from the prom."

"God, I didn't even think about that."

We paused for a while, and I listened to him breathe. Finally, I couldn't hold it back any longer. "I really like you, Cody."

"I really like you, too."

When school ended for the summer, Cody was going with Gus to Alaska to visit another one of their cousins. He was going to be gone for a month and they would be going hiking and looking for wild animals and all sorts of manly things that I had no interest in. I pretended to listen to everything he was saying about the trip, but secretly I thought it sounded absurdly boring to trudge around that state trying to sight a moose and being cold. The only thing that I thought about when I imagined the trip was how lonely I would be for twenty-eight days without him.

The day before he was leaving, he asked me if I wanted to do something special and I requested that we go to Carbon Lake, that place where my parents had spent one of their first magical days together, and he looked it up on a map and decided we could go. I packed a picnic and I told my dad where we were going. He lied to his parents and told them he was going to an amusement park with some of the guys. They still didn't know about me. I still hadn't met them, nor had I been to his house since the puking incident.

Carbon Lake was a quarry, on old blasted land that had been turned into a state park. It was a bit of a hike to the actual lake, but when we got there it was pretty. In the middle of the week, it wasn't busy, and we found a spot to ourselves and ate our lunch. He didn't talk much and neither did I. Sometimes we just liked to be around each other, no noise between us.

Finally, on the way home, he said it. "I'm going to miss you. It's kind of making me not want to go on this trip."

I tried to make light of it. "It's only a month. It's not forever. We can still talk sometimes or text. Maybe you don't want Gus to know we're talking, so just text me."

He didn't say anything.

"You're going to be having so much fun, you won't even be thinking about me."

He still didn't say anything.

"Maybe you'll meet some hot Alaskan chicks and forget all about me."

We were at a red light, and he looked at me out of the corner of his eye. "Don't sell yourself short."

"What does that mean?" I asked.

"Nothing," he muttered.

I pulled my sweater onto my shoulders, suddenly feeling a coolness that wasn't from the weather.

He dropped me off at home before dark and barely even kissed my cheek when he walked me to the door.

"You don't want to come in?" I asked, hopefully.

"I still have packing," he said quietly.

"Oh. OK." I debated with myself whether or not to give him the super big hug I had been wanting to give him all day. I wanted to be as cold and as hard as he was being, but I knew that sometimes you didn't get second chances, so I wrapped my arms around him and squeezed him and told him how much I was going to miss him, but that I hoped he would have fun.

I went straight to bed, depressed, but hoping that the next day would be a new day for me. Maybe I needed a month off from him. Maybe I just needed to be me again for a while. Being us could be exhausting at times. Lilly and I had planned to go to the pool where Skip was working as a lifeguard for the summer. I wondered if I would feel guilty when I looked at him.

When the sun went down, I fell asleep, looking forward to morning and a fresh start.

12

Any Other Summer

SKIP HAD a lovely birthmark on the back of his left leg. It was a discoloration, a tan spot on his creamy thigh. I noticed it when he walked past me at the pool and I looked for it when he climbed back onto the lifeguard tower. For over a week, I had been admiring that mark from near and far, and secretly, very secretly, I wondered what it would be like to run my lips over it. I pretended to read while I watched him, and while I watched the other girls watch him. The Circlers had their own corner of the pool, and I noticed that Libby had her eye on him and was pursuing him aggressively. She would wave him over to have a snack with her when he was on his break. She would touch his chest, feeling his pectoral muscles, running her french manicured nails over his biceps. It made me want to throw up. It was bad enough the Circlers had to keep a tight leash on their own boys, but they had begun intruding into our territory, too.

"Look at her," I said to Lil.

"I know."

"She can't have him. He's outside the Circle."

"Well, now, that's a bit hypocritical, don't you think?"

"Why?" I asked, still staring at Libby and Skip. He was rubbing sunblock on her back. It made my skin crawl.

"You're dating a Circler. You have Cody."

"That's different."

"Why?"

"Because she can have anyone. Why does she need Skip?"

"It's doesn't even matter, does it?"

"Why not?"

She laughed as if I were being crazy. "Because Skip doesn't want her."

"How do you know?"

"Skip doesn't want a girlfriend. Temptation, you know?"

"I guess," I said, remembering the incident in the basement, knowing that he had sexual thoughts just like any other boy.

"How badly do you miss Cody?" she asked, rolling towards me and giving me her full attention. "Do you feel like you're going to die?"

"No."

"Has he called or texted?"

I took my phone out and showed her the single picture I had received of Cody standing beside an American flag on a mountain peak. He was wearing a tank top and showing off his bicep with his typical half-grin. No text accompanied the picture. I used his lack of communication with me to justify my rekindled interest in Skip's wonderful body. "Only this."

"He's probably thinking about you and doesn't know what to say."

"I doubt it. He's probably having fun and meeting new girls."

"Maybe you should call him."

"I don't want to be pathetic."

"Admitting you have feelings and you miss him isn't pathetic."

"Yes, it kind of is. I'm home. I'm doing nothing. I'm always available. He's on vacation and he's busy. I don't want to bother him. He can call me if he wants me."

"Maybe he's *wanting* you to call."

"What if I call…" I started, my mind jumping to conclusions, "And he gets annoyed with me and he says something bitchy and I have to hang up and feel bad about it for the next three weeks until I see him again? That's what I'm trying to avoid."

"Is he ever bitchy on the phone?"

"This is different. It's a boy's trip. He probably wouldn't want to talk to me in front of Gus. I mean, our relationship status is still pretty unclear to the Circlers."

"If they don't see it, they're blind. I see it plain as day. He's in love with you."

"Love? That's a strong word."

Lilly kept herself covered at the pool. Had she worn a bikini the caliber of Libby's bikini, she would have blown Libby right out of the water. Lilly obeyed her dad's rules, though, and either didn't go into the water and donned a cute cover-up, or wore an over-sized t-shirt when she went in the water. The other girls chuckled at her. I thought it was a bit of a double standard that Skip could go around in his short lifeguard shorts and no shirt, but Lilly had to be miserably covered and burdened with weird tan lines. I didn't like to show my body, but at least I wore a bathing suit with a tank top to cover my lack of boobs. Lilly had everything she needed to wear a bathing suit well, though.

After the pool, we went to her house and messed with our hair, trying to make it look like we had just spent the day at the pool, but in a good way. Skip laughed at us. His tanned, glowing skin was hard to look away from. His super-genuine smile was harder to look away from.

When Lilly left the room for a drink, Skip stayed. I felt guilty for being alone with him given the way I had been feeling about him.

"How's Cody?" he asked.

"I don't know," I said, nonchalantly.

"He's in Alaska, right?"

"Right." I put some lipstick on and he laughed. "What?"

"You don't really need makeup," he said, matter-of-factly.

"Oh, please. That's just something boys say to make girls feel better about themselves."

"Why would I be patronizing you?"

I thought about it for a second, and decided to go with the old cliche. "Because that's what boys do."

"Where do you get your ideas about boys?" He was leaning against the door frame confidently and I always hated how boys had so much confidence and how it just came naturally to them. God should've spread that out more equally.

"I don't know," I said, giving up on the argument.

"Learn to take a compliment, Caroline. You're pretty. You'll be getting more of them."

I felt myself blushing. "Thank you, Skip."

He winked at me and walked away. Why did he always seem so mature compared to Cody? Maybe it was just the fact that he wasn't interested in the things that most boys his age were interested in. He didn't care about girlfriends or popularity or getting his license. He only really cared about Jesus.

Everything was so strange that June that nothing really surprised me. My dad and Kristi carried on like they were a couple, even though they weren't a couple. The three of us went to the flea market together, and went out to dinner together. She came over a couple times a week, but went home instead of spending the night. Sometimes he went to her place, and he came home happy.

I was able to put Cody out of my mind like he didn't actually exist. It was the only way to go on without hating him. He didn't text me or call me or send me an email, or even a postcard. If I thought about it too much, it made me feel worthless. Of course, I couldn't share my feelings with anyone. I secretly wondered how I could act like everything was OK when he came back. Everything was not OK and I could see that it was the beginning of the end. I began leaving my phone in my bedroom, under my pillow, just so I wouldn't be checking it constantly. I didn't need that compulsion. I tried to keep myself busy reading books and taking walks and thinking about where I could get a job when I turned sixteen.

I helped my dad at his office. I dusted and cleaned and organized his books. I liked being in his office at the college, because not only did I feel closer to him, but I appreciated everything he had accomplished in such a short amount of time. He was teaching a summer course, and I sat in on it. He was a brilliant teacher.

One day, when I returned from the college, there was a single text message from Cody on my phone.

I miss you.

How could I respond to that? He missed me? Two and a half weeks had gone by, and he had sent me one picture, with no explanation. Now he missed me? I wanted to completely ignore it and be heartless, but that wasn't me. I wanted him to know how much I had been hurting, but I wouldn't be that girl.

I miss you too.

That was all I could manage. I put the phone aside, not wanting to obsess over a response. It was a good thing, too, because he never responded.

I hated the fact that I wanted to validate myself by having the attention of a boy. Why are girls hard-wired to do that? Every day I loathed myself a little bit more because every day I felt a little bit crappier when I thought about how little he must have cared for me. Not only did it seem like he wasn't interested, but I was beating myself up over it, too.

When his return date finally arrived, my emotions were a mixture of excitement and pain and nausea. I didn't know what to do with myself. I wanted to tell him that I hated him for ignoring me, for ruining my summer, for making me feel worthless, but at the same time I didn't want him to know he had the power to do all of that to me. I *wanted* to be genuinely happy to see him, like the last four weeks were water under the bridge, but I had a dam building up inside of me and I was afraid it was going to break.

I thought about going to the college with my dad that day so that when Cody came around or called to ask about coming around, I would be busy. I didn't want him to think I was sitting around thinking about him for that month. But my want to see him, even though I was angry with him, outweighed the want to seem like I was above wanting to see him. I knew that he was coming in on a red-eye and that he would be home by the time I woke up, but I waited. I extended my wait and I allowed myself to wallow in self-pity a little bit longer while I waited for any sign that he was missing me. I hadn't picked up my mother's journals in a while. In fact, I put them away so I wouldn't constantly be tempted to look at them, but I decided to dig them out and read for a while.

December 15, 1993

Teddy's semester is over and we went to Rocky Ridge for the weekend to help Edie get ready for Christmas. Teddy likes to help Edie bake and they are so cute together. My boss wasn't too keen on giving me a weekend off so close to Christmas, but I begged because I didn't want to miss the trip. I baked with them for a little while, but when I got tired it was nice to just lie on the couch and fall asleep while football was playing in the background. It is such a safe space. Sometimes I never want to go back to the city. Teddy and I decorated the Christmas tree on Saturday night. He knows exactly how lucky he is to have that life and I love him for that. On Sunday morning we went to church and afterwards we went out for pancakes. Everyone knows Edie and Carl. Everyone is so friendly. On Sunday afternoon we went bowling with some of Teddy's friends from school and he's so proud to be with me. Even now that he knows that I'm not normal, he still wants to be with me and he's still proud to be with me. Every girl should get to have a guy like Teddy Bryant, who never finds your faults, who never loves you any less for any reason. Every girl should be as lucky as me. But most guys aren't like Teddy. That might be the entire problem with the whole world.

My mother knew that a perfect man was rare. Teddy wasn't even perfect, he just had an unconditional love for her and that was unusual. She was lucky enough to have Teddy and she still threw her life away. How were the rest of us supposed to get by with sub-par boys who didn't really love us? She couldn't even make it and she had that edge. It made me want to cry.

I dozed off picturing that weekend in my head, wishing I could watch it like an old movie. I was jarred awake by the knocking on our back door. I jumped out of bed, not thinking that it would be Cody.

He had changed. He seemed taller, more muscular, and his face had matured even more. His baby cheeks were gone, replaced now by cheekbones that hadn't been there before. He looked tired, and not very happy. He had no spark in his eyes for me. I wondered if we were over, but I tried to hide my concern.

If he was making any attempt to be normal, he was failing miserably. Instead of sitting in the kitchen, or on the couch, he awkwardly went around me and went straight to my bedroom and began to play with the necklaces that lay on my dresser. He always fiddled with things when he was nervous, or when he wanted to say something. I sat on the edge of my bed wondering if the break-up conversation was coming.

"We need to talk," he said.

I wanted to blurt it out. I wanted to tell him that I knew something happened in Alaska that was making him reconsider our relationship. I *knew* it. That had to be why he had ignored me the entire time.

He sat on the bed beside me. "I met this girl," he said, pushing his glasses up on his nose.

"Uh-huh." I could feel it coming.

"At a party. She's Danny's friend."

I shifted uncomfortably, already trying to plan what I would say or do if he was dumping me. I decided I would be stoic and act like I didn't really care.

"Well, I guess it doesn't matter how it got there, but something almost happened."

I wanted him to get it over with.

"We kissed."

I would have rather had the details than had to guess how they got to that point.

"She unzipped my pants and, well, I guess I was drunk."

"Then what happened?" I tried to remain calm. He wasn't my *real* boyfriend. We were just friends, barely hanging on to that relationship by a thread. We didn't *love* each other. We weren't serious.

"Nothing. She touched me and I couldn't feel anything." He seemed worried. "Something was wrong with me. Nothing happened because nothing could happen. I think it's because of the way I feel about you."

"Oh."

"I didn't want to. I was being dumb and drunk."

"Why even tell me, then, if nothing happened?" I was annoyed. "You didn't have to tell me anything."

"I'm telling you because I'm paranoid now."
"Why?"
"Because. Am I going to be like this for the rest of my life?"
"Like what?"
"Programmed to one girl."

I laughed, somewhat maniacally, because I wanted to punch him in the face, but I knew I couldn't react like that. "*That* is your concern right now?" I thought perhaps he should be concerned about my feelings.

"Yes," he said, simply.

I shook my head. "Well, what the hell do you want me to do about it?"

"I don't know."

I turned away from him and tried not to cry. I looked at the green leaves on the tree outside my window and wondered why it felt like everything good always seemed more suffocating than the bad thing that was happening in that moment.

He got up and looked at the necklaces again and touched the poem that was taped to my mirror. "Are you mad at me?"

"No."

"Then look at me."

"I can't."

"You're angry."

"I'm not angry," I said, trying to find my composure, and turning back to face him.

"I'll have to admit, I'd be angry if you had kissed someone. We should've went on a break before I left."

"A break from what?" I asked. "We're not official. Remember? We're just…whatever."

"Yes, but I think for intimacy we should be monogamous."

"We've not been intimate."

"We've been kind of intimate."

"We've kissed." I wanted him to leave so I could cry, but he didn't.

He ignored me, and went on with his own conversation. "I never really thought I wanted more than what we have. But you should expect more out of me. You deserve more."

Inside, I was in turmoil, but I felt like I was holding it together on the outside. I would never understand why he did what he did and why we couldn't just be or not be together in a simple way. All I knew was how much it hurt. I couldn't think of anything to do, of any way to make it better. So I kissed him. He stumbled back against my dresser, but didn't pull away. I had missed him too long, ached for him too long. In that second, his confession didn't matter.

"Where's your dad?" he whispered into my ear.

"He's at the college."

I pulled him to my bed and he climbed on top of me. I had to keep my eyes open to take in his changing face. His hair was longer and I ran my hand through it. I took his glasses off and put them on my nightstand. I tried to wrap my hand around his bicep. He was growing up and I had stayed the same. He was handsome and complicated and smart and I had to be very careful not to let myself fall for him now.

I wanted to distract myself from what I was feeling for him. I thought about the other girl. Now it was plural. The girl he kissed on New Year's Eve and the girl he kissed in Alaska. I had to make sure I had the upper hand. As I thought about it, my inner sense of self-respect told me to stop squashing it. But I thought about it anyway. I have to do *something*. I have to make him see me that way. I'd never felt competitive before, but when it came to Cody's attention shifting to another girl, the desire to win him stirred together with some jealousy and made me want to prove myself. I didn't want him to see me as a math partner and a watcher of cop shows. I wanted to be a sexual being, too.

"Stand up," I whispered.

"Now?" he asked.

I nodded.

He climbed off of me reluctantly and stood at the foot of my bed. I followed him. I got in front of him on my knees. The hardwood floor made it unpleasant.

"What are you doing?" Cody asked.

I unbuttoned his shorts, then unzipped them. He was wearing St. Patrick's Day underwear with four leaf clovers on them, and I thought it was ironic that he'd be wearing those on his lucky day.

"Caroline?"

"Do you want more?"

"What do you mean?"

"Let me give you more."

"Like what?"

"How far would you take it with me, Cody?"

"With you? I would do everything with you."

"I don't want to give you everything. But I want to give you something."

He pulled his pants down around his thighs and stared at me. There was something new in his eyes. It almost seemed like fear.

I told myself I was going to do it, to show him that I was game for more than he expected. I felt self-destructive, realizing I was degrading myself in an effort to keep a boy's attention. Knowing what I was doing didn't stop me from doing what I was doing, though. I thought about everything I'd ever read in *Cosmo* about blow jobs, and hoped I was doing it right.

"Oh my God," he said, and as soon as he said it, I heard the back door open.

He jumped, scraping it across my teeth, and pulled up his zipper. I pretended to be looking for something under my bed.

"Hi, Mr. Bryant," he said, cheerfully.

"Hey, Cody. How was Alaska?"

"I'm glad to be home," he said.

"What are you doing, Bear?"

"Have you seen my earbuds, Dad?" I asked, nonchalantly, looking up from under my bed.

"No, I haven't."

"Well, I have to go," Cody said, unexpectedly.

"OK. See you later," my dad said.

"Yeah, see you," I said.

My dad looked at me, maybe suspiciously, or maybe I was being paranoid, then walked away.

Two minutes later, Cody was tapping on my window. I tried to open it quietly. "I need my glasses," he said.

"Oh." I retrieved them from the nightstand. "Did you like it?" I just couldn't help but ask.

"I have to get home for dinner," he said, matter-of-factly.

When he left, I sat in the bathroom and cried for an hour, grieving the loss of the few ounces of self-respect that I used to have. When I came out, my dad poured me a shot of Pepto Bismol because he thought I had a stomach ache. I wondered where all the good guys like my dad were, because he was the only one I'd ever met.

My reunion with Cody was half-assed and I hated myself for doing what I did instead of yelling at him and telling him to get out, or demanding an apology. I stewed over the girl in Alaska. Was she pretty? Was she prettier than me? Was she smarter or funnier than me? Did she watch *Broken Blue*? I hated Alaska with every ounce of hate I had. I was pouring it out into my journal when he texted me.

Are you up?

I need some time to think.

About what? Aren't we good?

I'm sorry, but I don't think we are.

Look. I'm really sorry about it. I didn't like her. If I had to pick someone to do anything with, it would always be you, no matter what. I don't want anybody else.

It's not even that. You ignored me the whole time you were gone. Like I didn't even exist.

You could have called.

And looked like a nagging bitch? No thanks.

I'm sorry.

I don't want an apology. I just need some time. I'm going to my Gram's house for the Fourth. We'll talk when I come back.

Why can't we talk now?

I just want to say a bunch of mean things to you and that just makes me look pathetic. I want to keep my shit together and talk when I'm ready.

Lose your shit on me. I think I deserve it.

Whatever you did in Alaska doesn't deserve that much of my attention. You get it? She's not worth it.

I never wanted to lose my best friend over this.

You haven't. Just give me some space.

I'm sorry.

Why did you even tell me?

Because you're my best friend. I don't know how to separate it. I want to tell you everything.

I guess you shouldn't have to separate it.

I didn't talk to him again. The next morning I packed up my stuff and we went to Gram's house. I felt the same way about Rocky Ridge that my mother had felt. It was quiet and peaceful and beautiful, and on the first day, I wandered around in the park by myself, getting a little bit lost. I found a nice rock to sit on and I took out my journal and began to write down the truth about Cody, the truth about how I felt when I was around him, and all the truth about all of the things my body wanted to do with him and feel with him. I admitted to my journal that it didn't matter where Cody and I ended up in a year or so, but I wanted him to be every one of my firsts.

What are you doing?

I looked at my phone. Was he trying to make up for lost time? I didn't want to talk to him yet. I turned my phone the whole way off and continued writing. I spent time admitting to the journal that he had hurt me and finally, after hours of writing, I concluded that it was OK to let people hurt you sometimes because it's the only way you ever grow. Pain is a human emotion.

Gram was cubing potatoes for the potato salad she would make in the morning. She had a special way of pre-preparing things so that it all seemed effortless when she finally made her dishes. I couldn't imagine a life of standing over a sink cutting up food, but Gram seemed to love it. Gramp had put a birdbath in the backyard right outside the kitchen window and she kept an eye on it while she worked.

"What has you down, sweetie?"

"Nothing," I lied.

"A boy," she said, knowingly.

"Maybe."

"Tell me about him."

I wanted to gush about him, but I would have to end it on that sour note, so I kept quiet.

"Is he handsome?"

"Yes," I admitted. "I think so."

"How did you meet?"

"School. Math. We were doing a project together."

"He's a good student?"

"Very. He's smart and popular and athletic and everything I guess I should want in a boy."

"So, what's the problem?"

"He went on a trip and ignored me the entire month he was gone."

"Oh. I see."

"It hurt."

"I imagine it did." She looked at the birds, then went back to her cutting. "I suppose now you're ignoring him for payback."

"No. I'm ignoring him because I don't want him to know how much he hurt me."

"If he doesn't know he hurt you, he might do it again, accidentally."

"I just don't want him to have that power over me."

"It's not power. When you like someone, that's just how it is. Some part of you just has to surrender to your emotions."

"I don't want to lose control of my emotions."

She cut up her potatoes for a while, not disagreeing with me.

"I just don't understand boys," I finally vented. "They act like they like you, then they act like they don't. Everything is in such a gray area. Why can't people just say what they really feel? Why do boys have to be so mysterious and closed off and unreal?"

"You have the upper hand over most girls, sweetie."

"I do?"

"Your dad raised you. You probably understand men better than most girls do."

"My dad isn't like the rest of them. He's a nice, decent guy. Guys my age aren't like him."

"Guys are more alike than you think they are. Your dad went through that teenaged stage, too. He still can't figure out what to do with his women. We both know that, don't we?" She chuckled.

"He's just afraid to really love somebody. He's afraid of losing someone again."

She turned and looked at me. "Sounds familiar, doesn't it?"

I averted my eyes to the placemat on the table.

"I'm not telling you to fall madly in love. But let yourself feel something. You can't live in a bubble because of what happened to your mother."

"Oh, Gram." I started to cry. "It's not that I don't want to be hurt again. I also don't want to turn into her."

Gram came to me and put her arms around me. "You aren't her, Caroline. You won't turn into her."

"It's why I hang on to the control so much. I don't want to go crazy and sometimes Cody makes me feel like I am crazy. When I can't explain what I feel for him, it makes me crazy."

The nice thing about Gram was that sometimes she could just hold me and she didn't have to say anything.

I could hear the car pulling in as Gramp and my dad came back from wherever they had been. The old rotary phone on the kitchen wall began to ring and my dad came around the corner like a kid and answered it. He started a conversation with whichever of Gram's friends was on the other line, and ended the conversation telling them Gram couldn't come to the phone.

"What's the matter, Bear?" my dad asked upon hanging up. I think Gramp knew better than to ask. He quietly went to the

The Pastel Effect

living room. He never had to deal with girl-drama the way my dad had.

"Boy trouble," Gram said, sympathetically.

"What did he do?" He asked as if he could do something about it.

"Nothing," I said. "It's nothing, Dad."

"I'll talk to him if he did something."

"No. It's OK. I'll get over it. We're mostly just friends anyway. Maybe I expect too much from him."

He knelt down in front of me. "Are you sure?"

"Yes."

He smiled, then he kissed my cheek. I knew that no matter what happened with Cody, I had one of the best dads in the world, and suddenly Gram and Gramp were the best, too, because they made him.

I went to bed that night thanking God that I had the family I did. It didn't matter what I had lost, I knew that I was lucky for what I still had.

The Fourth of July was a big deal in Rocky Ridge. First there was a parade, followed by the crowning of "Miss Rocky Ridge," an outdated, but much celebrated tradition. Everyone decorated patriotically, just as much as they did for Christmas. During the middle of the day, you could have your own picnic or join the community picnic in the town square. We always had our own picnic. At night, there were massive fireworks. I always liked the Fourth of July because it felt like a time of possibilities. I liked feeling hopeful.

I could smell Gram cooking pancakes when I woke up, so I started down the steps and towards the kitchen. I could hear her talking and thought it was early for Teddy to be up. In fact, it was early for her to be cooking.

"We started dating right after Easter."

Every muscle in my body tightened.

"To be honest, I liked her for a while, though."

"You came quite a way to see her," Gram said, with her trademark chuckle.

"Well, I really missed her."

I ran back up the steps and put on the cutest outfit I had packed, then hurried into the bathroom to brush my teeth and put on some makeup. Sometimes, I didn't mind Cody seeing me at my worst, but I didn't want him to realize why he had ignored me for a month. I didn't want to look like a slob who had just rolled out of bed. I guess what I really wanted was for him to regret it.

I went down the steps again, quickly practicing how I would act surprised to see him.

Our eyes locked as soon as I went into the kitchen. His mouth was full of pancakes and he couldn't even say hello. He chewed, purposefully and slowly, and finally swallowed. "Hi," he said.

"Hi."

Gram was sitting beside him at the same kitchen table where I had sat crying over him the day before.

"You're, uh…you look nice," he said.

"Thanks," I said, remembering Skip's advice on taking compliments. "What are you doing here?"

He half-smiled, like he always did, barely ever committing to a full smile. "I missed you," he said.

"How did you get the address?"

"I asked Skip if he knew where your grandparents lived. He asked Lilly for me. I drove into town and they were making floats for a parade, so I asked a couple people until someone told me where they lived."

That seemed like a lot of trouble to go through.

He ate another mouthful of pancakes and Gram refilled his orange juice, then poured one for me.

"It probably could have been a lot easier, had your phone been on."

I had never turned it back on after I ignored him.

He continued eating as if I weren't even there. "These pancakes are delicious," he said with more enthusiasm than he said most things.

Gram looked at me, as if to say, *you need to fix this*, and she excused herself. I sat across from him and watched him eat. He didn't look at me. I stared at him.

"Why are you here?" I finally asked.

"I told you. I wanted to talk to you. I missed you. Your phone was off."

"I'm not trying to be contrary here, but do you think you've had a taste of what I've been feeling for the past four weeks?"

"Is that why you did it?"

"No. I did it because I just wanted to be alone. Shut off. Unplugged."

He seemed to consider it for a moment, then went on eating. "I would've answered if you would've called."

"You would have felt *obligated* to answer."

"No. I would have enjoyed getting a call from you. I mean, let's be fair. You ignored me, too."

How dare he call me out on what was fair? "You might've been too busy for me. That would just suck. We've been through this conversation. It's over. We don't have to talk about it any more."

The pancakes were finally gone and I had his full attention.

"Can we go somewhere and talk?" he asked.

"We can take a walk," I suggested.

I took his plate and rinsed it while he finished the orange juice.

"We're going for a walk," I called out to anyone who might be listening, and we went out the back door.

We began the two block walk to the park in silence. He seemed to be searching for words and I would give him time to let them come out. Eventually, Cody told me all about the trip as we made our way into the park and walked down the shady trails towards the creek. We stood on a flat rock and watched a school of tiny fish swim past. We watched the sun creep through the leaves and make patterns on the ground. We inspected the mossy hand-built rock walls. Some of the walls took forty years to build. I tried to imagine building one wall for forty years and it seemed boring. I stopped to look into a hole in a tree — a tree that had a hundred names carved into it over the years. Once my dad found the tree that he carved T&T into. He did it the summer she was pregnant with me. I never was able to find that tree again. We went further into the woods, into more seclusion, and we sat on the edge of a small footbridge for a while.

"God, you're pretty," he finally said.

I smiled. "Do you mean it?"

"Yes, I mean it."

"Was she pretty?"

"I don't even remember what she looked like. I don't think she was the kind of girl to have good conversations with or spend long periods of time with. She wasn't funny or interesting or…you."

He put his hand on my cheek and I looked away from him. I was afraid that I would feel something that I couldn't take back. I was supposed to let myself feel, but the fear of it was like the fear of falling off of a building. I was afraid that once I went over the edge, I wouldn't be able to stop until I hit the bottom.

"You're pretty," he said thoughtfully. "And I always thought you were. I was nervous those first days in class sitting beside you. I was afraid I'd never be somebody you would want. But now that I know you, it doesn't even matter how you look because I just like you so much. I missed you so much every day…I missed you so much that it hurt. I wanted to talk to you, but I only would have been able to talk about how much I wanted to come back to you. I know we're not really in love or anything like that, but more like — you're the only person who understands me — who cares about understanding me. And I find you intensely fascinating because you think about things in such a different way and every time I talk to you, it's something new and I love that."

I wanted to open myself up to that, to let it all in, and I pretended to for his sake. He had just poured his heart out to me, but something stopped me from absorbing it. I wanted to, but I couldn't. Maybe, when it came to boys, the truth didn't get much better than that. He kissed me after we were quiet for a while. His lips still tasted like maple syrup.

We walked until we came to a nearly grown over path and that path led to a small clearing by the creek. I sat down and he kissed me again. I felt the tall, soft grass under me as he gently pushed me down into it. He pulled his shirt over his head and put it under my head, like a pillow, and the sun warmed his back while he kissed me. I ran my hands over him, trying to memorize every muscle so I could write about it later. That day, his kisses were gentle and patient and I liked that. He always asked me first if he could do the next thing, if he could take it a step farther, and I wanted to please him, so I agreed. That's why I let him take off all of my clothes and see my body for the first time, even in the unforgiving sunlight.

Every time his skin touched mine, it was like a magical electricity running through me. I couldn't get enough of it. He lightly kissed me everywhere, from my lips down to my belly button. I loved the way it felt. I loved him, but I fought it.

I looked up at the leaves, at the sun fighting through them, at a spider's web catching the light between two trees. Would this be the most perfect moment of my life? I already knew that I would remember it forever, and I thought about that for a while. Thirty years later, when we were both in our own lives, maybe we would look back at that moment and remember it fondly, the way the sun felt, the way the grass smelled, the way the creek sounded, and it would be bittersweet. Lovely that it had happened, and sad because nothing like that could ever last.

He looked at me, kind of hopelessly, and that was something I liked about him — that I never quite knew what he was thinking. The next moment was always a bit of a surprise with Cody.

"Will you?" he asked, quietly.

"Will I?" My mind was deep into the thoughts of what it all meant.

"Finish what we started the other day," he half-whispered.

That summed it up quite perfectly. I was thinking about the moment, and he was thinking about sex. I would never stop wanting him to like me, though. So I said that I would. I was excited about it, but he was nervous. He fumbled with the button on his pants. I thought maybe I should do it for him, but part of me liked that he was struggling and nervous while I was calm and collected. I knew that he didn't deserve anything from me, but I was eager to please him.

He closed his eyes, tightly, as if looking at me was too embarrassing. He seemed uncomfortable and I almost thought it hurt by the look on his face. My first instinct was to ask. I remembered what *Cosmo* said, though. The number one sexual turn on for a man is a confident woman. I just acted like I knew what I was doing. Maybe he would believe it.

He was conscientious. He kept asking me if I was OK, if I wanted to stop, if I was getting tired. He was ruining it for himself. I had to stop him. I quit for a moment, looked up at him, and told him how much I really liked it, and that seemed to be the finishing touch he needed.

When it was over, he finally opened his eyes and looked at me with a fear I'd never seen in him before. I tried to ease his worry with an understanding smile.

He pulled up his pants. "I'm sorry."

"Why?"

"It seems so — like, wrong."

"I liked it, I told you."

"Did you, really?"

"Of course."

I wasn't lying. I did like the power of it. I had never been in control of anything the way I was at that moment.

We went back into town just in time to meet up with Gram and my dad to watch the parade. Gramp always marched with the VFW guys and Teddy and I fought over the Tootsie Rolls that they threw out from the fire truck. It was funny how Cody fit into our family so perfectly. He looked a lot more relaxed, and when nobody was looking, his hand would find its way to me. We held hands under the table at the picnic until my dad caught a glimpse of it. After the fireworks, Teddy wanted to know what Cody had told his family and he told them he said he went to a friend's house.

"It's getting late, Cody. It's a long drive."

He looked at me, pleadingly. "I wanted to stay for the fireworks."

"Why don't we give your parents a call? Maybe they'll let you stay. I'm worried about you driving."

"Stay?"

"Stay the night. We have a pretty comfy couch. Or you can stay in Jen's room and Bear can stay with me. I just worry about you — you look tired."

"My parents…"

"His parents don't know about me," I said, casually, as if it weren't a big deal, even though it was a big deal to me.

Teddy looked confused, but accepted it. "OK. I can call them anyway. I don't have to tell them about — whatever. I would just feel better if I talked to your parents."

Cody reluctantly pulled his phone out of his pocket and called his mother. He tried to explain where he was and why without explaining our relationship, and finally he gave the phone to my dad, who, a master of words, was able to convince Mrs. Kirby to let him stay. He ended the conversation with a bunch of niceties, a good laugh, and a pat on the back that he had played the dad game quite well that day.

He quickly gave the phone back to Cody and announced that he was going to "meet friends." He kissed Gram on the cheek, gave me an innocent-looking smile, and left.

Cody and I walked to the town square with our blanket. We spread it out and waited patiently, while more blankets went down around us.

"I'm sorry," he said again. "About earlier."

"It would be so much nicer if you sounded like you enjoyed it a little bit."

"I did enjoy it a lot."

"It's OK. It was a practice run. It wasn't supposed to be great."

"Practice run? Meaning, you want to try it again?"

"Sure, someday. Don't you?"

"Uh, yeah. Someday."

We stared at the blank sky, waiting for something to happen.

"You know, my dad was going to meet his fuck buddy."

"What? No."

"He hooks up with this girl from high school. Gram doesn't really like her, though."

"Why?"

"I don't know. I guess because, generally, maybe women don't like their son's girlfriends. Right?"

He looked at me. "Why do you ask me?"

"Why else would you not tell your mother?"

"I told you, she'd meddle."

"Meddle?"

"Pry. Butt-in. Investigate."

"I know what meddle means. I just don't know why she'd meddle. If you told her the truth, she wouldn't have to meddle."

"Look. I promise you. I'll tell my mom sometime between now and our wedding day. OK?"

He was too funny and too sweet and I didn't want to argue with him. "OK."

13

And Tomorrow, I'm Sorry

IT WAS bittersweet watching Cody drive away from Rocky Ridge the next morning. Gram filled him up on french toast and turkey sausage and he was happy enough when he left.

I waited until dark to text him.

Did you make it home OK?

No answer. No answer by midnight. No answer by morning. I texted first. I got no answer. My fear of looking pathetic stopped me from texting him again. I was so afraid of looking clingy and I still didn't want to admit that I liked him more. I had a sick feeling for the rest of the time we stayed at Gram's. I wished I could be casual like my father was. Maybe because he was a man, he could be so close to someone then be so far away from them and not even think about them. I wanted that. I wanted to be able to go home and run into Cody somewhere and say, "Oh, do I know you? Oh, yes, I think I did give you a blow job once, that's right. You are *that* guy."

Of course, it wasn't like that for me, a female, who carries every single thing that ever happened around in her heart forever. How do you let people, or things, stop hurting you? How do you do it? I wanted to know. I got emotional and felt like I was going to cry at every little thing. I rocked in the hammock reading and napping and reading some more. Like we always did, my father and I went to visit her grave before we went home. I chose yellow roses to put there. He had an excellent cry and I cried with him, probably over something else, though. We sat on the grass with her and he traced her name with his finger.

"Do you feel empty?" I finally asked him.

"What do you mean, Bear?"

"Do you feel empty without her? Do you still feel empty when you try to fill yourself up with something that is the wrong thing? Is that why you're so sad?"

He wiped his eyes and smiled. "A piece of advice about guys? Ask one question at a time, OK? Our brains can't handle all of that."

"Do you feel empty without her?"

"It's not empty. It's more just like crap. I feel like crap without her."

My dad, who knew so many words, liked to say things like *crap*.

"Do you feel empty after you sleep with women you don't love?"

He shrugged. "That, too, is more like crap. A different kind of crap, though."

"Do you keep doing the same thing over again expecting different results?"

"No. I like the pre-crap feeling. Guys are guys. Always remember that, too." His hand finally dropped from the stone and he shielded his eyes from the sun. "Why the questions?"

"I haven't heard from Cody since he left here and I feel empty and I hate letting anyone have that power over me."

My dad just smiled his sympathetic, knowing smile. Sometimes there was nothing to say.

"I wish I didn't care."

"Sometimes things just hurt. There's no way out of it." He glanced at the stone, the only permanent thing left of my mother. "I wish I could tell you it's easier than that, but it isn't."

"I know, Dad."

"You'll always have me. I'll always answer the phone. You know that."

I smiled. "I know. I'm not lonely. I'm just confused."

"Maybe Cody has never really liked a girl before. Maybe he fights his feelings just like you do."

I contemplated that and decided that my father was probably right.

"I just want to stop thinking about him."

"I know."

I decided to fight fire with fire. In the morning, I went to the pool and secured a spot where I could watch Skip climb up and down the lifeguard ladder in his beautiful swimsuit. I hid behind a book and pretended to read. He glanced left to right, then right to left, watching the screaming brats in the water. On the hour, he blew the whistle and everyone got out of the pool. I watched him climb down and admired the birthmark as he walked the perimeter.

"Hey."

I turned my head slowly away from Skip, realizing that Cody was settling into the chair beside me. He wore plain blue swimming trunks and put a plain blue bath towel down on the chair. That would be like Cody, to bring a plain blue bath towel to a swimming pool. Perhaps his dad was too cheap to splurge on a full-size beach towel, or perhaps Cody was too unconcerned to look for one.

"Hey," I replied, unenthusiastically.

"What's wrong?" he asked.

I couldn't believe he had the nerve to ask. "Your friends are over there," I said, eyeballing the corner where the Circlers hung out.

"It's just the girls."

"So?"

"What is your problem?"

"Here I am. You have somehow turned me into the girl who texts first and last and everything in between. I have somehow turned you into the guy who doesn't answer texts. You drive all the way to my Gram's to apologize for it and then you do it again, which makes me wonder if you didn't just drive all the way to my Gram's for a blow job?"

He turned his head to the side quickly to see if anyone had heard me.

"Of course, why do that when you have that whole squad of whores in your Circle who have probably guzzled more cum than I'll ever dare to."

He looked strangely amused, but hurt, too.

"I don't want any of them, nor do they want me."

I got up and rolled up my beach towel with all of my things inside of it, slid on my sandals, and headed towards the gate.

"Hey," he said, grabbing his single lame towel and following me. "Hey. Wait up."

He got in front of me when we were in the parking lot and tried to stop me. I dodged him and went around.

"Why are you doing this?" he asked.

"I don't want to play this game. You're mean, we make up, and you're mean again. I don't want it."

"Don't you think it's a bit more complicated than that?"

"How?" I asked, not really caring to hear the answer. My mind was already planning my next move, which would be to go home, get dressed, and spend the rest of the day feeling the ice cold air conditioning of my father's office on my sun-toasted skin. It would be comforting to feel the cold from outside matching the cold within me.

"Look," he said, nervously. "I've never been in love before."

I made a face. "What?"

"You heard me."

"That's not love. That's…" I moaned in disgust, trying to find words. "That's not even like."

"How do you get to say what I feel, Caroline?"

"Because even you, Cody, even stupid you could do a better job at love than that."

"This is the best I've got. I don't know what I'm doing."

"So, you went home so lovestruck that you couldn't text a one-word answer?"

"I went home so confused that I had no idea what to say or do."

"Oh, is that it? I confuse you?"

"Not you. Not you on purpose. The way you make me feel. I don't understand these feelings."

I stepped up to him and we were practically nose to nose. "Maybe you are so deluded by those morons that you call friends that you can't even see what is right in front of you. Do they not allow you to have feelings for anyone? Are you feeling too guilty because you stepped outside of your incestuous little Circle?" I began to tremble, and I didn't want him to see me cry, but everything was pouring out like a waterfall. "You know what, Cody Kirby? I liked you. I really did, but I'm not so sure anymore because I'm tired of putting it all out on the line for someone who can't climb out of the tiny box they live in and finally fucking feel something!"

"*Me*? It's *me* who can't feel? No, no, no, Caroline. It's *you* who can't feel. It's you who can't text twice in a row when I fuck up. It's you who has to act cool and unbothered and unfeeling. You are dying inside. You're mean and cold and at least I admit that I'm confused."

"Fuck up?" I laughed maniacally. "Well, isn't that grand? Because I'm pretty sure in the world I come from, that's cheating. That's kissing someone else, which spells out cheating pretty clearly to me! Do you want to know how I really feel about it?"

"Sure, sure, tell me," he said as if he were patronizing me, and that was something I truly hated.

I don't know where it came from, but it must have come from deep within me. I slapped him. I wondered if it looked like something from an old-time movie. His glasses flew off and he put his hand on his cheek, maybe stunned. "I kind of hate you," I said calmly. "There. I feel something now." I had never hit anyone in my entire life. At that moment, I realized the Circlers were staring at us. I wondered how much they had heard.

Libby, to my disgust, came to Cody's aid and picked up his glasses. "Are you OK?" she asked.

I rolled my eyes.

"I'm fine," he said, quietly. "I deserved it."

She busied herself with examining the handprint I had left on his face and as she did it, I realized something quite clearly. Cody had someone to be at his side. No matter how fake and phony she might be, he had someone, and I did not. I looked away from them and kept walking towards my house.

I took a cold shower. I always liked the way it felt to put on a warm cotton shirt after being hot, then being cold. Something about it felt really clean and new and I almost couldn't even feel bad. My mother's Aerosmith shirt almost felt like her arms around me. I wished I could remember her voice so I could imagine her telling me that boys suck, that I don't need them, that I should be stronger. I took out her journal, the closest thing I had to her voice.

December 31, 1993

I hate endings. The end of a year. It's hard to believe I only met him a few months ago. He changed my life so much. I'm safer now. I go to doctor's appointments — he makes sure of it. He's the voice inside my head. He's the light when I feel dark. I don't know if it's a good idea to let one person be so important in my life. I know that people leave, no matter what they say. The medicine just keeps me slow and steady right now. It's finally starting to get back to normal. I lack feeling. I don't know how to feel the right amount. How do you teach yourself how to feel? It's a fine mystery, I guess.

I took a nap for a little while, attempting to put Cody completely out of my mind. I was angry. I was really angry. But maybe he was right. Maybe I was too stubborn. Maybe if I wanted attention, I would just have to ask for it. But asking for something you wanted took away some of the importance of getting it. I wanted to be pleasantly surprised by Cody, not begging for him. But, it was idealistic thinking that someone could just fall so in love with me that they could read my mind. Maybe it wasn't the surprises that I wanted after all. Maybe I just wanted what I wanted.

I walked to the college, debating on whether to tell my dad that I had slapped Cody. Of course, if he wanted to know why, I'm not sure what I would say. I couldn't tell my dad about any of the things we fought about. Maybe I would just tell my dad that we finally broke up. Maybe if I had the courage to say it out loud, it would finally be real and I could just tell Cody that I didn't want it to be complicated. I enjoyed him, and I was attracted to him, but it was time to let it be what it was, which was just friendship. I would call him and he would call me, but my life would no longer depend on it. We wouldn't sit together at lunch next year. We wouldn't go to Circle parties together. We wouldn't do much of anything except text each other when we had something too good to hold in that nobody else would understand. And maybe we could watch *Broken Blue* together. *Maybe.*

I would spend some time with my dad and let it sink in and then I would call Cody.

I liked to watch my dad work, deep in thought at his old wooden desk. I sat in the windowsill staring at the words in the book, but not reading them. I looked out the window into the nothingness going on outside.

"Bear? What's wrong?"

"Nothing, why?"

"You haven't turned the page in ages."

"I think I'm breaking up with Cody."

"OK. Why?"

"I don't want to be with him. He doesn't make me feel as good about myself as I think he should."

"It's up to you. But you shouldn't rely on him to make you feel good about yourself. You need to figure out how to do that on your own."

"I know. But then maybe I should do it all on my own. Not be chained down by him."

Teddy smiled. "Chained down?"

"I don't like looking at my phone every two minutes to see if he texted yet. I don't like thinking about him all the time."

"And if you break up, that goes away?"

"I think so."

"Whatever makes you feel better, Bear."

"How do *you* feel about him?" I put the book down and sat in the consulting chair across from him.

"I like him. You know that. I think he's a good kid. You get along so well. Sometimes when I hear you talking, it just makes me feel good to know that you have someone to talk to."

"That was when we were just friends. We don't talk anymore."

"All relationships take work. Even friendships."

I contemplated it. "You and Tressa?"

He shrugged and leaned back. "Some things were easy. Some things were not. You appreciate things more when you work for them. It was always easy to love her when she danced around in that t-shirt."

"What do you think she would tell me to do about Cody?"

"I think she would tell you to give him a chance. Look who she took a chance on."

I looked around the tiny office, thinking of all the things my dad had accomplished to get there. "I think you took the chance on her, not the other way around."

"Look, Bear. You don't have to marry him. You don't have to love him. You can call a relationship whatever you want to call it — those are just words. You have an opportunity to have a good friend, a companion, and since you've met him I hear you laugh more than I ever have before and I think that's a good thing. All I'm saying is not to write him out of your life completely. Maybe you can reorganize where you put him, but don't throw the whole thing away." He looked at the ticking clock on the wall. "Let's say we get out of here and grab some dinner?"

"OK."

We went to the diner with the jukebox and instead of ordering dinner, we had milkshakes. It's funny how when you are trying not to think about someone, everything reminds you of them. Seeing the strawberry milkshake on the menu. A Temptations song making its way through the jukebox. A police officer picking up his dinner. I had to wonder if these things happened on purpose or if they just seem more obvious when somebody is on your mind. But at the end of it, I had realized that I would miss Cody far too much to just get rid of him like that. He wasn't a great boyfriend, but I would miss him nonetheless.

He was sitting on the step of our front porch when we came home. My dad smiled knowingly and went in through the back door. I went to the front and sat beside him. I knew I didn't have to, but I wanted to be the first to apologize. "I'm sorry I hit you."

"I deserved it."

"No. It was wrong."

He looked away from me, at nothing in particular.

"How long have you been sitting here?"

He looked at the ugly calculator watch. "Three hours."

I smirked, amused at his dedication. "Why?"

"Because I wanted to be here when you came home." He looked at me. Our eyes met. He had been crying. His eyes were bloodshot, but not how they were when his contacts bothered him. I could see where the tears had stained his cheeks. "Because I want you to know that I love you."

I looked, wanting to believe him.

"I know we're young. I know that. But somehow, I guess I told myself that being young means you don't know what you feel, and I'm realizing that's not true. I've never been around anyone who makes me feel as good about myself as you do. I'm a jerk and I was wrong. If you never want to kiss me again, I would understand that. But please, don't stop being my best friend."

He grabbed my hand and squeezed it. He was trembling, but just in the slightest way, enough that I knew I had to say something. "I'm sorry I said those things. I want you to be able to tell me anything. I just don't know how to be able to hear that stuff without getting jealous and angry. And I do love being your best friend. I miss the way it felt when you told me everything and I just liked to know you."

"We can just be friends again and forget about the rest."

"I like kissing you, though. I like the rest. But I don't like the way you are when you feel like you're tied down to me."

"I don't like the idea of you being free to see other guys, though," he said. "I want you to myself."

"Then why are you so weird about it? I can't go on like this. One day you're hot, the next you're cold. One day you're driving for an hour and a half to see me, the next day you can't even say hello."

"Because I don't think I'm ready to feel the way I feel about you."

"I think that loving you hurts and it shouldn't."

"Do you love me, too?" he asked, maybe hopefully.

"I think I felt it before you did." I put my head on his shoulder and inhaled his perfect smell. "Maybe it's not the way you feel about me. Maybe it's the way you think everyone else feels about *us*. You don't want to have to explain this to anybody. Don't you know that you don't have to?"

"I do, though."

"You love who you love, Cody. Case closed."

He wrapped his arm around me. "I won't ignore you anymore, C."

A lightbulb went off in my head. I don't know where the

thought came from, but at the time it seemed like a good idea, and it rolled out of my mouth. "Maybe it's better if nobody knows."

'What?"

"Maybe we can just keep it to ourselves. When we go back to school, we don't have to act like we're a couple. I'm not going to feel bad anymore about you not telling your mom. I'm not going to feel bad anymore about the Circlers making faces at me. What does all of it matter, as long as *I* know that I have you?"

"That sounds like it's not very fair."

"I'm tired of it, Cody. I'm tired of having to worry about you worrying about them. We have our world and I'd be just as happy if everyone else stayed on the outside of it. OK?"

"Is that really what you want?"

"Yes. What matters more to me is that I can text you and tell you whatever is on my mind and you'll say something funny. That matters more than holding hands in front of them. I don't want being with me to seem like a chore for you. I don't want you to have to drag me to parties. I don't want you to feel like a weight is on you."

"Sometimes I want to take you to parties."

"OK. Fine. Just don't treat me like an anchor."

We sat like that together for a long time, not talking, just staring at the street and the trees and the sky. The future was unclear. The future was scary. That was the road to adulthood.

14

The End of the Summer As We Know It

I STOPPED GOING to the pool after the incident. I'm not sure if it was because I felt guilty about looking at Skip, or if I was trying to avoid the Circlers, or if I just had had enough of the sun. I ran into Libby one day at Rachel's Coffee and she gave me a dirty look, then informed me that she had Cody's back. I attempted not to laugh at her. I never mentioned it to Cody. It didn't deserve mentioning. I was more on the outside of the Circle than I had ever been and it was liberating to know that I didn't have to try to fit in with anyone.

We also stopped going out for pizza. Kristi didn't come around anymore. My dad spent every other Friday at home. One weekend in August, he decided to take a spur of the moment trip to Gram's. I knew he wanted to see Becca. He was getting lonely. He needed a companion. I needed to find one for him, one that made sense. I started paying attention to every woman I met, wondering and hoping if they could be a match for my dad. I was tired of seeing him sad.

Cody continued to improve on every level. His hair got longer, his muscles got bigger, and if it really was pheromones, he threw out more of those than he ever had before. When he kissed me, my skin tingled. When he breathed on my face, it tickled, and when his hands nervously made their way to forbidden places, I welcomed them like they were long lost friends.

Shortly before school started again, Cody had called me on a Wednesday around noon and asked me to come to his house. When he opened the door, he was just the usual Cody in an ill-fitting t-shirt and khaki shorts. I was learning the importance of looking nice, and had realized a few weeks prior that I could grab Cody's attention much easier when I wore a cute dress. He looked me over, and I knew it had worked. He smiled and pulled me in by my hands. He had brought me there with the intentions of doing our summer reading together, but we both knew we wouldn't be reading for long.

He led me to a sunroom in the back of the house that contained a lot of plants fed by the sunlight pouring in through generous windows. He sat on the well-worn couch and put his feet up on the coffee table. He had chosen *In Cold Blood* from the summer reading list, so I decided to read it as well. I figured it would give us something to talk about when the conversation started lacking. We read for a little while, and eventually my foot touched his foot and my hand touched his hand and pretty soon I could smell him and we reached for each other.

I liked the way he never rushed a kiss. He kissed me like nobody would ever come home, like time was standing still, like seven minutes could be seven hours. He paid attention to little details, like not pulling away too fast, and like breathing at exactly the right time. In the back of my mind I knew he was just practicing on me. Maybe he was practicing for the college girls or the after-college girls, even. He did everything so perfectly that it was hard to believe he was an awkward guy who'd messed up all of his prior kisses.

We stripped down to our underwear and our bodies tangled together and everything about him felt new and familiar at the same time. I wondered if he would ever ask for more. He seemed content with the partially nude kissing. He seemed perfectly happy with it.

Eventually we had to get back to reading, though, but I wanted to be wrapped in him, so I put on his wrestling t-shirt and laid my head on his bare chest and the rhythm of his heart and the slow rocking of his breathing put me to sleep. I thought to myself, right before I dozed off, *this must be the peace you feel right before you die.*

I felt guilty when it happened, like it was somehow my fault, or all my fault. I suppose I felt a little bit slutty, not because of what actually happened, but because of what she probably thought happened. I woke up to his mother shaking him by the shoulder. He sat up quickly, giving me a little push.

"Mom!" he said, acting surprised. "What time is it?"

"It's almost six." She looked at him expectantly. "Are you going to introduce us?"

I felt like the proverbial deer in headlights. I had no idea how he would introduce me. I could come off as a friend, except for the fact that we were sleeping in a more-than-friends embrace. Also, I was wearing the shirt that he clearly should have been wearing, and my dress was somewhere underneath me and unobtainable from the position I was in.

He stuttered for a minute, so I decided to play it safe. "I'm Caroline. Cody's math partner."

"Math? It's summer."

"Now we're reading partners," he said.

She looked at us suspiciously. "*You* are Caroline?"

"Uh-huh."

"*The* Caroline?"

"Mom!" Cody said, getting embarrassed.

"The Fourth of July Caroline?"

"Yes," I said, reluctantly.

"You're Cody's math partner? I thought you were Cody's best friend."

He put his hand over his face, maybe mortified that I knew what he had told his mother, or maybe upset that I had just had my first conversation with her and I was caught in a lie. "Well, yes. That, too."

"Well, Cody, when you said it was complicated, I guess you weren't lying."

I looked at him, and he looked back out of the corner of his eye. "*Mom*. Please."

"Alright, alright," she said with a smile, but I wasn't sure what her smile meant.

As soon as she walked away, I put my clothes on and he put his shirt back on. "I should go," I said.

"You don't have to," he said.

"My dad — dinner. You know."

"Of course. I'll drive you home."

I agreed to it, only because I wanted to kiss him at least once more.

March 30, 1994

I've decided not to tell Teddy until he's done with finals. It should be no problem hiding it until then, and I don't want him to stress over it and mess up his grades. I've been sick in the morning and I told him that it is my meds and I made a doctor's appointment. I had to make one anyway, to tell him I have to go off the meds. Or that I did go off the meds. I see the difference already. Insomnia and a general feeling of panic. Everything seems loud to me. I'm doubting everything, but miraculously, I'm not doubting Teddy. I wonder what Edie and Carl will think. I wonder if they will be happy for us or disappointed in us. They should only be disappointed in me. It's my fault. I hope I'm not going to ruin Teddy's life, but something tells me that I should bring our child into the world. I wonder, had I asked to terminate it, if Teddy would have supported me in that. I think he loves me enough that he'd do anything for me, and I should do anything for him, and he would want this baby. I can imagine him as a father and he'd be a wonderful father. Teddy will fall in love with this baby instantly. I know him.

It was time for the final party of the summer, the we're-going-back-to-school-in-two-days party. Once again, Zack Fortner was hosting it. I remembered all of the other ill-fated parties. And now, Cody wanted me to go to a party again. I had spent the last couple of weeks enjoying our alone time, enjoying each other before we had to go back to school and face the masses. I had decided I would follow Cody's lead and we wouldn't talk about the relationship and how to have it at school. We had Wednesdays.

My dad was hard at work at the college and had been burying himself in work since Kristi didn't come around any more. It gave Cody and me a lot of time alone together, and we usually ended up in a make-out session before too much time passed. That Friday night was no exception. Cody came over an hour early, and we got straight down to it, kissing like we were taking our last breath. He was more eager than he had been before. The kisses were aggressive, and I liked his confidence. He stopped kissing me long enough for me to tell him that I wanted to get ready.

He smiled. "Maybe we shouldn't go."

"You don't want to miss it. I know you." I sat up on the edge of my bed. "You'll regret not going in the morning."

"I'm just really into spending time with you right now."

"Explain that to your friends, Cody. They'll start dinging your phone and you'll be miserable."

I tried to stand up, but he took my hand and stopped me. "I want to ask you something."

"What's that?" I was curious. Was he going to say he wanted to leave the Circle to be my full-time boyfriend? Was he going to say *I love you* again, but this time with less doubt? Was he going to suggest we run away together for the last weekend before summer ended? All of those were ridiculous thoughts, and I knew it.

"I've been having a hard time concentrating. Sleeping. I'm really preoccupied with this."

"What?"

"I think it's all this build-up, this tension, and nothing ever happens."

My heart dropped. Here it comes. I figured he wanted more from me, and I wanted to keep him enough to do something stupid like that. "I'm sorry, Cody. Why didn't you say something?"

"Oh, no. Don't be sorry. I just, I thought it'd be nice if you could do it this time. Maybe it would change something for me."

"Do what?"

"You know," he said, making the hand motion to signify that he'd been pleasing himself. "The other thing was good. I don't want to ask you for that, but maybe you could just do this. It won't take long. I promise."

He looked nervous and it made me feel pity for him. I liked the way it made me feel to make him feel something. Iwanted to know what it was like to have power for the tiniest moment, or to make someone feel. It was almost like a gift and I welcomed it. I didn't answer him, simply unzipped his pants and reached in.

Cody wanted to drink at Zack's house, and I worried that I'd end up dragging him home again, taking him home to his mother and giving her more ammunition to hate me. He refilled the flask from my dad's seldom-used bottle, and we went to Zack's.

It was the first time I had been around the Circle since I slapped Cody at the pool, and I'm sure word got around about that. Libby was trying to stab me with her eyes and Maia looked at me like I was beneath her. The guys didn't seem to care, but the girls were catty and protective over Cody. I just tried to imagine his face when he climaxed, and the fact that I gave him that look, not any of them, and it made me feel a little bit better. When we went our separate ways for a while, I even kissed him first, making sure that the girls saw it. He was mine, and suddenly I realized that I was going to have a hard time pretending not to care when they pawed at him. It made me angry, but I thought I knew how to deal with it.

The only person who really cared to talk to me at parties was Gus, and I was angry with him about the Alaska incident, and that was just another thing I tried to hide.

"How was your trip?" I asked, trying not to sound hostile. It was the only thing I could think of to say to him, though.

"Let me show you the pictures," he said, smiling, as he put down his red cup of beer. He got closer to me on the couch until our shoulders were touching, then he took out his phone and started telling me about each picture. Fishing, hiking, going out to eat, cooking dinner, camping. Everything with more explanation than I could've ever needed. "I'm sure Cody told you this already."

"No, we didn't talk about the trip."

"At all?"

"He mentioned a couple of things. He mentioned the girl."

Gus smiled. "He would, that stupid fuck."

"That's a long way to go to get a hand job."

"It doesn't matter what she said, he wouldn't have gone through with it. All he did was think about you and talk about you and wonder what you were doing."

"That's strange." I looked at Gus's checkered Vans and contemplated it. Why didn't he call me if he missed me so much?

"Did he ever give you the gift?"
"He didn't give me anything."
"He's such a pussy."
"What was it?"
"Act surprised if he ever gives it to you, OK?"
"OK."
"It's this stupid bluebird necklace. Because he said your favorite poem is about a bluebird or something. I don't know. We were making fun of him too badly to really pay attention. I hope you know that he takes a lot of shit for you."

I thought about it. How did he know my favorite poem was about a bluebird? I don't think I had ever told him that. It was just a little poem that was taped to the mirror in my bedroom, a room he'd hardly ever been in at the time he would've bought the necklace. I wondered how observant he really was, compared to how aloof he acted. An hour had gone by, and suddenly I missed him. I missed him like he'd been gone for a month again, and I told myself that this must be what love feels like. God, I hated that I needed him to make me feel whole, but I couldn't deny it, either. We had something, and maybe it was a little more than the puppy love that I made it out to be. Maybe it was actually quite real. I just needed to find him, and when I found him, I just needed to kiss him.

I went into the basement. He wasn't down there. I walked around outside. He wasn't outside. I went upstairs and checked the bathroom. No. Then I made my way down the hall. I could see a room with light peeking out from under the door, and something told me to open that door. I never expected to see what I saw, what I could never unsee, what could never be explained or justified in any way. I could see the bottoms of his shoes, but I knew it was him because of the calculator watch that was on the wrist that appeared to be reaching for the hook of her red lace bra. I could hear their mouths, the wet sucking noises that you don't notice when you're actually the one doing the kissing. It was like a train wreck — I couldn't look away; I was paralyzed in horror and disbelief. I was disgusted.

Libby turned to look at me. "Oh, hi Caroline," she said casually. "Don't you know how to knock?"

Cody looked out from behind her, and I knew I had to run

before our eyes met. I ran down the steps and through the crowd of all of the people I hated, and out into the front yard. Gus was leaning against his car casually talking to a girl. Our eyes met and he surprisingly seemed to get the hint that something was wrong. "Caroline…"

"Can you take me home?" I asked, a little out of breath and trying not to cry.

He seemed accommodating. "Yeah," he said, without hesitation.

I had this idea that Cody would come running after me, apologizing, asking me to fix things. He didn't do that.

"What's wrong?" Gus asked, as we drove away from Zack's house.

"I guess I forgot how much I don't like parties."

"I'm not the biggest fan myself."

"Then why do you go?" I asked, barely paying attention to the conversation, but trying to keep my cool.

"I want to fit in." He glanced at me quickly. "Go ahead, call me shallow."

"It's normal," I said. "We all want to fit in somewhere whether we admit it or not."

"Yeah. They're my friends, it's just that I have to do all the trying."

"Turn left," I said.

"Who tries? You or Cody?"

"Maybe neither of us try very hard."

"I think he tries, you just don't see it the way we do."

"Why wouldn't I see it?"

"He's obsessed with you."

"Why doesn't he show it?"

"I don't know, Caroline. He's weird and he's hard to understand."

"Stop here," I said, once we were in front of my house.

Gus pulled over. "Are you OK?"

"I am," I said. "Thank you for the ride."

He smiled and turned towards me. "I think you're pretty. If things don't work out with Cody…you know. I wouldn't mind giving it a try."

I just stared at him.

"A date. You know, I'll take you out somewhere. I'll buy you a steak. I wouldn't hide you if you were my girl."

"Thanks, Gus. But I don't think I could date his cousin. And I've had my fill of your Circle."

"What happened?"

"Ask him," I said, and I got out of the car and walked into my house.

I was relieved that my dad wasn't there. I would've burst into tears and had to tell him what Cody had done. Even though I was hating Cody, for some reason, I didn't want my dad to hate him. It would be like admitting to my dad that I had made a terrible mistake by trusting someone. I opened my drawer and took out the picture of my mother and Teddy, wishing she were alive, wishing I could ask her about it, wishing she could show me where to find my strength in all of this. Getting hurt was supposed to teach me a lesson, I thought. I didn't feel like I was learning anything.

I sat on the floor, wanting to be uncomfortable, and sat the picture down beside me. "Why did you have to die?" I asked her tearfully. "Why wasn't I good enough for you? Why am I not good enough for anyone?" I thought about it a little longer. "Why didn't Teddy replace you so I wouldn't have to be so alone?" I stared at her empty eyes, wondering if she had been dead long before Teddy came into her life. I wondered if she had *ever* been alive. I seriously had my doubts. But for the first time in my life, I longed to have a mother.

I went upstairs to my dad's computer, knowing that he merged his contacts from his phone to it. I hadn't been up there in a while, and if I could imagine a boy's dorm room, it would've been that, but with many books scattered about. I sat at his desk and pressed the space bar to wake up his computer. I clicked on his address book. Ninety percent of the names were female. Instead of last names, there were dates in that space. I clicked on one of them — Tawny. March 2010. In the address field it simply said, "laundromat." I clicked on another one. Isabella. May 2010. "American Lit 8 am." I clicked on enough of them to realize that these were either his interests, or his conquests, or both. I stopped clicking on random names and found the one I was looking for — Kristi.

I dialed her number, hoping, just hoping she would answer, and wishing that maybe my dad would've loved her and married her.

When she said hello, I couldn't hold back my tears.

"Kristi?" I asked.

"Yes. Who is this?"

"It's Caroline."

"Are you OK? Is Teddy OK?"

"He's OK. I just wanted someone to talk to."

"What's the matter?"

"It's Cody."

"Is he OK?"

"I hate him. And I can't talk to my dad about it."

"Do you want me to come over?"

"Yes," I said.

It was the Friday that she would've normally spent with my dad, and I wondered what she had been doing on those Fridays now. It looked to me like she had been lounging around at home. She showed up in her pajama pants and a big t-shirt, with her hair up in a messy ponytail. She went right to the freezer and scooped out two dishes of ice cream.

"If you only knew how many boy problems that ice cream has gotten me through."

I wasn't hungry, but the cold felt good on my lips.

"What did he do?"

I could feel the tears rolling down my cheeks, but I wasn't physically crying any more. "It's like every time he convinces me that he's into me, even that he loves me, he does something totally stupid to reverse it. He ignores me, he hides me, he does whatever he does. And it hurts."

"It does hurt."

"How do I accept that and get over it?"

"First off, you have to remember that guys are stupid. It's a fact, they just are." She licked her spoon. "Your dad always had good taste in ice cream, though."

"But he's stupid?"

"Yes. They all are." She looked at me. "What did he do this time?"

"Will you tell me what Teddy did if I tell you what Cody did?"

"I suppose so."

I sighed. "I walked in on Cody and some girl was on top of him, kissing him."

"That's typical. It's like their number one goal in life — to get off."

"That had already been taken care of."

"Oh," she said, as if that changed something.

"Why do you think he did that?"

"That's the second thing you need to know about boys — you'll never know why, so don't wrestle with that. They aren't logical, you'll never understand them. There is no way to bridge that gap between how we think and how they think."

"I don't understand how he thinks. We talked about it. He was the first one to say we're too young for sex, that we should wait until high school is almost over, when we're seniors."

"Good, I'm glad you decided that."

"We do stuff. We could've done that, if that was what he really wanted."

"Don't compromise yourself to keep a guy. Please, don't."

I leaned on my elbow, feeling the comfort of the ice cream kicking in. "What happened with Teddy?"

She smiled. "Nothing happened with Teddy. That was the problem. I started to fall in love and he didn't. I wanted to get exclusive, and he wasn't feeling the same way."

"How do you know?"

"He doesn't hide it. The panties in the glovebox gave it away."

"Did you ask him about it?"

"No. I just waited a day or two and I asked him if he wanted to get serious and he said no. I mean, in a nice diplomatic way, but the answer was no."

"It's not you, Kristi. You know that, right?"

She shrugged, and I could see that she was tearing up, too. "He's a good guy, down to earth, has a good job. You don't come across that all the time. I wanted it to work."

"Did you ever see a picture of them? My parents."

"No."

I got up and retrieved the picture of Teddy and Tressa. "I know it doesn't seem like it, but my dad is really a one-woman man. It's just that she's gone and he can't fill the void."

She looked at the photo. "She was the love of his life, wasn't she?"

"It sure seems like it," I said. "I almost feel sorry for him. She didn't love him back as much as he loved her and he's still paying for it. And that's why he's a jerk. And I'm sorry about that."

"He's not a jerk. He just can't stop looking for that perfect thing again."

"Nothing is perfect," I said. "Not even close."

"Maybe I could've been second," Kristi said. "I could've lived with that."

"You shouldn't have to be. And I'm sure Teddy knows that."

She looked at me. "You shouldn't be second either."

"At least you know what you're up against. It's a mystery to me."

She took my hand. "Caroline. You need to realize something. You're pretty. And smart. And you've got your dad's sense of humor. It's a good mix and you don't have to settle."

"I can't stop thinking about Cody. I can't get him out of my head. I feel like he's got a piece of me and I don't want that. I don't want anyone to own any part of me."

"Wouldn't it be nice to choose what you feel?"

Kristi convinced me to take a hot bath and go to bed. I turned off my phone because I didn't even want to anticipate a phone call from Cody. Of course there was still the expectation that he would come knocking on my window. I would probably just pretend to sleep through it. I couldn't look at him — I couldn't do it because I knew that I would still love him when I looked at him, and I didn't want to because I didn't think he deserved it.

I drifted into a light and anxious sleep. The sound of my dad opening the back door woke me up.

"Kristi? What are you doing here?"

"She called me. Boy trouble. Stuff a dad wouldn't understand."

"Thanks for coming."

"I always liked her, Teddy. But you knew that."
"I know you did, Kris."
"How've you been?"
"Busy. Work. You know. That time of year."
She laughed. *"Yeah. I know."*
"Could you stay for a drink?"
"Maybe one."

I heard the familiar sound of the squeaky cupboard door open, the glasses clanking.

"You're the only guy I know who drinks Johnny Walker from a Snoopy glass."
"I'm the only guy you know who does a lot of things, probably."
"I miss you."
"I miss you, too."

The talking stopped. I wondered what they were doing.
Finally, *"Do you want to stay for a while?"*
"No. I should go home. I hope you understand."
"I do. I'm sorry."
"I don't know how I ever thought I wouldn't fall for you."

I could hear the back door open and close again. My dad approached my door, peeked in, and I pretended to sleep. It did take a while, but I fell asleep.

May 7, 1994

He cried when I told him. I think he was crying because he was happy. I couldn't hide it much longer at all. Immediately after the shock wore off, he was concerned about my meds. I told him that I had already talked to the doctor about it all. I'm trying to hide the fact that I'm anxious and nervous as I try not to let the fear take over. I want to lock it out, and I'm trying. I just don't know how strong I can be. This child is going to be Teddy's whole world. How is he going to take care of both of us?

"I don't feel good."
    "You don't?"

I knew I looked tired, harboring dark circles under my eyes from the lack of sleep I'd been experiencing. Maybe he would buy it.

"Dad, please let me stay home today."

"You've never missed a first day of school, Bear."

I sat and stared at my cereal. "I know, Dad. Can I just have a day, please?"

He sighed, concerned, but gave in. "If you'd tell me what is wrong, maybe I could help you."

"Nothing is wrong."

"Something is wrong." He knew I was lying. I wasn't a great liar.

"I think we broke up, OK?" I finally said. "And I'm just not ready to face him and all his friends."

"Don't look at him, then."

"He's in three of my classes this year."

My dad hugged me, which only made me cry. "Geez, I like Cody, but I wish you didn't let him make you feel this way."

"So do I."

"Why don't we get you someone to talk to, huh?" He pulled away from me and looked at me like he was inspecting me and I didn't pass. "Please, let's not go too far down this road."

"Can you give me one more day? And if I don't do better tomorrow, you can call whoever you want to call for me. Give me a day to figure it out."

He kissed my forehead. "I'll call you at lunchtime to see how you feel." He swung his battered, brown laptop bag over his shoulder, picked up his blazer, and went out the door. I knew just how lucky I was to have him, and something in me got angry because Tressa never saw it.

Isn't it funny how an hour turns into a day and a day turns into a week and pretty soon the days all seem to have formed one day? You realize you haven't washed your hair in a while and you've been wearing the same pajamas for the same amount of time. By Wednesday, I wondered why he hadn't called or texted or tapped on the window. By Thursday, I felt like the biggest idiot in the world. I was so nervous and sad that I had no problem throwing up in the morning, which led my dad to allow me to stay home again. On

Friday I caught a glimpse of myself in the mirror and I wondered how I'd let it get that far. That afternoon, my dad came home, dragged me to the car, and drove me to a doctor's office.

It smelled like cinnamon in his office. I didn't particularly like that smell. He was younger than my dad and quite good-looking. How on earth would I talk to him about anything? He had blonde hair and blue eyes and absolutely did not look like a doctor. I looked at the diplomas on his wall and estimated him to be about twenty-six years old. He got up to go to the bathroom before the session even started, then sat across from me. He looked more nervous than I did.

"I don't think I want to take medicine," I said, ruminating on my mom's journals.

"OK. Well, I'm a psychologist, so I can't give you medicine." He looked at my paperwork. "Caroline. My name is Josh."

"Josh? Not doctor?"

"There was already a Dr. Parker. Just call me Josh."

I looked around his office. There wasn't much to look at aside from a couple of pictures. "Is that your girlfriend?" I asked.

"No. My sister."

"Do you have a girlfriend?" I was desperate not to talk about myself.

He chuckled. "Why do you want to know?"

"Sorry. It's none of my business."

"Are we going question for question?"

"Is that how it goes?"

"I'm pretty new at this. Anything goes."

"How new?"

"Like, about a month new."

"Oh."

"I'm still figuring out how to make these things work. You'll have to bear with me." He slid some books aside on his desk. "Why are you here, Caroline?"

"My dad is worried about me."

"Why?"

"He thinks I'll turn out like my mom."

"Why do you think he thinks that?"

"Because right now, I'm acting like her."

"How is that?"

"This is the first time I've been out of bed in a week."
"You know that's serious, right?"
"I think I know that, yes."
"So, why? Do you know why?"

I didn't make eye contact with him and nervously wrapped my hand up in my shirt.

"I like your t-shirt. Do you like Aerosmith?"
"My mom did. This was her shirt."
"Do you want to talk about her?"
"I can't really remember her."
"What do you remember?"
"She seemed very tall. I mostly remember that. She always seemed so tall."
"When did she pass away?"
"When I was five."
"Was she ill?"
"She overdosed."
"Is this hard to talk about?"
"Not really. It makes me feel bad for my dad when we talk about her."
"Why is that?"
"He still loves her and he can't love anyone new."
"And how does that affect you?"

I shrugged. "It doesn't, I guess."

He got up and stood by the window. "It's nice outside."
"Yeah."
"A good day for…you finish the sentence."
"Sitting."
"Sitting?"
"I just like to sit in the sun. I like the way it feels to be warm."
"Why didn't you get out of bed for a week?"
"A boy."
"And he was…a friend? Boyfriend?"
"I find it a little weird to talk to you about boys."

He loosened his necktie. "I am so nervous about this job. It was my grandfather's practice and I feel like I'll let him down if I don't wear a tie to work."

"Will he be mad if you take it off? If he comes in?"
"He passed away three months ago. I know he wouldn't have

cared, but there's some sense of reverence that I still have for him. Or some sense of obedience, maybe."

"Was this his office?"

"No. His was in the other room. I don't feel like I'm good enough for it yet. I use this one."

"What if a patient wanted you to take off the tie? Would he be OK with it then?"

"I suppose so."

"I think you should take it off," I said.

He smiled as if it were a huge relief. I wondered if it was part of an act. "Thank you," he said as he pulled it off and put it on the desk. "So, we can't talk about boys? My sister and I used to talk about boys all the time."

"And you don't anymore?"

"She's married now. Has two kids. Not much to talk about anymore. She's busy." He sat down again. "I miss it, though. She was my best friend."

"He was my best friend," I said.

"Who? The boy?"

"Yeah. I think so. I mean, we talked to each other. It was real."

"What did you talk about?"

"Everything. School. Friends. The future. We laughed and joked a lot, but sometimes he talked about serious things. And sometimes so did I. It was easy to talk to him, but we didn't have to talk. Did you ever just feel like you could understand someone without saying a word?"

"I don't think I've ever been that lucky, no."

"But sometimes I don't understand him at all. And he doesn't understand me."

"Do you think you understand yourself?"

I thought about it for a while. "No."

"Why not?"

"If I understood myself, I could stop myself from feeling this way. Don't you think?"

He leaned on his elbow and tapped his pen. "I don't think feelings work like that. You can't stop them. You can learn how to cope with them, maybe."

"How do I cope with them? How does that work?"

"That's what we're trying to do here. Figure it out." He wrote something down. "What do you think would get you back to school?"

"If I didn't have to see Cody there."

"Well, that's not really an option, is it?"

"No. Which is why I haven't been going."

"You don't want to talk about Cody. I get that. But he is just a person and you are just a person and he's just like any other person."

"I don't understand why he didn't call me. Why he didn't explain. I don't know if we're together or apart. I don't know anything."

"What is stopping you from asking him?"

I looked at Josh's diploma on the wall. He went to the University of Kentucky. I tried to picture him there, and I could see him in a fraternity, playing beer pong and flirting with girls. He looked like that kind of guy. "Did you like it in Kentucky?"

"It wasn't bad."

"Why Kentucky?"

"Same reason you don't go to school." He leaned back.

"A girl?"

"We were going to go to Ohio State together. People grow apart, though. I didn't want to see her everyday."

"So, you didn't cope with it."

"I had a choice. You don't. You go to high school. When you go to college, you can go to a different school than him. But right now, you're in high school and you have to see him."

"Maybe you'll see each other again and hook up. My dad does. Every time he goes back to Rocky Ridge, he hooks up with his ex-girlfriend."

Josh laughed. "I won't be hooking up with her."

"You never know. I bet my dad didn't think he'd hook up with Becca, but he does."

"I won't," he said. "She's not even my type any more."

"Cody wasn't my type. Not at all."

"Why not?"

"He's popular and athletic and cute. Like you probably were."

"I wasn't any of those things. Don't judge a book by its cover, Caroline."

I looked at him doubtfully, once again thinking he was trying to connect with me.

He took a photograph out of his desk drawer, then turned it towards me. "That's me, in high school."

He had long hair, down to his shoulders, was wearing black, ripped jeans, and a Metallica t-shirt.

"I played the guitar. I wanted to be in a metal band."

"Really?"

"Yes. People change sometimes."

"Why did you change?"

"That took a lot of effort and I ran out of energy for trying. Always trying to be different, it's exhausting."

"So you decided to become a doctor?"

"Yeah. I guess. I decided that I liked talking to people about stuff. And my grandfather was already a psychologist, so I thought I'd be a shoe in."

"Are you?"

"Not really. But I try. Is it working?"

"I don't know," I admitted.

"Maybe you've labeled Cody as this typical popular guy, and maybe he's not. You have that iteration of what you expected him to be and he's not living up to it."

"No, he's being exactly the guy I thought he'd be. He's not living up to my expectations that he's actually someone else. He's not a metal guy who is a doctor on the inside. He's a jerk who is a jerk on the inside."

"Then why do you even care about seeing him if you can write him off so easily as a jerk? What is stopping you from just confronting him and telling him he's a jerk and moving on?"

I wanted to change the subject again, but I was running out of distractions. "Pride, I guess."

"Pride?"

"I don't want to admit that he can make me feel bad. Or good. Or anything."

"Don't you think you're admitting it by hiding from him? If he saw you in school, saw that you are strong and can face the music, don't you think he'd realize that he has no influence on the way you feel?"

I let it sink in for a moment. I pictured myself going to school with confidence, not even caring what Cody thought of me, and the idea of it felt good. But for some reason, I was crying. Josh handed me a tissue.

"What I can't understand is, what does every other girl have that I don't have?"

He sighed. "Maybe the question you need to ask yourself is, what do you have that every other girl doesn't have?"

15

Know When To Walk Away

I HAD MIGRATED to the couch for my dad's sake. I think he was getting lonely while I hid in my room. I was watching reruns of crime shows practically on mute, but not *Broken Blue,* while he read a book. I was trying to see how long I could go without thinking about Cody. I had gone an hour, and I was proud of myself for that. My dad got up to put a frozen pizza in the oven, and I heard a light tapping on the back door. I knew it wasn't Cody — that wasn't how he knocked.

My dad opened the door. "Hey, Skip. Come in."

I turned my head. I hadn't seen Skip in a while, and he looked taller and cuter and more sun-kissed from his lifeguard job. I got up. "Hi," I said, wishing I didn't look like I just spent a week in bed.

He smiled his usual genuine smile that was irresistible. I loved the fact that it drove the girls mad that they couldn't have him. That might've actually been the number one thing I liked about Skip — that he didn't like anyone else.

I went to the kitchen table and my dad went back to the couch. Skip sat a pile of books on the table. "Are you feeling better?"

"Yes. I am. What is that?"

"It's from Cody. He asked me to bring it to you — his notes and the homework from the week. Math, English, I don't know. You probably do. He said you wouldn't want to get too far behind. He said you can bring it back on Tuesday."

"Tuesday?"

"Labor Day is Monday."

"Oh, yeah."

"I'm not just here for Cody. Lilly and I were worried about you, too."

"I feel better." I turned towards the refrigerator. "Do you want something to drink?"

"I guess so," he said. "Just water, though."

I opened the door and saw the strawberry milk that I had kept in there for Cody and tried not to let it kill me. I handed Skip a bottle of water and we sat down at the table. My dad made his way up the steps. I was lucky to have a dad who respected my privacy.

"I couldn't help but ask myself why Cody had *me* deliver this stuff. Is everything OK?"

"I don't know, Skip. I don't know what it is."

"That group — it must be hard to fit in."

"I don't even want to fit in. I want to just be OK with being me. Does that make sense?"

"Of course it does."

"How do you do it?"

"Do what?"

"Stay outside of the crowd and not go crazy."

He laughed. "I know it seems like a big deal now, but this is high school. In ten years, they'll all be different people. So, it just doesn't seem important to make a big impression on people now. You never know what is going to happen tomorrow. We're all just trying to get through it."

"I guess you're right. How's wrestling?" I asked, just to change the subject.

"It's like it always is." He took down the rest of the water all at once. "If it's on your heart, go ahead and ask about Cody. He asks about you."

"It's on my heart, but I'm stubborn."

"All I can tell you about Cody is that whatever happened, he seems really sorry for it." He looked at his watch. "I have to get home. Curfew."

"Uh huh. Thank you, Skip." I don't know why, but at the door, I wanted to hug him, and he awkwardly hugged me back.

I sat down again and opened the notebook to his familiar handwriting. How did he know that I wasn't so angry that I would just burn all of his notes and his homework? Part of me wanted to. I looked at Cody's familiar handwriting. Handwriting I'd never seen on a card or a love letter. I wondered if he would've done this for the girls in the Circle. He probably would've done it for them days ago, but he let five days go by before he sent the books to me. I took out my notebook and copied down everything he had written. I finally got to the end of the English notes and was surprised by what came next.

Dear Caroline,

Well, I told myself that if you made it this far, then maybe it was meant to be that you find this note, and if you didn't make it this far, then maybe it was meant to be that you don't. All I can say is that I miss you. We should've never complicated this with the physical stuff. We should've just been friends because that's what we were good at. I don't know why I can't seem to pick up the phone and call you. It's probably because there's nothing I can say to fix it. I was drinking. You know how I get when I'm drunk and you know how fast I get there and the only thing I remember is Libby grilling me about our relationship. I probably said something I shouldn't have. I honestly don't remember. If it makes you feel any better, I threw up on her about thirty seconds after you left the room. The fact that I had lost it so much that I got there combined with the prospect of losing you made the room spin and I just barfed.

So, I never thought your dad would have a two-hundred dollar bottle of scotch. And apparently that gets a person pretty damned drunk. And none of this is an excuse for what I did. And none of this can bring you back to me. I'm sorry I hurt you and I'm sorry I hurt our friendship. And whatever is going on with you, I hope you're OK. And whatever happened with Libby, I hope you know that I didn't want it and it didn't mean anything to me. I never liked her. Never. The truth is, I always liked you. I know that I tried to tell you this before, but I truly always liked you. On the first day of school of your first year here — freshman year — you sat two seats in front of me in Algebra. On that day, you were wearing black nail polish and mascara and a black dress with little white flowers on it and a black sweater. Your hair was dark and it looked soft and I stared at it for the whole class period and learned absolutely nothing.

I don't know why I never told you, but I've always had a bit of a crush on you. Maybe it's because you never believe anything I say when I say something nice about you. I don't think that's fair, though. I wish you would believe me. I wish for a lot of things.

I know this can't be undone, but I can ask that you would forgive me. I don't deserve it, but please forgive me.

Love,
Cody

I wanted to pick up the phone and call him. It was an impulse. I just wanted to see him and to touch him and to smell him again, no matter what he had done, no matter who he had done it with. I was learning the very hard lesson that my dad had learned years ago — you don't stop loving and missing people just because you want to stop loving and missing them. Instead of that, I penned a letter back to him.

Dear Cody,

I suppose you're just a boy. Boys are stupid. I know that now. We can't be friends. We can't watch TV together and we can't do things together when there is nothing else to do. I feel differently about you. I feel romantic about you. I can't seem to change it back to what it was. Maybe we can pretend we ended it on a high note. Maybe we can pretend we knew when to walk away, when it became too much, and maybe we can believe that we stopped it all by ourselves before it became a train wreck. Would that be fair enough? Maybe we can pretend it was a summer thing and revisit it next summer when all of the things of the rest of the year aren't there to get in the way. That seems to be when it was at its best, when there is nothing else to do. We weren't too young to know what love was, just too dumb to know that we weren't going to be any good at it. And that's just human error, not our fault. I hope you know that loving you felt good.

Caroline

I yelled up the steps for my dad.

"What, Bear?"

"Can you give me a ride?" I asked, gathering up the books.

"OK. Where to?"

"Cody's house. I want to take back his books."

"Now?"

"Yes, now. I don't want to be looking at them."

He came down and picked up his car keys. "Are you sure?"

"I'm sure," I said, with a new found confidence. I thought about Dr.Josh , how he believed that I could get over it, and that I was strong, so I believed it, too.

I looked in Cody's window, at the TV flickering, at his dad in a recliner chair, and I marched right up to the front door and rang the doorbell.

His dad looked me over from head to toe and I realized that I looked like a reject from the cast of *Flashdance*, but I didn't let it bother me. "Is Cody home? I wanted to give these back to him."

"It's late, he might be sleeping."

"OK. Can you just take these books, then? They belong to him." I offered to hand them over, but his dad declined.

"Come in, I'll get him."

"It's OK, I can wait here."

He left the door open and called for Cody.

"What?" I heard him yelling as he came around the corner. He was in the usual too-tight t-shirt and khaki shorts. He stopped when he saw me and then approached cautiously. "Hey," he said quietly.

"Thank you for thinking of me," I said, offering the books back. "You're a good note-taker."

"Look, Caroline," he said, putting the books inside and shutting the door behind him.

"I read the note. My dad is waiting, though. So I should go."

He looked over my shoulder and waved to my dad. "We should talk, though. There's more I wanted to say."

"I'll see you at school," I said.

He grabbed me and hugged me and I held my breath and did not hug him back. I knew that I would melt if I smelled him or touched him. I pushed him away gently. "Caroline, please?"

"I'll see you at school," I said again.

I got back into the car with my dad.

"Are you OK?" he asked.

"Yeah. Can we stop at the convenience store? We're out of ice cream."

I knew that in reality my dad was all I had, so I decided to finally talk to him about it. Mint chocolate chip ice cream was a decent way to break the ice. I dished it out. He slid the newspaper towards me. "I've been saving the crosswords."

"Thanks."

He took out a pen and filled in 1-across. "Acorn," he said.

"Can we talk instead?"

He looked surprised and put the pen down. "OK."

"Thanks for taking me to see Josh."

"Josh?"

"Dr. Parker. He says not to call him that. Dr. Parker was his grandpa."

"Oh. I see."

"Will you tell me about your first break-up?"

"My first break-up?"

"Veronica. From summer camp. You know."

"Oh, yeah. Veronica." He groaned. "It wasn't much of a break-up. Rather a can't-stay-together."

"What made you like her?"

"Well, during counselor orientation, we ended up in a rowboat together. I was rowing and when I stopped rowing, she leaned forward and kissed me. She said she wanted to be my girlfriend, and I said OK. It was simpler back then. You were or you weren't. That's all. She was always wearing cherry lip gloss. I remember that."

"And when it was time to go home?"

"I wanted to write to her, but she said no. She said it was time to get on with our lives and it was just a summer thing and we had to go back to our real lives, and I accepted that."

"Breaking up was that easy?"

"No. It wasn't easy. It just wasn't that long before I met Becca, which then made it easy."

"So, you replaced her."

"No, no. They were nothing alike. Veronica was bubbling over with something. Some kind of appeal, something sexy. I don't know. Becca was sort of so-so. She wasn't that into me. I wasn't that into her. So that wasn't a hard break-up either. I guess I never really broke up with anyone."

"Did you ever break up with Tressa?" I knew the answer. I wanted to hear it from him.

He looked into his ice cream dish because I knew he didn't want to talk about it. But I needed him to. "Once."

"Once? Why?"

"She had one of her episodes and she got mad at me. That's why. It lasted a couple of weeks. Up to that point, the worst two weeks of my life. I was lost without her. I felt like something had been ripped out of me. Like my heart had been ripped out of me. I didn't eat, didn't sleep, barely made it through work. I decided to read something sad. I read *Jude the Obscure* and I cried every ten seconds. It hurt."

"And then you got back together?"

"Yes."

"Why?"

"I don't know why. For the wrong reasons, probably. Probably because I desperately loved her and she had nowhere else to go." He smiled sadly. "I convinced myself that the only reason she didn't totally love me was that she couldn't. She wasn't capable. She was too broken to do that. And then I wondered why it was better to live with the pain of knowing that than to be alone. And then I got my answer."

"What was the answer?"

"You, Bear. You were born."

"I think she loved you, Dad. She loved you as much as she could."

A tear rolled down his cheek, but he quickly regained his composure for my sake. "Are you going to tell me what's going on with you?"

"He doesn't know what he wants. And I think I realize now that he can't help it. I don't think we should be in each other's lives. Once and for all. I really don't think so. We are too different."

"Does he feel that way?"

I knew he didn't feel that way. "I don't want to be the person who holds him back."

"And someday he'll thank you for it, right?"
"I doubt it. He's Cody."

On Labor Day, Gram and Gramp decided to come over and have a picnic. There was a never-used picnic table in our backyard that had been there since we moved in. Gram covered every base, even the table cloth. Sometimes she cut corners, and today she did so by buying grocery store potato salad. She made baked beans, and Gramp brought his charcoal grill to cook on. I always liked to stare at Gramp's military tattoos. They interested me. I liked to hear his Vietnam stories, too. He told the same couple of stories over and over, but I never got tired of hearing them.

I didn't mention my week off of school or my breakup with Cody to Gram because I didn't want to worry her. She worried enough about my dad, and she didn't need the added stress of worrying about me.

When my dad was around Gram and Gramp he turned into a kid again. I guess it's just because that's what your parents expect of you no matter how old you are. He wore his old jeans and a Skid Row t-shirt and Gram mentioned how he needed a haircut. Gramp always enjoyed a good t-bone steak, and he put five of them on the grill, leaving me to wonder why for about twenty seconds until I realized why. I had come to recognize the sound of his Jeep and it sent a little shiver up my spine to hear it again. I felt sour, and it wasn't just the lemonade.

He approached cautiously, but Gram waved him over and opened her arms for a hug. He seemed relieved that she was accepting him. Of course she was — if she had known about him kissing Libby just a little over a week ago, maybe she wouldn't have been so welcoming. My dad simply raised an eyebrow and looked away, as if he was about to see something horrific go down.

He sat beside me at the picnic table. "She invited me," he said matter-of-factly.

"How?"

"I gave her my phone number when I was at her house. She texted me. I think that's cute that your grandma texts. Even with the smiley face."

"You answer my grandma's texts?"

"Yeah."

"She doesn't know, Cody."

"Doesn't know what?"

"Seriously?" I whispered. "What do you think? None of them know."

"Oh. OK."

"Didn't you get my note?"

"Yeah, I did. But I disagree with it completely."

I got up and pulled him with me into the kitchen. "How can you disagree with my feelings?"

"I'm not disagreeing with your feelings. I'm just saying my feelings aren't the same. Can't we work something out? Wednesday nights? *Broken Blue*? Talking about college and stuff?"

"You have a hundred friends. Can't any of them talk to you?"

"No."

"I kind of hate you right now."

"Does your dad know? I feel like I should apologize to your dad."

"No. Why would I tell him about *that*?"

"I don't know. You tell him a lot."

"Well, I didn't want him to totally hate you."

"Because there's a chance?"

I crossed my arms. He had me there. "No. There's no chance."

"There must be a chance or you wouldn't say that. You wouldn't care if he hated me."

I turned away from him because I couldn't look at him anymore. He put his hand on my shoulder. "Don't touch me," I said, but he didn't move his hand.

"I honestly don't know how she got me into that room. I don't know how any of it happened."

I had to look him in the eye again. "Why didn't you ask her?"

"I don't want to talk to her. Ever again."

"Why? Because she'll seduce you or because you're embarrassed for barfing on her?"

"Uh, a little of both. I just walk away from her at school. As soon as she comes around, I walk away."

"You shouldn't have to," I said.

"I want to."

"You shouldn't have to make a decision between having a girlfriend and having friends."

"I shouldn't be drinking at parties."

"Everyone drinks at parties." I turned around to face him. "I told you before, I don't want to be the thing that ties you down. You shouldn't have to feel guilty if you want to be with another girl."

"I didn't *want* to be with her, C. I don't know what I was doing."

"Even if you were drunk, something in you wanted that or you wouldn't have done it."

"Every guy wants that, sure. I want it with you, though."

"I'm not ready for that kind of thing."

"Well, clearly, neither am I." He ran his hands through his hair, frustratedly. "Look, I need you in my life, C. It's just shit without you."

"And I told you, I can't put aside the way I really feel about you."

"Which is what?"

"Attracted. How can we be friends when I'll always be thinking of how good it feels to kiss you? And what you smell like? And the way you touch me? We can't, Cody."

"Then let me kiss you again. Let it go back to the way it was."

I started to cry. "It hurts. I can't kiss you without thinking about you and her."

He pulled me against him and I hated the fact that he was using my sadness to get close to me. "I'm sorry," he whispered.

"You hurt me," I said. "I trusted you when everything inside of me told me not to trust you and you hurt me. You let me down. You made a fool of me."

"No, I didn't. Who thinks you're a fool?"

"Libby. Me."

"I'm the fool." He squeezed me tightly. "I am, C, not you. I don't want to do life without you."

"That's a little dramatic, Cody."

"No. It isn't." He let go of me and I noticed how tired he looked.

"Look. You can eat dinner with us. I'll think about the rest."

He hugged me again. "Thank you for giving me another chance."

"It's not another chance yet. It's just not being able to hate you as much as I want to."

I had never realized how much I missed his laugh. Or the really smart things he said. Or his hair or his eyes or his awful sense of style and how his shoes didn't match his personality. Or the way he savored his food when he ate it. I noticed a million things I hadn't noticed before. He talked to my dad about our summer reading and remembered everything I said about the book. I sat there taking it in, and at the same time thinking about how to explain it to Josh when I saw him again. Knowing I would be talking to Josh was like having someone to answer to and I felt like it was going to keep me in check. Josh would expect me to stand up for myself, to be truthful, and to respect myself. Oh, who was I kidding? I barely even knew Josh.

It got dark and Gram and Gramp packed up and went home, Gram promising to be back for one of Cody's wrestling tournaments in the winter. I didn't know where to go with Cody now that he had nobody to entertain except for me. He asked me to take a walk with him and I did it, simply because I missed him and I knew that tomorrow in school, everything would be different. We walked through town and to the college, down to the small lake on campus. There was an amphitheater facing the lake, and Cody and I sat on empty benches facing the stage.

"It's hard to believe summer is over," he lamented.

"Yes. It is."

"It's like, I'm getting older and growing up and I don't know how much I really want to."

"You're always talking about the future."

"Yeah. I know. But it hurts a little bit, that feeling of growing up. Sometimes I want to curl up in a ball because it settles right in the pit of my stomach and it's almost like a panic attack or something."

"Well, nothing will change for me. I'll still live with my dad. Probably go to school here. It won't be different. A new set of jerks to see every day, that's all."

"Go away, then."

"I don't know if I want to. I'm all my dad has. He's all I have.

And I'll get a decent discount. Maybe if I can get him a nice girlfriend by the time I apply, then maybe I'll go."

"You really love him."

"He really loves me. Imagine being a couple years older than you are now and having to take care of a baby. My mom was sick. He had to take me to work with him and put me in daycare when he was in school. My dad did all of that and still got good grades and graduated with honors and got good jobs. He always had so much to do, so much to worry about, and he was still the best dad. And a really good teacher. Even after he was heartbroken, he was a great dad."

"I don't think my dad would've done it."

"I know how lucky I am. Maybe that's why I set the standard so high."

"For me, you mean?"

"For anyone. When you know that people can be good, can have a lot of good inside of them, why should you take any less than that?"

"I guess I never had an example like that."

"That's why I said, I'm lucky."

We were quiet for a while.

"Can we kiss?" he finally asked, breaking the silence.

I looked at him. He looked sincere, but I didn't really want to. I knew it would be a whirlwind of emotions for me and I was just coming out of my funk. If I didn't kiss him, I could control the situation. If I did kiss him, my heart would get wacky and I'd slip down a few pegs. I hated listening to my heart and I hated not listening to my heart. You can't do both.

"If I kiss you, and you don't like it, we can stop."

"Did you kiss her first? Or did she kiss you?"

"I think she kissed me, but I honestly don't remember."

"You're asking me to compromise what I know is right."

"What do you think is right?"

"I should be really mad at you. And hold a grudge. And never forgive you. And I certainly shouldn't kiss you."

"That's really how you feel?"

"It's logical."

He laughed. "What is logical about anything, ever? What is

logical about this relationship? It's totally weird. It's unconventional. It's kind of against the odds, don't you think?"

"Why is it weird?"

"We're different. We don't seem like we'd go together very well. But we do."

Talking to him was mentally exhausting me and I decided to give him what he wanted. I realized I'd have to pay one emotional price or another. "Fine. Kiss me," I said, unenthusiastically.

He twisted his whole body into it, but I merely turned my head as if it really didn't matter to me. He only kissed me gently on the lips and hovered for a moment, then leaned back. It took me a second to open my eyes. I was expecting more.

"I didn't want to overdo it," he said.

I thought of something. "The bluebird. How did you know that?"

"What do you mean?"

"Gus said that you knew my favorite poem was *The Bluebird*."

"It's taped on your mirror."

"You paid attention to that?"

Quietly, Cody recited the entire thing, from beginning to end, every last word.

"You memorized it? Why?"

"I liked it. I would've never known it if I hadn't seen it in your room. You show me things I never would've known. That's one of my favorite things about you. You open me up to things I never would have seen. I want that in my life because without you, it's the same old parties, the same old people, the same old thing day after day. I can have adventures with you."

I got up and he followed me. It was getting late and I didn't want my dad to worry.

"I can't believe Gus brought that up. Why?"

"I don't know." I didn't tell him about the necklace. I decided to keep that to myself.

He took my hand and I let him hold it while we walked back to my house. He gave me a hug at the doorstep and asked me if he could pick me up in the morning.

"I don't think we should do this at school."

"Do what at school?"

"Be close."

"Why not?"

"Because we're not close," I said. "Not that close. Not close enough to take the shit for this."

He looked away from me for a second as if he were thinking of a way to contest it. "I want to earn your trust back."

"You don't have to, Cody. I'm not putting myself in a position where I need to trust you."

"Even as friends, you need trust."

"Not the kind of trust that you broke."

He looked down. "I deserve this. I know."

"I'm sorry," I said. "I have to go in, now."

"But you're coming tomorrow, right?"

I quickly thought about Josh. "Right."

He leaned forward and I could feel his cheek touching mine. "I love you," he said.

I went inside. I didn't want to know that.

16

Wake Me Up When September Ends

THERE WASN'T enough room in the halls of Newbury High for me, Cody, and our weird tension. It just felt like a ton of bricks sitting on my chest and suffocating me. I loved him. I knew that I loved him. I hated it when girls talked to him, no matter how uninterested he looked. I watched Maia reach up and tuck in his shirt tag, and even though he pulled away from her, I got jealous. I was thankful that I didn't have any classes with Libby, except for gym class, and Lil was there to take my mind off of her.

Eventually, I told Lil what had happened, and she said it didn't even seem real, not even like Cody. She was probably right.

There was a new guy at Newbury High, and his locker happened to be beside Lil's. He approached us on Tuesday morning as I talked with Lil, and she introduced us. He was like the old Josh, in ripped jeans and a band shirt, and he had the remnants of a stamp on his hand, as if he had been at a club over the weekend, which only made me wonder how it wasn't washed off by now. His name was Jordy and I thought that was a funny name for a boy. I could see how he looked at Lil, like he didn't know any better and might've thought he had a chance with her. Anyone else watching would have thought that he was coming on to *me*, forgetting that a new guy would never know that Lil was unobtainable.

Every morning he stood by the lockers with us, then he sat with us at lunch. He didn't fit into any group yet, so it made sense to stand by the only two other people who had no group. He didn't really talk to us since he always wore headphones, and they were usually loud enough that I could hear some of what he was listening to. He wasn't interested in conversation, just in not standing alone. I couldn't blame him for choosing to spend that time standing beside the prettiest girl in school, the totally off-limits Lilly Waters.

Every day I could see Cody staring at us. He didn't even try to hide his disdain for Jordy. He made the angriest face he could make when Jordy approached, and on the fourth day, Friday, Jordy came without headphones and asked Lil what she was doing over the weekend. After she replied with, "Nothing," he must have chickened out and turned towards me, at which point he touched my necklace, commenting on its coolness. I suppose from where Cody was standing it could've looked like he was touching something else.

I wondered what Cody's breaking point would be, and that answered my question. Cody crossed the hallway and Lil told Jordy to watch out. He turned and saw Cody coming and got out of his way.

"Caroline? I can't do this anymore," he said.

"What?" I asked, but before I could even finish saying the word, his lips were on mine, his tongue was in my mouth, and he was breathing on my face. The back of my head was against the locker and I had nowhere to go. I allowed myself to smell him, the sense that made me the weakest for him. Then, I came to, realizing that people were watching, commenting, and even whistling. He must have realized what he had just done, and pulled away.

Jordy smiled the biggest smile I had seen from him since I met him. "Dude! That was awesome, man." He looked at Lil. "Is that normal here? I hope so."

"No," Lil said.

Cody turned towards him. "Whoever you are, don't do whatever you've been doing. She's my girlfriend. I still love her."

Jordy continued his smile, from ear to ear. "It's cool man." He looked at Lil. "Do you have a jealous wanna-be boyfriend, too, or are you single?"

I laughed out loud.

"I'm single," she said.

"In that case, you want to do what they just did? I could be into it, you know?"

"You liked *her*?" Cody asked.

"Um, yeah. Now that I see it's not a thing to be cool about who you like at this school. Yeah, I like *her*."

"Sorry," Cody said, half-heartedly.

"You're cool," he said, offering a fist bump, which Cody accepted.

Jordy was the only person who couldn't feel the weirdness, simply because he didn't know it existed. "So, like, what's with that weird group that always sticks together? What is with them? Are they a cult or something?"

Lil laughed. "I've got a lot of explaining to do."

"I'll walk you to homeroom," he said, draping his arm over her shoulders.

"Wow. I feel like an asshole," Cody said.

"You don't own me, you know."

"It sucks, C."

"Welcome to my world. I have to watch those girls petting you all day. Messing up your hair, tucking in your tags. You don't like being on this side of it, do you?"

"It looked like…"

"He was admiring my necklace."

"Right," he said. "I'm sorry." The bell rang, and I looked away from him, excited and disappointed all at once.

I had been looking forward to seeing Josh all week. When we got there, the waiting room and the reception desk were empty, and after about five minutes, the receptionist emerged from Josh's office, a little disheveled and red in the face.

"I am *so* sorry," she said. "I have to make a note to get that doorbell fixed." She picked up a pen and I stared at her. I had seen it enough times with my dad to know what it was. "Just go ahead in," she said, when she realized I was waiting for the okay.

He was standing in front of the open window, and I watched him quickly flick a cigarette away and pick up a can of room deodorizer. "Sorry," he said. "Bad habit I picked up in college. I don't smoke a lot. Maybe twice a day."

"I can't judge you for that," I said. "It doesn't bother me."

He was dressed down, in a button down shirt and jeans.

"Where is your tie?"

"Sadly, I only had a handful of patients today. Fridays are dead. I knew you'd appreciate this." He took off the button down to reveal a Van Halen t-shirt. "I guess you don't outgrow it completely."

I nodded.

"What's on your mind?" He sat down and slid his notebook in front of him. It was the one thing that looked official about him.

"Honestly?"

"Yeah, of course."

"Were you just having sex with your secretary?"

"How long were you out there?"

"Long enough," I said.

"Oh. I'm sorry."

"It's fine. My dad is a single guy, so I get it."

He laughed.

I smiled. The fact that he had just done three very un-doctorly things made me like him more. He took an apple out of his desk drawer and a Swiss Army knife from his pocket and made some nice even slices. He sat them on a napkin and pushed the pile towards me. "I'll share."

Josh had perfect teeth and when he ate the apple, it showcased them. I quickly realized that I should not form a crush on him. "You went to school this week?"

"Yes."

"How was it?"

"I lived."

"How was Cody?"

"Weird. He sent his notes over for me to copy and then my Gram invited him over for Labor Day because she didn't know that we broke up. And then he kept asking me why we couldn't stay together and I kept telling him it was because I have some self-respect. Even though I really don't. He kept hugging me. He kept trying to flatter me and tell me that I'm special and different and all the usual garbage that I guess somebody says to you so you stop feeling bad."

"You don't think he actually thinks that you're special and different?"

"I think he does think it, but that's just because he's so used to — I don't know. Basic girls? I don't know them so I shouldn't judge them, but they all seem alike. So, I'm not really special, just not what he's used to."

"Maybe you're special to him?"

"Aren't you supposed to say that I shouldn't put up with his crap and stand up for myself and never take him back?"

"I'm not telling you what to do with Cody. I'm only telling you that maybe everyone is not as patronizing as you think they are. Maybe everyone is not a liar. Maybe some people are sincere. Isn't it tiring to think that everyone has an ulterior motive?"

I decided that he was right. I wasted a lot of time trying to figure out what people really meant when in reality they just meant what they said most of the time.

"Is she your girlfriend?" I finally asked.

He clasped his hands together and looked down. I knew he must have been frustrated with me. I always changed the subject. "I thought we were on a roll there for a second."

"I'm just wondering."

"No. She's not my girlfriend. She's my receptionist."

"Was that in the job description?"

He laughed. "No. I don't think it was."

"It must just be an unspoken thing — available bodies must be magnetically drawn to each other."

"Nobody wants to be lonely. Maybe alone, but not lonely."

"You're right, I guess."

"Can we talk about you now? We can talk about my love life later."

"I tried to avoid him all week, but today he thought this guy was hitting on me and he just came over and kissed me like he had something to prove. It was very strange."

"How did it make you feel?"

"I'm not really sure yet. I know that I miss him, but I don't think he's good for me."

"That's for you to decide." He crunched down on another apple wedge. "He's probably as confused and mixed up as you are. Do you think that whatever he did to hurt you — whatever it was —

that for your own sake it is time to let go of it, to forgive him, and to move on? You don't have to take him back or be his friend, but let it go inside."

"I'm not sure that I know how to let things go."

"You can pray or meditate or just write it down in a journal and hope that it leaves you and goes where you put it. And if it doesn't go the first time, keep trying. If you carry it around with you, eventually it will get heavy. Heavy and uncomfortable. Don't let it grow."

I could hear the drums playing at the football game and I imagined that Cody would have to be in whatever gear the Spirit Club would be in tonight, whether it be superhero day or hula day or pink-out day. I never knew what the theme of the week was because I failed to pay attention to the announcements most mornings. I was always reading during home room to escape the reality that was school. My dad had a date. I was happy for him since he seemed to miss Kristi on his Friday nights. I had no idea who it could be, but I hoped it was someone good enough for him. I decided I would use the time alone to catch up on some reading, and maybe do what Josh told me to do and let out my feelings into my journal.

I decided to be honest with myself and list all of the things I liked about Cody. On the opposite page, I listed the things that I didn't like about Cody. Then, on the next page, I took the things I didn't like about Cody and narrowed them down to the bad things I *thought* were true about Cody, versus the things I knew for sure about him. *Cody wants to try a variety of girls.* Cody denies this, therefore, it was an inference on my part based on the things he had done. Perhaps *Cody tries to fit in* would be a better way to put it. He does try to fit in sometimes. He went into the bedroom with the girl in Alaska to fit in. He got drunk to fit in. I doubt he really enjoyed any of it.

At ten o'clock, once I finished all of my lists and decided to make myself dinner, I heard a tapping on the back door. It was Cody wearing camouflage and looking like a somewhat nerdy version of Rambo.

"Can I come in?"

"Why?" I asked.

"Why are you being this way?"

"Because I'm trying to get over you and you make it insanely difficult."

"Fine. I'll stand here on the doorstep and we can have a conversation." He crossed his arms, unbudging.

"Come in." I moved aside and allowed him in and he sat at the table.

"What're you doing?"

"Making dinner."

"I'm kind of hungry, too. We could go for pizza."

"Everyone goes for pizza after the game. I'd rather stay home."

"I'll cook for you," he said. He went to the cupboard and took out a box of macaroni and cheese.

"That's not cooking."

"I'll prepare some macaroni and cheese. Is that worded better?"

"Fine." It was annoying that he knew where our pots and pans and dishes and silverware were. I watched him put the water on to boil, realizing that he had infiltrated my life and I had barely put a dent in his.

He sat down again and faced me. "You missed the game."

"I'm not a big fan of the games. And I'm not in a club that requires me to go."

Everyone in the Circle who wasn't a cheerleader or a football player was in the Spirit Club. They couldn't detach long enough to go somewhere without one another.

"No party tonight?" I asked.

"Yeah. There's a party. You wanna go?"

"Not at all."

"I didn't think so. Neither did I."

"You? Miss a party?"

"I'm not drinking anymore. And I don't feel like making an ass of myself tonight."

"Did you look in the mirror?"

"OK, C. Everyone in Spirit Club wore camo. I don't look like an ass when I'm with everyone else."

"If you say so."

"I'm sorry about today in school." He reached across the table and touched my hand with his fingertip, as if he were testing the water. "I can't put aside the feelings I have for you."

"OK. Apology accepted."

"Really?"

"Yes." It was easier to forgive him.

"Where were you for that week?" he asked. "Why weren't you in school?"

"I just couldn't go."

"Because of me?"

I hated that he was giving himself so much credit. "No, Cody. Because of me."

"So, were you sick?"

"I just couldn't. I don't know how to explain it."

"How did you get better?"

"My dad took me to a doctor. He's afraid I'll be like her."

"Who?"

"My mother. Mentally ill."

"I'm sorry," he said.

"My dad was always trying to get her better. I don't want him to have to do it for me. I have to work on it."

"What does it feel like, C? What does it feel like to not want to get out of bed?"

"Nothing. It feels like nothing. You wear yourself out thinking and then you go blank."

"And your mom? That's how she felt?"

"I don't really know how she felt. I was five."

"I'm sorry for all the things that have happened to you."

"I don't want you to feel sorry for me. I don't like that feeling. That's just how my life unfolded. You have challenges, too."

He shrugged. "Like what?"

"Like finding your own identity. I know you're part of the Circle and I get that, but you are someone else, too. You don't let that person shine through sometimes. Is it hard to stifle that?"

"Why do you think I like to be around you? Because I can be me."

We stared at each other for a moment, then he realized the water was boiling and tended to the macaroni and cheese. We made small talk about the game until the food was done, then he finally asked me if he could stay for a little while. "Because I just really miss you," he added.

I thought about it for a moment. "If I say we can be friends again, will you stop this weirdness?"

"I want to be your boyfriend."

"What does it say about me if I just take you back after what you did? It says that I'm pathetic and stupid and that I'm just asking to be hurt again."

"It says that you know who I really am, C. And you do."

"I can only be your friend right now."

"Can I kiss you sometimes?"

"Let's see what happens. Can we do that?"

"Yeah," he said, reluctantly. "When can I ask you about this again?"

"At the end of September. After my birthday. When I'm sixteen."

September went by quickly. So much was happening. Cody got a job washing dishes at The Tavern, Lil and Jordy terribly covered up their budding romance, and my dad went out once a week with his new secret girlfriend. I laughed when she called him and he left the room to talk to her. I didn't walk into any awkward moments between Josh and his receptionist again, and the next two Fridays he dressed casually and wore his band t-shirts. Things were getting better for me, but I sugar coated them even more for Josh. I felt obligated to allow him to think he was doing a really good job. In exchange for my progress, he gave me bits of information about himself, and I wrote the facts about Josh down in my journal along with anything that Cody said or did.

Josh's ex-girlfriend's name was Missy and she was going to be a veterinarian. She was a cheerleader in high school and he was a metal guy, so they were kind of doomed from the start. But his grandpa was a doctor and his dad was a doctor, and he was good boyfriend material because of that. The hair and the clothes could be changed over time and she credited herself with persuading him to become a doctor. She liked to introduce him as doctor this-and-that's son or grandson, but everyone in town knew that Josh's dad was a free-clinic doctor at Planned Parenthood in the next town over and he gave away most of his money to charity. Josh's mom stayed home and took care of foster kids, mostly ones who had special needs. He had about twenty brothers and sisters come and go over the years. He kept in touch with about five of them. That was as far as I got with Josh's life story.

"Why don't you just go out with Reagan?" I asked during my last September appointment.

"My receptionist?" he asked, sitting in the open window, smoking again. I wasn't sure if he smoked in front of me to be cool and relatable or if he just trusted me enough not to tell on him.

"Are there a lot of Reagans in your life that we both know?"

"She's seeing someone, I think."

"Will I be that casual when I'm older?"

He flicked the cigarette and sprayed an aerosol can around the room. "Maybe it's not casual. Why do you have such a fascination with other peoples' relationships? I think we need to dig into that."

"Why do you say it's not casual?"

"Maybe it's not casual, just desperate."

"Desperate for what? Sex?"

"No. Not that. A connection. A human connection with a real person you can reach out and touch. That's all."

"You have to admit, there's an element of casualness about having sex with your receptionist."

"We never did it. Not the whole shebang." He smiled and sat at his desk, finally. "You should be the psychologist. You're getting too much information out of me. More than I get out of you, for sure. You want a notepad so you can write it all down?"

I always did that when I got home, anyway.

"Anything new with Cody? If I'm dishing about my non-existent love life, you have to dish about yours."

"I want to be friends, but I don't know how you do that after I've been his girlfriend. The season premier of *Broken Blue* was on Wednesday — that's our show — and I could just feel his eyes on me. Like he was watching me, not the show."

"Why that show?"

I smiled because thinking about Cody made me feel warm and I let myself feel that. "He's going to be a cop. He says he wants to be CIA or something, but I just know him. He'll be a cop someday. He's intelligent enough to be in the CIA, but when I picture him years down the road, I just see him as a regular guy fighting crime, not like a secret agent or something."

"Do you always take things ten years ahead?"

"I've thought about whether or not you'll invite me to your wedding to Raegan."

"I won't. Because there isn't going to be one."

"Huh. OK."

"If Cody is going to be a cop, where are you going to be?"

He stumped me. I hadn't thought about myself. I could see my dad, hopefully settling down, and if he met a younger woman, maybe having another kid. I thought about Skip and pictured him as a pastor, like his dad. I thought about Lil — she would get married, too, and have a whole slew of kids. I even thought up terrible futures for some of the Circlers. Libby would get fat and her husband would be a chronic cheater and Maia would become a prostitute and a breeding ground for VD. Gus would be a stand-up comedian, but not a very good one, and his parents would pay his rent. And Josh would marry Raegan and their kids would stay in a play-pen in the corner of the waiting room.

"Caroline? Where are you going to be?"

"I don't think about it."

"Why not?"

"I don't know why not. I just can't seem to think past maybe seven or eight years."

"In eight years you'll be turning twenty-four, right?"

"Yes."

"You don't think about being thirty?"

"No."

"You don't think about being twenty-five?"

"No."

"How old was your mom when she died?"

"Twenty-five."

He looked at me as if we had made some sort of a break through.

"I don't think that's why. I just never think too far past college, is all."

"You don't remember her. But you were five years old, weren't you? Wasn't she around much?"

"Do we have to talk about that?"

"I'd like to talk about that. Do you think today we can?"

I felt like I owed it to him. He had confessed that he hadn't gotten lucky with Raegan after all. "I don't know how to talk about somebody I don't know."

"It's sad that she died. I'm sorry for that."

"I want to be mad at her, but my dad says it's easier not to be."

"He's probably right. But are you mad?"

I always stared at his diploma when I didn't want to look him in the eye. "I don't know. I mean…" I sighed loudly, so he would know how inconvenient it was for me to explain it to him. "I didn't know her that well. It's like saying that I'm mad at someone I don't even know for stuff that I'm not even sure they did."

"Well, you did know her. She was your mother. And you do know what she did — she overdosed and stole your time together."

"I don't think her time was ever my time or our time. I don't know how glad she was to have me. Maybe I was part of the problem."

"You can be mad at her. And then you can forgive her. You're skipping some steps. It's perfectly fine to be mad at her. Work through it and forgive her."

"It'll hurt my dad if I'm angry at her."

"Why is that?"

"Because he's not."

"Do you think he's really not? And never has been?"

"Love is blind," I said flatly.

"Is it?"

"Obviously. Or he should be super mad at her. I mean, he's ruined his entire life, never let himself love anyone else. He had a nice girlfriend. One I liked. And when she fell in love with him, he just — I don't know, tossed her out the window. Because he can only love Tressa."

"It sounds like you're a little angry with him."

"I just don't understand any of them. I mean, my Gram — she doesn't like Becca, my dad's high school girlfriend. Why? I don't know. She didn't do anything wrong to my dad. It was a mutual break up. They went away to different schools. Nobody broke anyone's heart, but Gram doesn't like her. But my mother, I mean, she was never good to my dad. She was crazy, went crazy on him, left him to take care of me even before she offed herself. And then, she hated life so much, she hated him and me and the way living made her feel — hated it all so much that she would rather poison herself in a crackhouse than be alive to see the rest of us live. And nobody, and I mean *nobody* is mad at her, not even one little bit? It's ridiculous. I don't think I'm angry at her; she was just a crazy fool. But, God! Why am I the only one who sees it? She's not an angel. She's not perfect. She's not anybody special at all. She's just another addict who croaked one Thanksgiving because she couldn't stand to stuff down one more goddamned piece of turkey with the morons who loved her in spite of all of her shit."

I could feel tears on my face, but I felt almost nothing inside. At least I had said it.

"Am I mad? Yes. I'm mad because they are all blind to what she did to herself and what she did to all of us. I could understand, maybe, if she got mowed down by a drunk driver or something, but she was just a stupid drug addict. And do you know what else I think about sometimes?"

"What?"

"Drugs aren't free. And Teddy loved her. And what she did to him was so wrong. I mean, how do you buy drugs when you don't have any money and you're young and pretty? I see it on the cop shows. I know how young, pretty girls get drugs. And my dad, God, he just loved her so much, you know?"

"I'm sure he did."

"But he's not mad. He just forgives her. Doesn't even blame her. Blames her illness. And now he thinks I have it."

"What's the difference, do you think, between you and her, if you were to have it?"

I wiped my eyes on the back of my hand and a smear of mascara came away with the tears. I wondered how many mascara streaks Josh made in his office. "I suppose, the difference is that I care about everyone enough to do something about it."

"Who do you care about?"

"My dad. And Gram and Gramp. And Jen. And even stupid Cody."

"You get yourself better because of them?"

"Because I don't want to hurt them. And I just don't want to be like her."

"Well, your dad is right about it — she was sick, Caroline. It's not really an excuse, but an explanation. And they've all coped with it in that way, but I don't think you've really coped like that. Maybe you're a little more analytical than all of them. That's OK, to be that way. This is you. It's alright to be angry. But you have to forgive, too. Maybe not just a blind forgiveness, the way your dad does, but maybe a thoughtful sort of forgiveness."

I sunk down in the chair. "How?" I asked, exhausted from thinking.

"If you'd have given her ten years, do you think she'd look at you now — not just you, but you and your dad — and wish she'd have done things differently? Do you think she wanted it the way she had it?"

"I don't know. I think she wanted to be well. I think she wanted to be normal."

"She would be sorry, don't you think?"

"Yes."

"She would be sorry, and you understand that enough to forgive her, don't you?"

It dawned on me at that moment. My mom had never apologized to me for what she had done to me and to all of us and everyone forgave her, even me. Even Teddy, who she hurt the most. Why couldn't I just forgive Cody for the thing with Libby?

"Can I tell you something? Because I trust you now. You've told me things you didn't have to, and I know you did it to gain my trust, and I trust you, Josh."

"OK."

"There are three things I don't forgive Cody for and it's why I can't be his girlfriend anymore."

"OK."

"There was a point when we knew we weren't just friends anymore, but we weren't a couple either. We were just close in a special way and we both knew it. And he kissed someone else."

"And how did you find out?"

"He told me."

"OK."

"Then, he went on a trip over the summer. He ignored me. And he met a girl that he kissed."

Josh raised his eyebrows. "And how did you find out about that?"

"He told me that, too."

"OK," he said, again, as if he were tallying up points as to whether Cody was going to pass some sort of slime ball test or not.

"I got over that, sort of. Maybe not in the best way, but I did. But this last one, I just can't get over. This bitch — this girl who is a complete bitch to me — I don't know how it happened or why, but I walked in on them and I just keep seeing it all the time in my head, when I look at her or him. Or anything. She was kissing him with her shirt off. He wants to kiss me and I think about him kissing her. He can't remember it because he was drunk, and he doesn't know how he got in the room with her or anything."

"And this was the unforgivable?"

"It's not like I'm purposely holding a grudge. I guess it's kind of like my mother. How does life go on just like normal, the people around you go on, but something has changed drastically? In *my* life something has changed drastically and I can't play along with acting normal anymore. And that's why I stayed in bed for a week. Because it seems like life is a game and I can't play it sometimes."

"It's not a game, Caroline. And you know that. People make mistakes. People hurt each other. But you have a choice of how you react to that. That's the only thing in this life you can control. And sometimes that's not easy, but it can be done. Should we work on that?"

That night I found an empty box and I decided to put away her journals and her t-shirts and her polaroids and her jewelry. Trying to figure her out wasn't my job. It wasn't mine or Teddy's or Gram's. That had been her job, and she had given up on it. Just like Josh didn't want to fill in his grandfather's space, I didn't want to fill in Tressa's. I wanted my own space and my own style. And sometimes I even needed to open the window and look outside.

Sometimes it stops, just like that. Like a switch was flipped and a light came on. I woke up one morning and there was something good in me and it was too much not to let it out, not to let it show. It was happiness. And it wasn't just a little bit of happiness, it was a lot of it. I was bursting at the seams with it and I didn't know what to do. Everything seemed too small. Just having cereal for breakfast was too small — I whipped up some egg whites, sliced a tomato, and served it on a piece of wheat toast with light butter. Just wearing mascara was too small — I decided to use the eyeliner. And the eyeshadow. Just wearing a dress was too small. I put on the suede wedge boots that I had bought on a day I felt confident, even though I had never actually felt confident enough to wear them.

Just like that. I was better.

"Where do you want to go for your birthday tonight, Bear?"

It wasn't because it was my birthday that I felt good. I usually felt low on my birthday since the person who gave birth to me died. So, it certainly wasn't that.

I knew he'd expect me to say Alice's or maybe even the diner, but I decided to do something different. "The Boat House."

"The Boat House?"

I knew my dad had taken dates there. It was slightly nicer than most places, but not nearly as nice as The Tavern. I guess they wanted you to feel like you were in the belly of a ship — the floors and beams were made of rustic-looking wood and there were nautical decorations that looked authentic, not the replicas like the chain restaurants had. And when they served your drinks, whether it was water or a margarita, it came on a little navy blue cocktail napkin with *The Boat House* embossed in silver, and that's why I felt like it was a classy place.

"Well, it's your pick. We can certainly go to The Boat House if that's what you want."

I watched him drink his orange juice and decided that he needed to hear how much I loved him. "You know, Dad? I probably don't tell you this enough, but a birthday is a good time to say it, I think. You were a much better dad than you ever had to be and I appreciate it." I hugged him. "I have to go now. Bye."

Walking to school, I smiled the whole way. I waited outside for Lil since I knew her dad would disapprove of my "special" new look. I didn't even mind when we ran into Jordy at the corner, and he and Lil stopped every two seconds to kiss. Their kissing was limited to whatever they could sneak in at school when nobody was looking, and sometimes after school in whatever corner they could find that nobody was occupying. It didn't even look like real kissing, just pecking about each others' faces, and it was humorous and entertaining.

Part of me hoped that Cody would leave a note in my locker, perhaps a birthday card or a gift of some sort. I knew I couldn't let him disappoint me, though. He was Cody and I'm sure he would do absolutely nothing. He might not even have remembered that we were supposed to revisit our relationship status on my birthday.

I saw him walking down the hall, not really paying attention to anything, being his angry old self, and I noticed that he was wearing my favorite shirt. His jeans, as usual, were too tight around the thighs, and he had one side of his shirt tucked in and the other side hanging out. I was pretty sure he hadn't combed his hair, either. He didn't mean to be so disheveled; it just came naturally to him. I watched him turn towards his locker and I decided that I wanted a little bit of him in that moment, so I approached.

He smiled at me. "Good morning."

I leaned towards him until my nose touched his shoulder and told myself I wouldn't lose my shit over his perfect smell. "Do you want to come over right after school?" I asked, quietly.

"For?"

I turned my head slightly and kissed his neck, gently. My lips barely touched his skin, but it was enough for him to understand what I wanted from him.

"Fu-uck," he said, slowly, frustratedly.

I leaned away from him. "Well? Think you can drive me home?"

"Yeah," he whispered.

I smiled as slightly as I could without looking weird, then I walked away from him.

I could feel his eyes on me whenever he was near me. I felt warm and happy and everything felt good. I felt confident and older and in control of myself and it was a new and wonderful feeling. He came to my locker at the end of the day looking expectant, but hesitant.

"What?" I asked with a laugh as I loaded my backpack.

"What is this?" he asked, suspiciously.

"My dad's class is until four thirty. We can have some time."

"Time for what?"

"Didn't you get the hint?" I started to walk away while he stood there in deep consideration of it.

He caught up to me. "I don't understand."

"You will," I said, exercising the tiny bit of power that I knew I had over him. It was like I had become a different person overnight and I wondered if that was what it felt like to be a woman. Certainly turning sixteen didn't change a person just like that. It was something else and I didn't care to figure it out because I liked it and I didn't want to ruin it.

He remained nervous and I reveled in it. I liked that he had to worry about where things were going with me. Usually I was in that position. Usually I worried and questioned myself and wondered what he wanted and if he liked me. I liked turning the tables on him.

When we got out of the Jeep, he slung his backpack over his shoulder.

I looked him in the eye. "You won't be needing that."

He looked scared and I had to try not to laugh at him. I took his hand and led him to my bedroom and closed the door behind us. "You looked so good this morning," I said.

"I did?"

"You know this is my favorite shirt."

He smiled. "It is?"

I nodded.

He looked around. "The necklaces are missing," he pointed out.

"I didn't really want my mom's stuff lying around anymore."

"Why not?"

"Why are we talking so much?"

"What should we do?"

I looked at him for a split second before I started kissing him. It was like a floodgate opened and every sexual feeling I ever had or ever should have had spilled out at that very moment. I fumbled for his belt and he unzipped my dress. I unbuttoned his shirt and he pulled the dress down over my shoulders. I pulled down his pants and he took off his shirt and in a minute I was straddling him on my bed. I was in love with Cody — it was true. But at that moment it could have been anyone, any half-decent looking guy, and I probably would have felt the same way. He got on top of me and kissed me harder and I enjoyed thinking about how his body worked. I wondered if it was just instinct when he pushed his hips into mine, the way he rubbed against me, the way he whimpered when he stopped kissing me.

"You're so hot," I blurted out. I wasn't even sure why I said it.

"So are you." He finally smiled.

"It feels good."

"For you, too?"

"Keep doing what you're doing," I requested.

I had read in *Cosmo* that you should tell a guy what you like and what you want. That's why I was laying it on thick, I suppose. I just let it come right out — whatever wanted to come out of me, and he just continued doing things and looking at me as if I were some sort of mystery that he was hell-bent on solving.

I didn't bother to tell him that he'd figured it out.

"Stop," I finally said.

He looked at me wide-eyed. I smiled and kissed him.

"What happened?" he asked. Confusion was a good look for him. He always looked cute when he struggled to understand something and his little brain wheels worked overtime.

"Caroline," he said seriously. "What's gotten into you?"

"You don't like it or something?"

"Does it seem like I don't like it?"

"Now it does. It seems like you're disappointed." I looked away from him, the caving-in feeling of not being good enough washing over me again.

"Disappointed? No. Confused? Yes." He turned my face back towards his. "Yesterday you would barely even look at me. What is this?"

"Today I felt good."

"Are we together? I need to know."

"How together?" I asked, as if I were some kind of expert on casual dating.

"Like, *together* together."

I faced him and put my arms around him. "Together, like, 'you don't ignore half of my texts' together?"

"I won't do that anymore," he said. "And it was never intentional."

I laughed out loud so he would know that I didn't believe that.

"Together, like, 'you don't kiss anyone else' together?"

"I never wanted to kiss anyone but you."

"Together, like, 'what your friends think doesn't matter' together?"

"Together like I love you and you love me together," he said, just to make sure I had no doubts.

"I do love you, Cody. And maybe you do love me. But the world just can't handle us." I turned away from him to put my bra back on.

"What world? We are in high school. There is no world for us. We're kids."

"You have a world, Cody. And I have a world. And I don't want you to leave yours and I don't want to leave mine. And let's face it, you're going away to school someday, I'm staying. It'll never work out. We're kids, you're right. We should be having fun, though."

"What just happened was fun." He said it desperately as he watched me get dressed.

"It was," I agreed.

"But it doesn't feel right because we're not together."

"We're best friends. Isn't that enough?"

"It's more."

I sat beside him on the bed and took his hand. "We have an expiration date," I said.

"I know," he said sadly, looking down.

"So let's not make it too serious. And let's not shove it down anyone's throat. Let's just feel what we feel and not worry about it. Isn't that fair?"

"Does it mean I can be with you the way we used to be? I want you to be the first person I call when something good happens. And the first person I call when something bad happens. I just want you to be — with me."

"Then stop cheating on me," I said seriously.

"I'm sorry," he said.

"And don't apologize for it anymore."

"OK."

"And don't be so uptight and miserable about our relationship. It is completely separate from that abyss of friends that you have. I don't want to be a part of it."

"I understand."

"I want to be happy now, Cody. Can you let me be happy?"

"I want to be the one who makes you happy, C."
"Then be that. OK?"
He smiled. "So, we're back together?"
I shook my head. "Just let it be what it wants to be."
"What are the rules? Can I hold your hand? Can I kiss you whenever I want to?"
I realized that I had really done a number on him. It was only fair since he had really done a number on me, too. "There are no rules," I said. "Do what you feel like doing. But do it with me."
He smiled and started kissing me again, I guess because there weren't any rules.

My father and I celebrated my birthday at the Boat House. I could see the relief in his eyes when he saw my improvements. We talked and laughed and he told me stories about summer camp and I told him what had been going on in school. We talked about books and music. I could always count on my dad to remind me of everything that a man should be. Usually in situations like that, I thought about my mom and what he had wasted on her, but that night, I felt hope for him. His life wasn't over.

After dinner, I took off the makeup and soaked in a hot bath for a while. It had been a good day. I thought I had straightened things out with Cody, I had spent some time with my dad, I was relaxed, and I was happy. The only thing still weighing on me was that I wondered how long it could possibly last. Nothing good lasts forever.

I smiled at the familiar but unexpected tapping on my window. I opened the window and he climbed in — he now had it mastered.

"I didn't forget about your birthday," he said.
"OK."
"I didn't know what to get you. I'm sorry."
"It's OK. You didn't have to get me anything."
"I got you something a while ago. I never gave it to you, though. I don't know why. I guess I was just afraid it was dumb or you wouldn't like it. I don't know."
"I wouldn't think a gift from you was dumb."
"So, it's not really a birthday gift I guess."

He reached into the pocket of his jacket and handed me a small box. Of course, I knew it was the bluebird necklace, but I took the lid off and tried to act surprised. "The bluebird," I said. I looked at him and smiled. "Well, I needed some necklaces, I guess."

"Yeah. I guess you do now." He helped me put it on and I looked in the mirror at the way it sat slightly below my collarbone. I never expected Cody to buy me a personal gift — a gift that meant something.

"Thank you," I said. "I really love it."

"I didn't know, at first, what that poem meant. It was you, for me. The bluebird was you. That's why I bought you this, when I realized that. But I didn't know what to do with those feelings, so I hid them."

"You can do whatever you want to do with those feelings. They belong to you."

"You're probably right. It doesn't matter if anyone else knows. But it is important that you know. I love you."

I turned around to face him and I put my head on his shoulder.

"Can I stay for a little bit?" he asked.

PART II

Cody
SPRING 2014

17

Her

I THOUGHT I remembered my mom having blonde hair, although I couldn't be sure. I knew her, I knew it was her, but in my head she didn't have brown, permed hair. My dad was big. I didn't exactly remember his facial features, but I knew his voice. It was him. Ricky seemed older than I remembered him. How much time had gone by? "Not much," was the answer I kept getting. Like they didn't want to quantify it for me. They told me not to worry about it because I needed the rest. It wouldn't have mattered anyway because I don't even remember having the accident. I don't remember any of it. I don't remember getting in the car. I don't remember where I was coming from or going to or what time it was or what day it was or what week it was. I sometimes wondered if they were lying to me. Maybe it was no accident at all. Maybe it was all lies and they performed some kind of brain experiment on me, donated me to science because they couldn't pay their mortgage.

So, I guess that's why they kept telling me it was a car accident. Because I kept asking. Because I didn't really believe them. I think I'd feel something. Maybe. If it were that bad.

I didn't know the date or who the president was at first. Maybe they ask you those not-so-important questions first so you don't realize right off the bat that you've forgotten your entire life. I remember my fifth birthday party and my fifteenth birthday party. I can't remember graduating from high school. I took a guess at it and told them that I thought maybe I went to Baylor College because I could see it in my head, the poster and the t-shirt. My dad cried and left the room. My dad didn't look like the crying type. My mom, a nurse, just held my hand and smiled.

It doesn't matter how it all unfolded and how I almost didn't even care that I didn't know these things about myself. The worst part was people telling me who I was. *Something, something, something...do you remember that? Something, something, you remember. You remember, don't you? You have to remember that.* And when I didn't remember I let people down. I made people cry. So I pretended to remember some of it. I guessed and when I got it even close to right, they saw a glimmer of hope.

She didn't do that.

She wasn't there when I woke up. She came later when the others left. It could have been days or a week later. It was hard to recognize the passing of time when I had forgotten years and years of my life.

She knocked lightly on the door and I looked up. When I looked at her I could feel something. I didn't remember her, but my body tingled. I was trying to be conscientious about my expressions matching my feelings, so I smiled. She smiled. *I hope I know her.* That's what I thought.

"Cody?"

Was she asking because she didn't know me or because she thought I didn't know me? "Yes?"

I was sitting up in my bed and she made a cautious approach and sat on the bed beside me. *I must know her. I must.* She was pretty, in a different way than a lot of girls. Her dark hair was the perfect frame for her face and her equally dark eyes looked like they veiled a certain kind of pain. She was edgy and delicate all at the same time and I felt warmer as she got closer to me. I really wished I wasn't wearing grey sweatpants and a nondescript t-shirt that my mother had brought for me. I wished I looked nice.

"I don't know how to do this," she said, nervously.

"What are you doing?" I asked. I had a feeling I knew what she was doing, but she was the first one who came into my room and did it. A couple of times I caught glimpses of people, probably my friends, loitering in the hall, maybe trying to figure out what to say to me. She was the only person who came in.

"Do you remember me?" she asked, quietly. I wasn't very perceptive after the "accident" but I could hear something sad in her voice. Guessing was getting me nowhere. She looked like the kind of person who would see through that, like she didn't carry around false hope with her like a security blanket.

"I feel like I must have known you," I said. That was true.

She inhaled sharply and clasped her hand over her mouth like she was holding back a sob. Not a big dramatic gesture, just what she couldn't help but let escape.

"I'm so sorry," I said. "They are saying it will come back. Maybe most of it and most of the time." I had grown weary of apologizing to my family, but I felt like she deserved it. After all, she came in.

"No, I'm sorry," she said, gaining composure. "I mean, I tried to be prepared, but, oh, God. Why am I telling you? You're lucky to be alive."

"Why?" I asked.

"The accident."

"Are you sure it was an accident?"

"Yes."

"Were you there?"

"No."

"I don't think it was an accident," I said. "I think I would remember something."

"Was that a joke?" she asked.

I smiled. Humor had been my crutch since I lost my memory. My family didn't appreciate it, but it gave the nurses a laugh sometimes.

"What is your name?" I finally asked.

"Caroline. Sometimes you would call me C."

"Where? College? Or high school?"

"They told me not to overwhelm you with information."

"How do we know each other?"

"So, how are you feeling?" she asked, ignoring my question.

"Why aren't you answering me?"

"Is any of that important now?"

I wanted her to tell me, but the room was full of energy. I wanted to insist she tell me, but I was too busy feeling something new and trying to understand where it belonged with me. I memorized her face — I did that now; I memorized things that I didn't want to forget with an urgency and a fear of losing it again. She sat beside me and eventually her hand touched mine and I watched a big tear roll down her cheek. We were silent for a long time. The noises in the hallway, the footsteps, the chatter of nurses, the beep-beep-beep of equipment, it all seemed miles away and she was close. All I knew was that I must have known her well. She was the first person who wasn't trying to make me be somebody that they used to know.

"I brought you something," she finally said.

"What?" I asked.

She reached into her bigger-than-necessary purse and handed me a hat. A gray stocking cap. "I didn't know if your head was going to get cold. You gave me this hat once when my ears were cold."

She must have been referring to the third of my head they had shaved when they decided to drill into my skull. I put the hat on over the bandage. It smelled like coconuts.

"Also, I wrote this down for you. You used to like it."

Next, she gave me a thick piece of paper, folded in half, and a poem was written inside. "Did you write this?"

She smiled. "No."

We had another silence.

"Would you like me to read it to you?" she asked.

"I remember how to read," I confirmed, in case she was wondering.

"I know. You don't have your glasses, though."

"My glasses?"

"You always wore glasses. Maybe you should ask your mom to bring your extra pair? They are in the right hand drawer in the desk in your bedroom."

"You've been in my bedroom?"

She nodded. "I've been in yours and you've been in mine."

"Oh," I said, wanting to guess, but having to wonder why. It seemed like she meant something by it, but I was rusty at the art of reading into things. "Why?"

"Why, what?"

"Why was I in your room?"

She laughed a little, a confirmation that it was best left undiscussed. I wanted so badly to know who she was to me. "I've not trusted anyone who has told me anything so far. But I feel like I can trust you."

"You always seemed to trust me," she said.

"Did you always trust me?"

"Mostly. Even when you did something wrong, you never lied. We didn't really have secrets."

"Did I do something to you?"

"Nothing worth talking about."

I extended my finger to touch the side of her hand and she looked at me.

"Are you really OK?" she asked. "You can tell me. You used to tell me everything."

"I'm getting tired," I said. I didn't want to admit to her that I hated that everyone was disappointed in me. That everyone was angry and sad about me and what they lost. I didn't feel like I lost anything. I didn't know any better. But for the first time, I felt like something was missing for me, and I felt like that something was her.

"I'm sorry," she said. "I should go."

I looked at her, trying hard to remember her, anything about her — about us. "Can I have your phone number?"

18

Waiting

I WAITED about an hour before I texted her. Just a simple, *Hey...this is Cody.* And she texted me back, *I missed getting texts from you.* I wondered about it for a while, then I asked, *Were you going to come back again?...Would you like me to?...Yes...I can come tomorrow...Maybe at dinner time? That's when my parents go home...Why do you say that?...They're just annoying is all. Everyone is so annoying, but you're not...Why?...They bug me to try to remember things and I just can't. You didn't ask me that...I don't want you to feel bad...I actually don't...I will see you tomorrow then.*

I refused to stay in bed all the time. I sat in the chair, I wandered the halls, I got put back in my room. I texted Caroline and asked her to bring me a good book when she came. I snuck out again. My mom brought me more clothes that I didn't remember having. Nobody else came to see me and nobody bothered to stand in the hall. Just my parents, my brother, and finally Caroline.

She brought me macaroni and cheese and strawberry milk. How did she know that I liked those things? Furthermore, how did I know that I liked those things? We didn't talk much while we ate our dinner. She didn't seem like the type who would burst into tears if I asked her questions that I should already know the answers to, like my parents did.

"Did I not have friends?" I finally asked.

She smiled. "I always thought you had too many friends."

"Really?" I poked at my food, because eating and thinking at the same time proved to be too much for me. "Then why are you the only person who has come to see me?"

"I don't know. Maybe they are busy and I'm not. Or maybe you didn't keep in touch with them much after you went away to college and they all went away to college."

"Then why did I keep in touch with you?"

She shrugged and looked out the window. I decided to leave it alone.

I asked her to come back the next day and the day after that, and pretty soon I didn't ask anymore, she just came. We usually sat quietly. It was as if there was no need to talk. We sat in the courtyard and enjoyed the sunlight. I wanted to be near her. I knew there was something about her, I just didn't know what. We were connected somehow, but I didn't know how.

At night, when it was as quiet in the hospital as the hospital could be, I worked on remembering her. I didn't try to remember family vacations or my friends or my college. I thought about her inky hair, soft but sharp around her face. I thought about the way her eyebrows rose right before she laughed. I thought about how her eyes were so dark they were almost black. I thought about her perfect little upturned nose.

I was moved to a rehabilitation facility. It was much farther away and people didn't come to see me all the time. They gave me little tests to see if I could function, to see if I could comprehend things. Yes, I could follow the directions on a Betty Crocker box to make a cake. Yes, I could balance a checkbook. The injury hadn't affected my speech or my motor skills. Everything seemed to be fine, but I had to stay, like a jail sentence. As if having an accident wasn't bad enough, I had to be locked up with a bunch of people who *really* had problems. The thing I didn't mind was that it was like school, with little lessons and little tests. It was like elementary school, which I remembered just fine. The thing I did mind was that Caroline came only on Saturdays instead of everyday. I surprised her by being able to recite part of the poem, and for some reason that made her cry, but it seemed like a good thing when she cried, not a bad thing like when my dad had cried. She hugged me very tightly and I could feel her tears running down my neck.

19

Home

HOME. It was familiar, but different. I didn't recognize some things, and some things I did. In my room I found my Baylor t-shirt, which I knew that I had, and the poster was on the wall. I sat still on my bed, afraid to open any drawers, or the closet, for fear that I might not know the things I found. It was the first time since the accident that I was scared of the memory loss. Maybe every day I would open one drawer or one box or one notebook.

Sleepless, I sat at my desk, trying to decide what to do. I thought about my consultations with neurologists and psychologists and whoever else they could find to try to figure out a rhyme or reason to my memories. I wasn't remembering things like brain injury patients usually did. Things weren't coming back to me. Times and dates didn't matter. They concluded that I was subconsciously choosing what to remember and not remember. I couldn't understand it. If it were a choice, surely I'd want to remember Caroline — I'd choose to remember Caroline. What was stopping me? They placed the blame and the burden on me, and it didn't sit well with my parents. They seemed to have forgotten that I almost died and decided to be resentful towards me.

I heard the baby crying and it sounded familiar and ordinary, but I didn't remember my nephew Rocky at all. I didn't remember my brother's girlfriend, Shelby. She was a short blonde with a puffy face and a bubble butt. She wore her t-shirts too tight. I remembered that my brother had been a college student and was not very good at it. He dropped out to sell car stereos, wore a large watch, and used a lot of hair gel. He used to wear backwards hats and listen to rap music.

At the rehab, I had a therapist who told me to start writing things down. Dreams, memories, feelings. Maybe something would trigger me to remember. I was starting to hate that word — *remember*. I opened the desk drawer and found the extra pair of glasses Caroline had told me about. When I put them on, I could see everything much better. *Get glasses*. I wrote it down in the notebook. I decided to tackle the drawer. I found ticket stubs to a movie from three years ago. A community pool pass, expired. A few trifold college pamphlets. Colleges I didn't go to. Maybe I would look into them again. I wasn't sure if I could return to Otterbein, since I didn't remember going there and I couldn't really remember wrestling, which was what my partial scholarship was for. I was also told that my major was in criminology and that I wanted to join the CIA someday. Messy longish hair, now lopsided. Smile, crooked when I could manage one. I looked at myself in the mirror and laughed one night after they told me. I did not look like a CIA agent, not by any stretch of the imagination. I looked like the less attractive brother of the drummer from a punk-pop band. I wrote the next thing down in my notebook. *What does the CIA even do?*

The last thing, under the pamphlets and other stupid junk, was a photograph of me, my hair a little shorter, and Caroline, looking a little younger. We were sitting together on a step, maybe. The house was unfamiliar. I had my arm around her and I was looking at her more than at the camera. I flipped the picture over, and in nice cursive handwriting:

July 4, 2010 Cody, I thought you would like this. Love you, Gram

I knew that my grandmothers, both of them, were dead. I remembered that. And I never called either of them Gram. I flipped the picture over again and looked at us. My body language said that I really liked her. The look on my face said it, too. I tried to remember the moment.

I made the final note in my journal. *Who is Caroline to me?*

Even though I had "learned" how to take care of myself in rehab, my mom insisted on staying home with me the first day. I felt like a visitor in their world. Shelby and Rocky sat at the kitchen table while my mom put pancakes down in front of us. She looked at my t-shirt then looked away quickly. I wondered what that meant. *Why does Baylor irritate my parents?* Rocky hit the tray on his high chair and Cheerios flew up and back down to the floor. He squealed. I tried to smile at the strange little alien. He made baby noises. Shelby went on talking about something like it was any other day, and like I knew what she was talking about. I learned to just nod and agree, which got me through a lot of conversations.

After breakfast, my mom asked me if I wanted to go anywhere or do anything or if I needed anything.

"I need new glasses," I said. "I think these are old."

She smiled. "Of course. I'll make an appointment for you."

"Also, I'd like a hat." I knew I had a lovely scar on my head that was barely being covered by the short hair growing around it. "Maybe a haircut."

"I'll cut your hair," Shelby volunteered.

I looked at her, unconvinced.

"I'm a licensed beautician. I can cut it," she said, somewhat less enthused by my doubt.

"Yeah, OK."

"Anything else?" my mother asked.

"Yes. I'd like to go see Caroline today."

She pursed her lips. I grew to realize when she was getting a short fuse with me.

"She's probably at work," Shelby offered up. My mom shot a glance at her.

"Where does she work?"

"Rachel's."

"That's a coffee place, right?"

Shelby smiled. "Yes. You remembered?"

"Yes," I said, basking in the glow of the small victory. I closed my eyes for a moment and tried to remember how to get there. The full effect of losing my driver's license didn't hit me until that moment. Because of my injury, my license was suspended for six months. I didn't think it would be a big deal since I didn't remember ever driving in the first place. It would pass quickly; the three months would be summer months, and once I figured out what to do in the fall, I'd only have three months to go. I could get my license again by Christmas. But the moment that I realized I'd be given a hard time about seeing Caroline, I felt the sting of my wings being clipped.

I tried to take it all in as we drove to the mall. I had to make a conscious effort to think about my surroundings. It would help me to remember, the therapist said. I never remembered my mother being so generous, although I couldn't be sure, but she insisted on buying me not only a hat, but some shirts and socks, too. I put the hat on right away so nobody would stare at my head. It wasn't that I took offense to it; I was afraid that it offended everyone else.

When we got home, Shelby was eagerly waiting to cut my hair. She did it all very gently, from shampooing around my scar, to wrapping a towel around my shoulders, to the precise way she cut it. She took a couple of inches from what was left, and it was quite close to the length that it had been in the picture of me and Caroline. When she was entranced with the slow snipping of the scissors, I decided she might let down her guard enough to tell me something.

"Why don't my parents like Caroline?"

"It's not that they don't like her. Maybe they just don't think that you're good for each other."

"Why not?"

"Because you're young."

"So when you're young, you're not supposed to have feelings?"

"I thought you didn't remember her."

"I don't. But I feel something when she's around, so I think we must have liked each other. Did we?"

She didn't answer right away. "I never asked questions about you and Caroline."

"You can't tell me? That's fine. I'll find out eventually. I already found a picture of us."

"I thought Pam took them all down." I could tell that she knew immediately that she wasn't supposed to let that slip.

"She took them down?"

"I mean, all the pictures of all your friends. She thought it would be too confusing for you."

"I had a lot of friends?"

"You did seem to have a lot of friends. You had a big group of friends."

"And none of them came to see me?"

She sighed. "No offense, Cody, but really, what are people supposed to say to you? It's not easy."

"Do I make it hard?" I asked.

"Not on purpose. It just...is. It's hard to always have to think about it. It's hard to remember that for you, it's starting all over again from the beginning."

She was right. But why, then, was Caroline so willing to do it?

"It wasn't always on," Shelby finally said.

"What?"

"You and Caroline. It wasn't that serious. On again, off again. OK?"

"Why did you tell me?"

"Because I don't think it's really fair to keep your own life a secret from you. It isn't right. I don't know a lot about it, but I know it wasn't that serious. You were together sometimes."

"Were we together when the accident happened?"

"I don't know, Cody. You were — are — a pretty private person when it comes to that stuff."

20

Friends

IN MY ROOM, I went through my closet, remembering some clothes and not others. I had a lot of wrestling shirts. I couldn't remember ever wrestling a day in my life. It didn't even appeal to me when I thought about the prospect of wrestling. Or of *needing* to wrestle just to go to school. It sounded like a job, and not a very good one. And, as far as jobs went, I knew I was going to have to find one. It would have to be within walking distance, and maybe one where I didn't interact much with the general public, to avoid the risk of running into someone I'm supposed to know.

Somebody was ringing the doorbell and when I realized I finally was alone in the house, I decided to answer it. I grabbed my hat from the dresser and adjusted it on my head so the scar wouldn't show.

He stood taller than me and had a blonde buzz cut and a good tan. He wrapped his arms around me and I awkwardly reciprocated the gesture. It certainly didn't feel natural. When he let go, I really didn't know what to say. "Hi," I offered.

"I feel like I haven't seen you in so long," he said.

"When did you see me last?"

"Gee, it must have been around Christmas."

"Oh," I said, trying to act like I knew what he was talking about. I wasn't sure how to react — to just admit that I had no idea who he was, or to act like I did and hope he'd go away before he realized I didn't.

"I'm sorry." He extended his hand. "I'm Skip."

I shook his hand. "Cody."

"Yes, I know."

"Come in," I said, since I obviously knew him. We sat together on the couch and I offered him a drink. He would only accept a glass of water.

"I really wanted to see you in the beginning, but I wasn't sure if you were ready for visitors. I asked Caroline about you all the time."

I immediately put my guard up. Why did *he* see Caroline all the time? "How do you know her?" I asked, almost standoffishly.

"She's my sister's best friend. And we all went to high school together. The four of us. Lilly is in Belize now. A missionary. When this happened to you — Lilly can't get in touch all the time. She asked me to keep checking in on you. And on Caroline. I came to the hospital and sat with Caroline, but it was before your parents allowed you to have visitors."

"Allowed?"

"There was a list. But we sat in the waiting room quite a bit."

"OK." I wasn't sure how to feel about my parents making a list and not putting Caroline on it.

"You and I were grappling partners in wrestling for years."

"We were friends?"

"Well, you had your own friends, really. But we got along pretty well."

"My parents don't tell me anything," I admitted.

"It's fine. We don't have to talk about any of that. I just wanted to see you and to see if you needed anything or see if you wanted to hang out sometime. I don't know where to go from here. I prayed for you a lot, though, buddy. A lot. And look. You came through."

"I came through," I agreed, but my mind was already elsewhere. "I do need something, actually."

"What's that?"

"I'd like to see Caroline."

He smiled. "Oh. You like her?"

"Well, I think she was my girlfriend. Was she?"

"It wasn't quite that simple, but yes. At times."

I instantly liked Skip since he didn't seem like he wanted to hide my life from me. "Why only sometimes?"

"I think you should ask her that. I never knew all the details of it."

I felt like Skip was someone I could talk to. "I text her, but I'm embarrassed to ask where she lives. It feels like I should know and I don't want to hurt her feelings."

"I don't think she'd expect you to know."

"I want to surprise her," I said.

I tried to remember the way to her house. I lived on Denver (I remembered that, but was made by my mother to carry a card stating it nonetheless) and from there, we crossed a state road, made one left and two rights, and pulled into the driveway of a gray four-square with lackluster landscaping. I got out of the car and waited for Skip to knock on the door.

Sometimes I thought maybe I remembered someone a little bit. Caroline's dad looked familiar, but I didn't know his name, and had I seen him on the street, I wouldn't have associated him with Caroline. He hugged me — everyone wanted to hug me — then took a step back and looked at me. "Wow," he said, quietly. "Wow, Cody, you look great. Come in, come in," he said, stepping aside. Many things felt like deja vu since my injury, and being there felt like it, too. "Can I get you anything? How do you feel? Sit down."

Skip followed me in and we sat at the high top table together. Caroline's dad went to the refrigerator and got out a half gallon of milk, a bottle of water, and a canister of strawberry Nesquik. He mixed the powder and milk in a glass and sat it in front of me. He gave the bottle of water to Skip. He must have known me if he knew that I liked strawberry milk. Caroline knew it, too.

"How are you?" he asked again.

"I feel pretty good. Is Caroline home?"

A smile slowly spread over his lips. "You get right to the point, don't you?"

Skip raised his eyebrows. He seemed sympathetic to my condition, and realized he'd have to introduce us. "Cody, this is Caroline's dad. Mr. Bryant."

"I'd say you can call me Teddy, but you never would." He sat across from me and reached over to shake my hand. He was younger than my parents, by what I would guess to be a lot. He had a kind face, and I could see the resemblance between him and his daughter.

"I'll call you Teddy."

"She's not home, though. She's at work."

I tried to hide my disappointment.

"It's alright. She'll be home in an hour. Do you want to wait?"

I looked at Skip. He was my ride.

"Well, there I go thinking again. Thinking about how you used to wait, to listen to records and wait for her. I'm sorry for assuming that you'd still want to do that."

"I came here with Skip. He drove me."

"It's fine. I'll take you home later. Or maybe Caroline will. Are you staying for dinner?" Teddy got up and opened the cupboard next to the refrigerator. "She said you'd be coming around, so she bought your favorite." He turned around again with a box of macaroni and cheese.

I must have spent a lot of time with them.

"Or we could just get pizza," he said. "Do you still like Alice's pizza?"

"Who is Alice?" I asked.

He looked like he was sorry for saying it. "It's just the name of the pizza place."

I wanted to stay and Teddy had let Skip off the hook for being my chauffeur. I asked Skip to put his number in my phone before he left, then I sat quietly in the kitchen with Teddy.

"So. I used to like records?"

"You like records," he assured me. "Come with me," he said, going to the large collection of vinyl in the living room. "You like Led Zeppelin. And anything Motown."

"Motown?"

"Smokey Robinson. The Temptations. Listen." He carefully slid a record from its sleeve and placed it on the turntable. There was something familiar about the crackling of the needle on the vinyl coming through the speakers. Then the music began.

"I liked this song?" I asked.

"You like this song," he said, talking over the loud music. "Maybe it's the English professor in me, but you shouldn't talk about yourself in the past tense."

"I can't remember anything," I reminded him.

"Maybe you've lost your memory, but you're not dead."

He had a point. When it came to the chorus, somehow I knew the words. Remembering small things gave me hope that I would remember more. After we listened to a few records, we started to have a conversation. Mostly because I wanted to ask some questions.

"Did I come here a lot?"

"You spent some time here, yes."

"I think I was, am...was...Caroline's boyfriend. Am I? Or was I when I had the accident?"

"I don't know. I could never tell when you were together or not together."

"Why not?"

"Because you were best friends. And I don't think, for Caroline, that there was ever anybody else."

"For me there was?"

"I don't know. What I do know is that you are very special to her, whether you are just friends or more. I don't think she ever loved anyone else."

"She loved me?"

"Maybe that's a conversation for you to have with her."

"I try having conversations with people. Nobody wants to talk to me. The therapist says I should have my memory jogged. But nobody will tell me anything, I think on account of it being too hard for them to see that I can't remember. It's easier to ignore it. And sometimes I think my parents think I'm faking it. They think if they hide all the truths from me that one day I'll slip up and let it out."

"They think you're faking it?"

"The doctors told them that pure retrograde amnesia is rare."

"What does that mean?"

"That I just don't remember things about myself. I can remember facts, like things I've learned in school. I can remember how to make scrambled eggs and how to write my name. I remember my birthday. I can remember a lot of my early childhood and some things from my early teens. I don't remember anything, really, after turning fourteen or fifteen. Not personal things, but I do remember the things I learned. I just don't remember learning them. And then college — I don't remember anything about college. I didn't even know my major."

"I'm sorry. It has to be hard for you."

"Aggravating sometimes. I keep asking everyone about Caroline. Nobody will tell me. She doesn't even tell me. I don't know why."

"So, the doctors told them to jog your memory, but they won't?"

"No. It's too hard for them to realize that..."

He looked at me, patiently, as if he were used to these kinds of conversations.

"That maybe I'm not exactly who I used to be. And the only person who seems OK with that is Caroline."

"Caroline is a very understanding person. She's been through a lot."

"She has?"

"She will tell you about it, I'm sure. Eventually."

"Isn't there anything you can tell me about her — or about us?"

He smiled. "You had a favorite show you watched together on Wednesday nights. *Broken Blue*. Even the reruns. You guys liked to watch it."

I made a mental note of it. She came home after a little while, and something felt complete about me when she was around. I was a little nervous, the way a person might feel if they had a crush on someone. I don't remember ever having a crush, though.

Teddy looked at his watch. "Well, I think I'll head over to my office for a while."

Caroline looked at her dad as if she was surprised.

He opened his wallet and put two twenties on the coffee table. "You kids get some dinner. OK?"

"OK," she said.

When he left, I approached her in the kitchen. "Hi."

"Hi," she said.

"Are you mad that I came here?"

"No. Just surprised."

"Skip brought me."

"Oh."

"Sorry I didn't text you yesterday. It was...annoying. My mom was hovering around. And Shelby."

She looked at me, puzzled. "It's OK."

"Is something wrong?" I sensed that something wasn't quite right, but then again, everything felt that way.

"No."

"Can we talk?"

"Let me get a shower and out of my work clothes first."

"OK."

I looked at Teddy's records while she was in the bathroom, but I was drawn to the door of her bedroom. I had been in there before. Maybe I would remember something. Of all the things I wanted to remember, I so desperately wanted to remember her the most. The pastel walls didn't seem familiar. The necklaces. The clothes. The pictures — pictures mostly of us. And a picture of a gorgeous blonde woman with a younger Teddy. I stared at the pictures. School dances, graduation, other moments. The poem, the bluebird poem, taped to her mirror. The soft stack of pillows. The slightly opened window. I wanted to remember it. But I didn't.

I touched the pillow, just to see if maybe the feel of it would reawaken me.

"Are you OK?" I heard from behind me.

"I'm sorry. I just want to know so badly." I looked at her dripping hair and the way she had the towel wrapped around her body.

"What do you want to know?" She began to busy herself with getting dressed and asked me to turn around. I obeyed, but just knowing she was behind me, naked, did something very real to me.

She sat on the edge of the bed and invited me to sit with her. "How much am I supposed to even tell you?"

"I want to know everything."

"It wasn't always good."

"Was it me?"

"Sometimes it was you. Sometimes it was me. Sometimes it was us."

"Did you love me?" I had to know.

She smiled, a little sadly. "I did love you, actually. Still do. I never stopped." She looked towards the window. "Not for lack of trying to stop."

"Why did you try?"

She took my hand. "Don't you know how lucky you are to get a clean slate and not to remember the bad?"

"Lucky?"

"OK, that was a bad choice of words." She sighed. "We were always thinking that the best thing would be to split up. And we would. And we tried. But we were always drawn back together for some reason. Like magnets or something. When we started college you went away to school and I spent a month with a broken heart, trying to get over you. Pretty soon it was Thanksgiving and we made plans. Then it was like walking on air until you came home for winter break. Then we fell totally in love again. Then we sucked at the long distance thing because I felt like I was holding you back. We split again. Then you came home for spring break and we couldn't stay away from each other, then I had summer to cling to. And sophomore year was the same exact thing. Once we were within a few miles of each other, there was an attraction. I tried to let you go, but there you would be, at that window right there. At two o'clock in the morning, when you would realize that what we were doing — breaking up — felt awful. Do we have to go into the details?"

"No." I stared at our intertwined hands, her black nail polish, her veins. I wanted to be the blood that was rushing through her body. "What about before college? Look at the pictures. We were together in high school."

"You were just a boy. I was just a girl. It was kid stuff."

"Tell me how it started, at least."

"A geometry project. I did the math. You drew the graphs. We were partners."

"And we fell in love over graphing?"

She laughed. "Not quite. It took time. You had friends who always pulled you in another direction, and your parents, too. And wrestling and a job. We fell in love when we got the chance to, I suppose. And you always, no matter what you did wrong, you always told me about it; you told me the truth. We didn't have secrets because we were friends first and we needed that."

"What did I do that was wrong?"

"You'd disappear sometimes, not call or text. Other stuff. Let's not talk about it."

"I was a bad boyfriend. God, that's embarrassing."

"You didn't know what you were doing. I found it charming in a way."

"Did we ever..."

She looked at me. I thought maybe she was hurt.

"I'm sorry if we did and I don't remember. I don't remember anything."

"I know you don't remember, Cody. I just feel weird telling you about it."

I flopped back onto her bed, exasperated.

"I'm sorry. It just feels like I'd be telling you my version of it."

"I don't have a version. As far as I know, I'm a virgin."

"You're not."

I stared at her ceiling for what seemed like forever, wondering if I'd ever been in her bed before.

She lay down beside me.

"Can't you tell me something? Just one story about us?"

She giggled and turned towards me. "You had this shirt you always wore and...it was my favorite shirt on you. One time we went to a party and you got drunk and I walked you home. You threw up on that same shirt and I took it home and washed it for you so your parents wouldn't find out. And before I loved anything else about you, I always just loved the way you smelled."

She gently took my hat off and ran her finger around the outline of the scar. "I don't care how I got you back, Cody. The point is, I got you back. And whether you remember me or not is beside the point because I think there is something deeper that connects us, not just crappy high school memories."

I hoped she was right because I didn't know how to make a person fall in love with me, and I didn't know how to fall in love either. She made it sound like it didn't happen on purpose, though, so there was a chance.

21

Family

WE LIKED to take walks down to the college campus where she went to school and where her dad taught. Around the little lake. Through the rows of seats in the amphitheater. Past the painted rock. Up the hill and the back way to her house. Sometimes we visited Mr. Bryant in his office and looked through all of his books.

Mr. Bryant, or Teddy as I was supposed to call him, gave me a great book called *The Bell Jar* and I read it in two days after I got my new glasses. He told me it was an amazing book, and it was. He told me he had given it to me once before to read, and when I asked him why, he told me it was one of his favorite books because it reminded him of Caroline's mother. When I asked him what happened to her, he simply told me that she died. She was the pretty woman from the picture and Caroline didn't even slightly resemble her. He gave me a lot of good books to read that summer, like *In Cold Blood* and *Tender is the Night*. I began to realize that every book he gave me was a book I had already read and that maybe it was his way to try to jog my memory — with books and records.

Caroline didn't want to come to my house. I never got the whole story; I just knew it was on account of my mom and dad not seeming to like her too much, but only because they wanted what was best for me and being tied to a girl, I guess they thought, wasn't best for me.

"Let's not tell them we're spending so much time together," she said.

I begrudgingly agreed to it.

Caroline helped me with everything. She helped me pick out the clothes I had liked to wear. She helped me get a job at Alice's Pizza. She bought me the DVD collection of all seven seasons of *Broken Blue* and on Wednesday nights, we watched it and she told me all of the reasons I wanted to join the CIA. None of it sounded very intriguing to me. I laughed when I thought of myself as a secret agent. It seemed awfully ridiculous to picture myself as one, and that's why I couldn't help but laugh.

Another thing really bothered me was the thought that I was expected to get back into the sport of wrestling. I had absolutely no interest in it. It didn't make sense to me and nothing about it felt familiar. My dad brought it up almost every day and I talked to Skip about it to see if I could get even a glimmer of recognition for the sport I supposedly loved and excelled at. The only thing that came out of it was bi-weekly trips to the gym with Skip where I realized that I was stronger than I thought and I started to enjoy working out. I tried to get him to show me some of the maneuvers, but he was afraid because the scar on my head reminded him that he could possibly hurt me. Couldn't everyone be hurt?

It was the middle of July when I started working at Alice's. Teddys ex-girlfriend was the manager, and she agreed to keep me in the back, simply because I was uncomfortable about seeing people I couldn't remember.I stayed in the back mindlessly topping pizza with pepperoni and washing dishes and sweeping and mopping at the end of the night when everyone was gone. I liked putting the chairs up on the tables and seeing the shiny floor when it was all done. I think I mostly liked that task because I was alone.

Caroline was so protective over me that she insisted on picking me up after work, even at two o'clock in the morning. She had thought up a bunch of scenarios of things that could happen to me if I walked home in the middle of the night, everything from getting hit by a car to being abducted by evil-doers.

When I was working, I could see out into the restaurant and I had to wonder when I looked at people, did I know them, were they my friends? I thought it everywhere I went. At Rachel's I wondered if everyone in the room knew me and knew about the accident and was afraid to talk to me. I didn't go out without my hat because I knew that the scar would even further deter people from approaching me if they knew me.

By far, the worst day of the entire summer was the day I told my dad that I didn't want to go back to Otterbein. He was not happy at all. I raised my voice, pretending to be just as frustrated as he was. "Do you think I wanted to lose my memory? Do you think I wanted it to be like this? Do you think I wanted to throw away years of my life and everything I worked for? It's not that I don't want to do it, Dad. I *can't* do it. I *can't*!"

He looked at me, his face turning red, his cheeks puffing up, but all he could say was, "You're spending too much time with that girl."

"She's done nothing but help me. She's tried to help me remember. And she's never said one word about me staying here. Not one word. I haven't even talked to her about it. She doesn't even know. For all she knows, she thinks I'm going back to school."

He sat at the kitchen table, weary from arguing with me. I had a feeling I might not have put up much of a fight in the past. The accident had changed me.

"If I don't fill out my transfer paperwork, I'm going to have to take a semester off."

"Just go back, Cody. Go back to your life and maybe you'll remember."

"I don't have a life."

"You're not even trying."

"I can't do it. I've just found out that life can be very short. I am not spending what I have left of it trying to remember the past. Some people have learned to live with that. Why can't you and Mom?"

"Alright, Cody. So, what is your major going to be?"

"I'm going to leave it for now."

"Why? You don't remember wanting to be a cop, right?"

"I don't think I wanted to be a cop."

"So, you know that but you don't know how to wrestle?"

"I have to withdraw from Otterbein and my scholarship. Dad, this isn't junior varsity wrestling. If you make me do this, go out there against these college guys, I'm going to get hurt."

"You're psychic, right? That's how you know all of this."

"I don't want to fight with you. I'm just not ready to go and figure out a whole life again in September when I just started to figure out my life here."

"I don't think you've tried to figure out anything."

I couldn't do anything but walk away.

22

Clues

ONE DAY we sat in front of the lake staring at the ducks swimming around. I took off my shirt to work on my tan.

"Why don't we ever go to the pool?" I asked.

"I didn't think you'd want to. I mean, some of your old friends might be there."

"I'm not even sure why I'm avoiding them at this point. I mean, my own parents can't even accept this. Do you think it's going to hurt anymore if my friends don't understand? Why haven't they come around yet? Why haven't they called to see if I'm OK? What kind of friends were they?" I waited for any signs that she would tell me what was going on with them, but she just stared out into the water.

"Three times you kissed someone else."

"Huh?" It caught me off guard.

"Before you wanted to know how it was between us. And I told you that you always told me the truth even when things were bad. Well, that was what you did. Three times, you kissed someone else."

"Why?"

She laughed a little. "I don't know why. I guess because you wanted to. Or because you were drunk. Or both. Or because everyone always made you feel like we didn't belong together. Even when we were just friends."

"My parents."

"Not just your parents. They didn't even know about us for ages. Your friends. And later, your parents, too."

"That doesn't make sense."

"Does anything?"

I thought about it for a long time. That night I sat in my room thinking about it. I couldn't sleep and I stared at the Baylor poster and I thought about it. I found my high school yearbook and I flipped through the pages and I still thought about it. If it didn't make sense then, how the hell would any of it make sense now? Maybe it was time to let it go. Maybe it was time to just go forward and not think about the past at all.

When a person looks at a high school yearbook, it becomes clear who is popular and who is not. I suppose I was moderately popular while Caroline was not. I was in the National Honor Society. I lettered in wrestling. I was in the German Club. I was on the Homecoming Court. I was in the Spirit Club. I did a lot of things. I must have been pretty busy. I tiptoed into the living room and turned on my parents' desktop computer. I clicked through photos. I had the same friends at every birthday party. They were the same friends in my graduation photos. They were the same friends that it seemed like I did everything with. My parents had an abundance of pictures of me with my friends and very few pictures of me with Caroline.

I slipped on my shoes and a hoodie and walked to Caroline's house. I texted her to wake her up and she let me in. I liked the way she looked with sleepy hair and no makeup and pajamas. Something felt familiar about it, but I was starting to get used to that almost familiar feeling.

"What are you doing here?"

"I couldn't sleep." Honestly, I usually couldn't sleep. My neurologist wanted me to see a counselor. I had put it off, not wanting my parents nagging me about something else, nagging me to get help for my problems and at the same time denying there was a problem when it was convenient for them. When they wanted me to go back to Otterbein, to wrestling, to my scholarship, to my dorm, and away from Caroline.

"OK. Why?"

"I'm confused. I'm curious. Or something. I don't know. I want to know about my life, and it's not like I even care that much about it. I'm just tired of being in the dark. It's like — if we would've started watching *Broken Blue* in the middle of the series. Right? That's why you bought me the DVDs. I just need to know a little bit. Just anything." I handed her the yearbook.

We went into her bedroom and she shut the door part way. "OK. What do you want to know?"

"Who were my friends?"

She flipped through the first few pages until she came to someone I should've known, and ended up patiently telling me about my group of friends, who did what, which ones I liked more and which ones I just tolerated. She told me about my first kiss during a game of spin the bottle. She told me about my second and third kiss, too. I asked her how she knew about it and she said that I had told her. I asked her about the first time we kissed and she said it didn't matter. We lay in her bed after a while staring at the ceiling.

"I'm glad I told you everything."

"You are?"

"Yes. I'm glad that you can tell me. It seems kind of weird that I told you all of those things, but this must have been the reason for it."

"You told me a lot. You kept a lot in, too. There were plenty of things I didn't understand."

"Well, I guess that's all gone now."

"I guess so," she agreed.

"Why won't you tell me about the two of us?"

"I don't want you to feel obligated to be what you were to me before."

"I don't feel that way," I said, quickly. "I spend time with you because I want to, not because you were my girlfriend."

She rolled towards me and touched my face. "We never really had a name for it, Cody. I just couldn't stop it from happening."

"What?"

"The way I felt. I'd get mad at you. I'd swear, I'd promise myself that I'd never fall for you again, but I always did. Some way, somehow. I always did. Being near you was just irresistible. I just wanted to be near you."

"Do you still?"

She smiled with a certain sadness. "I'm not the one who lost my memory. What do you think?"

I stared at her, face to face. Almost nose to nose, and I wondered if I should kiss her, but it didn't seem like the right time. It felt like a time to wait.

23

Escape

WHEN I WOKE up in the morning, she wasn't there. I wondered if she had gone to Rachel's to work, and if she had, how awkward it would be if Mr. Bryant found me in her bed. I reached for my glasses and looked at my phone. It was six o'clock. I thought I could sneak out without him hearing me. I got up and quietly made my way towards the kitchen, but I heard her in the bathroom and it sounded like she was throwing up. I pushed on the unlatched door a bit.

I startled her and she knocked a bottle of pills to the floor.

We both bent down to reach for them, but she grabbed them first and put them into the medicine cabinet. "Are you OK?" I asked.

"Who, me? Yeah."

"Were you sick?"

"No," she said. She wasn't a good liar.

"Are you sure you're not sick?"

"I'm fine," she insisted.

"Do you have to go to work?"

"I'm off today."

"Me, too. And tomorrow." I had an idea. "Let's do something today."

"Like what?"

"What would *you* like to do?"

"I'd like to visit my Gram. My dad is too busy right now, though."

"Let's go. Can we?"

"I'll have to see if I can use my dad's car."

I went home to get a shower and change my clothes. My mom had already left for work and Shelby and Rick sat at the table feeding Rocky. My brother liked to act important, crunching numbers in his notebook. He had deadlines and quotas and he liked to frequently use those words. He scowled at me when I came in.

"Mom was worried," he said flatly.

"Sorry. I fell asleep at Caroline's."

"Right."

I didn't feel like explaining myself to him. I got a shower and shaved, wanting to make a good impression on Caroline's grandparents. They were going to be the first people from my forgotten past that I was making an effort to meet. I wanted to look presentable. I wrote a note to my mother: *Don't worry about me. I went with Caroline to visit her grandparents. I'll be back tonight or tomorrow.* She wouldn't like it, but I needed to get away. I needed to spend time with the one person who wasn't nagging me to remember her. But still, a little part of me wondered why she didn't seem to care about it.

One thing I realized when I lost my memory was that it was awfully hard to have conversations with people because they knew me and I didn't know them. I didn't know what I should or could talk about. Either way, I was completely lost and lacking in words. It was never like that with Caroline. She knew that I didn't know her and that she no longer knew me and that it would have to be like starting over, so we used the hour and a half drive as an opportunity to talk about things. She told me about Gram and Gramp, not about the times I had met them before, but simply that they really liked me. She told me about her Aunt Jen in the Peace Corps and how Gramp was a Vietnam veteran and how Gram was a wonderful cook. She told me that when we got there, Gram would surely make me chocolate chip pancakes and get out the Vermont maple syrup and it was one of my favorite things to eat. She told me that we could take a walk and lie in the hammock and that when you were in Rocky Ridge, doing nothing wasn't boring. It was a good reason to go there. It was a good place to relax.

I recognized the front steps from the picture of me and Caroline. It was a nice old house, well maintained and wonderfully lived in. Gram was waiting for us on the porch and when she saw me, she cried and she told me that she was so glad to have me and so glad that I was OK and something about it all made me want to cry, too, but I didn't. I wasn't wearing my hat because from the way Caroline had made it sound, there was no need to hide anything in Rocky Ridge. Once I was in Gram's embrace, I knew it. After she gave me the once over, she looked at Caroline, who looked away. I wasn't sure exactly why.

We had the pancakes and I remembered tasting them before, but I didn't say anything. I wasn't totally sure how taste fit in to my memories, but oftentimes, I could remember what I liked to eat and drink.

"This reminds me of the Fourth of July," Gram said, smiling.

It didn't feel threatening, like it did coming from my parents who were always testing me.

"What happened then?" I asked, curious about the picture.

"I'm not sure exactly what happened, but Caroline didn't answer her phone when you called her."

"I had turned my phone off," she corrected.

"Right. And so you drove the whole way here to talk to her."

I smiled.

"You made it right, Cody. You always made things right. You're a good kid."

I pushed my new wire-framed glasses back up on my nose, having to wonder if that part was true.

Gram got up and busied herself in the kitchen again until Caroline decided to take me to the park, a beautiful forest within walking distance of Gram's house, just down the street. She told me that we went to the park every time we went to Gram's and that she'd show me our favorite spot, where our initials were carved into a tree; everyone carved their initials into the trees. Even her mother and father had when they were young.

It was a small clearing near the creek where the grass hadn't been matted down yet. The sun poked through the leaves, through the holes in our protective forest roof, and warmed little spots on the ground. She laid out a blanket, then sat down and stretched her legs out in front of her. I watched the sunlight dance on her body. When it swept over her hair it reminded me of the color of coffee beans, that rich blackish color with a hint of brown. Her eyelashes were long and practically touched her cheeks when she blinked. I so desperately wanted to remember her. Maybe I could start there and move backward.

I stared up at the sun, hands behind my head. I imagined her putting her face to mine and kissing me. I had thought about her like that before, but always as a means to an end, not tenderly, not romantically. It came to me quickly, almost seemed like a memory and not just a wish. If I told her I thought we had kissed in that spot before, she would know it was simply conjecture. After all, it was our spot. We had gone there often enough, we had carved our initials in the tree, and certainly if we had loved each other we would have kissed there. Our spot would loan itself well to a rendezvous. It felt safe and protected and off the beaten path.

"After I came home from college in May..." I hesitated, not quite sure how to ask. "Did we see each other after I came home, but before the accident?"

She didn't answer right away, not because she was trying to remember, but because she wasn't sure if she should answer at all, I suppose. "Yes," she finally said.

I had deduced from calendars and paperwork that I had been home for three days before the accident. The day that I came home, then one whole day, and the next day which was the night of the accident. That was the second week of May. Now it was the beginning of August. Nearly three months had gone by. "On which day?" I asked.

She looked down at me, skeptical of my asking.

"I'm just trying, trying pretty hard, to figure out what happened. You're the only person who has tried to really help me. The ways the doctors are doing it, they aren't working. If I can't remember it, I at least want to know."

"On the night you came home, we saw each other. That was the last time I saw you before the accident. I can't be the one who tells you what led up to it. I didn't see you again." She didn't seem to want to give me details.

"Why didn't we see each other after that?"

"I don't know, Cody. Just as much as you don't know, I don't know."

"Why not?"

"Because that's just how you were."

"What do you mean?" I sat up and we were face to face. She almost seemed angry.

"I'm not going to tell you who you were, who you used to be, so you can try to turn into him again."

"I've changed?"

She bit her quivering lip. A tear rolled down her cheek. I felt something different inside.

"I'm sorry that I don't know what you're talking about."

"I know you are. I'm sorry it bothers me."

"I'm sorry for whatever I did to you to make you feel this way about me."

"It wasn't what you did to me. You just always seemed to back off when things got too real. You would disappear, not talk to me for days. It was hard, emotionally, to feel so close to you then just be completely ignored. Then, when it cooled down again, you'd be back like nothing ever happened, either way, the good things or the bad things. And you never told me what you did when you were absent. I never asked and you never told me."

I looked away, embarrassed for my actions. "It sounds like I was a real dick."

"Only when the feelings got to be too much."

"Do you think it was the pressure from my parents?"

"You remember something about that?"

"No. It's just that obvious."

"I don't know what it was, Cody. But you were like that from day one."

I couldn't imagine feeling anything but infatuated with her after knowing her for years. I barely knew her again and she was the only person I cared to see, talk to, or spend time with. If I didn't feel that way about her before, why did I feel that way about her after? I wanted to know exactly what I had done to hurt her, to make her cry when she thought about it. I wanted to understand. I didn't want to make the same mistakes again. I didn't want to cause any pain. "I don't remember how I was or who I was back then. I just know that it sounds pretty awful to me now and I'm not going to be like that anymore." I put my arm around her and tried to pull her closer.

"I've heard that before, Cody. But you wouldn't know that. You can't know that. So it wouldn't be fair to you if I didn't trust you now. But it doesn't just go away. It takes time. I'll need to forget it, too." She put her head on my shoulder. "I'm sorry that it's still so fresh."

"What happened that night?"

"Nothing," she said.

And I left it at that.

24

Eavesdropping

SHE WAS right about Rocky Ridge and about relaxing and about losing yourself there. We played Battleship on the back porch. We ate at the picnic table in the backyard. We took a nap in the hammock. I was infatuated with her in her summer sundress and the bra straps that peeked out from beneath it.

When I woke up from the nap, Caroline wasn't there and I went inside to look for her. Through the door I could hear Gram talking to her.

"You don't look well, honey. Have you been taking your medicine?"

"I'm OK," she said, as if she were tired of the conversation.

"Has your dad said anything? You look pale."

"No. I'm fine."

"Has Dr. Josh said anything?"

I wondered who Dr. Josh was.

"No. Not really."

"If you weren't feeling well, you would tell Dr. Josh at least, right?"

"Of course, Gram. You worry too much."

"How can I not? Once you lose someone, it's hard not to worry about everyone you love."

"Oh, Gram! You don't think I'd do that, do you?"

"No, dear. Of course not. I just...well, I know how your dad feels. He couldn't take another...heartbreak. If anything happened to you, I'd lose you both. You know that, right?"

"It's just a little bug, is all."

"You can't keep anything down."

"It's just a bug," she insisted.

"Have you considered..." Gram paused. "No, no. That's none of my business." She almost sounded relieved. "Have they fixed your medication?"

I could hear them moving around, a cupboard door opening, a drink pouring. "Not yet, Gram," she finally said.

"How is Cody? Is he OK?"

"He's OK," Caroline said.

"Does he —"

"No," she said abruptly. "I don't really want to talk about any of it. I promise I will talk to Dr. Josh, OK? I promise I'll get my medicine fixed."

Gramp came in the front door and I pretended to be looking at some knick knacks in the dining room. He chuckled. "Well, you know that it's best to stay out of those conversations, too, I see."

I nodded.

"Something you learn after a while of being a man. Better to stay oblivious to most things until you're dragged into them. They talk and, Jesus God, half the time I don't even know what it all means. I guess that's the enchanting thing about women. They have this secret language, this secret way of doing things, this thing that we can only admire."

His gaze fixed on a picture, one that, had I actually been looking, I would have been looking at, too.

"He never quite got over her," Carl said of the angelic blonde beauty in the white cashmere sweater.

"Who?"

"My son. Never got over Caroline's mother when she passed." He looked at the picture pensively for a moment. "Well, I can't say that I blame him. She had a certain thing about her that just made you want to love her. I don't know. It crushed us all a little bit, I would say. You don't get over those things. Not one hundred percent. Not ever."

"What happened to her?" I asked. Now I was concerned about

Caroline. Her grandmother worried that she was going to end up like her mom. Was it cancer? Some terrible disease? An "accident?"

"To tell you the truth, I'm not sure what actually killed her. One sickness leads to another and...I think in due time Caroline will tell you about her mother. She was only four years old, but I think she understands it better than we think."

I settled for that answer, none of my worry about Caroline eased.

25

Dreams

I DRIFTED off to sleep in Teddy Bryant's childhood bed, awakened first from a light slumber by Caroline's chronic retching in the bathroom. Too tired to devote my whole self to worrying, I drifted off again. I hadn't slept quite right in weeks. I slept well the night before in Caroline's bed, and probably would again after the filling day in Rocky Ridge. Even after relaxing nearly the whole day, I still felt like sleeping. Until I realized why I probably hadn't been sleeping.

I also realized why it may have been better not to hear anything about my past. When I had nightmares, I faced the real possibility that they were simply memories, and not fiction at all.

It started as a dream. I'm driving home in a nondescript vehicle. It could have been a scene from a movie. My stuff, my treasured belongings piled high in the backseat. My mother serves chicken. It's quite dry. I wash it down with ice water. Rocky smashes baby food into his tray. Does he ever stop squealing? I have to get reacquainted with the sounds of home. My mom goes through the happenings in town, what my old friends are up to, relatives who got engaged, had babies, graduated, died. I am half not listening to her, only one thing on my mind. I want my phone to buzz, ring, light up, whatever it does. And I want it to be her, not friends, not family, only her.

It's two o'clock in the morning. I can't sleep. If this is a game of endurance, as it usually is, I am prepared to surrender. Deny it as I may, I need her. I just do. Just like I need air or water, I need her, and it is obvious that she doesn't need me. Thirty-three days, once. For thirty-three days she didn't call or write or text. I can't win. On the thirty-fourth day I was defeated; I broke the silence. Clearly, I care more, I love her more than she loves me. That is what scares me. It took me a long time to figure it out, but I inadvertently invested more, placed higher stakes in the relationship than she did, and I was always at risk of losing my investment, of being a fool. I knew that at fifteen, sixteen, seventeen, and beyond, I was a big enough fool. I didn't need another thing to remind me that I didn't know anything.

I thought about her when I woke up and when I went to sleep and a lot of moments in between. I stared at blank notebook paper, wanting to say something, to write it down, the way we used to. I apologized for my actions in a variety of ways. I made mediocre gestures by coming to her window at night. I only used the word love when I had to, when I absolutely had to, as a bargaining chip. *But I LOVE you. I won't, I wouldn't, I can't, no, no, no, I won't do that again. I'm just confused because...well, because I love you.* But I really did — really do — love her. I want to crawl into her mind and know that she loves me, too. She keeps some things inside. She keeps them tucked away with the feelings about her mother and the sting of my many betrayals. Funny that love should find a home, should snuggle up in a space where she hid (and she hid it quite well) her anger towards me, albeit well-deserved. Had I any control of this dream, I would go to the place where I had cultivated that anger and things would be clear to me again, but that wasn't the intention for this nocturnal thought.

It's two fifteen. I walk to her house so I don't wake my parents with car doors and jingling keys. I tap on the window. She's sitting up in bed reading. She was waiting? God, how I hope she was waiting. She instructs me to come to the door; Teddy has spent the night with his latest nubile post-graduate. Caroline hates it when her dad beds down former students. She has an excuse for him, though. He's still a man.

I wonder if that's her excuse for me, too.

She tells me I've changed. She also doesn't like it when I wear contacts. They make my eyes red. She likes me with my flaws, with my bad eyes and the gap between my front teeth and my unruly

The Pastel Effect

hair. I don't even know who I am in this dream. I have false confidence, though. I am a lot like her, but I don't want her to know that. She thinks that I'm somebody else, and I've shown her slivers of who I really am, bits and pieces, and when those real things come out, well, that's when I tend to want to disappear. It's a facade. I prefer to keep it that way. If she knew what I *really* felt, that my parents drive me crazy, that I don't care if I ever see any of my friends again, that I'm only an athlete because I'm afraid I'm not smart enough to be recognized for anything else...if she knew that, she'd realize that I'm the world's biggest liar and that if she did love me, she loved someone who she merely thought I was.

We go to her room even though Teddy's not home. It's where she feels comfortable, where the soothing pastel walls provoke me to strip the veil away, to be myself, for those moments, for those hours. She knows it and I know it. It wasn't meant to last. But tonight, in this room, we are ourselves and it Is like we were never trying to be anyone else.

She doesn't ask me the obligatory questions about what I've been up to. With her, it goes much deeper than that. When she asks questions, to answer them means to take your heart out, to serve it up on a platter, to open up your skull and garnish it with whatever was on your mind. Words meant something to her, to us. We didn't use them to fill in spaces, we didn't waste them. We didn't lie to each other. I lied to her once, but other than that, we had never, ever, ever lied to each other, even when it meant hurting each other. Even when it put everything on the line. That was the definition of trust. Maybe I am wrong about my investments. My truths hurt and she is such a forgiving creature. For the times when my eyes wandered, for the times that my mouth followed, only for the sake of proving to myself that I hadn't fallen as hard as I thought I did. I never meant it, though. And she was still my only. And I intended to keep it that way. I had kissed other girls, but I never went any farther than that. I didn't want to, and my body didn't work for anyone else. Not even for the buxom blonde senior who felt me up at my first freshman taste of a college party. *Sorry*, I said. She walked away, disgusted at the eighteen-year-old boy with too tight pants that allowed her to be sure of his temporary case of erectile dysfunction. I immediately half-staggered back to the freshman dorm and drunk texted Caroline that I couldn't get it up for anyone but her. *How do you know?*

Because I tried, of course. Even then, she didn't hate me. Even in a jealous fit of rage over something that was said or done, when I told her that I had accumulated several conquests (my solitary lie), only to confess the next time we were in this room, that it was in fact a lie, even then she didn't hate me. She laughed at me and asked me if they didn't want me or if I didn't want them. I wouldn't even know. I didn't even try. And then, out of pity or relief or just because she loved me, she invited me in. I kept track of them all, and that was the third time.

That was the past. Back to tonight. She opens the drawer of her nightstand. She has the tattered, nearly threadbare black and white plaid shirt — the one I threw up on and she tenderly washed and returned so my mom wouldn't know how drunk I liked to get. The one I wore when we sat next to each other in Geometry class. The one I was wearing at the unfortunate party when we ended up in a closet together, where we had the most passionate kiss of my life, before or since. *Sorry*. I was always sorry. I was always being stupid. She asked me if she could have the shirt on the day I left for college, and I obliged, and here it still sat, close to her bed and her heart, proof that she still loved me, too. I smiled and put my head into the soft, downy pillows. It was like coming home. She unfolded the shirt and wrapped carefully inside of it was a copy of *The Beautiful and the Damned* from our senior English project. We were partners. Our final days of high school were spent waiting for prom, the blessed night that we had set aside for the monumental first time. It started as a joke. It was a joke, until we realized how much we wanted it. How hard it was to write a term paper when every word and every sentence seemed like it was about sex, simply because it was the only thing we thought about in those months. Of course the book and the shirt would be together. Because on that silly prom night we stood there, suddenly modest, afraid to touch each other, afraid we might feel something. And the only thing that would, that could, come out of my mouth was that famous phrase from Anthony Patch, *Things are sweeter when they're lost*. She blinked so slowly and her lips parted for a sigh and I found my courage in that second.

And now, here it was nearly two years to the day, the tenth time ever, each one better than the one before, when I finally found myself only by losing myself to her. Only because I allowed it, stopped trying to control it. Now it was so perfect, so good, so close, that I couldn't stuff it down for one more second. Everything was different that time. Focused, and letting myself be in love, I felt closer to her than I ever had, and our bodies came together like they never had before to form some kind of majestical, molecular, phantasmic bond. I had never been so scared as I was in that moment. Scared because I knew that she now had a part of me and I had a part of her and in that second, I realized that she was my life — she was the rest of my life. I was supposed to want other things. I was supposed to want everything. But I only wanted her, and that scared me.

With her asleep in bed beside me, I sat frozen in fear, until that same fear compelled me to run. I picked up the book and I ran all the way home. I got a shower and when I looked in the mirror, I cried. I cried because I knew that I had lost myself, that I would never, could never, be the same again. I loved her too much and nobody understood that. Not even her. Especially not her.

So I did what I was good at doing, what I always did. I shut her out. But not with intentions of ignoring it until it went away. Not with any bad intentions. I decided I would read the book. I would think about the whole thing. Then I would admit it. I would admit to her that she was it for me, that she was my end. She had killed the Cody that once existed and let this new, no — the real Cody — come out. It was the last time I would ever disappear. It was the last time I would ever leave. I went into the woods, spent the next two days there, where I could be alone and I read it and re-read it until I found the words...*It happens that I want you, and so I just haven't room for any other desires.*

One last midnight drive to muster up the courage that I need to lay it all out. I drive past our high school, where we met, where the friends and the parties and the politics got in the way. Past the pool, remembering that day we had the big fight and she slapped me. Past all of the places I longed to forget when I longed to stop loving her so much. One loop through the country, and I was going to her, ready or not, it had to come out. It was time to give in to what I had known since the day I sat beside her in school and felt my stomach do the flip flop that it would never quite recover from.

Rounding the bend, it happened too fast to react. All I saw were headlights coming at me fast, coming at me head on — on the wrong side of the road. I woke up what felt like hours later with bright lights around me, hot sticky blood drying on me in the cool night air, seeping into the grass beneath me after it soaked my hair and my shirt and dripped from the back of my neck. People were rushing around me. I heard the words. Are they supposed to say it? Someone said it. *He's not going to make it.* I began, screaming, screaming at the top of my lungs to let them know that I was alive.

26

Awake

HER ARMS WERE AROUND ME, tightly. Tight enough that I could only take short breaths, gasps.

"Stop, stop. It's OK," she insisted.

I'm alive, I thought in a loop in my head.

"You're shaking. It was a nightmare. Calm down."

That was why I didn't sleep. Night terrors. Sleep paralysis. Anxiety. Some doctor along the way had prescribed Xanax. I was tired of medicine and I didn't want to take it. Caroline didn't know about the pills — I hadn't told her. I was drenched in sweat. It felt just like the blood. The bed beneath me felt like the grass under me when the person who could've passed me by stopped and dragged me out of the car. I was hanging there, by my seatbelt, upside down and barely alive. A doctor, of all things. A stroke of bad luck and good luck pushed into a solitary moment. My parents wanted to thank him, but he wished to remain anonymous.

I had no way of knowing how much of it was reality and how much of it was conjecture and how much of it was a residual brain injury acting up again. Pure retrograde amnesia at its finest — when your memories are nightmares quite possibly peppered with truth. But how could they be? Was it starting to come back? Or did I make it up, a grand story based on the things I'd heard and seen? I was afraid to ask Caroline for fear that I'd have it all wrong, and she'd wonder what life I might have lived — what life looked like to me. No, we were one and I couldn't put that between us. When she left the room, I tried to catch my breath, to stop shaking and sweating and figure out how to speak.

She came back with a cool, damp washcloth and a glass of water.

"In the front pocket. My pills," I managed.

She found them in my backpack and looked at the bottle. I thought she would judge me, but she was simply reading the directions. The relief came pretty quickly from the Xanax. I sat at the desk while she changed the sheets — they were too soaked to salvage. She had made the bed again, folding the corner back, signaling my return. Then she came to me and peeled my drenched shirt over my head, an old t-shirt from some bygone wrestling match, and wiped off the sweat. She didn't know the part that had happened below, the part that happened when I dreamed of her, of us, before the terror began. I couldn't explain that part when I was forced to tell three different doctors every embarrassing detail of it after the nurse got sick of sedating me and cleaning me up for the third night in a row.

Still hot, I lay on top of the sheets and the blankets, the slight summer breeze blowing over me, drying off the parts she had missed. She continued dabbing at my forehead after refreshing the sweaty washcloth with a new and colder one. I think she was afraid to leave me.

"Does this happen often?"

"Not since the hospital."

We stayed quiet for a long time.

"Do you remember *The Beautiful and the Damned?*" I finally asked.

"Yes. Why? Do you?"

I didn't want her to know I might have remembered, so I made something up. "I found an old notebook. I think I really liked that book, even used it for a project."

"Yes. You did."

"Did you read it?"

"We read it together."

"You know, I think it's the same for my memory. Maybe things are sweeter when you lose them. Maybe the past wasn't so great after all."

She paused, then made a long rectangle of the wash cloth and placed it across my forehead. "You should get some sleep," she said. She kissed my cheek. "Sleep well," she whispered.

I touched her lips, suddenly wanting to feel her eyelashes against my skin. "We loved each other," I assured her.

She ran her finger around my ear and down my jaw. "We did. We do."

I started to fall asleep before she was out of the room. It occurred to me that these things should be written in the journal. And with that thought, I was out.

27

Try

I COULDN'T TELL anyone that I may have remembered something. In the morning, I wrote down the little bits that I could remember, from the good to the bad. To give someone the false hope that I remembered them was just cruel. She had told me about getting drunk and she had told me about the closet. I could have made up the dream around it. And I didn't even remember Caroline totally, just the moments that brought us to what we ended up doing, what most teenagers want to do, I suppose. So, how important really was that? I was convinced that it was my body's way of taking care of itself.

I *had* remembered something, though. I knew I did. Two days after we came back from Rocky Ridge, a package arrived on my doorstep, and within the package was a copy of the book I'd mentioned. Surely, a gift from the one person who could possibly know what it meant to me.

Leaving Rocky Ridge left me with a ton of questions, not just about my dream, but about Caroline. What was her illness? Who was Dr. Josh? How did her mom die?

I made a deal with my parents. I would resume counseling if they allowed me to transfer out of Otterbein. And I would also pursue my criminal justice degree since I wouldn't lose any credits if I kept my major. I wanted to stay with them, with Caroline. My father, still not keen on it, only agreed so he wouldn't have to hear it from my mom. My mom only insisted when I asked her to get my Xanax prescription refilled, proof that the nightmares had returned. I heard her whispering to my dad one night, coaxing him to look away from the TV and listen. *He has PTSD, Rich. The classic signs of it.* My dad scoffed. *I'd hardly compare his experience to what those guys go through.* She, getting more emotional by the second, snapped back, *He almost died. I almost lost my baby and I want him here.* That was the end of it. I transferred.

That was how I met Dr. Josh for myself. The sign out front said Dr. William Parker, but Dr. Josh Parker inhabited the building. When he invited me into his disheveled office, he introduced himself, and only then did I put it together — Dr. Josh was Caroline's doctor. He didn't seem to be much older than me, probably not even thirty yet. He had perfect teeth, a strong, square jawline, good hair and oceanic, crystal blue eyes. The window hung open, a can of aerosol spray on the window sill. I'd have guessed he'd been smoking, but I didn't ask. He didn't look like a smoker, but we all had our secrets. As if my entrance had sparked him to realize his disorganization, he quickly put some effort into tidying his desk, setting aside his discarded lunch, closing two thick medical books, and after an awkward minute of that, the awkward minute when I wondered why he had paired a necktie with jeans — comfortable meets formal like oil and water — I wondered if he was as suited for psychology as I was going to be for the CIA.

When he finally sat down across from me, legal pad open, flipped halfway through, cheap pen with chewed-on cap in hand, only then did I see the spark of recognition. Did he know me because he knew Caroline?

"Will you be my doctor, or..." I wondered if it was a mixup, if Dr. William was simply absent.

"I need to change the sign, but I just can't. This was my grandpa's practice and he passed a few years ago. It doesn't feel right to change it. Weird, I know. I'm sentimental."

"Well, I'm not," I said, humorously trying to break the ice, waiting for the punchline to be absorbed.

After a moment, he got it, smiled, and shook his head. "Good one." He flipped back and forth through a medical chart. I found it odd that he didn't use a laptop, like the hospital doctors did. "Look,

I'll be honest with you. I haven't dealt with an amnesia case before, and yours is...severe," he said, searching for words. "I can refer you to someone really good, really seasoned with this."

"I lost my driver's license," I said. "Is he within walking distance? My parents missed a ton of work after the accident. I don't want to bother them to drive me."

"I guess you can't walk to Cleveland," he said.

"I just want to do this, here. With you. It's not really the amnesia that bothers me. It's the night terrors. That's why I'm here. In the dreams, in the nightmares, I might be remembering some things. I'm scared to sleep. The amnesia is what it is. I accept that."

He stared at me, debating whether or not to believe my laid back approach to forgetting everything. "OK, then. Let's talk about the dreams. Let's talk about the nightmares."

I told him everything: from driving home, to tapping on Caroline's window, to sitting in the woods reading, to the blood seeping down my neck and shoulders. I told him that I believed it was real, but I didn't want to tell anyone about it, to have anyone else confirm or debunk it. I told him that I thought it was my job to do those things, and that I would learn to know the difference between a memory and a fantasy and a dream and a nightmare. When he scribbled on the legal pad, I wondered if he would tell me it was a conflict of interest. I wondered if he'd send me off to someone else, not wanting to accidentally spill my secrets to Caroline or hers to me.

I said her name, just so he could be sure.

Maybe she didn't talk about me.

28

Investigation

I BEGAN to think the CIA might suit me after all when I realized that the only way to know anything for sure was to become a detective, to prove my theories on my own. The first thing I set out to do was find out about the accident. I tried the newspaper and online searches. I tried tricking Shelby into telling me something. I thought if I could find out exactly where it happened or find the wreckage in a junkyard, that maybe I could prove my dream to be at least partially true. A newspaper article from the next day left me half-wishing I hadn't looked. *Alcohol a Factor in Fatal Accident.*

Fatal?

The guy who hit me was a repeat drunk driving offender. He went through the windshield, and his body came to rest thirty feet from the car. A good samaritan passing by, a doctor who witnessed the accident, told police he made the decision to work on me since I seemed a more viable candidate for survival. *The victim is in critical condition.* The victim, that was me. I survived. The drunk had died. The police had interviewed the doctor. The newspaper had obtained the police report. Maybe I could obtain the police report.

So I did.

In hindsight, there are some pains I could've saved myself from had I not set out to prove that my subconscious was correct. And the only reason I wanted to know — the only reason I cared — was to connect to Caroline and to be able to feel a history with her. I couldn't settle for it being brand new.

I had the location of the accident. And now I had the location of my car.

I went to the accident site first. I asked Skip to drive me. He cautioned me against it, but I insisted. It was a bright sunny day and I might have been able to spot any loose evidence the police could have missed that night. I wasn't sure what I was looking for, just any sign that it was real. I couldn't prove my love story with Caroline, but if I could prove that the accident happened the way I dreamed, then chances were I loved her the way I thought I did. So revisiting the accident was the easiest way to satisfy the conviction that I was really that much in love with her.

We came to the sharp bend about forty yards past a cemetery, of all things. I quickly thought, *had I died, they wouldn't have had to take me too far.*

"What are we looking for?" Skip asked.

"I don't know. Anything."

Skip turned up a penny, heads down, dated 1972. I turned up nothing. I decided it was a bit much for Skip to take me on two errands in one day, especially emotionally draining ones. We retreated to the gym to lift weights.

I debated, really weighed the options about going to see the car, but I finally decided to do it. I stood there, staring, amazed at the wreckage, amazed I had lived. It was my brown Jeep and I had a flash of it sitting in the driveway in one piece. I thought I remembered flinging my backpack into the backseat on early school mornings. Then I imagined the drive — the fated drive past the cemetery and around the bend that stole my mind and my past from me.

The roof was off. I remember that. Comfortable old jeans with the ripped out knee. My t-shirt fluttering against my bicep in the night breeze. My hand reached for the shifter. I downshifted into the bend. And then the blinding high beams from the oncoming car.

The front was smashed, mangled engine exposed from under crumpled metal. Front wheel on the driver's side, gone. Front bumper, gone. Mud scraped down the passenger side from the slide before the flip. Windshield, shattered. Steering wheel, bent. Seat belt cut, buckle still firmly in place from when I snapped it in. I refused to see the blood. The roll bars must have saved my life. And the doctor.

Funny how some things remain unscathed. A perfectly preserved red tree air freshener hanging from the mirror. An oil change sticker still stuck to the ruined windshield. Spare tire attached to the back in perfect condition. License plate GPA 4142. Sticker good until next February, on my birthday.

I avoided the driver's side and went to the glove box. Inside, an Otterbein parking pass. Registration and insurance card. A blue ink pen. My debit card. I put these mementos in my pockets. They all seemed vaguely familiar. I took the air freshener, too.

I was like Lopez and Shields on *Broken Blue*, secretly cataloging evidence from my illicit investigation. I put them into Ziplock bags for preservation thinking that when I had enough evidence from high school yearbooks and college pamphlets and glove box items, I could sit down and piece it all together, stick it on one of those boards with a large diagram of how each item relates to the other, leading to the top of the pyramid, my memory. At first it was just a big empty brick, the supporting bricks underneath just starting to stack up. Unless they were all imaginary. But, no. That's why I had those things, those real things that I could see and smell and touch. Cherry air freshener, scent sealed in the bag in case I ever needed to smell it to jog a memory of sliding, rolling, hanging upside down.

29

School

I TOOK naps during the day to combat the insomnia. I slept on the sofa in our sunroom. The sunlight kept me from the nightmares of that night. Now the parts with Caroline were hurried, rushed, and the part with the accident was elongated. Every time I had the nightmare, I was driving slower, anticipating the accident longer, sliding, rolling, and hanging longer and longer. In the bright daylight and the warmth of the sunroom, there was no way for the terror to find me. Soon school would start and maybe it would occupy my mind enough to stop thinking about the accident, the investigation, the clues.

But school starting only brought a slew of other feelings, like the way the disappointment in my dad's eyes made me feel guilty for not trying to go back to Otterbein. On campus, everywhere I turned, I wondered if I knew people. Between classes, I hid at the library where nobody would talk to me. Caroline described me as a guy who was always surrounded by friends. Now I couldn't look anyone in the eye. And part of it wasn't even the embarrassment that would come when I didn't know a person — part of it was paranoia that everyone knew me and I didn't know them and it was a big secret.

I spent a lot of time in the library, doing homework and reading books. I had always been a straight A student and I wanted to keep up on that so my parents would realize that they made the right choice by not forcing me back into my scholarship. I spent a lot of time thinking about why my friends never came around. Some days, when I was lonely, I wished there would be someone to talk to. Skip didn't talk about guy things, probably because he was practically married to Jesus. I would never be able to tell him some of the things I was feeling about Caroline. Everyone in my family seemed against our relationship, and I could talk to Caroline about everything except that. I wanted a confidant, I suppose. I wanted somebody unflappable, who I couldn't scare away with the scar and the lack of memories.

I did have Josh, though. I made a point of being hyper observant during the dream phase of the nightmare, even in its reduced state. Every little thing I remembered seemed like a breakthrough. I wrote down every new detail and brought the notebook to the bi-weekly sessions. In the most recent rendition of the nightmare, I noticed her velvet lavender bra strap sliding down her shoulder. Maybe it had happened since the accident and I incorporated it into the dream. Another time I specifically remembered the necklace -- the long silver chain with the moon and stars dangling from it. Maybe I had seen her wearing it in a picture. I tried to debunk all of my memories by making excuses for how I came to them. I couldn't accept the fact that maybe I remembered something, because then I just felt like I was deceiving myself. And a little part of me worried that she didn't want the old me back anyway. She didn't want to talk *about* him, so why would she want to talk *to* him?

"How are you today?"

That was how Josh typically started every session. I guess it was a generic way to feel things out.

"I feel OK."

"How's school?"

I shrugged.

"Are you participating in anything?"

"No."

"You've said so yourself, you used to be a busy person."

"It doesn't appeal to me. I don't feel like engaging. I have a lot on my mind."

"Anything you want to talk about?"

I looked at his diploma from the University of Kentucky. "Why did you go there?"

The Pastel Effect

He glanced over his shoulder at the diploma. "A girl."

"You went there because of a girl?"

"No, because I had my heart broken. I went to OSU with my high school girlfriend who promptly discovered frat boys. I transferred out after my first semester. Kentucky was close enough but far enough."

"You loved her?"

"I thought we would get married, buy a house, have kids. I saw this whole future ahead of us."

"I do that, I think. I do that sometimes and then I realize I've never even kissed her. I mean, not that I can remember. I realize there is so much I haven't done. This me, at least."

"You feel like you are two different people?"

"Sort of."

"Explain that."

"I feel like it's me before the accident, the one I don't remember, and then me after the accident. This one now. There is me who loved Caroline and who knows her, but who has done things to her that she didn't appreciate. Things that were hurtful and mean. But it's OK, because she says I was just a kid — we were just kids. Then there is the new me, the one who has been good to her so far, but who doesn't remember the prom and the school projects and our first kiss and our first...everything."

"So you want to remember the good things? The important things? And nothing else?"

"I think I want to remember everything, just not turn into a jerk again. I'm afraid if I remember who I was, I'll start acting like him again."

"But in the dream you've already changed from that person into the person you wanted to become. You decided you wouldn't hurt her anymore, that you wouldn't fight the feelings anymore."

"I don't know if that actually happened."

"Would you want to remember yourself if Caroline wasn't in the picture?"

I had to think about that. It wasn't something I could answer quickly. "I don't know. I mean, would I suddenly wish I could remember a sport that I have no interest in? A career I have no interest in? I don't even know how that's possible. I only wished I remembered Caroline because she came into my life again. She didn't give up on me the way my friends did. My friends who I wouldn't even know if they were standing beside me."

Josh leaned back in his chair.

"Are you going to be like my parents and tell me not to make my whole life about Caroline?"

"No. I'm not going to say that because I don't think you have. And, I know that love, being in love, is a powerful thing."

"Trying to remember things just feels so fake."

"What feels fake about it?"

I stood up and looked out the window, Josh's smoking window, that looked out on a bird feeder, some birds, and a scattered array of cigarette butts. "I don't want to remember the other things. I don't need to. The only thing that comes naturally to me is the sense that I knew her. It's the only thing I know about myself that doesn't feel forced. I am supposed to remember these facts and these details. With Caroline, it's like I just know. I know that I don't *actually* know, but I don't even have to remember. I feel it. And that's enough to believe it, maybe for both of us."

"If the dream is true, then it was the biggest thing you were feeling in the days leading up to the accident."

I stared at the birds for a little while, recalling the blue bird poem silently to myself. "Sometimes, since I remembered or had the dream or whatever, I think to myself that if I hadn't been being my usual old self, like such a little shit, that I wouldn't even be in this situation. I would've never had the accident."

"You can't blame yourself."

"Do you believe that everything is predestined?"

"Yes, I suppose. To a degree. Do you?"

"I guess I have to. If not, I'd have to just wallow in this, have pity on myself, blame people. And what is the point of all of that?"

Josh smiled. "You're on the cusp of overthinking."

"I know I am."

"I don't think I like you repressing these memories just because you might not like what you remember about yourself. Maybe this is where I stop believing in pre-destiny — nothing is written in stone. Maybe you were a jerk sometimes, but you don't have to be one. Maybe you don't have to like the things you liked. People change whether they have brain injuries or not. If you don't like the way something in your life is heading, you don't have to let it pull you along, and I think you realized that before the accident."

"I guess so. If it's true."

"So, what comes next for you?"

"Honestly?"

"Yeah. Honestly."

"The only thing I want out of life right now is to be able to kiss her."

"What's stopping you?" he asked, half-grinning.

"I suppose it feels a little weird that it's my first time kissing her and not her first time kissing me. And I don't know why it's even such a big deal. I am twenty years old. It's just kissing."

"It is a big deal. Maybe you were never one to take relationships, or any part of them, lightly."

"I don't think I was, or I would've just let my relationship with Caroline be easy, I guess. And I find no evidence that I ever had any other girlfriends. And if the dream is correct, I never wanted anyone but her and we made a big deal out of everything. Kissing and everything."

"There are some parts, Cody...some parts that are just you. Some things you don't forget, it's your personality. All of this is important to you. Do it at your own pace."

"Something about almost dying makes me feel like I'm running out of time, though. What if I walk out of here and get hit by a bus? What if that good samaritan guy only delayed the inevitable? What if I'm dead meat no matter what? And I die and I've never kissed a girl. I die a virgin. I die an un-kissed virgin with a scar on my head? What life is that? And that's why I feel like I need to do something."

"You were meant to live," Josh said. "Or you wouldn't be here."

"Are you telling me I have all the time in the world?"

"That's not really a measurement of time. And, no, I'm not telling you that. We all have numbered days. I'm just saying that if you die and never kiss her or never make love, or whatever it is you're worried about missing out on, does that mean you loved each other any less?"

"No."

"Then take it at your own pace."

30

Found

KRISTI WAS Teddy Bryant's ex-girlfriend, and also my boss at Alice's. She was younger than Teddy, with no hard feelings about their mutual break-up. Some nights when it was slow, she talked to me only for lack of having anyone to talk to. She told me about how Teddy tried to hide the relationship from Caroline for a long time, but she caught onto it. She told me about how they weren't really a couple, but she caught feelings. She told me that Teddy would never have a relationship because he was stuck on Caroline's mother, the beautiful blonde woman who died at a very young age. Kristi had never found out how she died because it was such a sensitive subject with Teddy that she was afraid to ask. And she also believed that he was a great father and he loved Caroline more than anything.

It was nearly closing time and I pushed the mop around the floor while she sat counting her tips and talking — she loved to talk and I was fine with that because I didn't want to have to talk. I had no memories of anything to talk about. It was dead and we closed at eleven on weekdays, so in ten minutes I could turn the sign around and Caroline would be there to pick me up. As Kristi talked, my mind raced about making up a way to kiss Caroline, the same thing my mind had been racing about since I met her. Maybe I would ask her if I could come in for a while and do homework. And then, maybe, I could reach out for her hand. And then, maybe, our eyes would also meet, and our lips could meet in the middle. I had a hundred scenarios of how to kiss her and zero of them had panned out so far. I had also been debating on telling her about the dreams, but when I got close to saying it, something always told me not to.

I looked up when the door opened, expecting it to be Caroline, but it wasn't. It was a taller guy in nice clothes with dark brown hair in a stylish cut. He approached me, until he was face to face with me — too close. Even with my diminished people-skills, I could tell he had a problem with me, but instead of being scared, I was intrigued. Clearly, he was from my mysterious past and maybe he would provide a clue.

"It *is* you," he said.

I wasn't sure how to respond.

"Are you kidding me?"

"What?"

"You've got nothing to say to me?"

"Sorry. Should I?"

It happened fast. He punched me in the face, in the jaw to be exact. I felt it crack a little as I stumbled back, dropping the mop. Before I could go the whole way down, he grabbed me by the shirt and yanked me back up. Kristi tried to intervene, but he pushed her back with his free hand.

"You can pretend you don't remember shit so you can never say what really happened. I know how you are, though."

"What are you talking about?"

"You are fucked up in the head, Cody. None of this was my dad's fault. None of this went down the way you say it did. We were *friends*. How could you do this?"

"Do what?" I asked, again.

"Don't you wonder why nobody will talk to you? It's because nobody believes you."

"Believes *what*?" I didn't hate losing my memory most of the time, until it felt like picking up in the middle of a really complicated book. Or like taking a test I didn't study for in a class I had never attended.

He pushed me against the wall and pinned me.

"I don't even know who you are," I countered.

He looked at me, our eyes met, and it seemed like he was trying to figure out whether he was right or I was. "Are you really clueless?"

"I don't know you," I reiterated.

He raised an eyebrow and I wasn't sure if he was amused or mad or sad, but at that same moment, the door opened again and Caroline ran towards us and wasted no time in pushing him away from me.

"What is wrong with you, Zack?" she asked. "Get out of here."

He looked at her with disgust. "I always thought you were a bitch, Caroline."

"Get *out*!" she said.

He looked me in the eye. "This isn't over."

"What isn't over?" I called out as he walked away and out the door.

I stared at the door, not even realizing right away that Kristi and Caroline were making a fuss over my bloody lip. They sat me down in a booth. The ice pack against my face finally jarred me out of my thoughts.

"Are you okayOK?" Caroline asked.

"Yeah," I said. "What was that?"

She looked worried but continued to dab at my face, much like she did when I'd had the nightmare. She brushed her hand over my scar. "Where did he hit you?"

"Just here," I said, holding the ice to my jaw.

"Just once?"

"Yes. Who is he?"

"He's an idiot. He always was."

We didn't talk on the drive back to Caroline's house. I sat on the edge of the bathtub while she continued wiping away the blood from my lip. Every time I opened my mouth it started bleeding again and I kept opening and closing my mouth because my jaw hurt.

My new coping mechanism was humor, which everyone who knew me seemed to find strange because I was told that I was a pretty serious person before the accident.

"Look. You're in the bathroom and for once you're not throwing up."

She shook her head.

"Have you been feeling better?" I asked.

"Why are you asking about me?"

"Because I worry about you."

"I told you that I'm fine."

"I keep telling you that I'm fine, too, but you keep asking. For me, it's just some blood and a little bruise, but you've been sick for weeks."

She turned around and rinsed out the washcloth in the sink.

"Tell me who that guy was. Please. I got punched in the face. It's not fair that I don't even know why."

She didn't look at me. She kept herself busy at the sink. "His name is Zack. You used to be friends. He'd throw big drinking parties and back then you liked to drink. He was on the wrestling team. He ran in your Circle."

"He said that he knows why none of my friends will talk to me. Why won't my friends talk to me?"

"Maybe it's awkward."

"Why?"

"The accident. It was his dad."

I didn't know what to think. It felt a bit like a whirlwind, like it always did when pieces fit together and something suddenly made sense. "Does he think it was my fault?"

"I don't know what he thinks. But it wasn't your fault, Cody. We all know that. He probably even knows that. The police know that. You know that, right? He was drunk. You were sober."

"I know." I stared at her reflection in the mirror. She looked tired. I wondered if she was getting tired of me. That's what made me think that maybe it was time to come clean. "He was on the wrong side of the road. Coming around the bend. I had just passed the cemetery."

"What?"

"It's the nightmare. It's a memory. I know what happened."

She turned to look at me. "You *remember*?"

I looked at the floor. "I've been remembering some things. Only in the nightmare."

"You didn't tell me." She sounded disappointed.

"I'm sorry," I said. "I just wasn't sure if it was a memory or a nightmare."

"And now you are?"

"No. Because there is only one person who would know that."

"Who?"

"You."

"How?"

I held her hand. "Because I can tell you what I think happened and if it's not what happened we would know it's a dream and if it happened then it must be a memory. Or I just put it all together."

"I wasn't there."

"I remembered everything from the three days before. And then I remembered what I was thinking about the three days before. I was thinking things about you. So if they really happened, then..."

"You remembered *me*?"

"I am not totally sure."

"What happened?"

"I came home from school. I knocked on the window. Your dad was out. I had been thinking about our senior prom. The book. You had my shirt. I loved you so much and I was scared and I had to figure out what I was going to do because it was really clear to me that I couldn't go on being in denial of it all. So I had to be alone, like I always had to be alone. On the night of the accident, I was coming to see you. I was coming to say that we can't be apart anymore and that I can't not love you. I was going to tell you that it wasn't going to be a game ever again."

I immediately regretted telling her as she began to cry the most pathetic sob that I'd ever heard, or remembered hearing. I realized something. The worst sin a man could commit was making a girl cry. It was heart wrenching, and I couldn't think of anything to do but pull her against me. "Don't cry," I said. "I'm sorry." I felt that I must've had it all wrong and it was a bit of a relief to know that I had been dreaming, not remembering in that way. My brain must have pieced together random bits and made something up to entertain me. "I'm sorry that I didn't remember, Caroline. I want to, though. I really do want to remember you."

She pulled away from me and wiped her eyes. "What do you mean?"

"I had a feeling it was all a dream."

"It wasn't a dream. That's exactly what happened. The window and the shirt and the book."

"Why are you crying then?" I was confused.

"Because I don't want to lose you," she said, beginning another round of tears.

"Why would you lose me if that was how I felt?"

"Because I didn't know you felt that way. The last thing you did was disappear on me. For the millionth time. What was I supposed to think, Cody? How was I supposed to know? I thought you'd left me. Again."

"I was coming back." I looked down, realizing that I must've been a real jerk to her more often than not. "I got scared because I knew just how much I loved you."

"Do you remember everything?"

"No. I remember little pieces of some things."

"Like what?"

"I don't know exactly. Just what I told you and what I was feeling. I know whatever happened that last night, it took me by surprise. It made me see something I couldn't un-see and I know that at that point, I really, completely loved you."

She wrapped her arms around me and I could feel her tears on my neck. For some reason, it aroused me. Maybe because I'd not really been touched in this lifetime and she'd never been that close to me.

"When did you have the dream?" she asked, when she finally let go.

"I'd been having it. I just couldn't remember the part before the accident until that night in Rocky Ridge. That's when I remembered the whole dream. I started having it when I was in the hospital. I didn't know how much of it was true, or how much I just made up because I wanted to believe it. That's why I asked you about the book." I sighed. "It does feel like a dream, though. Or like a movie. Like it happened to someone else. Like I'm still not him."

"It's okay OK, Cody," she said. She took my hand and pulled me up, giving my face the once over before dabbing something on my bloody lip until she was satisfied with it.

"My mother is going to ask a thousand questions about this."

"Do you want to stay here tonight?" she asked.

Sometimes, she could read my mind.

31

Love

AFTER THE PASSIVE aggressive thumbs up from my mother, Caroline made up a bed for me on the couch. Eventually, Teddy would be home and neither of us wanted to show him any disrespect. The truth was that on some days I just didn't want to go home. And on some days I just wanted to know she was five steps away from me. And on other days it was a little bit of both.

We sat together in the dark with just the flickering of the television, silenced. I watched as the black and white turned to technicolor during that magical moment of *The Wizard of Oz*.

"Do you like this movie?" I asked.

"I'm not sure," she said. "It's kind of scary if you think about it. I mean, there she is, in another place, not knowing anyone. Not knowing how to get home. Not fitting in. People accusing her of killing witches and stuff. You know?"

I laughed. "I know exactly how Dorothy feels."

She looked at me, her long lashes making shadows on her cheeks. "I'm sorry. I suppose you do."

"Nothing to be sorry about, C. It's not your fault."

"Maybe it is. Maybe I made you feel like..."

"You only ever made me feel good, as far as I can remember. My confusion was my fault."

"Was it?" she asked, and I had to think about that. Maybe it was just the pressure of what everyone else wanted me to do weighing down on me that confused me. Maybe it wasn't her. I already felt it again, with my parents.

"Well, it wasn't yours. Was it?"

"I was never very confused about any of it," she said.

"Full circle. It's not your fault."

"I learned something from this, Cody."

"What?"

"I'll never turn my back on you again. I have to hear from you every day. I have to know you are alright. Is that fair?"

"More than fair. I expect the same from you. I don't want to be without you."

"No more tests of endurance. No more grudge matches. I quit with that. OK?"

"That's fine. I barely remember it anyway."

She giggled and put her head on my chest. "I'm sorry," she said. "I know I wasn't easy to put up with."

"Was I?"

"No."

"Then we are probably even and we can start fresh again." I ran my fingers through her soft, silky hair. Even that was erotic. "Can I ask you something?"

"Yes."

"I still don't remember our first kiss. And I've been thinking about —"

She pressed her finger over my mouth. "Don't talk about it."

I stared at her, wondering how bad it could have been. I could barely finish the thought before she was climbing onto my lap, straddling me. She pushed me back into the cushions, cupped my face in her hands and pressed her lips to mine. I opened my mouth to let her know she was welcomed there. He lips tasted sweet, like cherry pop, and it tickled when her tongue brushed across my gums. Next, she was kissing my neck. Then back to my lips again. Her hands slid under my shirt. She pulled it over my head. She kissed me more. My head was spinning and I couldn't think of anything to do but let her kiss me. I tried to kiss her back, but I was sinking into something and I couldn't grab hold of anything solid. I was sinking into her fast.

We kissed until my lip was bloody again, then I went to the bathroom to clean it up. I stared at myself in the mirror. In the beginning, I looked at myself, wishing I could remember. I would stare into my own eyes. *Remember*. I willed myself to come up with any memory, any tidbit to take back to my parents, to ease their pain. Later, when Caroline started coming around, I did it again, only trying to remember what holding her felt like, what kissing her tasted like. I turned on the water and watched the watered-down pink blood swirl down the drain. It wasn't the hot blood of death that surrounded me on the night of the accident. It was a pastel version of it, a lighter and less ominous reminder that there was more than one kind of death.

When I came back out of the bathroom, Dorothy and her friends were in a field of poppies. She was staring at the screen with tears in her eyes. "What's the matter?" I asked, foolishly thinking I could solve all of her problems.

"Nothing. I just...had a thought."

"What?" I sat beside her and put my arm around her.

"I wonder if that's what it feels like to die."

I watched Dorothy lie down and fall asleep and I hated to break it to her, but I knew the answer. And it wasn't at all like that.

32

Remember

THERE WAS something totally divine about waking up with her in the morning. There was a warm, wet spot on my chest where she had been breathing on me all night. My arm was asleep. I didn't have any dreams or any nightmares and I hadn't even taken the medicine. I smiled. It was just a natural thing, something that happens to your face when you're too happy not to let it show. I heard a noise in the kitchen and I gently shook her to wake her up. She looked up at me.

"Your dad?" I whispered.

She sat up, maybe a little embarrassed.

"Good morning, Bear!" he said, almost delightfully.

"Good morning, Dad."

I sat up, too.

"I made blueberry pancakes," he said, proudly.

"Sorry, Dad. We fell asleep."

He was humming an unfamiliar song as we came to the table. Everything in their kitchen — in their entire house — was dark. Everything but Caroline's room.

"Who's the lucky lady?" Caroline asked.

He shook his head.

Caroline looked at me. "He only hums that song when he gets

all domestic because he's going to bring a lady home. It's his house cleaning song."

I looked at Teddy.

"For your information, Bear, I always listen to nineties rap when I'm cleaning. Not just when I'm cleaning because a lady is coming over."

"You only clean when a lady is coming over," she said matter-of-factly.

He turned up the music on his phone so I could hear it. He was lovingly trying to irritate his daughter.

"What is it?" I asked.

"Dr. Dre," Caroline said, rolling her eyes. "He's so nineties."

As we ate, he noticed the clock on the microwave. "Time for work." He straightened his necktie and looked at her once with concern. "Are you feeling OK today? You're just moving the food around on your plate."

"I'm just not that hungry." She smiled to be more convincing. I was catching on to the way she protected her dad from the truth. I just wasn't sure what the truth was.

She washed the dishes and I dried them, trying hard to figure out a way to ask her about her illness. Eating disorder? Ulcer? Cancer? I never thought much about sickness or had to deal with it on my own and when I finally blurted it out, I immediately realized I should've said something else. "How did your mom die?" I asked abruptly, regretting it instantly. "I'm sorry. I didn't mean for that to really come out. Not that way, at least."

"It's OK. I never really talk about it."

"Why not? I mean, except for the obvious reasons."

"The obvious reasons?"

"Like, it hurts too much."

"It doesn't hurt that much. I barely remember her," she said, putting the plates away. "I guess I never talk about it because nobody ever asks me."

"Did I ask you?"

"I told you. I don't remember if you asked or not."

"I'm sorry that I don't remember."

"You don't have to keep apologizing, Cody. It's not something you did on purpose."

I sat at the table again. "Is it something we can talk about, though?"

She put away the last dish and turned towards me again. "Drug overdose," she said.

It wasn't what I was expecting, and I wondered how Caroline's sickness related to her mother's.

"It's kind of embarassing to say it. I always thought had anyone asked me when I was younger, I would make up something less embarassing. You think about drug addicts and you think of this certain thing and that's not ever how I thought about her. Or how Teddy thought about her. Or anyone, for that matter. Drugs were just a symptom of her disease."

I didn't quite understand what she meant. "What disease?"

"Manic depression. Bipolar. Whatever word they use for it now." She sat beside me. "You know, this may sound really mean, but you've seen her. You've seen my dad. And when you see a picture of them together and she's a ten and he's a six or a seven, you must wonder why she would be with him. How could he get her? I'd never say it to my dad, but sometimes I think he must've been head over heels or stupid to think that somebody like him could get somebody who looked like her unless something was wrong with her."

She looked guilty for even saying it.

"God, I've thought that for so long, and now saying it feels so wrong. Maybe this is why I don't talk about it. In my dad's eyes, it's this great, tragic love story. To me, he's a fool for thinking that someone perfect would want him."

I did think it was mean when she put it like that.

"Like us," she finally said.

"How is that like us?"

She grabbed my hand and squeezed it. "It doesn't matter anymore. Does it?"

I didn't know if I should be happy about that statement or not. "If it doesn't matter to you, then it doesn't matter to me."

"I called Alpha Sig today. They said you didn't request a transfer."

I racked my brain trying to remember what that meant.

"I paid almost five thousand dollars so you could pledge Alpha, and you haven't even transferred."

My mom looked at my father, then me, then him again. "Your fraternity, Cody."

I looked at Rocky, who was eating mashed potatoes by the handful.

"I'm sorry. I don't remember."

My dad slammed his fist on the table. "Damn it, Cody! That's a lot of money."

Rocky started screaming.

"Tell me what I have to do, and I'll do it tomorrow." It was the first time I'd heard anything about a fraternity.

"I've got doctor's bills up to my eyeballs, I've got tuition payments due, and all you can say is, *I'll do it tomorrow*? What the hell, Cody? Get your head out of the clouds. There is nothing wrong with you. The doctor said it, the MRI said it, all of the brain scans — the brain scan that I got a forty-two hundred dollar bill for — said that there is nothing wrong with you."

"I'm sorry, Dad. I wish I could remember."

"You don't *want* to remember."

I got up, fueled with anger by with his accusation. "I don't *want* to remember? I sit in the library all day. I don't have any friends. I mop floors at a pizza store and I can't drive. Before this, I had a scholarship at a good school. I was an athlete. I had tons of friends, and I guess, apparently, I was in a fraternity. I'm struggling at school because I'm a junior and I can't remember what I've learned for the past two years. I can't remember what I've learned since my freshman year in high school. I have no idea what anyone is talking about, ever. I live with people that I don't even know. I can't remember any of it, and it is *not* my fault. And I am sick of *you*, Dad, making me feel like I can control this situation. I can't. OK? I can't. I don't know how to make any of it come back. If I could, I would. So, a doctor told you I should remember. Well, I'm sorry, but the doctor isn't inside of my brain, and he doesn't know what's real. OK?"

My mom grabbed me by the shoulder. Rocky's screams seemed deafening, and I couldn't take them any more. I went out the front door. Rick was getting out of his car. "Hey, bro, what's up?"

"Why don't you have to take any of his shit?"

"What? Who?"

"Dad. You're a bigger fuck up than I'll ever be. Why doesn't he come down on you?"

"Hey, watch it."

"This isn't my fault," I said, and I walked away.

Caroline's house wasn't very far on foot, and I walked there, hoping she'd get out of work early. I sat on her front porch and waited until an ominous roar of thunder clapped. It started to rain, hard and fast. Big raindrops hit my face. I tried the door. It was locked. I went to the side door and turned the knob to the door near the kitchen. It opened.

"Hello," I called out through the empty house. "Mr. Bryant?" His car wasn't in the driveway and I knew he usually worked late on Wednesdays. It was his office evening.

I went into the bathroom and dried my hair with a pink towel that was hanging on the back of the door beside Caroline's nightgown -- the gray one with the yellow moons that she'd been wearing the last time I was there. I looked at my scar in the mirror, happy that my hair had almost grown over it. For a moment I wished I could have it all back — the memories, the scholarship, the life I had. Wishing was a waste of my energy, though, and I knew it. Someone had told me that once. I remembered the words. I just couldn't remember who said it.

Caroline was the only person I had a recent memory with. Our prom. Our bodies. Our life.

I was swallowed by the grief that losing that part of me caused. I needed to know Caroline. Everything shot through my head, just like the lightning outside, and I remembered the white bandage. And I remembered my mom's voice. And I remembered the bright light. And I remembered the lightning, the leaves against the window. And I remembered Teddy. And I remembered leaving. Some things were my fault. Maybe that was one of them.

What had happened? Caroline was sick. Caroline had always been sick.

I opened the medicine cabinet. Three orange bottles from the Village Pharmacy with Caroline's name on them. I took them out and searched the names of the drugs online. Caroline was sick. Caroline *is* sick. I looked up the side effects to the medicine. Upset stomach and vomiting.

I put the pill bottles away carefully.

I stood in her pastel bedroom, with the lavender blanket and the pink chair and the bluebird poem taped to the mirror.

The desk. *Sometimes I just wonder where my mind goes compared to other peoples' minds.*

The dresser. *Do you think I look like her?*

The bed. *We have an expiration date.*

I breathed in with the pain of my memories, the pain so severe that it took me to my knees. I pressed my face against the light blue rug and felt the tears running down my cheeks. I contemplated trying to forget everything. I had hurt her. Some things weren't my fault and some things were. I had always wondered if the bandages were my fault, too.

When I come back in May, I'm never leaving you again.

These are my wounds. These are not your chains.

It happened in February. I came home when I heard. She was tranquilized. I could only stare at her. Teddy talked to me because the silence was deafening. On Monday, I had to go back to school. My parents were on my case. So, I left her that note. *I'm never leaving you again. I promise.*

And she wrote back to me. *This wasn't your fault. I have this illness. I have this disease. These are my wounds. These are not your chains. You are free, Cody, and you will always be free, and you should embrace that.*

We didn't talk about it again after that, until I went to her that night. I knew, though. I always knew. I knew when she sat in front of me that day in her black dress with the little white flowers, when she turned around to pass the papers back to me, the way she blinked, like it was in slow motion, because she had the most beautiful dark eyes I'd ever seen. I knew when I kissed her in Libby's storage closet, and my heart beat hard against the wall of my chest, and my body wanted to melt into her body. I knew then that nobody would ever be able to make my heart beat the way she did. I always messed it up, though. I was scared of myself, and I was scared of her, and I was scared of not being normal. So I always messed it up.

I turned my head and saw the stack of books under the bed. Composition books, spiral notebooks, and leather-bound diaries.

I had remembered something, but I hadn't remembered everything. She wrote everything down. *Everything.*

I wiped my eyes and reached for the books.

He's cute and he smells good. I can't describe it. It's fresh and tender and clean and cool. Every day he smells the same, so it's not his laundry detergent or his cologne. It's just him. I want to put my face against him and live there for a minute and remember it forever.

I don't know why he always seems so angry. Sometimes he laughs, though, and it's like a whole world opens up. I can't fall into this. The Golden Circle would eat me up.

I've never really been interested in anyone that I could probably have. This is something new.

I put the book down and opened another one.

It's not fair to remember things the way I do. I have to be sure to never let myself remember another smell or another taste. I can't stop thinking about the way his hair feels between my fingers, the way his lips taste like strawberry milk, the way his shirt brushes against my cheek. I want to forget him. I need it to end.

Dr. Josh makes me laugh when I don't want to. He doesn't even mean to. He keeps a pack of Newports in his desk drawer right next to his grandpa's fountain pen. He keeps a Swiss Army Knife in his pocket. When Missy dumped him, he put all their pictures in box and marked it "Do Not Look" because he didn't have the heart to just dispose of everything. Dr. Josh isn't perfect, and that's why I like him.

. . .

I'm not scared. Maybe I am, but not out of fear that it might hurt, or because of cold feet, or second thoughts. No. I know that Cody will feel something, and when he does, he'll stress out and he'll run. He'll disappear. He'll leave. He can say the words, but when it all becomes obviously real, he'll hide from it.

I reached for the black leather-bound book.

Everything is so bleak, and I know what she meant now. You either feel everything or nothing and there is no in-between. I'm scared of going overboard, so I stay in bed. Because if I did everything I felt like doing, everything I thought about doing, I would hurt too many people. I would hurt Cody, and if there is ever a chance with him, I want that preserved.

Cody called me today to let me know his body still doesn't work for anyone else. This made me simultaneously happy and sad. I wanted him to go off and experience things. I never wanted to be his anchor. Maybe we have something a little bigger than what we want it to be, and it sabotages our efforts to sabotage it.

I flipped to the halfway point.

Josh says I need the medicine. I asked him to give me one more chance. I don't want to talk to someone who is only listening because he has to write a script for me.

I don't know what made me finally do it. I couldn't stand to drop any farther. I suddenly had no fear of the pain or anything like that. I pushed the blade right into myself and dragged it along my wrist. When it became real, when I saw the amount of blood, I realized that I couldn't be like her. I had to say something. So I called my dad and I told him that I loved him. I guess he knew. And maybe I didn't want to die, after all. I just didn't want to take the medicine, to make every feeling go away. If every feeling was going to go away, there was no use staying around for any of it. Dr. Josh brought me pink roses and I told him that it was the first time a boy ever bought me flowers and he said there are easier ways to get flowers from boys and we had a good old laugh. Then it came to the serious stuff, and he got me set up with one of his friends who was going to prescribe my medicine and he'd keep close tabs on it, too. I didn't see Cody, but Dad said he sat beside me for two days. I always thought that old thing about setting free the things you love was some fluff, but I have to give Cody a chance at his own life. And I have to give myself a chance at mine.

He checks in sometimes and we don't talk about what happened. He sent me a t-shirt from his fraternity that said "Alpha Sigma Phi — Spring Break — Fort Lauderdale or Bust!" It smelled like him. He sent it because he said it would save me from having to steal it later, and I'd have something to remember him by until May.

There was one more book, and it was sitting on her nightstand. I opened it to the day she came to see me in the hospital.

I waited three weeks. I went to the hospital plenty of times, but I never went to his room. Once, after he was stable and awake, I mustered up the courage and tried, but Pam stopped me. "Do you really want to do this?" she'd asked me. "It's not easy. Let me tell you. It hurts." I thought I could give him this gift, this freedom. He would never have to know about me, about us, about what we put each other through and what we did to each other. For three weeks I sat in the hospital lobby reading his favorite book over and over again, remembering how he'd read certain things out loud. Remembering that I was on page seventy-two when he put his arm around me, and page one hundred thirty when he slid his hand under my shirt and said, "I don't feel like reading right now." But I saw him today, and nothing changed about how I feel, and I still love him. I don't know how to tell him, because if I tell him this, I have to tell him everything, and he seems so fragile, and who can make a decision like this on a good day, let alone when you don't even know what got you there?

I feel the difference now with the medicine changed. I have to make a choice. We have to make a choice, but Cody won't remember or understand.

We spent the weekend in Rocky Ridge. My mother wanted that life. I am part of a family. I have all of this behind me. What else can I do?

Everything is spinning sometimes. Cody has no memory. My dad doesn't know. I can't keep changing my medicine. Time is getting away from me and I'm afraid of the fallout. I'm afraid of the hurt and disappointment this will cause everyone. I don't know why I ever thought it would be right to put it on Cody. Maybe because I thought it would be wrong to not at least give him a choice in any of it. But now that's exactly what I have done. It's all spiraled out of control.

I flipped through every page of the book trying to understand it. I looked under the bed for another book. I looked in her desk drawers. I opened the nightstand drawer. My shirt. I remembered it. I held it. Something in the shirt pocket crinkled in my hand. What was it? I took it out of the pocket. It was a photo. It was an ultrasound photo, like the one I'd seen on *Broken Blue* when Lopez found out that Emily was pregnant. I studied the photo. *Bryant, Caroline. October 1, 2014.*

33

Storm

IN THE THUNDER, I couldn't hear my own thoughts, and that felt good. With the lightning I remembered things. I remembered taking the chance. I remembered the app on my phone, and checking it afterwards. I remembered trying to wake her up, to tell her. *Caroline,* I'd whispered, *we might have fucked up.* I could never fall asleep after sex like she could. My heart was always beating too fast. My mind was always racing. And it was always racing to places like that. I knew that sometimes Caroline felt responsible for her mother's problems because she had to quit her medicine when she got pregnant. And when she quit her medicine, everything went to shit. I remembered telling her that it wasn't her fault. *You were five years old when Tressa OD'd. She had plenty of opportunities to fix her meds. Don't blame yourself.*

My mind stopped dead in its tracks — I could muster only one last thought. What the hell are we going to do? I was standing in front of Rachel's in the pouring down rain and I had a choice to make. I could walk away now. Now that I knew what I knew. Now that I saw what I saw. I could walk away and let everything be as she thought it was. She'd always thought I was running from her. I wasn't. I was running from the things I couldn't control, like how I felt about her. The lightning struck and a tree branch crashed to the ground in the green behind me. I turned my head to see it, and someone grabbed my arm and pulled me inside.

"What are you doing out there?" she asked, quickly grabbing a towel from behind the counter to dry my face. She took my glasses off, dried them, and placed them back where they belonged. "You don't even have a jacket on. You're going to get pneumonia."

"That's not exactly how pneumonia works." I looked behind the counter, and Skip stood there smiling. "Workout could've waited until morning. There's an indoor track at the Field House."

"Let me make you something to warm you up." She busied herself with the coffee machine. "You almost got struck by lightning. What happened? Why did you walk here?"

I held the crumpled, wet picture out to her. "What is this?" I asked, trying not to shiver from the cold and the shock.

She took it from my hands, but didn't speak.

"What is it, Caroline?"

A single tear escaped the corner of her eye.

"You're lying to me about everything, and that doesn't protect me." I raised my voice, yelling at her just like I'd yelled at my dad.

"I'm not lying, Cody. I just didn't tell you everything."

"Now you don't have to. Because I remember."

"What do you remember?"

"I remembered the Valentine you gave me, and the day you showed me Tressa's picture, and the day we got back together, and the day you did...that," I said, noticing the scar across her wrist for the first time. "And I remember the night..." I grabbed the picture from her hand. "I remember the night that *this* happened because I remembered why I left."

"Why. Why did you leave, then?" she asked, practically sobbing. "Was it the same reason you always leave?"

"Because I knew that it happened."

"How could you know? I didn't even know until right before I visited you."

"Because I kept track and you didn't. And after you went to sleep, I looked on the app to see, and I knew we messed up. I tried to wake you up so we could talk about it, but you didn't want to talk. So I had to think about it by myself."

"How were you so sure?"

"I just was."

"So you think that gives you the right to go through my things?" She stood back up to me, surprising me. "It doesn't, Cody. You always thought you had some kind of right to do what you wanted to do with me, with my feelings. And you thought you had something over me. This..." she said, using a slicing motion across her wrist, "this had *nothing* to do with you. You give yourself a bit too much credit. That night you left me, I prayed to God that you'd never come back, that you'd never do that to me again. And then you had the accident and I thought God was punishing me again. I thought He was punishing me for wishing you'd go away. So I sat in that fucking hospital and waited and waited and waited for you to wake up. And when you woke up and they told me you couldn't remember anything, I wanted to give you a fresh start, I wanted to let you forget about me. By that time, I knew I had a piece of you that I could keep if I really wanted you. I couldn't let it go, though. I had to see you. I *had* to see you one more time, so I could try to make up my mind. And that only made it worse, because some things aren't about remembering. Some things, I guess you just feel, and you still felt it, and God knows, I still felt it. And now, here we are. But now you remember, don't you? You remember how there was always something else you should be trying or doing. And how I was holding you back. You remember everything, right?"

"No, Caroline. I don't remember everything. I remember you. I remember how much I love you. And how everything else always felt totally wrong, and how I fought with myself to go in any other direction, and how I separated myself from what I really wanted because that was supposed to be best for us. And how I promised you that I would come back and never leave, and I did. And I'm here. And I'm keeping that promise."

"I'm not holding you to a promise you made when you thought it would save me."

"You always had it wrong."

"What was I wrong about?"

"Who needed who."

"You don't need me, Cody."

"Yes, I do." I looked at the picture. "We both do."

She turned away from me. Skip looked from me to the customers in wide-eyed horror as some kind of coffee drink spewed from the machine onto the floor.

"Caroline, turn around."

She reluctantly turned back to me.

"I love you," I said. "I have for a really long time."

"Cody, I'm not OK. You know that right? I'm sick, like my mom was."

"I have unexplainable memory loss. I'm not OK either."

She stared at me and I couldn't think of anything else to do, so I kissed her.

The door flew open behind us. "What's wrong?" a worried voice called out from behind me. A familiar voice.

I turned. "Oh, shit," I said, out loud.

"What happened? Someone said lightning struck Rachel's? What's going on?"

"Dad. Nothing. It hit the tree out there and Cody was standing there and he's...OK."

Mr. Bryant grabbed me by the shoulders. "What do you have, like nine lives?"

I tried to smile.

"Thank God you're OK. Why were you out there in a thunderstorm?"

Skip bowed his head, probably saying a silent prayer for me.

"It's a really long story, Mr. Bryant," I said.

"Let me get you some coffee, Dad."

34

Saved

THERE WAS nobody in Josh's office at the reception desk or in the waiting room. His door was partially open, so I peeked inside. Nobody was in there, either. I looked at his bookshelf, not just full of medical books, but of fiction, too. He had a bunch of novels and poetry books, which led me to believe he liked to read in his spare time. I wondered if we'd read any of the same books. I scanned them, trying to take note of anything that looked interesting enough to read.

One book caught my eye. It looked familiar and I tried to figure out exactly where I'd seen it. *The Beautiful and the Damned* was the book I'd read for my Senior project with Caroline. I took it off the shelf and looked at it. Dust and dirt blew off the cover and into the air. The dust lingered in the sunlight for a while before settling. I opened the cover. There was something written in pencil inside the front cover.

I love you.

And then in different handwriting: *I love you, too.*

. . .

Three days until the prom.

They better play our song.

I remembered. She asked me that question. It was the best question anyone had ever asked me, and I texted my brother and asked him what it meant when a girl asks you what song you'd play at your wedding, and he texted me back, *Run.*

I flipped the book over. The pages had been wet. The book was dirty. There was a dark brown stain on the spine that had bled into some of the pages. I opened the book and flipped through the pages. The handwriting was my own. The writing was in pencil, because when it came to finding the meaning in things, I changed my mind a lot.

"Sorry about that. Raegan's out sick today, and..."

I turned around, the book in my hand.

Josh didn't speak.

"Why do you have this?" I asked.

He sat down at his desk and leaned back. Then he looked out the window.

I sat across from him and sat the book on the desk.

"I was coming home from my parents' house, took the shortcut off the state route because I didn't feel like sitting through all the lights in town. He crossed the center line and swerved towards me. I slammed on the brakes and saw it in my rear view mirror. I heard it. I've never heard a sound so terrifying. I think you remember it from your nightmare, don't you?"

I nodded.

"First, I called 9-1-1. He was lying on the ground, well, you don't need to know the details. So I ran to you. You were hanging upside down, unconscious. I cut you out of the seatbelt because I had to stop the bleeding. You faded in and out a few times. You weren't speaking. Your pulse was dropping, but you were breathing. And then the paramedics and the helicopter came. And when they moved you, this book was under you. So I picked it up. I thought I'd give it back to you if you pulled through. I went to the hospital the next day to check on your condition and that's when I found out who you were. And I know that you know that Caroline is my patient. After I saw the book, what was written in the book, I just put it away."

"You saved my life."

"You probably would have lived anyway."

"No. I don't think I would have."

"Then one day, you're standing in here. Raegan made the appointment, and I thought I could just send you to someone else, but you wanted to be here, so I let you. It's probably some kind of conflict of interest. I'll have to report it."

"No. Why? Why would you have to report it?"

"Because it isn't right."

"I don't want you to report it."

"Cody, if it comes out later..."

"Caroline needs you. I'm begging you. Don't report it."

He leaned forward. "How did you pick that book off the shelf?"

"I remembered."

"How much do you remember?"

"I remember a lot about Caroline. I remember it like little pieces, like moments, and pieces of dialogue."

"That's fascinating, Cody. Did you tell anyone?"

"I told her. She knows."

"When did this happen?"

"Yesterday. Last night."

"We should call the specialist. Order a scan. Maybe something changed."

"I don't need a scan. My dad's already broke from this accident. And I don't really care about the rest of it."

"Do you remember college?"

"Not really. I remember a little, but not the specifics. That's not what I came here to talk about, though. It's something else."

"What's that?"

"I think it's another thing you already know about."

He sat back again. "We can't discuss Caroline. You can talk to me, though."

"I know that Caroline is pregnant."

"How do you feel about that?"

"I'm worried about her and her medicine. I'm worried that she'll end up dead. I'm worried that someone with Bipolar Disorder and someone with brain damage won't make the best parents. I'm just...worried. My dad is going to kill me. How am I going to pay for any of this? God, it's so heavy."

"It's a lot to deal with coming back from where you've been."

"But I'm happy, too. Because I love Caroline and I remember loving her. But I remember some of the stupid shit I did, too."

"Something tells me you're not that person any more."

"Caroline always worried about tying me down, but I don't think of it like that."

"What do you think of it as, then?"

"Roots."

35

Beginning
SUMMER 2016

"I TOLD you I would marry you," I said quietly. I held her hand in mine while we danced.

"I know. I never said you were a liar."

"Man of my word." I looked at our families, finally being slightly less awkward than they usually were. "Imagine what this would've cost your dad if we had any friends."

She giggled. "At least he only had to rent twenty chairs."

"One for my mom, one for my dad, and one for the chip on his shoulder."

"One for the prostitute that Gus hired as a date."

"One for your dad's flavor of the week, and one for the other girl he's sleeping with."

"And Dr. Josh, who I have strategically sat by Aunt Jen. See that? Don't they look cute together?"

"Killing two birds with one stone there, since Josh brought his mom as his date. Meeting the future in-laws."

Skip, who had dropped out of school in the middle of junior year to join the Army and become a chaplain's assistant, was getting the attention of Gram's friends, and he took turns dancing with them. Skip was a perfect gentleman, and the older ladies loved that.

"I did have one fear," she said, putting her head on my shoulder.

"What was that?"

"That you might revert back to your old ways and leave me at the altar."

"Now, by altar, do you mean that bird bath over there with the Little Tykes sliding board tipped over behind it?"

"How much did you want to hit up our parents for? Your dad is still trying to get his Alpha Sig money back, and mine had to pay for our bastard kid so we could finish our useless liberal arts degrees."

"I'm never leaving," I assured her. "This backyard wedding confirms it, don't you think? I mean, if not, your dad just wasted a good four or five hundred dollars."

"I wonder who paid for Shelby and Rick's wedding."

"I don't know, but I'm sure they won't have to hear about it for the rest of their lives."

"Who has Cal?" she asked. It was something we said often when we were in Rocky Ridge. He got passed around quite a bit.

"Kristi."

"Does she miss you yet?"

I laughed. "How can she miss me? I eat there three time a week."

"I'm glad you don't remember wanting to be a CIA agent. Working at a bail bonds shop might seem a little lackluster compared to that. Plus, being on the other side of the badge might suit you better."

"My biggest influence was a dirty cop. Rest in peace, Lopez."

"That he was."

Gus picked up a microphone as the song ended. "Funny story about the bride and groom, here."

"Oh, God," I said. I never knew what would come out of his mouth.

"The first conversation they ever had was about what song they would dance to at their wedding. Very first conversation, folks. No lie."

"How does he know that?"

"I spent a lot of time being drunk around him. You know how it gets."

"Cody and Caroline, this song is for you."

Also by Arly Carmack

Nineteen

Nick Charming's Guide to Breaking Hearts in Twelve Easy Steps